Abaddon's Curse

Niall Illingworth

Grosvenor House
Publishing Limited

This book is published by
Grosvenor House Publishing Ltd
Link House
140 The Broadway, Tolworth, Surrey, KT6 7HT.
www.grosvenorhousepublishing.co.uk

A CIP record for this book
is available from the British Library

ISBN 978-1-80381-994-5
eBook ISBN 978-1-80381-995-2

Dedication

For Jean and Alan, a finer couple you couldn't meet

Also by the Same Author:

Where the Larkspur Grow
A Parcel of Rogues
Dead Birds Don't Sing
Hard Rain, Cold Hearts

Acknowledgements

As usual my grateful thanks go to Deborah and Eunice. Deborah, as she has done for all my previous books, was good enough to read the early draft and provide useful feedback. She assures me that the story hangs together quite well. Let's hope so.

And Eunice, with her usual good grace, took on the unenviable task of correcting my grammar. You might think that by now I would be getting to grips with it. Judging by Eunice's fluorescent pen I still have some way to go in that regard.

Chapter 1

Queen's Park Glasgow, April 2004

The tops of the beech trees bent and swayed in the biting north-easterly that whipped viciously across the park. It was now the second week of April, but the icy blast still carried the threat of a wintery shower. It had been, certainly by recent years, a particularly cold winter and a week after Easter it remained unseasonably cold. Spring was digging in its heels and stubbornly resisting making an appearance. The pieris and camellia shrubs that populated the border above the boating pond were yet to bloom and the first clutch of tiny mallard ducklings, hatched only last week, rode the choppy waves of the pond like a rollercoaster as they frantically tried to keep sight of mum. Discarded food wrappers, assorted detritus from overflowing bins spiralled skywards in the gusting wind before plummeting back to earth or becoming impaled on the branch ends of trees. Everything, it seemed, was just a little out of kilter.

On the west footpath near to Pollokshaws Road, a small knot of people stood peering into the murky waters of the boating pond. It was still early, just after eight, but the number of onlookers continued to grow as more and more people stopped to see what was going on. Now there were at least twenty people, all with their

1

eyes firmly set on what was in the centre of the pond. The rough water made it difficult to see but that didn't stop the speculation. Drew Watson had spotted it first and now he was in his element, holding court to anyone who would listen.

Watson was the coordinator of an eclectic band of dog walkers who met each weekday morning at 0730 hours at the park gates on Balvicar Street. Mostly retired, the group of both men and women had been meeting at the same spot for the last three years. Strangely, some of the group still didn't know the names of their fellow walkers, although everyone knew all the dogs' names. For some reason it didn't seem so important to know each other so intimately. The old lady who owned Fudge, a caramel-coloured Maltese terrier with chronic halitosis, had hardly said two words in the eighteen months she had been part of the group. But that didn't seem to matter, they enjoyed the companionship and security of each other's company as they meandered their way through the myriad of paths that dissected the park.

Nearing the end of their walk the group were coming down the path that led down from the mansion house when Watson stopped abruptly. He pointed to something floating in the centre of the boating pond.

'Feck me, look, there's a body in the pond!'

The other walkers stared open mouthed as they tried to make sense of what they were looking at.

The owner of the Maltese Terrier was first to speak. 'Are you sure it's a body?'

Hearing her speak was almost as unusual as finding a body in the Queen's Park boating pond. Watson gave the woman a withering look.

'Course it's a body. What else could it bloody well be?'

A man holding the lead of an overweight Labrador shrugged his shoulders.

'Looks more like a mannequin dummy if you ask me. Especially the way its dressed. Tweed sports jacket, dark trousers and the shoes look like brogues. It's the sort of clothes you see on mannequins in charity shops. If you ask me, it'll be teenagers having a prank. Got hold of a tailor's dummy from somewhere and tossed it into the pond for a laugh.'

Watson looked unimpressed.

'I'm telling you it's a body. Look at its arms. Mannequin arms are stiff, rigid. They don't flop and bend and those arms look floppy to me. I'm telling you 100%, it's a body.'

'So, where's it's head?' asked the lady with the Maltese Terrier who had now said more in the last two minutes than she had in the previous eighteen months.

'Under the bloody water I should think. It's floating face down so it's difficult to tell, if the water wasn't so damned choppy, we'd be able to say for sure.'

'I thought you were sure.' replied the lady. '100% you said, that sounds pretty definitive to me.'

A tall man with an ancient brown mongrel interjected waving his mobile phone in the air before Watson had a chance to reply.

'Just for everyone's information, I've contacted the police, they're on their way. They said they'd be here ASAP, so one way or another we'll find out what it is.'

The consensus amongst the remainder of the crowd seemed to be swinging behind the theory that it was a tailor's dummy and therefore must be some kind of prank. Other than a Lycra clad couple who had broken off their run and were now being buttonholed by Watson, no one appeared to be convinced that it was a

3

body. This was Strathbungo, bodies turning up in boating ponds might happen on the set of a TV drama, but not in Strathbungo, not in the douce southside.

No more than five minutes had passed before a marked police vehicle pulled up at the gates at Balvicar street. Two uniformed officers, an older male and a much younger female, exited the vehicle and approached the pond. Athletic would not be the word you would reach for to describe the male officer. Heavily overweight, he appeared incapable of running the length of himself. Too many fast-food dinners hung in layers around his middle like a series of rubber rings. His appearance wasn't helped by the state of his uniform. His trousers hadn't felt the touch of an iron in months, they were baggy and at least a couple of inches too long. Various food stains gave the black serge a mottled grey appearance; it was as if some culture in a petri dish had escaped from a lab and set up home on his trousers. It was not a pretty sight. To round things off he walked with a hirpling gait, a sure sign he was suffering from back and hip problems most likely brought on by his bulk and the weight of the protective equipment and other apparel that hung from his utility belt. Years of unsociable hours and poor eating habits had taken a heavy toll, policing can be an unforgiving environment for the unfit and aging officer.

By contrast the young female officer looked the epitome of health. Small and slight of build she moved purposefully and swiftly up the path towards the group gathered by the pond. 'Morning everyone, my name's Constable Mellish.'

'Morning.' murmured the crowd.

Constable Mellish peered towards the centre of the pond. 'So, you think you may have found a body?'

4

The crowd nodded in unison. Shielding her eyes Constable Mellish peered again.

'Well, there's definitely something there, but it's difficult to say what exactly it is. It might be a body, but it could just as easily be a shop dummy, looks a bit like one to me.'

'That's what we thought.' said the owner of the Maltese Terrier throwing Watson a knowing look.

Constable Mellish took out her notebook. 'Who was it that found it and can you tell me when that was?'

Watson's hand shot into the air. 'That would be me. Drew Watson's the name, (69) retired civil servant, Flat 2/1, 128 Pollokshaws Rd.' The smugness in his voice dripped from every syllable. 'And it was 0802 hrs exactly when I saw the body. I immediately checked my watch because I knew you'd ask me that. And I'm sure it's a body and not a dummy because if you look at the arms, they're floppy, now if it…'

'Ok, ok let's not get ahead of ourselves.' said Constable Mellish holding up her hands. 'We'll establish that in due course.' She scribbled a few details in her book and returned it to its pouch. Picking up a large stick that was lying under a nearby tree she made her way to the edge of the pond. Carefully she plunged the stick into the muddy depths.

'Any idea how deep the pond is? It's about two feet here but it would be useful to know if it gets deeper towards the middle.'

The man holding the Labrador shook his head.

'I'm pretty sure it's about the same depth all over. They sail boats on the pond at the weekends. I've seen folk wade out to retrieve boats when they break down or get stuck. They wear thigh waders, like the ones fishermen wear, so it's not very deep, I'm pretty sure it's about two feet all over. I don't know how solid the bottom is, but I suppose it can't be too bad if they wade out to get their boats. If they were sinking into mud, they wouldn't be able to do that so it must be fairly solid.'

'That's good to know.' replied Constable Mellish pulling out the stick.

Her colleague who hadn't said a word up till now suddenly piped up.

'You're not thinking about wading in are you?'

Constable Mellish threw him a look of disdain.

'And don't look at me like that, because I'm definitely not going in, that's a health and safety nightmare. We should call out the Support Unit, we've got specialist officers to deal with this kind of thing.'

Constable Mellish looked unimpressed. She knew only too well that her colleague just wanted rid of this call. If he didn't make it to the Ewington Hotel on Queen's Drive by 0845 hrs he could forget getting breakfast. Sausage and bacon rolls passed out of the back door of the kitchen by John the chef. But it had to be before the dayshift manager started at nine. Miss the time slot and greedy old cops would go hungry.

'No, I wasn't suggesting that you volunteer to go in, why change the habits of a lifetime. I can't remember the last time you volunteered to do anything work related.'

Her overweight colleague harrumphed and looked at his watch.

'Look, it would take ages for the Support Unit to get here if we called them out. I've got an idea that will save me getting wet feet and might just get you your breakfast. You know the fishing tackle shop on Pollokshaws Road, just up from the BP garage. Nip up in the panda and see if they can lend us a pair of waders. I've been at the shop for an alarm call before and I know he opens early. The guy who owns the shop is a decent guy, I can't remember his name, but I know he's got new and second-hand gear in there, some of the boys from the station get their fishing tackle there, I'm sure he'll lend us some waders if you explain what it's for.'

Her colleague didn't need to be asked twice. By the time she had finished explaining her plan 'Mr Blooby' was halfway down the path to the panda car. Amazing what the thought of a freebie breakfast can do to kick start someone into action.

Within ten minutes he was back. The crowd by the pond watched as he scuttled up the footpath carrying a pair of grey waders with yellow elasticated straps. Crimson faced and blowing hard as he struggled to catch his breath, he handed his colleague the waders.

'The guy in the shop said these should do the job they're chest waders.' He spluttered as he fought to catch his breath. 'The straps are adjustable apparently, so you can shorten them if they're too long and they've got cleats on the soles of the boots to prevent slipping.'

Having delivered the necessary information, he slumped onto a nearby bench, a sweating and exhausted spent force. Nearing 28 year's service, and still only in his late forties he was seriously in danger of not seeing his 50th birthday if he didn't change his ways and lose some weight. He sat perspiring, pondering his mortality as his athletic colleague took off her boots and stepped into the waders. They were far too big for her 5'3 frame, but by shortening the straps as far as they would go, they would just about do. The top of the nylon waders came up to her oxters and her small feet slid about inside the capacious size 10 boots.

'I wish I had my camera with me hen,' said Drew Watson trying to suppress a laugh. 'You don't see many Poli women dressed like that. You should go out guising at Halloween with that gear on, you'd be guaranteed to earn a few bob.'

Constable Mellish smiled. 'It's functional rather than fashionable.'

Taking small steps, she slowly moved towards the edge of the pond clutching the large stick.

Without hesitation she stepped down into the water. Disconcertingly, her feet sank a couple of inches in the soft mud. She prodded the bottom with her stick. The ground beneath the surface layer seemed solid enough and she was able to lift her feet from the mud without difficulty. So far so good. Using the stick to check the depth she moved gradually towards the centre of the pond. The water reached halfway up her thighs, it appeared that the man with the Labrador had been right, the pond couldn't be more than two feet deep. The crowd on the footpath held their breath as she approached the thing floating in the water.

Whatever it was it had remained almost motionless. Even though the gusting wind was making the water choppy it had hardly moved position. She was now no more than three feet away, but it was still impossible to tell what it was. Well, no time like the present, she thought, girding herself. If nothing else, she was going to have a cracking story to tell the girls at the hen night she was going to on Friday. But right now, she needed to remain professional, a surge of adrenalin coursed through her body heightening her senses, a combination of nerves and raw excitement at what was about to unfold. This was why she had joined the police, the out of the ordinary experiences that you won't find in civvy street. All eyes were on her, she had the stage, and her audience were transfixed.

Bracing herself with the stick in her left hand, she leant forward and with her strong hand grabbed the back of the jacket. She felt the leaden weight as she tried to lift it out of the water. She had only been able to lift it a foot or so, but it was enough. She swallowed hard as her eyes focused like laser beams on the water in front of her.

This was no dummy, this was a human body, and it was missing its head!

Chapter 2

Between the railway bridge at Cathcart and the traffic lights at Sainsbury's at Muirend there are 17 premises where you can get your hair, nails or other beauty treatments done. Their proximity and the choice they provided was a principal reason why Maureen Goodall enjoyed living in the southside. Most things she cared about were just a short walk from her flat in Tankerland Road. Newly turned sixty and now fully retired, Maureen was intent on enjoying the good things in life. She had never married, but that had been a deliberate lifestyle choice on her part. She'd had offers, plenty of them, but Maureen preferred to keep her options open, play the field, and live a little.

For someone entering her seventh decade she was remarkably fit. Tall and slim, she swam at the Eastwood baths at least twice a week and played tennis throughout the spring and summer months. Every Tuesday she did pilates, and on a Thursday evening she was part of a ladies tap dance class that she had faithfully attended for the last ten years. All in all, you get a picture of a lady who, in terms of fitness, could cut it with most men or women, half her age.

Her looks were very important to her, and she spent a large part of her disposable income on her beauty regime and updating her wardrobe with clothes that many might say were inappropriate for a woman her age. Skirts above the knee and tight-fitting tops were not your typical attire for a woman of 60. Not that that bothered Maureen, although she hated people thinking she was mutton dressed as lamb, she dressed, as she always pointed out, to please herself. If her appearance caught the eye of an admiring male, then all well and good, she wasn't going to complain.

One thing Maureen Goodall couldn't be accused of was being a cougar. She hardly ever dated younger men, and on the rare occasions she did, she employed a strict five-year policy. If they were more than five years younger than her then they were deemed to be off limits. That, for a large part, was done for financial reasons. Experience had taught her that older suitors were much more likely to splash the cash and as her own income was strictly limited, she preferred to keep the company of deep pocketed retired men. Particularly men of a certain social class who had the time and financial wherewithal to lavish her with attention and gifts. It was a formula that had served her well.

Honing her skills over many years she had learned other tricks to help snare her prey. Loitering in the food aisle of Marks and Spencer's in Newton Mearns had proved a fruitful hunting ground. Retired bachelors or more particularly widowed or divorced men in their 60s and 70s were in plentiful supply. Unsurprisingly they were not natural cooks, consequently they spent considerable time shopping for ready meals that they would later wash down with a decent bottle of wine.

Bridge was the other ace up her sleeve. She'd once read a book about a woman who had spent her retirement years cruising the world picking up wealthy men. She swore blind that on several occasions the thing that gave her the initial in was her ability to play a hand of bridge. Maureen had taken the woman's advice to heart and years before she retired, she'd attended evening classes at Langside College to learn how to play. It hadn't always worked, but her ability to make up a four, while on holiday or at the tennis or golf club, had paid handsome dividends on more than one occasion.

With a high maintenance lifestyle and a limited budget, you had to find other means of financing your interests. It wasn't for everyone, but what she was doing wasn't illegal and for Maureen Goodall it provided the perfect solution. She had fun and got to enjoy some of the finer things in life.

It was only just after nine when she opened the door of 'Pamper and Shine,' on Clarkston Road. A girl in her late twenties, hair pulled tightly back from her forehead and wearing a crisp white tunic greeted her with a ready smile.

'Maureen, great to see you, come in, come in. And the best news, I've got you all to myself for the next two hours. Unless someone walks in off the street, I don't have another appointment till eleven, so oodles of time for you to tell me all about your trip, when is it again, and let me take your jacket.

Maureen removed her jacket and handed it to the girl.

'Leave tomorrow afternoon. We fly to Naples where we pick up the cruise ship. Then two weeks cruising the Amalfi coast, Corsica, Nice and Cannes. For the last few days, we head to Barcelona then down to Valencia finally ending up in Lisbon. That's where we fly home from.'

The girl put her hands across her chest.

'Sounds absolutely divine, and all paid for by that sugar daddy of yours, you really are the luckiest lady.'

Maureen frowned.

'He's not my sugar daddy. Actually, I first met him about ten years ago, but I've only recently started seeing him again so we're really just friends, it's purely platonic, I'm just going as a companion.'

The girl started to giggle.

'Of course you are, no romance, just companionship, aye right Miss Goodall, that will be the frosty Friday, I know you too well.'

Maureen laughed shaking her head.

'No honestly, I'm being serious. He's booked us separate cabins, he's a widower, I think he's just lonely.'

'Bet you've got adjoining cabins though. And look at you. You're gorgeous, no hot-blooded male is going to leave you all alone in your cabin, I'll bet you all the tea in China.'

Maureen smiled. 'We'll see, but I think he's too much of a gentleman. Anyway, regardless of any of that I've still got to be looking my best, it's cocktail dresses for dinner at night, and if I'm really lucky we might get to dine at the captain's table. I've always wanted to do that, so here's hoping.'

'Ok cool, fingers crossed for that then. Right, let's get down to business. Hair first I thought, then pedicure and shellac and we'll do your eyebrows last. Unless of course you want me to tidy up that bikini line, as I said, you just never know, you might get lucky.'

Chapter 3

In the CID general office at Aikenhead Road police office, Conway Niblett was searching for a pair of clean mugs while he listened to his new DCI extolling the virtues of coffee drinking, in all its varied manifestations. DCI Elaine 'Mini' Cooper was clearly an authority on the subject and now she was in full flow there was no stopping her.

'I got addicted to coffee when I was at school, one of the girls in my dorm's father was a coffee merchant. He imported coffee from all over the world and she always had small bags of exotic coffee in her wardrobe. We thought we were the height of sophistication, 13 years old and drinking Arabica coffee from a cafetiere. You know I wasn't so keen on it to begin with, took me a little time to get into it, but within a term I was an absolute pro. And it's stayed with me ever since. First at Uni and now in this job I've never looked back. I wouldn't thank you for a cup of tea but coffee, it's the drink of the Gods, Conway, and this one is a particular favourite.'

Elaine Cooper, universally known as Mini was a highflyer. With just over 11 years service she had arrived at Aikenhead Road on promotion only three weeks ago. She had spent the last 18 months working in Policy Support in Headquarters and before that she had been a uniformed Inspector in Paisley. Her last CID experience had been as a Detective Sergeant four years ago. Her appointment to DCI in a busy Division raised more than a few eyebrows, it was not what they were accustomed to. Also, while the flitting from department to department, uniform to CID, might not be the norm, it was far from unique for an officer on the Accelerated Promotion Scheme and someone who had been identified for high office.

Elaine Cooper came from a wealthy background. Brought up in rural Aberdeenshire where her family farmed 3,000 acres of rich arable land near Kintore, she had been sent to secondary school at St Leonards in St Andrews where she had boarded from the age of 12. Boarding school had given her an independence and strength of character that had served her well both at university and now in her police career. She was intelligent, single minded and sporty. At school she had excelled at both hockey and lacrosse, gaining representative honours in both. In fact, it was only in the last year that she had stopped playing hockey competitively; a troublesome knee injury which had first reared its head while she was at university finally got the better of her and now her sporting activities were restricted to swimming and the occasional pilates class.

A graduate in psychology from Glasgow University, her choice of a career in the police service had come as a surprise to her family and friends, but thus far it had proved a pretty shrewd decision. Still only thirty-three and with three ranks under her belt, she was on course to make it to the ACPO ranks. That at least was the goal but there were potentially any number of pitfalls on the way that could prevent that from happening.

A DCI's job in a busy city division was not for the faint hearted, but Elaine Cooper was a resolute and resilient character, you don't grow up on a farm in the middle of nowhere and spend six years at boarding school without being able to problem solve and stand on your own two feet; she was determined that she would make a success of it. It helped that she was currently single, her last relationship with a former university colleague had fizzled out six months ago, so now she was able to direct all her energies into her job. She wasn't going to fail for not putting the hours in.

Since the retiral of DCI Bob Fairbairn fifteen months ago the DCI's position at Aikenhead Road had been filled by an acting rank, who while stabilising the patient after the debacle that had surrounded Fairbairn's departure, had hardly set the heather on fire, he'd kept things ticking over but it would be fair to say that he'd kept a low profile. His efforts, however, had been recognised and rewarded with a move to a specialist role at Headquarters, so the timing of Elaine's promotion was, from her point of view, perfect. She had the substantive rank and, most importantly, the opportunity to make her mark in a busy high-profile job.

Her nickname, Mini, was not something that she was called growing up. She became Mini when she joined 3 Group at Cranstonhill Police Office on her very first day of operational duties. Her Tutor Constable back then was a car enthusiast who drove a souped-up orange Mini Cooper. It tickled him no end that his new probationer was called Cooper. In a job where nicknames are ten a penny, it just seemed natural to call Elaine, Mini. And like many nicknames it stuck. From that day onwards everyone in the job knew her as Mini Cooper.

She was about to press the plunger on the cafetiere when the door opened and in walked DI Campbell Morrison. In his mid-forties, a stone overweight and with a healthy dose of cynicism, the career detective from Lewis in the Western Isles could not have been more different to his exuberant young boss.

'Better find another mug Con, the DI's arrived and I would imagine he'll appreciate a cup of this nectar, it's Fazenda Santa Ines from the Mantiqueira mountains in Brazil. My parents gave me some as a birthday present. I particularly like it in the mornings, it's robust with just a suggestion of sweetness, just right to kick start the day with.'

Campbell gave Con a bemused look and shrugged his shoulders. Con mouthed something inaudible in return and busied himself looking for the extra mug.

'Are you sure you haven't got me mixed up with someone else, I like a cup of coffee but I'm certainly no expert. I'm a bit of a Gold Blend man when it comes to it. Now whisky on the other hand, I could tell you a few things about the water of life.'

Mini laughed and handed Campbell a mug of the steaming liquid.

'Best drunk without adding anything to it I'd say, much like whisky in that regard, not that I'm in any way an expert, but I like the odd malt, a good Speyside preferably, and served just as it comes.'

'Well, you'll get no argument from me on that, although I prefer the peaty Islay malts, or something like a Talisker. I like my whisky to pack a punch.' He took off his jacket and took a large mouthful of coffee. 'A bit like this coffee then, which I have to say is pretty damn good.'

Mini grinned and raised her mug as she sifted through a pile of crime reports.

Over the next five minutes half a dozen detectives drifted in and found seats in the spacious office. A couple had brought their own beverage, but there was something that everyone was in possession of, a pen and a notebook. Three weeks ago, at the DCI's first morning meeting, two DC's arrived without the means of writing anything down. The gutting they very publicly received for arriving ill-prepared was not likely to be forgotten in a hurry. The DCI was irked and said so in no uncertain terms. In part, it may also have been a show of strength and intent on her part. Setting her stall out early. Whatever the motivation it clearly had the desired effect, no one was going to make that mistake again. Gone were the days when you could relax at the morning meeting and sit back in your chair with your feet on a table, this was a different regime altogether. Last week's reprimand had immediately been followed by a grand inquisition. A series of questions spat out randomly in the manner of a teacher testing ten-year-olds their times tables. What was the registration number of the white Volvo seen dealing drugs in Prospecthill Square? What was the suspect's description for the indecent exposure in Cathkin Park? Those unable to answer were embarrassed in front of their colleagues, they would not be so lackadaisical again.

Fortunately, Campbell had been spared any humiliation as the DCI hadn't asked him a question. Had he been asked he'd like to think he would have been able to answer but, being honest, he wasn't 100% sure. Fortunately, his prodigy, Asif, had been paying attention. He was the only detective asked a direct question who had got the answer completely right. That wasn't altogether surprising, Asif was always well prepared and never without a notepad and pen. What was more of a surprise was he was currently nowhere to be seen. Campbell had spoken with him in the bottom corridor when he'd arrived half an hour ago, so he was somewhere in the building. But where the hell was he? If the DCI hadn't noticed, although he suspected that she had, she would go off on one if he walked in late. Poor timekeeping was another of her pet hates.

The DCI looked at her watch.

'We appear to be one short, where is Detective Constable Butt? This meeting is already late, anyone got any idea where he is? I don't see why the rest of us who managed to be here on time should be inconvenienced by his tardiness. DI Morrison, any ideas where he is?'

Campbell was about to say he didn't have a clue when he caught sight of Con gesticulating towards the door.

'He appears to be standing outside the door, ma'am.' replied Con desperately trying to make eye contact with Asif to suggest that he should come in immediately.

'For God's sake someone open the door and tell him to get in here before I lose the will to live, we are already 5 minutes late and I've a meeting with the Divisional Commander in half an hour so can we get this bloody meeting underway?'

A detective sitting close to the door leant forward and opened it gesturing for Asif to come in.

Asif stepped into the room head slightly bowed so he didn't make direct eye contact with the DCI.

'Apologies for being late, but I'm not sure if you're already aware ma'am.' Asif held up a printout in his right hand.

'Aware of what?' asked Mini eyeing Asif suspiciously.

'Aware that the uniforms have recovered a body floating in the Queen's Park boating pond. Inspector Brough and Sergeant Pearson are on their way down to the locus, they're asking for CID to attend, that's why I was late ma'am, I was speaking to them in the corridor.'

Mini sat back in her chair putting her hands behind her head.

'No, I wasn't aware, but of all the excuses I've been given for people being late, that is one of the better ones I've heard.' she held out her hand.

'Show me the incident?'

Asif handed her the printout which she started to read. 'And do we have any idea who the deceased is? Gender, name?'

Asif shook his head.

'There's no indication on the incident, it just says it's the body of a male and was fully clothed. Oh, and identification might prove a little tricky as apparently it's missing its head!'

Campbell spluttered a mouthful of coffee over his desk. That was not what he was expecting his colleague to say. And yet the casual way Asif dropped it in was, in many ways, so typical. It was only a small detail, but a crucial one nevertheless and to Campbell it spoke volumes. Asif had added that the body was missing its head as if it was some incidental minor detail or even an afterthought. Campbell or most experienced detectives would have answered the DCI's question by saying they had found the body of a headless male, or words to that effect. The important detail that the body was missing its head would not have been an, oh and by the way, I should have said, it's missing its head.

Asif was a bright boy, much smarter and harder working than most other detectives in the office, but whether it was his experience growing up in Lahore or other cultural differences, there was a streak of naivety and innocence that ran through him. Sometimes he came away with the most bizarre things. That was largely borne from inexperience; he just wasn't what you would call 'streetwise.' That wasn't his fault, it just meant that on occasions he could be exposed or even taken advantage of. As a detective it was a trait you could well do without. Detective Constable Asif Butt still had a great deal to learn.

Slowly shaking her head, the DCI finished reading the incident and looked at Asif.

'So, it's missing its head, apparently.' Asif nodded and swallowed hard, even he was able to detect the tone of sarcasm in the DCI's voice.

'Yes, ma'am, that's correct, it was found without his head. Just a body, no head.'

Con and Campbell winced willing their colleague to shut up immediately. He was in danger of digging a hole for himself that he might not be capable of getting out of.

Campbell had heard enough; it was time to step in and try and save Asif from further embarrassment.

'Well ma'am three weeks in and it appears you've got your first murder. Not sure we can find any other explanation for a fully clothed headless body being in the Queen's Park boating pond.'

DCI cooper stared at Campbell contemptuously.

'Indeed not Detective Inspector. But before you give me any more glimpses of the blindingly obvious get your jacket on and get yourself down to the locus.

And take Detective Constable Butt with you, I'm sure being part of a murder investigation will do him the world of good.'

The barbed retort stung Campbell like a wasp. It was all he could do not to bite back. Everyone in the room had heard it, but that, as Campbell well knew was the point of it. It was someone very publicly and deliberately asserting their authority. It appeared that the only person who hadn't picked up on it was Asif, he was just delighted to be getting first-hand experience of a murder enquiry.

The DCI stood and gathered up her folder.

'Con, take the crime and incident reports from my desk and cover the meeting for me, you know the script. I'm going to grab a quick word with the Divisional Commander and after that I'll come down to the locus. And let's make sure that the incident is properly and accurately updated, everything by the book. I don't want to be getting asked questions that I can't answer.'

Campbell gave a perfunctory nod but didn't reply. If nothing else the last ten minutes had shone a light on the true character of his new line manager. The inconsequential and friendly small talk while drinking a cafetiere of fancy coffee had disappeared quicker than snow off a dyke. He should have seen it coming. He was annoyed with himself for letting his guard down. That wasn't like him, he'd been bitten too many times before by egotistical line managers. Quietly fuming, he grabbed a set of car keys and ushered Asif towards the door. If this morning was anything to go by, his working relationship with his new line manager was going to be a testing one.

Chapter 4

Asif found a parking space on Pollokshaws Rd across the road from the entrance to the park. An overweight cop wearing a fluorescent jacket that looked fit to burst stood looking thoroughly fed up by some blue police barrier tape that had been loosely strung across the gates suggesting that no one should be entering the park. The group of dog walkers and other hangers on who had been watching events unfold had now been moved out of the park. Most had drifted away to get on with their day, but Drew Watson and several others had positioned themselves on the pavement by the railings, where they continued to watch proceedings. Watson had managed to find a milk crate which he was now standing on affording him an unrestricted view over the top of the railings. His dog, thoroughly disinterested, lay curled up and asleep by the crate.

The cop at the Balvicar Street entrance looked a picture of misery. It was now well after nine and any chance of free scran from the Ewington Hotel had passed for that morning. The disappointment of missing his breakfast was etched large on his face.

'Morning Dave.' said Asif breezily as he and Campbell made their way through the gates and up the path towards the boating pond. The cop frowned thrusting his hands into his pockets.

'A friend of yours?' asked Campbell sarcastically.

'No not really. We used to work on the same shift for a short time. Dave Cunningham's his name, or Slypig as everyone calls him, although I never understood why. I knew he was here as I saw his name on the incident. I know his neighbour Natalie Mellish better, I worked with Natalie a few times in the past, she's a cracking cop, I really enjoyed working with her. She was the cop who waded into the pond and discovered the body. Must have given her a right old shock when she saw its head was missing.'

Campbell stopped walking and put an arm across Asif's chest.

'Slypig, it's a nickname, right. Cunning Ham, get it?' he lifted up his hands and waited for a response.

Asif smiled and shook his head. 'Nope, no idea what you're on about. Anyway, it's not important. Look, that's Natalie standing on the other side of the pond with Inspector Brough.'

The two detectives followed the path around the pond to where their colleagues were standing. Campbell stopped for a moment to look at the body that was still floating motionless in the centre of the pond not more than 25 feet away. The strong wind of earlier had eased slightly making the water less choppy and visibility better. The light brown jacket the body was wearing had the appearance of tweed with a thin red check running through it. The trousers appeared to be dark green, possibly corduroy, and the shoes tan coloured leather brogues. He would wait for confirmation, more than 20 years as a detective had taught him not to jump to conclusions, nevertheless, his initial impression was these looked like the clothes of an older gentleman, and a well-dressed one at that.

Inspector Brough smiled as his colleagues approached. 'Morning Campbell, morning Asif.'

'Yeah Morning', replied Campbell pulling up the collar of his jacket. 'Damned cold for April isn't it, and I never learn, should have put the old Barbour on, well at least it isn't bloody raining, that makes a change. Now what can you tell us?'

Inspector Brough shrugged his shoulders.

'Not much I'm afraid. Still very early days. After Natalie discovered it was a body all we've been able to do is secure the locus, well, the area close to the pond. I've got a cop up at the mansion house and you would have passed Slypig down at Balvicar Street. Other than that, we've called out SOCO, a photographer, and the Underwater Unit are on their way. And that's about it. We've got the details of the group who reported finding the body but obviously no statements yet. We had to move them out of the park as they were starting to get in the way if you get my drift.'

Inspector Brough threw a sideways look towards the group of rubberneckers standing by the fence.

'Is that one of them standing on the crate peering over the fence?' asked Asif scribbling notes in his pad.

Inspector Brough nodded.

'Yep, that's the guy who first saw the body, lives further up Pollokshaws Road, goes by the name of Drew Watson, bit of a 'Sweety Wife' and know-it-all, likes the sound of his own voice.'

Campbell grinned.

'Yeah, I know the type, funny how one always seems to turn up at a murder locus.'

'Absolutely.' said Inspector Brough. 'And they've always got something to say about how we should be doing our job, they can be a right pain in the arse.'

'You've got Watson down to a tee.' giggled Natalie.

'Ok, before we get sidetracked completely, any sign of the missing head?' asked Campbell.

Inspector Brough shrugged his shoulders.

'Nope. But to be fair we've not had much of a chance to look yet. Sergeant Pearson and a cop are checking the borders around the pond, just a cursory look, but it will need to be properly searched when the Unit get here. They're the experts, they'll undertake to do that.'

Asif looked up from his notepad. 'Could the head still be in the pond or is that unlikely?'

Campbell rubbed his chin.

'Could be, difficult to say, and of course the pond will have to be searched, but equally it could be anywhere, I wouldn't be surprised if it's not in the pond.'

Inspector Brough looked confused.

'Funny place for a body to turn up, a boating pond in a busy city park, most bodies are found hidden away, dumped somewhere out of sight. But not this one, it was always going to be found quite quickly, but perhaps that's what whoever did it wanted of course. I'm just thinking out loud, but it's a strange one don't you think?'

Campbell rubbed his hands together.

'It's unusual I'll grant you that, but let's not get ahead of ourselves, it's very early days. Right, Asif, I want you to get onto the control room and get them to contact Blochairn and get them to pull all the CCTV tapes for cameras that cover this park. There must be several of them at least.'

'Roger that.' replied Asif excitedly. This investigation promised to be his first proper exposure to a murder enquiry, and he was relishing the prospect.

'Any particular timeframe you want covered?'

Campbell pondered for a moment.

'Let's start from dusk last night, say 2000 hours. If the body had been dumped during daylight, I'm pretty sure someone would have noticed it, it's a busy park after all. And do me a favour and make sure the incident gets fully updated to that effect. We don't want to give our new leader any opportunity for criticism. We'll make sure we cover all the bases, one logical step at a time.'

*

By 11 o'clock the area around the pond was a frenzy of activity. Mini Cooper had arrived an hour ago and was busy issuing instructions to seemingly anyone and everyone. This was her show, and she was making it abundantly clear who was in charge.

The deceased, a white male of average build, whose clothing and liver spotted hands, suggested he was aged between 60 and 70. He had been photographed in situ, as he lay in the water, and more detailed photos of his clothing had been obtained when the body had been removed to the grass on the far side of the pond as far away as possible from Watson and the other onlookers whose numbers had swelled to more than twenty.

In truth there really wasn't much to see now that the body was sealed in a body bag. A private black ambulance, referred to as the Shell in police circles, was now in attendance. Much to the annoyance of Watson it was parked on the path immediately in front of the body bag. Now he couldn't see a thing. The deceased's remains would be removed to the city mortuary where Asif and another DC were going to be in attendance to check the body in, seize its clothing and any valuables or other items that might be of evidential value.

It hadn't taken long for the Underwater Unit to complete their initial search. As they had said themselves it had largely been a waste of time. The water was so muddy it was like looking into a bowl of Mulligatawny soup. They couldn't see their hands in front of their face. The Unit's Inspector had already moved to plan 'B'. Eight Support Unit officers all kitted out in waterproof suits and armed with garden rakes were standing in the pond about six feet apart. Very slowly and moving in complete unison, they started to make their way down the pond dredging the bottom with their rakes as they went. Slow sweeping movements, first to the left and then to the right. It was like watching some weird sort of aqua aerobics. Their sergeant carried a large wipe board onto which he had drawn the outline of the pond. Taking line of sight markings from landmarks like trees, benches, or wastepaper bins, he drew an accurate grid which allowed him to divide the pond into four separate sectors. This gave him confidence that the officers wouldn't go over areas they had already searched. It was a methodical and painstaking process, but it made sure that every inch of the pond was searched.

The first trawl of the pond took about 20 minutes. A rusty pushchair, a fire extinguisher and a kiddie's bicycle lay on the grass at the south end of the pond. The second trawl completed walking in the other direction added more items to the haul. Another bike, a fold up chair and several pieces of corrugated sheeting together with an assortment of smaller items including several lengths of copper piping, which had probably been dumped after being ripped out of one of the nearby flats when they were renovated several years ago. The trawl had revealed an impressive collection of items, but there was still no sign of any head.

With the body safely aboard the Shell, Campbell was deep in conversation with Asif making sure he understood what he needed do when he checked the body into the mortuary. Getting the deceased identified was the most pressing need. A quick search of the body had not found any wallet, bank cards or other paperwork that might help identify who the dead man was. In the absence of anything with a name on it, and while the head remained missing, formal identification was going to prove problematic.

DC Bob Thomson had now arrived to accompany Asif to the mortuary. He was parked in an unmarked Astra immediately behind the black ambulance. Asif listened carefully and made numerous notes as Campbell issued him with a long list of instructions. A visit to the mortuary was not a new experience, Asif had been there many times before. But on those occasions, it had been for routine sudden deaths, he had never had to accompany a murder victim before, so naturally he was apprehensive. His nerves calmed somewhat when his mentor assured him that DC Thomson had undertaken the task several times before.

The ambulance switched on its engine and sidelights; it was time to go.

'Message me from the mortuary if you get an ID.' shouted Campbell as Asif opened the passenger door of the Astra. 'I'll want to know before a certain DCI gets to hear about it.'

Asif wound down his window.

'No worries, I'll make sure you'll be the first to know. Well, that's a lie, actually you'll be the third person to know because Bob and I will know before you!' He started to giggle.

Campbell shook his head and smiled to himself, that was a typical Asif response. For all his idiosyncrasies, there was something immensely likeable about him. He had a ready sense of humour and didn't take himself too seriously. Also, he didn't see the need to act like most of the other detectives, he was his own man, comfortable in his own skin. Perhaps most importantly of all, his moral compass was almost always on point. That, above everything else, was what Campbell most admired about Asif.

Campbell watched as the vehicles disappeared down the path and out of the park gates. He was aware of voices talking behind him. It was Mini Cooper and Inspector Brough.

'Do you think it was wise to let Asif go to the mortuary without you? Responsible job that and even more so given we don't know the identity of the deceased.'

He fixed his new boss with a dead pan expression.

'He'll be absolutely fine, he's with Bob and he's an old hand. And as I'm sure you'll be the first to appreciate, we all have to learn.'

It was a cheeky remark, but Campbell couldn't help himself, it was payback for the put down she'd given him earlier.

Mini threw Campbell a look that could have cut glass, she didn't reply, but the meaning behind what Campbell had said was not lost on her. Inspector Brough was completely mute, he didn't want to get involved in any internal spat, so he tapped his fingers together nervously while looking at his feet.

Mini cleared her throat.

'I've made a decision. I've decided that we need to shut the park. The whole park is a potential crime scene.

We need to find the missing head as a matter of urgency and the best way to do that is to clear the park of all members of the public, secure each entrance and create a sterile area. We can use the expertise of the Support Unit to systematically search the entire park.'

Campbell raised his eyebrows and stared at Mini. A deep, penetrating stare that said, you can't be serious! Seconds of painful silence passed.

Eventually, Mini spoke.

'Judging by that look and your lack of response you're clearly not convinced by that suggestion. So, go on, enlighten me Detective Inspector Morrison, what would you suggest?'

Campbell thought for a moment.

'Well, now that you've asked, I certainly wouldn't rush to close the park. There's nothing to suggest that the head will be in the park, well nothing other than proximity to where the body was found, but if that is our benchmark, then why don't we search all those flats across the road or the houses and gardens in the street behind the flats, they are all closer to where the body was found than most parts of this park. I'm not saying we shouldn't search the park; I think that's a given, I'd just be wary of closing everything down, doing that brings huge logistical considerations into play.'

Mini looked annoyed.

'What logistical considerations? This is a murder enquiry for God's sake, it must take priority.' replied Mini tersely.

'And it will. But it can't be to the exclusion of everything else. I reckon there must be about a dozen ways into this park, each one would require a police presence to prevent entry and for how long? A day,

3 days, a week? And if you're asking my opinion, I don't think using exclusively Support Unit officers would work either. We've got half their contingent here today, their Inspector was telling me the other half are up in Oban doing a series of search and seals ahead of a Royal visit. So, this is your lot in terms of personnel from the Support Unit. Those are the sort of logistical challenges I was meaning.' added Campbell.

Mini still didn't look convinced.

'I could request mutual aid. Bus officers in from other Divisions if you're worried about the number of resources that would be taken away from our own Division.'

Inspector Brough had been listening intently, overcoming his earlier reticence it was time to add his tuppence worth.

'Ma'am, what you're suggesting isn't unreasonable, I don't think anybody is saying it is, but there's another consideration here that's not been mentioned. The financial costs. The overtime costs for bringing in that many officers for an extended period of time would be astronomical. I know the Divisional budget is already overspent, that would potentially decimate it.'

'I'm well aware of the Division's budget situation Inspector, I attend the management meetings, I hear about it every week.'

Inspector Brough didn't reply, he reckoned he'd probably said enough, he wasn't looking to pick a fight with the new DCI.

Campbell tried to clarify his position.

'Chief Inspector, neither of us is trying to undermine your authority, but I think you'd have to admit that the missing head could quite literally be anywhere. The only place we're confident that it isn't is in the pond. For what it's worth, I think we should search the park today. With our own resources, a couple of dog handlers and utilising the Support Unit officers that are already here we could conduct a pretty comprehensive line of sight search by end of play today. You won't be able to do that if you use up 12 resources standing by entrances. And on the plus side, we're fortunate that spring is so late, most of the trees and shrubs are not even in full leaf yet, searching the wooded areas should be relatively straightforward.'

Mini gave a weary sigh.

'But what about contamination of a crime scene by members of the public. That goes against all the principles I remember being taught on my detective training courses.'

Campbell nodded. What the DCI said was correct, but occasionally there are times when you have to use your experience and go against the perceived wisdom. For Campbell, one of those times was right now.

'Honestly, I wouldn't be too concerned by that. I'd look upon it as having many extra pairs of eyes helping us. If a dog walker finds a head behind a tree, they're going to come running for us pretty damn sharpish, they're not going to interfere with it, I don't think you've got much to be concerned about on that score.'

Through a half smile Mini gave another sigh.

'Their bloody dog might!'

Campbell smiled at the use of humour. He sensed the DCI might just be starting to mellow. She appeared to be taking on board what he and Inspector Brough had said.

'Ok, having listened to the pair of you we'll go with your plan, Campbell. It'll certainly save us a lot of time and it won't burst any budget. And on reflection I think you're probably right, it is likely to end up achieving the same result.'

Campbell was reassured to hear that. For all her confidence and bullish leadership style, she had, in that moment, shown herself ready to listen and to change her mind. That was more than some senior officers he could mention. It was still early days, but it was the first sign he had seen that might suggest they could enjoy a positive working relationship. He had never doubted her ability, she was clearly smart and quick on the uptake, she just needed some of her rough edges smoothed out, and he reckoned he might just be able to help her in that regard.

'Inspector Brough.'

'Yes ma'am.'

'I want a briefing here in ten minutes. You, Campbell and the Sergeant and Inspector from the Unit. And have Natalie Mellish attend, it'll be good experience for her. She looks well capable of taking on some leadership responsibilities.'

'On it, ma'am.' replied Inspector Brough. 'Briefing here in ten.'

Chapter 5

Yesterday's search of the park had not revealed anything untoward. There was certainly no trace of the missing head. DCI Cooper had stood the search team down at 1930 hours. By then the light was starting to fade, and it had been a long and tiring day for everyone.

Mini had made another decision that had impressed Campbell. She had decided to restrict the search to the open areas of the park, and to the woods and herbaceous borders. She had organised for nightshift officers to guard the mansion house, the bowling club that bordered the park on Queen's drive, and the compound that housed the park keepers' offices and vehicles. These premises could all be searched the following day with additional resources. The nature of the buildings with their numerous rooms and storage areas meant the search would be quite involved and take time. The decision to delay it till the following day was a wise and sensible one as far as Campbell was concerned.

*

It had just gone 0700 hrs and as usual Asif and Con were the first ones in. For Asif that was just his habit, but for Con it was a necessity. Each morning, he had to collate all the crime reports from the previous 24 hours, any long-term missing person enquiries and any other issues that were crime related. All this had to be pulled together ahead of the CID morning meeting. Today he was even busier than usual. With help from a colleague, he had spent yesterday afternoon setting up the Major Incident Room which would be used to coordinate the murder investigation. This had involved setting up computers and phones as well as whiteboards, flipcharts and the obligatory kettle and coffee mugs.

This morning with the help of Asif he was filling the stationery boxes with production bags and schedules, statement forms, and any number of clipboards, pens and fluorescent markers.

'Ok, time for the first cup of tea of the day, I reckon we've earned it. Just after seven and I think that's everything done. Mini said she'd be in for 0730 hrs so just time for a brew.' said Con switching on the kettle.

Asif pulled up a chair.

'Sounds good, and while it's just the two of us, run that past me again will you, I just want to be sure I picked you up right.'

Con chuckled as he looked for the teabags.

'As I told you, Sly is another word for cunning. It means the same thing. And ham comes from a pig, so Cunning Ham, becomes Slypig. Get it?'

Asif scratched his head.

'Yep, I think I've got it, you've explained it better than Campbell did. It was the word sly that was confusing me, it's not a word I'm familiar with or have ever used. At school in Lahore, they were very particular about vocabulary in our English lessons, I don't think sly ever got a mention. But I get it, Cunning ham, Slypig. Quite clever now I think about it.'

Con handed Asif a mug of tea.

'The polis has some cracking nicknames. I used to work with a cop we called 'Hip Hip'. Hugh Rae was his real name, so he was known as 'Hip Hip'. Always liked that one. Another fellow on my shift was called Harpic because he was clean round the bend.'

Asif started to laugh.

'Now that's funny. And you know something, my mum still buys Harpic to clean the bathroom.'

'Same with my missus, done so ever since we were married, and that wasn't yesterday, old habits die hard, eh.'

The door opened and in walked Campbell carrying a copy of the Daily Record. He put the paper down as he rummaged through a cardboard box looking for a mug.

'Well, I see we've made the front page.' said Con staring at the paper. 'Headless horror in Queen's Park. They just love a bit of alliteration in their headlines, don't they?'

Campbell guffawed as he hung his jacket on the back of a chair.

'Indeed. Bet that sweety wife who was rubbernecking over the fence all day will be chuffed; he's made page 2. A photograph and a quote. He'll be dining out on that for years. Anyway, no surprise that there's been a lot of media interest. Did you see the DCI being interviewed on the news last night? The Duty Officer says it was on both the BBC and STV late bulletins.'

'Caught the one on STV.' said Con who was now reading the story on the inside page.

'I thought she did bloody well. Unflustered, factual. Didn't get drawn into speculation although their line of questioning was trying to get her to. If the top brass from Pitt Street were watching, they would have been well impressed. The lassie did well.'

'I'll take your word for it, but I didn't get to see it. I'm not surprised though, she speaks well and doesn't lack confidence, I'd imagine she would come over well on TV. Anyway, enough of that. How did things go at the mortuary. I know we don't have an ID but did everything else go to plan. Did you seize all the clothing and other property?'

Asif looked up and nodded.

'Yep, got it all. I've got his jacket and trousers in the drying room; it's all been properly marked so it won't get touched. And I've let the production keeper know. Malcolm will keep an eye on it and let us know when it's dry. Oh, good morning ma'am, I was just updating Campbell and Con with what happened at the mortuary.'

Asif and the others hadn't noticed the DCI coming in.

'Yes, I heard what you said about drying his clothing.' remarked the DCI between sips of coffee from her thermoflask. 'And are those his shoes in the plastic bag?'

Asif nodded. He removed a pair of tan coloured brogues from the bag and placed them on a table.

'They're still wet but I thought you'd like to see them.'

The DCI picked up a shoe and examined it carefully.

'Church's brogues, eh. Nothing but the best for our man. These are expensive shoes; my father had a pair of Church's that he kept for his Sunday best. Cost a fortune apparently, and he only ever wore them on special occasions.'

Campbell picked up the other shoe and inspected it.

'The leather sole on this looks almost new. There're hardly any scuff marks. The actual shoe on the other hand looks much older. Look how creased the leather is.'

The DCI turned over her shoe to examine the sole. She pursed her lips.

'Yeah, you're right enough. Looks like someone's had these resoled very recently.'

Campbell put down the shoe and picked up a smaller plastic bag that was lying on top of Asif's folder.

'And what have you got in this bag to show us?'

'That was the jewellery he was wearing. A gold wedding band and a gold signet ring. Both 18 carats according to the hallmark.'

'Any inscription on the rings?' asked the DCI.

Asif shook his head.

'And what about the watch?'

'Nope, no inscription on it either. But it's an expensive watch, I know that much. A Rolex Yacht-Master with a silver-coloured bracelet, and it looks fairly new wouldn't you say.'

Campbell blew out his cheeks as he started to examine the watch.

'This must have cost thousands, you don't get cheap Rolexes and this one is the genuine article, it's no fake rip off. You can tell by the perpetual motion of the second hand. Yep, 100%, that's a genuine Rolex.'

Mini sat down at a desk.

'A Rolex watch, 18 carat rings and a pair of Church brogues, it seems our man had money. What make was his jacket and trousers?'

Asif opened his folder to refer to his notes.

'A Brook Taverner Harris tweed jacket and his corduroys were Gant. They're both expensive brands, aren't they?'

Campbell nodded in agreement.

'But yet it doesn't appear to be the reason why he was murdered. The killer didn't bother taking his watch or other jewellery. Easy pickings that could have earned them a pretty penny.'

'Yeah, that is strange.' said Mini taking a mouthful of coffee. 'Ok, so that's his clothing, what about the body itself. Any other marks or other injuries?'

Asif referred to his notes again.

'You'll get proper photographs in due course, but according to Joe, the mortician, the head must have been severed using something extremely sharp, there were no ragged edges on the neck and the spinal column was cut very cleanly. He said he'd never seen anything like it before and he's worked at the mortuary for 27 years and has booked in over 2,000 bodies in that time.'

Campbell sighed sarcastically. 'But that's not that surprising, is it?'

Asif looked confused.

'Not sure I'm following you.'

'Look, your mortician friend may have booked in over 2,000 bodies, but not many of them would have been missing their heads, he's not likely to be an expert in the field.'

Asif raised his eyebrows.

'You'd be surprised, I asked him that and he said he'd had quite a few over the years. Mainly road accident victims, particularly prevalent amongst motorcyclists apparently, occupational hazard he said.'

Mini lifted her hands in the air.

'Ok, you two enough. Before we go completely off track, were there any other injuries we should know about?'

Asif nodded.

'Again, you'll see better when you get the photographs, but there was significant bruising across the top of his back and shoulders. Joe said it looked like he'd been struck with some sort of blunt instrument.'

Campbell grunted.

'Hmm, so our mortician is also a part time pathologist now, is he?'

Asif rolled his eyes.

'I didn't say that. But I reckon he knows what he's talking about, he's seen enough murder victims over the years and assisted at hundreds of PM's.'

Conway looked at Asif and shrugged his shoulders. It wasn't like Campbell to be so tetchy, and certainly not with Asif. Perhaps he'd got out of the wrong side of the bed that morning, whatever it was, he didn't appear to be in the best of moods.

'As you say, we'll know more when we see the photographs and when we have the results of the PM, which for your information, I'd like the pair of you to attend. So can we have an end to the bickering and move on please.' added Mini.

'Fine by me.' replied Campbell without making eye contact. Asif simply nodded.

'Good, now we've got that out of the way did he have anything else on him that might give us an ID. I know he didn't have a wallet or anything with a name on it, but did he have anything that might give us a starter for ten?'

Asif reached into his folder.

'Three other things. Firstly, he had this scorecard for Greenbank Golf Club in his jacket pocket. Could be that he was a member there. It's got AM written in pencil at the top of the card and a series of scores for each hole. Some are very faded, but others, like the 5 at the third hole are quite clear.'

Mini studied the card.

'Seems like AM might be a half decent player, that's a tidy looking scorecard. They got a birdie 2 at the par 3 thirteenth. I don't think I'd be able to give them much of a game, not with scores like that, I'm strictly a holiday golfer.'

'AM might not be initials; could it not indicate that it was a morning round? Just a thought.' added Campbell.

Mini looked sceptical.

'Doubt it. Much more likely it's initials, either the deceased's or his playing partner, either way it's something for us to follow up on, find out how many members have AM as their initials.'

Asif nodded as he jotted some notes in his folder.

Mini continued.

'Like most murder investigations, we just need to catch a break and get him identified. Then we can start to make progress. I was half hoping to come in this morning and find that someone had reported him as a missing person.'

Con shook his head.

'No such luck ma'am, it was the first file I looked at this morning.'

Mini sighed wearily.

'Ok, let's move on. What else have you got, Asif?'

Asif held up a bedraggled piece of white card.

'He had this ticket in his trouser pocket. Well, I think it's a ticket. Like the scorecard it's saturated, but I can't think what else it could be. There appears to be a number on the bottom corner. Looks like 263 something. Could be an eight, but I suppose it could just as easily be a six.'

'Let's have a look?' asked Mini holding out her hand.

'Yeah, difficult to say. The first three numbers are definitely 263. If I was guessing, I'd say it was an eight. Pity the writing at the top has been washed away. Impossible to make out what that said. We'll get forensics to have a look at it, see what they might be able to tell us.' She turned the ticket over and studied it closely.

'Some more writing on this side. It looks like the first two letters might be RE, and there looks like what might be a £ sign, within the outline of a box.'

Campbell's ears pricked up.

'RE and a £ sign. That could be the first two letters of Repairs. If it is, might it be a ticket for a shoe repairer. We've just seen that his shoes have new leather soles, not beyond the bounds of possibility.'

Mini bit her bottom lip.

'That's a decent shout Detective Inspector Morrison, yeah, I think you could be on to something, it could well be a ticket for a shoe repairer. You and Asif are going to be busy boys, plenty of actions to follow up on.'

'And what about the third thing?' asked Campbell, 'You said there were three things.'

Asif reached into his jacket pocket and pulled out a glass phial which he placed on top of a desk.

'And this was just the strangest thing, we found this in his inside jacket pocket.'

His three colleagues stared at the glass phial for several moments. Inside was the corpse of a frog, dark brown and about three inches long, it lay motionless with its limbs outstretched.

'It's a frog.' announced Conway stating the obvious. 'And what's more it appears to have shuffled off its mortal coil, it's as dead as a dodo.'

Mini looked unimpressed.

'Man's body found in a pond in April. Frog found in jacket. I bet we could find any number of frogs in that pond if we went looking for them. We had a pond on our farm in Aberdeenshire and it was always hoatching with frogs at this time of year. Not sure finding a dead frog helps us greatly.'

Asif smiled and stroked his chin.

'I take it was dead when you found it?' asked Mini.

'It was. And I think it had probably drowned. You see I looked it up. Frogs are amphibians so they need to breathe air. If they're under water for longer than seven minutes without oxygen they are likely to drown.'

Mini scrunched up her nose.

'I'm not sure I'm following this. Why do you think it drowned? It could have died in any number of different ways; it might have got squashed on the way to the mortuary. Anything could have happened to it. And anyway, it can't have drowned, it would have swum up to the surface and taken a breath, frogs won't be any different from us or any other animal. Its survival instincts would have kicked in, it would have surfaced for air.'

Asif smiled again.

'Well, you might have thought. But this unfortunate frog couldn't do that, you see we found it in his inside jacket pocket. A pocket with a zip on it that was zipped shut.'

Campbell and Con looked completely bemused.

'Inside a zipped jacket pocket?' exclaimed Campbell.

'That's what I'm telling you.'

Con scratched his head.

'Well one thing's for bloody sure, the damned frog didn't get in there by itself!'

Chapter 6

Asif's rabbit out the hat moment, or to put it more aptly his frog out of a zipped pocket moment, had caused much pondering and debate. The one thing that everyone agreed on was the unfortunate creature must have been put there by a human hand. The problem was it wasn't possible to say by whose hand. It was feasible that the deceased may have been responsible, it certainly couldn't be discounted. The more likely explanation was that it had been put there by the killer. It was all very strange, and nobody, not even Campbell, could think of a reason as to why it was there.

After the revelation about the frog, DCI Cooper had spent the next half hour writing actions on a whiteboard in the incident room. For the moment, she intended to keep the enquiry team quite small. Just Campbell, Asif and two other DC's. That could be scaled up as and when necessary, but for now and in the absence of the body being formally identified, the DCI deemed that a larger team was unnecessary. What was abundantly clear was that she was firmly in charge, she was overseeing the enquiry, she called the shots. No actions could be given out or decisions made without her explicit approval. It felt like one step forward and two steps back as far as Campbell was concerned. Yesterday's change of heart, when she'd listened to his advice and changed her mind, now seemed like a false dawn. Today she was back to her controlling ways and asserting her authority. Campbell was unaccustomed to working under such close supervision, he felt the scrutiny was overbearing and unnecessary. He was a highly experienced detective; he'd been involved in numerous murder and high-profile investigations. He would admit to being a little set in his ways but over the years he had become accustomed to doing things his own way. He was finding the new regime claustrophobic; he wasn't used to being micromanaged and he certainly wasn't enjoying the experience. He was irritable, a fact all too apparent to his colleagues.

To make matters more complicated, Campbell had received a short notice citation for a Sheriff and Jury trial that was starting today. He'd managed to speak to the Fiscal who agreed to put him on standby, but only on the understanding that he would be at Glasgow Sheriff Court within half an hour of being summoned. It wasn't ideal, but with the PM scheduled for 9am tomorrow, it was the best he could hope for.

Asif had spent the last fifteen minutes studying a map and making a list of all the shoe repairers he was aware of within a 5-mile radius of Queen's Park. 5 miles was a purely arbitrary number, there was absolutely no science behind it. If the deceased's shoes had been recently repaired as they suspected, then they could have been repaired literally anywhere. Asif simply reckoned that the dead man might prove to be local, and if that were the case then it was likely that his shoes would have been repaired somewhere close at hand. It didn't seem an unreasonable proposition, and in the absence of any other evidence it was where he intended to start.

'Con, is the shoe repair place just up from the bridge at Pollokshaws East railway station, still on the go, there certainly used to be one there?'

Con looked up from his computer screen.

'Yep, it's still on the go, been there for donkey's years, never been in but I pass it every day coming to work. Is that you plotting up all the local shoe repairers?'

'Thought it might be helpful.' replied Asif marking a cross on Kilmarnock Road near to the railway bridge.'

'Have you got Timpson's at Silverburn, next to the Tesco. And the one in Morrison's on Fenwick Road?'

'Yeah, got both of them, and I know there's one on Burnfield Road, near Giffnock Police office. Any others?'

'Not that I can think of on the southside. Pretty sure there's not one on Vicky Road. There's bound to be others North of the river. But close to here, I reckon that's your lot.'

Asif folded the map and put it in his pocket.

'Excellent. But it'll need to keep for later. Campbell wants us to start by making enquiries at Greenbank Golf Club, he's keen to establish how many of their members have the initials AM.'

It had taken Campbell and Asif nearly twenty minutes to get from the police office to the golf club. The rush hour may have passed, but the roads were surprisingly busy, the slowness of the traffic not helped by the appalling weather, it was teeming down with rain, and it showed little sign of letting up.

The terrible weather had deterred most of that morning's golfers, there must have only been a half dozen cars in the car park when they arrived shortly before ten. A cleaner emptying rubbish bins directed them to the secretary's office that was up a stair on the first floor. The secretary, an affable character in his early sixties, seemed eager to help when Campbell explained the nature of their business. Photographs of the clothing worn by the deceased was still to arrive from the Identification Bureau at Force Headquarters, so Asif did his best to describe them. Brown tweed jacket with a thin red check, dark green corduroys, and a pair of tan brogues. The secretary smiled and looked down at his feet. He was wearing tan brogues and a tweed jacket. All that was missing were the corduroys. The secretary told them that the description of the clothing could apply to any one of dozens of club members who were aged over 60. On any given day the clubhouse would be full of middle-aged and elderly men dressed in tweed jackets and brogues. The description of the clothing had drawn a blank.

Neither detective was unduly surprised. It was always likely to be a long shot, their best chance was to strike lucky with the initials. The secretary ushered them into the lounge and ordered them some coffee. It would take him a few minutes to print a list of members names and addresses. He would be as quick as he could, but his ancient Del laptop took an age to warm up.

Asif helped himself to a custard cream from the plate of assorted biscuits that the young waitress had brought in with the coffee. Campbell stared out of the window to the first tee, where a lone golfer dressed head to foot in blue waterproofs was taking a few practice swings ahead of teeing off.

'Must be off his rocker, going out to play in this weather, the rain's almost horizontal.' said Campbell dismissively. 'Never saw the attraction of golf personally, and certainly not in this bloody weather, he must be mad.'

Asif took a bite of his biscuit and sipped his coffee.

'You ok boss? It's just that you seem a little out of sorts. I'm not trying to be cheeky, but I've never seen you this grumpy before.'

Campbell turned back to face Asif. Shaking his head, he sighed wearily.

'Being honest, I'm not feeling on top form, seem to be permanently tired since I had that virus a couple of weeks ago and now my bloody teeth are playing up. Gnawing pain in my wisdom teeth these last few days. And before you say it, I know I should go and see the dentist. I hate the dentist, so I guess I just keep putting it off.'

Asif smiled.

'And what the hell are you smiling at? I've just told you I'm in failing health, and now you're smiling about it.'

The grin on Asif's face was now even wider.

'I'm sorry, I wasn't trying to make fun of you, I'm just relived that it's just toothache. I thought it might have something to do with the DCI, the two of you seem to be at each other these last couple of days.'

Campbell reached for a ginger snap and made a play of breaking it in half.

'Well, she's certainly not helping. Even you must have noticed. She's a complete control freak, she needs to know everything. But she can't go on like that, she's going to have to learn to trust people.'

Asif took another biscuit.

'I quite like her; you know where you stand with her. She's a damned sight better than that maniac Fairbairn who we used to have to answer to. At least she's not a bigot or a racist, and for what it's worth I had Fairbairn marked down as both.'

Campbell was about to explain his misgivings about their new boss when the secretary walked in carrying several sheets of A4.

'Sorry to have taken so long, but they're all here now. Names and addresses of all 330 members and that includes men and women. You won't leave them lying about will you, it's just that I'm not sure of my legal position in handing them over to you.'

'You've nothing to worry about, it's part of an investigation into a serious crime. But as it happens, we are likely only going to be interested in a few particular names, so if you give me the sheets, we'll take down the details and then give you your list back.'

The secretary seemed reassured and handed over the list of names.

'They're done alphabetically by surname. Starting with A's obviously, so you shouldn't have any difficulty finding what you're looking for.'

Campbell studied the list.

'Here they are, Page 4, and there only appears to be three of them, this shouldn't take us too long.'

He handed the relevant page to Asif.

'An Arthur Mitchell, 73 Hillend Road, Clarkston. Andrew McLean, 24, Barlae Avenue, Waterfoot and an Audrey Milne, 16 The Oval, Stamperland. Any of those names ring any bells?'

The secretary thought for a moment.

'Hillend Road isn't far from here, but now I think about it I haven't seen Arthur around the club in quite some time. He used to play regularly, but as I said, that was a while ago.'

Asif glanced at Campbell who raised an eyebrow.

'Andrew McLean is a regular, he plays as part of a large group every Tuesday and Thursday. In fact, I'm sure I saw Andrew here yesterday. Don't think I know an Audrey Milne, I don't tend to know as many of the lady members and I'm afraid there's none about who I could ask, the weather seems to have put them off today, usually Wednesdays are a busy day for the ladies.'

Asif took down the details of the names they were interested in.

'That's not a problem and thank you you've been very helpful.' Campbell handed the list back to the secretary. '

'Just one last thing before we go. If you do become aware of any of your male members, aged in the 60-70 years bracket who, perhaps quite recently, have suddenly stopped coming about the club, give us a call at Aikenhead Road Police office, we'd be interested to hear from you.' Campbell handed the secretary his card.

The secretary nodded.

'I'll do that officer, you can be sure of that, always happy to help the boys in blue.'

Asif laughed to himself. He'd always found that a strange expression. Police uniforms are black not blue, and his remark was even stranger as today, both he and Campbell were wearing grey suits.

Twenty minutes later Campbell and Asif were sitting in their car outside 73, Hillend Road.

'Well, bad news for the secretary, it looks like the golf club membership will be down to 329 any day now. It didn't sound like old Arthur has any intention of renewing his membership. Can't say I blame him. £450 is a lot of money, and like he said, if you're not playing, it's just money down the drain.' said Campbell.

Asif nodded in agreement.

'Debilitating thing arthritis, my grandfather had it. Extremely painful. That poor old fella didn't look like he was capable of walking the length of his garden, let alone play a round of golf. But I suppose we've learned one thing; Arthur Mitchell definitely isn't our mystery man.'

Campbell smiled and switched on the engine.

'Right, Barlae Road next, it's just a couple of miles from here. I know where it is. I used to have a colleague who lived in Waterfoot, used to drop him off occasionally, he lived just round the corner in Brackenrig Crescent.'

There was no one in at the smart white painted bungalow. Asif stood admiring the neat garden and pots of multi coloured tulips that stood either side of the front door as he rang the bell for a third time. He was on the point of giving up when a blue coloured Mercedes pulled into the red chipped driveway. Asif fumbled in his pocket for his warrant card, as the lone occupant, a middle-aged man with white hair, peered at him through the windscreen.

'Asif, Asif,' shouted Campbell from the driver's seat of their vehicle parked on the street.

'I'm going to have to leave this one with you, that's the Fiscal on the phone, she wants me down at the court, pronto, looks like I'm going to be required to give evidence.'

Asif waved his arm acknowledging his boss.

'Fine, not a problem, I've got this. I'll catch a bus down the road, I'll see you back at the ranch later.'

The man in the Mercedes was now unloading bags of groceries from his boot as Campbell, screeching tyres, took off at considerable speed.

'Apologies about that.' said Asif showing the man his warrant card. 'Detective Constable Butt, Aikenhead Road CID, and that was my boss DI Morrison. He's required urgently at Glasgow Sheriff court, hence his rapid departure.'

'Well, I hope he gets there safely, but that doesn't appear to be a given, he took off like a scalded cat.'

The man chuckled as he placed his bags of messages on the front step and searched his pocket for his house key.

'Come in officer and speak to me inside. Andrew McLean's the name, but if I don't get this frozen stuff into the freezer there will be hell to pay when Mrs Mclean gets home later, she's out for coffee with her friends. She was meant to be golfing, Wednesday is usually her day, but the weather earlier was dreadful, at least the rain's eased off now.'

That at least was something, thought Asif, as he realised that Campbell had taken off with his coat on the back seat.

'Come in, come in, I'm putting the kettle on for a brew have you time for one?'

Asif looked at his watch. He had no idea how frequently the buses ran from Waterfoot, but he assumed it wasn't often. Anyway, with Campbell now away he wasn't in a particular hurry.

'Sure, why not. Just a drop of milk would be great.'

'Have a seat in the lounge, I'll not be a minute.'

Asif sat down on the settee by the bay window. The wall to the side of the fireplace was adorned with what appeared to be numerous family photographs, taken over several decades judging by the changing colour of

Mr McLean's hair. Asif's attention was drawn to one particular photo, that of a very small boy attempting to kick a large orange ball. The ball was almost as big as the boy. Asif smiled. The child in the photograph looked about the same age as his own son, Caelan.

*

Asif's son had just turned 14 months. He was already walking, and he just loved to try and kick his ball when Asif took him to the park. Asif's romance with Caelan's mum, Roisin had been a bit of a whirlwind. They'd first met when she was working as the Roma Liaison Officer in Govanhill, and he was investigating the suspicious deaths of several young Roma men. In the weeks that followed things moved quickly and romance blossomed but after Roisin unexpectantly fell pregnant, it was time to do the right thing and get married. She was a proud Catholic from Donegal, and it was what she and her family wanted. That was fine by Asif, he loved Roisin, and he was going to take his fatherly responsibilities seriously. Getting married was the right thing to do. He'd offered to undergo instruction classes, to allow them to get married in her local church in Killybegs. But in the end, they opted to get married in the local registry office, Roisin knew that Asif's Muslim faith was just as important to him as her own was, she didn't want to ask him to compromise that, so they settled on a civil ceremony in the registry office. They'd set up home in a two bedroomed flat in Crossmyloof. It wasn't ideal, it was on the first floor, so they had to lug a pram up and down a flight of stairs. Also, they didn't have a garden, but until they were in a position to afford a house, it would have to do. It did, though, have some compensations; it was close to the shops, a train station, and both Queen's and Pollok parks were within easy walking distance.

*

Mr Mclean came in with the tea. He noticed Asif staring at the photograph.

'Cracking photograph isn't it and taken just last month in the back garden. That's Oliver, my daughter's boy, my first grandchild. He's a bundle of joy and a right old warrior, 15 months, into everything and absolutely fearless. Do you have family yourself?'

'Got a boy about that age, Caelan Yusuf's his name. His mother's Irish and my family hails from Pakistan. He's Yusuf after my grandfather.'

Mr McLean nodded and smiled.

'Well, that's just lovely, I hope he brings you as much joy as our grandson brings us, they're just at a lovely age, every day's a new adventure. Anyway, before we get completely sidetracked that's not why you're here. If fact, I don't believe you said why you're here.'

While they drank their tea Asif explained the nature of his enquiry. Andrew Mclean was clearly not their unidentified man. But just like the secretary, he couldn't think of anyone at the club who it might be. He scratched his head.

'Nope, I can't think of anyone. I play every Tuesday and Thursday, weather permitting. We call ourselves the 'Coffin Dodgers.' Most of the guys in that age range play then, but I can't think of anyone who hasn't been around for a while.'

'Not to worry. He may not even be a member, he might have been at the club as a guest, in fact we can't be 100% sure he was even at the club. We're just at the very early stages of our investigation.'

'With regards to the other name you mentioned, Audrey Milne, I can tell you something about her. She plays in the same group as my wife. Useful player in her day was Audrey. You won't get her at home though, she's currently in Australia with her husband visiting her sister. She left ten days or so ago and I think my wife said she was away for a month.'

Asif took out his notebook and scribbled down some notes.

'Well, that's saved me a trip, no point in calling just now, not if she's away in Australia.'

Asif looked at his watch again.

'You don't happen to know the times of the buses do you, I'll need to jump on one to get back to the office.'

Mr McLean looked at the clock on the wall and smiled ruefully.

'That's a pity, they pass here at ten past the hour. You've just missed one, its just gone quarter past. Look, I've an idea. I've got an optician's appointment at Clarkston Toll at 1145 hours. I'll run you down to the toll if you'd like. If you go to the bus stop just down from the railway bridge, opposite Clarkston Hall, you'll have your choice of three buses. The 6 that comes down from East Kilbride, the 4 which comes from the Mearns or the one that runs past here, the 4A. With three to choose from you shouldn't be waiting too long.'

'Now that sounds like a decent plan to me.' replied Asif, 'I'll take you up on that lift if that's ok.'

Ten minutes later they found themselves stuck in slow moving traffic heading down Busby Road from

56

Sheddens Roundabout. Mr McLean tapped his steering wheel impatiently.

'This road is always a nightmare, just needs someone to inconsiderately double park like that silver Lexus, and the whole road backs up, happens all the time.'

'And where's the police when you need them, eh?' replied Asif sarcastically.

'Aye, good one Detective Butt.' chortled McLean seeing the funning side of Asif's remark.

'Look, I'm intending to park in the car park next to the library and walk back across the railway bridge.' He pointed out his window as they approached Clarkston Toll.

'That's my optician's there, your bus stop is just round the corner opposite the car park. Hope that's ok?'

'Perfect.' said Asif peering out the window. He noticed the sign of a shoe repairs business three doors down from the opticians. Asif made a mental note. That was another one to add to his list.

Chapter 7

In the incident room at Aikenhead Road police office, four detectives perched themselves on chairs spread out like a fan in front of DCI Cooper's desk at the far end of the room. Between them the officers had more than 75 years police service. Campbell burned with embarrassment scrunching his toes in his shoes to distract himself from the humiliation. It was like a scene from an infant school, where teacher gathers her charges around her desk to listen to a storybook. Clasping his hands on his lap, Campbell breathed slowly through his nose as he tried to remain calm. It was difficult to say whether Asif or the other two detectives felt the same level of discomfort, but one thing was certain, nobody was saying a word.

DCI Cooper had called a meeting of the enquiry team for 1300 hrs, principally, so that Campbell and Asif, who had attended the postmortem of the unidentified male earlier in the day, could update the rest of the team with the findings of the examination.

It was now nearly three days since the body had been discovered in Queen's Park and they were still no closer to establishing its identity. That was most unusual. There were no missing person reports that fitted the race, gender, or age profile of the deceased. Fingerprints taken by the Identification Bureau had now come back negative. He was not on any police file. Mini's second round of television and radio interviews had been equally unproductive. Nobody had come forward with any information. Well, nobody if you disregard the old fella with mental health issues from Maryhill who phones police headquarters after every appeal claiming to be the culprit. It was all very frustrating.

Jan Hodge, who had been of great assistance to Campbell during the Chris Swift murder enquiry, had again been drafted in to run Holmes[1], the Home Office approved computer system that coordinated all the information gathered as part of a large investigation such as this. Having spent an hour updating the logs from yesterday's endeavours, Jan was now busy photocopying today's actions that Mini had agreed and signed off at the morning meeting. Nothing, absolutely nothing, was to be actioned without the say-so of the boss. That way, at least according to Mini Cooper, nothing would get missed.

A large cafetiere of freshly made coffee sat in the middle of the DCI's desk. Smiling, she leant forward and with the palms of both hands pressed the plunger into the dark abyss.

'This is black insomnia. Very strong and not for the faint hearted. Came into its own around exam time when I was at university. Now who's up for trying some?'

Asif, like an excitable toddler grabbed his mug and leapt towards the desk.

'Sounds intriguing ma'am, I'll give it a go.'

---

[1] Home Office Large Major Enquiry System

Campbell slid Asif an icy stare as he squirmed uncomfortably on his chair.

'Sounds intriguing ma'am! It's a cup of fecking coffee you're being offered, not an invitation to solve the Rubic Cube.' seethed Campbell silently.

Mini held up a cup towards Campbell.

'Do you want to try some of this? It's excellent, comes from South Africa.'

Campbell shook his head. Unlike his younger colleague, he didn't want to appear overly enthusiastic. And anyway, his tooth was playing up again, it jangled painfully at the touch of anything hot or cold. He'd managed to get a short notice cancellation so he had a dental appointment for later that afternoon, but for now he would make do with a couple of paracetamols washed down with a swig of tepid water.

'Fine, your loss. Looks like it's just you and me then Asif, but be careful, don't have more than two cups or you'll be climbing the ceiling. Now let's get on. Ok, Campbell, what can you tell us about this morning's PM?'

Campbell stood up and turned to address his colleagues.

'Well, according to the pathologist, Mr Roberts, our man was struck several times across the back of the neck and shoulders with a blunt heavy instrument. Roberts thought it was likely to be something like a crowbar. There were at least four different bruise marks, so it was a brutal and sustained attack. Roberts reckons it was very likely that the trauma to the back of his neck would have killed him. At the very least he would have been unconscious before his head was removed.'

Mini twiddled her thumbs.

'Well, I suppose that is some kind of blessing, but what a horrible way to die.'

'It was absolutely fascinating.' added Asif excitedly, 'when they pulled back the skin from his back you could see the purple bruise marks on both his shoulder blades.'

Mini looked at Asif putting a finger to her lips. In the manner a teacher does when trying to kerb the enthusiasm of a child who can't keep their hand down and repeatedly blurts out answers.

'That's what they mean by a bruised bone, there is quite literally a bruise mark on the bone. And I'm delighted you found it so interesting, but if you don't mind, can we just let Campbell explain without you interrupting.'

Chastened by the DCI's rebuke, Asif shut up and quietly sipped his coffee.

'The head would appear to have been cut off using a very sharp knife or perhaps a scalpel. The pathologist was fairly certain that the cut hadn't been made by a saw. We'll know for sure when IB examine the photographs. I had a close look myself and couldn't see any serration marks on the bone, it doesn't look like it was done with a sawtooth blade.'

Mini stroked her chin.

'Interesting. Just thinking out loud now but does the fact it was such a neat cut suggest it was done indoors, away from prying eyes but with time to complete the job properly, and by the sound of things, done by someone who knew exactly what they were doing?'

Campbell nodded.

'I had that same thought. This was no amateur job. The person who did it knows how to wield a knife. But why go to all that trouble and then dump the body elsewhere, it's doesn't make a lot of sense.'

Mini jotted down some notes.

'Anything else of interest?'

Campbell looked up.

'Just one last thing, Mr Roberts found some sort of residue around the neck area, just small deposits but it was right around the neckline. We've got samples for forensics but from looking at it I think it might be lead. It was the right colour, slightly oily appearance. Anyway, forensics will tell us one way or another.'

Mini took a large gulp of coffee.

'Indeed. I'll await that report with interest. Right, now time to crack on. You and Asif are taking Actions 12 through 16. Enquiries at shoe repair businesses and including the additional one you told me about this morning. Is that action 16, the one at Clarkston Toll?'

Jan handed Asif and Campbell copies of the action log.

'That's correct ma'am, action Number 16. I added it on this morning.'

'Ok, fine. I'll catch you for an update before end of play. Oh, and make sure you sign out the shoes with the production keeper. I presume you'll be taking a shoe with you?'

'I was intending to ma'am.' replied Asif politely.

'Not a problem, as long as you sign it out properly, you know the bother you can get into if productions go astray, well I can tell you that won't be happening under my watch, so make sure everything you take out is properly accounted for. Ok, everyone that's all for now.'

*

By 1545 hrs Asif and Campbell had completed the first four of their visits. The story appeared to be the same in each one. No one recognised the photo of the ticket Asif showed them with the serial number on it, although all on them stated that they issued similar type tickets to customers handing shoes in for repair. Furthermore, it appeared that none of the four shops had repaired a pair of leather soled shoes in weeks. In fact, the fella who ran the shop near to the railway bridge on Kilmarnock Road said he'd stopped stocking leather soles altogether because there just wasn't the demand for it anymore. At more than £40 for a pair, it was cheaper to buy a brand-new pair of shoes. It certainly was for the customers he dealt with. The story was much the same with the cobblers on Burnfield Road. He scoffed mockingly when Asif produced the tan coloured Churchill brogue. The man said in all seriousness, that in nearly 12 years working in that shop he'd only ever had to repair two pairs of Churchill's. They were clearly not your run of the mill make of shoe. It was all very dispiriting.

Campbell looked at his watch.

'My dental appointment is at 1620 hrs. I don't think I'm going to have time to fit in the last visit up in Clarkston and get back in time. I can't afford to miss the appointment; this tooth is giving me jip!'

'Sure, no problem, I can cover it,' said Asif dejectedly. 'I'll drop you back at the office and head up from there.'

Campbell shook his head.

'No need. The practice is in Shawlands, it's right on the main road. I can jump a bus from here, it'll take me right to the door. And anyway, I want to brush my teeth first and you look like you could do with a cup of something. So why don't we grab ourselves a quick cuppa and I can freshen up.' said Campbell removing a plastic bag containing toothpaste and a toothbrush from his inside jacket pocket.

Asif shrugged.

'Fine by me, but you could just as easily freshen up in Giffnock office, it's literally across the road.'

Campbell laughed.

'And risk running into Ruaridh MacLeod, he's the bar officer in Giffnock, he's related to half of Stornoway and the half that he's not he knows through his wife who worked in the post office before they came down here. He's a crushing bore, harmless but just deadly dull. He was the year above me at school, I daren't risk it, if he saw me, I'd never get away.'

Asif was sitting staring into space when Campbell came back with the two coffees.

'You, ok? Or is the reality of detective work starting to set in. This is beginning to feel like Groundhog Day isn't it, I bet this wasn't what you thought you were signing up to when you joined the CID.'

Asif smiled.

'Well as you've told me many times, you've got to be prepared to do the hard yards if you're gonna get a result. I'm just a bit tired being honest. Roisin's had a heavy cold for the last week so I'm trying to do my bit with Caelan, but getting up twice through the night is taking its toll. I now appreciate how tough it is for Roisin when I'm on nights. But I wouldn't change it, he's a wee belter, I just wish he would learn how to sleep!'

Campbell nodded sympathetically.

'Aye, a lack of sleep is a curse. Soon takes its toll. This tooth is keeping me awake so I literally feel your pain. Anyway, before we digress further, I meant to ask you earlier, any word regarding your application for the Accelerated Promotion Scheme, I thought you said you would hear this week. Remember I'm banking on you reaching the ranks that I failed to achieve. We need folk like you to change the job for the better, I'm not confident our illustrious leader is going to be a force for good, not judging by some of the nonsense she seems obsessed by.'

Asif finished the last dregs of his coffee.

'I think I might hear tomorrow, that's what some of the other candidates have been told. But you know, I think I'm going off the idea. The more I think about it the less attractive it seems. For a start there are all the courses at the police college that you have to attend. Being away from home isn't ideal, not when you've got a young child. Then, more importantly, there's the clash of the egos. It appears getting a place on the scheme makes you think you're the creme de la creme and you're going to be the next Chief Constable. And believe me, Mini's far from the worst in that regard. So, you see in many ways it might be better if I got a rejection letter, might save a lot of hassle.'

Campbell stood up shaking his head.

'Nonsense man. That's defeatist talk, you'd be great. Right, I'm away to brush my teeth and get this bloody tooth sorted. Phone me if you turn anything interesting up, otherwise I'll see you back at the office later.'

*

The only person who appeared to be in the shop was sitting at a bench grinding the rough edges off a pair of boots with an electric sander. The man looked up and smiled.

'I won't be a minute. Just want to smooth off these heels then I'll be right with you.'

'No hurry.' replied Asif taking the shoe from a brown paper bag and placing it on the counter. The man

65

switched off the machine and approached the counter wiping his hands on a small towel.

'Now, what can I do for you?'

Asif showed the man his warrant card and explained why he was there.

A quizzical expression spread over the man's face as he eyed the shoe on the counter.

'That's a Churchill brogue if I'm not very much mistaken.' He picked the shoe up and turned it over. 'And that's one of the leather soles I use, I'd recognise it anywhere even though it doesn't have a hallmark on it. I can tell by the colour of the stitching.'

The man lifted a leather sole from a small pile at the side of the counter.

'It's the same as one of these. I don't do many these days but I've a couple of regular customers who bring their shoes in looking for leather soles. It's an expensive business, not really worth it unless it's a quality shoe.'

The man examined the shoe more closely and smiled.

'Yep, this is definitely one of mine. And I can tell you without looking it up whose shoe this is. The only Churchills I repair belong to Magnus DeVilliers. Yep 100%. I did a small additional repair to the seam at the heel which was starting to split. Just half a dozen stitches but if you look closely, you can see the stitching is newer.'

The man handed Asif the shoe so he could see for himself.

Bingo! Finally, he'd got the break he'd been looking for. He took out his folder and handed the man a photograph of the repair ticket.

'Yep, that's one of my tickets. Even though it looks like it's been through a washing machine.'

Asif stopped short of telling the man that it had been in the pocket of a headless corpse that had been found floating in a boating pond.

'You said the shoe belonged to a Magnus DeVilliers; you wouldn't happen to have an address for him, would you?'

The man thought for a moment.

'I can't remember the exact number, but he stays in Pollokshields, Glencairn Drive. It's a big, detached sandstone villa. It's got an enormous copper beech tree growing in the front garden and if I remember rightly, it's almost directly across the road from the bowling club.'

Asif scribbled down the information as quickly as he could.

'I've dropped shoes off for him in the past on my way home. He was a very regular customer, his wife used to own a ladies' boutique just up from the Sheddens roundabout.'

Asif scribbled more notes.

'I'm very grateful to you, this is going to be very useful to our enquiry.'

The man stared at Asif, then a look of horror swept over his face as the realisation of what was unfolding took hold.

'Tell me this isn't about the body that was found in the Queen's Park pond. I keep reading about it in the paper and a female detective was on the tele again the other night appealing for witnesses. They said it was a well-dressed man in his sixties. Mr DeVilliers was in his late sixties, and he was always immaculately dressed.'

Asif looked at the man and nodded sombrely.

'I'm sorry.'

There was no point in lying. It was now almost certain that the unidentified man was Magnus DeVilliers.

The man slumped down onto a chair shaking his head.

'Bloody hell that's horrendous. A nicer gentleman you couldn't meet. Always so polite and friendly.'

Asif wasn't sure how much more he should say. There was still no formal identification, but there was little doubt in his mind that DeVilliers was their man. Asif was keen to find out what else the man knew about Mr DeVilliers.

'I'm sorry, I haven't even asked you name?'

The man sighed.

'It's Scot McAuley, that's Scot with one 'T'. You see my father was a diehard Rangers supporter, I'm named after Scot Symon the great Rangers manager of the fifties, he spelt his name with only one 'T'.

'I never knew that.' replied Asif taking care to ensure he kept his own football allegiance firmly under wraps. 'Now, I'm keen to know what else you can tell me about Mr DeVilliers. For a start, can you say when you last saw him?'

Scot reached for his receipt book and flipped through the stub of tickets.

'Here it is, DeVilliers, ticket number 2638. 23rd March, so less than a month ago. That's when I repaired his Churchill's. That was the last time I saw him. In fact, it's probably the only time I've seen him in the last year. I know his wife died after a short illness just over a year ago, I heard that it had been cancer. Very sad. Understandably he wasn't in so often after that. You see he used to bring his wife's shoes in for repair as well as his own. Mainly just re-heeling but after she died, he didn't need to do that, so he was in less often. Jeezo,

I still can't believe it. What a horrible way to go, somebody must really have had it in for him!'

Asif nodded sympathetically.

'Do you happen to know what he did for a living?'

'He was a retired doctor, a surgeon I think, but I don't know any more than that. Oh, and he wore a Rolex Yacht-Master watch, very expensive. He lost a pin from the bracelet once which I was able to replace for him. Saved him having to send it off to Rolex to get it fixed. God I can't believe that he's dead.'

Asif put his notebook into his pocket.

'Look, I'm going to have to come back later, probably tomorrow, and get a full statement from you if that's alright. And I'd really appreciate it if you kept this conversation to yourself for now. We have procedures to follow and next of kin to trace.'

Scot held up his hands.

'No problem officer. I won't be saying anything and I'm open till five- thirty tomorrow, so come back anytime. I'll be here.'

'Appreciate that, I'll see you sometime tomorrow. And just to confirm, Glencairn Drive, the house with the large copper beech opposite the bowling club.'

'That's the one, I don't think you'll have any difficulty finding it.'

*

By the time Asif pulled up outside the bowling club it had gone 1645 hrs. The house with the large beech tree was number 48. He tried phoning Campbell, but it went straight to his voicemail. He reckoned he must still be at the dentist, so he left a message asking him to rendezvous with him as soon as he was clear.

Asif crossed the road and stood looking at the blond sandstone villa from the entrance to the driveway. It was a handsome property, with all the hallmarks that it had been well maintained. The perfectly aligned slate tiles suggested it had recently been re-roofed and the cream-coloured paintwork on the windows, guttering and downpipes was in pristine condition. The story was much the same in the front garden. A neat and tidy lawn surrounded by red and orange Azaleas, ready to burst into a riot of colour at the first suggestion of warmer weather.

The house itself showed no obvious signs of life. There were no lights on and all the curtains to the front of the house were open. There was no car in the driveway. Asif walked slowly up the path to the imposing oak front door straddled on either side by a pair of impressive Doric pillars. He rang the bell. There was no reply. Peering through the front window into the spacious lounge he could see a brown leather Chesterfield chair sitting in the far corner of the room next to a large bookcase. On an occasional table next to the chair, he could see an empty wine glass and a book with what appeared to be a pair of glasses sitting on top. Finding nothing untoward he followed the gravel path around the side of the house to the rear garden. The garden was enclosed on all sides by a substantial eight-foot brick wall. Three mature silver birch trees, each at least forty feet high, obscured the view to the houses in the street behind.

Jutting out from the rear of the house was what appeared to be a utility or laundry room. Through a side window he could see clothes hanging from a pulley fixed to the ceiling. It was then that his heart skipped a beat. The white painted door was lying slightly ajar.

Several large splinters of wood lay on the stone steps. Slowly, Asif moved towards the door. Just below the mortice lock he could see the tell-tale teeth marks of where a jemmy had gouged deep into the frame of the door splitting it apart a couple of feet above the doorstep.

Gingerly he pushed at the open door. Lying on the linoleum floor was a broken section of doorframe. Adrenalin surged through his body. Like a moth drawn to a light, he felt an irresistible urge to enter the house, he desperately wanted to go in, to be the first and discover for himself, the truth of what had happened to Magnus DeVilliers. But something, that little voice of reason that occasionally pops into your head stopped him dead in his tracks. Perhaps it was his police training; don't put yourself in unnecessary danger, don't risk compromising important evidence. Whatever it was he could slowly feel his sensible head taking back control, he decided against doing anything rash. In truth, he feared incurring the wrath of his mentor, Campbell, or even worse having to listen to the criticism and caustic comments of his DCI. He desperately wanted to avoid that. He wanted to impress, to prove his worth as a detective and to his team. He couldn't afford to mess up, not now, not after everything he'd been through in the last eight years. One false step could undermine all the toil and hard graft he'd put in, he was within touching distance of a promotion. The poor boy from Lahore might soon become a sergeant. A promotion that could become the launch pad for a successful career, one that would provide financial stability and a decent pension for his wife and young child. It was that thought, more than anything else that made him step back from the door and reach for his radio. He knew he needed back up.

He was about to contact Govan control when he heard the crunch of footsteps on the gravel path that ran round the perimeter of the house. He pressed himself against the wall and held his breath. Letting out a sigh of relief he smiled weakly as a familiar face appeared round the corner of the building.

'Jeezo, Campbell you scared the bejeesus out of me, there's been a break-in, look the door's been forced, for a minute I thought you were the intruder.'

Campbell shook his head and scoffed.

'I picked up your message and got here as quickly as I could.'

He bent down and picked up one of the large wooden splinters from the step.

'Hmm. I don't think we're likely to disturb any intruder. Whoever broke into the house is likely long gone.'

Campbell showed Asif the splinter of wood.

'Look, this wood is soaking wet, it's been dry all day today, and come to think of it most of yesterday as well. This splinter is saturated. It must have been lying here for some time. Probably got soaked from all that rain we had a couple of days ago when we went to the golf club, it could, of course, have been even earlier than that, but it didn't get like that today.'

That thought had simply not occurred to Asif and yet it was the first thing that Campbell noticed. That was what set Campbell apart from the other detectives, he was just brilliant at noticing the small details. The kind of details that make the difference between solving a case or not.

'So, you've got us a name, somebody DeVilliers you said in your message. That's a good bit of detective work on your part.'

Asif smiled.

'Magnus DeVilliers. Retired surgeon apparently. The shoe repairer at Clarkston Toll recognised his shoe straight away and was able to direct me to his house.'

Campbell nodded.

'Excellent. Well, no time like the present, let's check the house out.'

Asif pointed at his radio.

'Shall I call for extra back up, just in case?'

'Na, I think we've got this.' said Campbell opening his jacket to show his PR24 baton strapped into a leather shoulder holster.

'I take it you've got yours.'

Asif patted his jacket. 'Affirmative. I'm good to go.'

'Ok, so here's the plan. We'll search the house according to the book. From the ground floor up. That way nobody can get out without us seeing them, not that we're anticipating that just to be clear. I'll stand at the doorway as you clear each room, got it?'

Asif nodded.

'Fine. We'll start here with the laundry room. And make sure every cupboard and recessed area is checked.'

For the next ten minutes they systematically searched each of the rooms on the ground and first floor. Other than the empty wine glass in the front lounge the only other thing of interest was a dinner plate with a lump of congealed cottage pie and some peas on it that was lying on the central island in the kitchen. The half-eaten meal suggested that someone had perhaps left in a hurry. As far as they could tell, nothing had been stolen from the house. No drawers had been ransacked; everything was just as you would expect it to be. There was even a ten-pound note under a vase in the hallway with a window cleaner's card sitting next to it. Whoever had broken into the property, theft didn't appear to be a motive.

'Well, that's the ground and first floor bedrooms clear, looks like there's two rooms up this stair to the attic.' announced Asif climbing a narrow staircase that led to the top of the house.

To the right-hand side at the top of the stairs was a small box-room. The door was lying open, and Asif could see that the room was filled with filing cabinets and numerous box files neatly stacked in small piles. In the corner by the Velux window was an old computer and console sitting on top of a wooden table. Nothing looked like it had been disturbed. Asif looked at Campbell and shrugged. They still had no clue as to why the house had been broken into.

'Ok, last chance saloon.' said Campbell putting his hand on the door handle to the room to the left of the stairhead. Unlike most of the other rooms the door was shut and when Campbell opened it the room was in darkness with the curtains at the dormer window drawn. Flicking on the light switch he recoiled in horror, stepping back from the doorway onto Asif's foot which nearly sent his colleague crashing down the stairs.

'Holy shit!' exclaimed Campbell standing bolt upright. 'Fuck me, I've seen it all now!'

'Seen what?' asked Asif trying to see over Campbell's shoulder.

'Ah, and watch where you're putting your feet, they're everywhere, the place is crawling with them.' said Campbell inching his way into the room.

Asif stood open mouthed as a frog hopped over his shoe and onto the landing. He felt the weight of Campbell's arm across his chest.'

'Right, brace yourself, 'cause this ain't pretty. Just take a look but don't touch anything. This is going to need the full forensic examination, whoever did this wasn't messing about.'

Asif stared into the room in disbelief. Sitting in a pool of solidified blood on a silver platter on a desk set against the rear wall was the head of a middle-aged man. Clean shaven and open mouthed with thinning grey hair, the man's eyes, sunken and bloodshot held the horror of what had befallen him. Asif's mind flashed back to Caravaggio's painting of Salome with the head of John the Baptist that he'd seen on a school visit to the National Gallery in London. That picture of blood oozing from a severed head remained imprinted in his brain. Now, twelve years later, he found himself standing ten feet away from the real thing, the bloodied head of Magnus DeVilliers, it was truly gruesome.

Strangely he didn't feel nauseous, he was sure he wasn't going to be sick, but he could feel his body reacting to the repulsive sight. He felt lightheaded and hot. Tiny beads of sweat trickled down from his temples. His pulse quickened, racing almost uncontrollably and his mouth felt dry the way it does after you've eaten dry crackers. He fought to control his breathing, taking deep regular breaths, in through the nose, out through the mouth. He recognised his symptoms; he was having a panic attack.

Campbell caught sight of the stunned look on Asif's face, he put his hand on his colleague's elbow.

'You ok?'

Wide eyed, Asif managed the merest of nods.

'Look, why don't you step out for a minute, find yourself a seat or get some fresh air. There's no hurry, this poor fella ain't going anywhere.'

Asif raised his hands.

'No, no, honestly, it's ok. It was just the initial shock, I think I got distracted by that bloody frog, but I've got this, really, I'm going to be fine.'

Campbell smiled.

'As long as you're sure, but still take your time. And watch your feet, I've seen at least half a dozen of the damned things, what the hell are they doing in here?'

'No idea.' replied Asif with a shake of the head. He moved carefully to the centre of the room. On the wall over to his right were three shelves which housed a collection of model boats. Between two and three feet long, the motorised boats immaculately painted with shiny brass rudders rested on wooden cradles. Standing on its own in pride of place on the top shelf was a magnificent twin sailed sloop, much larger than the other boats, its white headsail smeared in what appeared to be blood. More alarmingly, the magnolia painted wall next to the shelves had also been daubed with blood. Although some of it had run down the wall, it was still possible to make out the letter 'D' and the numbers 8 and 5.

'Campbell, look at the front sail of the yacht on the top shelf and the wall next to the shelves. That must be blood don't you think? Whoever killed DeVilliers used his blood to write those letters and numbers. That's plain weird. Those numbers must be two feet high. It's got to be some sort of message, has to be. The killer's trying to tell us something, but what the hell does it mean?'

Chapter 8

Two hours later the property was swarming with officers. Several police vehicles were parked outside the bowling club and a small group of local residents and dog walkers had started to gather on the far pavement wondering what on earth was going on.

Mini Cooper had hot footed it down the moment she received the call from Campbell. She immediately assumed command and for the last hour had been fully engaged issuing orders and instructions. She had brought Constable Natalie Mellish to act as her 'bagwoman' and she was now busy scribing each instruction given out by the DCI. It was obvious that Mini had taken a shine to Natalie since their first encounter in Queen's Park. Having made discreet enquiries Mini had learned that Natalie had stated an interest in joining the CID, so today, with the approval of Inspector Brough, the DCI had suggested that she came with her to the locus to gain valuable experience of how a major enquiry was conducted.

Up in the attic, a photographer and several scenes of crime officers, clad head to foot in white protective suits, were examining the crime scene in minute detail. It was apparent from the laptop and the piles of bank statements and receipts that the room was being used as an office.

Having taken general shots of the room, including several of the letter and numbers daubed on the wall, the photographer's attention shifted to a large bloodstain on the Paisley patterned carpet below the dormer window. The kidney shaped stain, three feet long and nearly two feet wide was clearly significant. Campbell was firmly of the opinion that it was here that the decapitation took place. It had to be. How else could so much blood have got there?

The photographer, a youngish man with long blond hair tied back in a bun, appeared nervous and ill at ease. It wasn't the blood that was bothering him, it was the presence of the frogs which seemed to be everywhere. One of the unfortunate creatures had already perished under the size ten boot of a scenes of crime officer. So, in one of her better decisions, Mini had decreed that all evidence gathering was to cease until all the amphibians had been cleared from the room. This held things up for a while, but with the help of a trout landing net, located in the garage, eleven very much alive frogs and one corpse were removed from the study. It had been eagle-eyed Asif who had spotted the plastic basin of water underneath the desk. Its discovery at least provided an explanation as to how the frogs had been able to survive for so long out of water, but it remained a mystery as to why they were there.

While the photographer went about his work, Asif studied the room from his position close to the door. The room itself appeared to be a shrine to all things nautical. As well as the shelves with the model boats there was a free-standing bookcase which, from what Asif could see, contained nothing except books about boats. On the walls around the room were several framed photographs of Royal Naval Ships. Most prominent among them was a large photograph of a man in full naval uniform which hung in an ornate gold frame above the desk. Gold braid dripped from his cap and the lanyard over his right shoulder. A row of medals, with multicoloured ribbons, hung proudly above his left-hand breast pocket. The inscription at the bottom of the photograph simply said, Admiral Guy DeVilliers, Royal Navy. The photograph was dated August 1960.

Asif took out his phone and googled the name. Wikipedia confirmed what he already suspected. As well as being a decorated war hero and a very senior officer in the Royal Navy, Guy DeVilliers was the father of two children, namely Constance and Magnus DeVilliers. The same article went on to say that in December 1943, Guy Devilliers had captained HMS Enterprise during the Battle of the Bay of Biscay. For that endeavour he had been awarded the Distinguished Cross, his ship being responsible for the sinking of two German Destroyers.

Out the corner of his eye, Asif caught sight of Campbell standing on the landing behind him. The flick of his fingers indicated that he wanted him to join him.

'What's up?' asked Asif putting away his phone.

'Look, until SOCO have finished doing their stuff there's not much we can do here. I want to have a good root around in that room, but it may be a while before we can get in, but I've been thinking.'

Asif grinned. If his boss had been thinking, he better switch on and concentrate, there was every chance it would be important.

'Did you see the blood stain under the dormer window?'

Asif nodded.

'Well, I reckon that's where the murder took place and I'm almost certain it's where his head was cut off.'

'Sure, even I had worked that out. So, what are you getting at?'

Campbell stroked his chin.

'Before we discovered the head, we searched this house thoroughly, bottom to top.'

Asif nodded. 'Yeah, we did.'

'And yet we found nothing out of place, and unless we missed it, we didn't find any blood, not even a speck.'

'Good point.' replied Asif trying to work out where his boss was going with this.

'We know Magnus DeVilliers body turned up four days ago floating in the pond in Queen's Park. So how did he get there? And why there? Maxwell Park is only a quarter of a mile from here, I've walked in it several times over the years. There's a large pond in the park, why didn't whoever murdered Magnus DeVilliers dump the body there. You would have thought it would have been easier?'

Asif pondered what Campbell had said.

'Not sure that's necessarily the case. If there was more than one murderer, and there could easily have been several, then it won't really have mattered. Either way they probably would have needed a vehicle of some description to move the body away from the house, so if they put the body into a car or van then it wouldn't matter if the pond was just down the road or a couple of miles away, does that make sense?'

Campbell screwed up his nose.

'Nothing wrong with your theory except one thing.'

'Oh, and what's that?'

'Come and take a look at this.'

Taking great care to stand only on the line of blue police tape that had been laid on the right-hand edge of the stairs to indicate the single path of entry and exit, the two detectives carefully followed the stairs down to the first-floor landing.

'Ok, now look back up the stairs, what do you notice?' asked Campbell.

Asif scratched his head.

'I don't think I'm noticing anything, what is it I'm supposed to be looking at?'

Campbell pointed at the stairs.

'Look at the centre of each stair and look at the nap of the carpet, do you see how the grain of the carpet is smooth and pointing towards us.'

Campbell bent down and brushed the edge of the landing carpet back the other way.

'Can you see the difference? The nap from the top of the stairs is pointing towards us and it's the same all the way from the attic to the ground floor. The grain is all going in the same direction. Also, look at the width of it, I'd say that was about the width of a body, wouldn't you?'

'I guess.' replied Asif once again staggered by his boss's eye for detail.

Campbell continued.

'That suggests to me that the murderer was acting alone. They murdered Magnus DeVilliers in the attic, cut off his head and put the body in some sort of bag. Probably something similar to the body bags used by the Shell. I think if there had been two or more people involved then they would have carried rather than dragged the body down the stairs. He wasn't the biggest of men, and without his head two people our size could easily carry him down the stairs.'

Asif nodded several times. 'Impressive. And all that from noticing the way the grain of the carpet was lying.'

'I'll let Mini and SOCO know,' added Campbell. 'I know they would have checked the stairs anyway, but I want them to be extra thorough with this one. Remember Locard's theory, every contact leaves a trace, you never know, we might just get lucky.'

Nearly three hours had passed before SOCO and the photographer finally finished their work. There was an eerie silence as all present stood respectfully still as the head of Magnus DeVilliers was removed in a large black box to the Shell waiting outside.

Before she returned to the office, Mini had arranged for three uniformed officers to remain overnight at the locus. One to be positioned at the front drive, another at the back door and a third on the landing outside the study where the head had been found. The DCI had also informed Campbell that she wanted a hot de-brief with the team at 2100 hrs in the incident room. She wanted everything logged and updated on the Holmes system before anyone finished for the day. That timeline gave Campbell and Asif a little over an hour to go through the room and get back to base.

'This is going to take way longer than an hour.' muttered a frustrated Campbell as he sifted through the pile of paperwork on the desk. 'This will just have to be a cursory look through, plenty time tomorrow to come back and do the job properly.'

'Sure.' replied Asif who was now examining the model boats on the shelves.

'Campbell, according to the inscription on this wooden plinth, this grey coloured ship is a scale model of HMS Enterprise. That's the ship his father Captained during the Second World War. That's his father in the photograph above you. I looked him up on Wikipedia earlier.'

Campbell glanced up and stared at the photograph above the desk.

'I know this sounds a bit macabre, but you can see the family likeness. The eyes and the shape of the nose are the same.'

Asif winced, but it was hard to disagree. He had noticed the likeness too. He put down the model ship.

'And I'll tell what's strange, other than one framed certificate on the wall next to the bookcase, that I think marks his appointment as a consultant, everything else in here is either a homage to his father or the Royal Navy. Unless I've missed it there isn't even a photograph of him with his wife.'

Campbell looked up.

'Good observations Detective Butt. It's clear he held his father in high esteem, there are more photographs of his father and I assume the ships he commanded in a drawer in the desk. But don't tell me you missed the photograph by the side of the bed in the front bedroom?'

Asif raised an eyebrow.

'I'll grant you it was small, but it looked like a photo of Magnus with a lady who I assume was his wife. It was taken on a golf course somewhere abroad, the trees in the photo looked like Almond trees, like the ones you get in Spain or Portugal.'

Asif shook his head. He hadn't clocked the photograph in the bedroom, he had been too busy looking for an intruder. But that was just another example of Campbell's detective skills. Very little went unnoticed by him. Unlike his own, Campbell's radar appeared to be permanently switched on.

Campbell picked up and studied a bank statement from the pile of papers on the desk.

'Well, he wasn't struggling to pay his electricity bill, according to this he's got over £115,000 in his current account. And I've already seen statements for investments with Santander and Standard Life, no wonder he could afford a pair of Churchill brogues, clearly had plenty money.'

Asif rolled his eyes.

'No shit Sherlock, even a baby detective like me could have told you that, look at the size of the house and the quality of the furnishings, it's all the best of stuff.'

'Hmm, Ok, perhaps that wasn't my most illuminating observation.' said Campbell taking off his glasses. He picked up another piece of paper. 'Now this, however, will be well worth following up on.'

Asif walked over to the desk.

'What have you found?'

'It's just a receipt for some butcher meat, Cranston's the butchers, in Pollokshields. It's only half a mile along the road, great butchers apparently, my old boss from my surveillance days was forever popping in when we were in this neck of the woods. He was on first name terms with the old fella who ran the shop. Went by the name of Connell. Connell Cranston. I've never forgotten it as it's such an unusual name. Anyway, I digress. What's interesting about this is the date. The receipt's dated April 11th. That's the day before Magnus

DeVilliers body was recovered from the pond. Old Cranston may very well have been the last person to see our man alive!'

Campbell picked up several other items from the desk.

'Ah, now these are also interesting. A couple of membership cards. One for Whitecraigs Golf Club and another for the bowling club across the road. And this appears to be a letter about the annual subscription for the Glasgow Academical Club. It seems our man was privately educated, no real surprise there I suppose. But with the boats and these clubs it appears he had plenty of interests to keep him busy. Anyway, there's enough here to keep us occupied for a couple of days, unless of course Mini has other plans for us.'

Asif looked at his watch.

'On that note I think it's time we were heading back, you know what she's like, we don't want to be late. Oh, and I meant to say to you earlier, were you aware that SOCO took a sample of the water from the basin for analysis. They let me have a good look at it, now I'm no scientist, but I can tell you something for nothing, that water didn't come out of a tap, there were any number of wee beasties floating in it, I reckon it's pond water, that will be why the frogs appeared to be so at home.'

*

'Ok, listen up. If you've given your updates to Jan, you can stand down, but I want everyone back tomorrow for a 0730 briefing. That's 0730 hrs, not 0745 or 0735 hrs. In here and ready to go at 0730 hrs. Is that clear?

Everyone in the room nodded.

'Good, well I'll see you all bright and early tomorrow, we've got the house to house and plenty of other stuff to get stuck into. Campbell, Asif can you both hang fire I want a word.'

Campbell pulled up a chair. What now? It had already been a long day and he still needed to get to a supermarket and get some painkillers. The dentist had told him he had an impacted tooth that would probably need extracting. However, that wasn't the worse news. The acute pain he had been experiencing was from an abscess that had formed under a molar. Years of avoiding the dentist had taken its toll, he needed root canal treatment to drain the infection. With luck the tooth could be saved, and he'd been given an appointment for early next week. Till then he would need to get by with a course of antibiotics and painkillers. There was also the cost. The treatment was going to set him back several hundred pounds. All in all, he'd had better days and now he just wanted to get home. He wasn't sure he was up for another verbal spat with his line manager.

'Right, you two, I just wanted a word on our own.'

Campbell rolled his eyes biting his bottom lip.

'Excellent bit of work Asif, getting us the name from the cobbler, and once again it just goes to show, if you don't make the calls, you don't get the results. And that was your initiative, and it's given us the break we were needing. So good effort and well done.'

Asif beamed a big, satisfied smile. That was the first positive endorsement he had received from the new DCI and boy did it feel good.

Campbell braced himself, he wasn't sure what he had done that might have annoyed his boss, but he was sure he was about to find out.

'You too Campbell. I just wanted to say well done. That was an excellent observation about the nap of the carpet. I've been thinking about it since you mentioned it and I think you're absolutely on the money. I think it's likely that our murderer was working alone. Of course, we'll keep an open mind, but all these seemingly insignificant details will help us build a picture of who killed Magnus DeVilliers. So today has been a good day, and in a large part that's been down to you two. I just wanted you to know I appreciate that.'

Campbell blinked and swallowed hard. You could have knocked him down with a feather. DCI Cooper had a heart and was shrewd enough to recognise and acknowledge good work. He'd worked with plenty of irascible old bosses who would never praise their staff like that. They would regard it as a sign of weakness. In the short time he'd known her, DCI Cooper was proving to be something of an enigma, she blew hot and cold, but credit where credit was due, she might be quick to criticise, but she was also big enough to praise and thank her team. That was the sign of a leader who might actually achieve something.

'Appreciate that boss, just doing our jobs as you know, but do you mind if I shoot? I need to get to Asda and get some painkillers for this bloody tooth, it's still aching, the antibiotics the dentist gave me aren't touching it yet, so if you don't mind.'

'No, no we're done, you shoot off. Asif, you might want to hang about, there's a letter for you from personnel on my desk. I think you'll know what it's about.'

Asif puffed out his cheeks and sighed.

'Oh, I'd cheer up if I were you. It's a fat letter and fat letters are good. Thin ones on the other hand, well let's just say you don't want one of them. It only takes one sheet and two paragraphs to tell you were unsuccessful.

I remember receiving my letter and my colleagues who were successful were exactly the same. We got the fat letter, the letter with all our joining instructions and details about the course. Now I've gone out on a limb here, but I don't think I'm wrong. Why don't you go and see and put us all out of our misery, as I said it's lying on my desk.'

Asif nodded and scuttled off in the direction of the DCI's office.

Campbell put on his jacket and sat down.

'I'm hanging on for this and I just hope you're right, the boy deserves it. He works hard and has a good brain, he's just what the job needs.'

They didn't have long to wait. The door burst open, and in strode Asif holding the letter aloft with a with a smile as wide as the Clyde.

'You were right boss, I've been accepted, I'm going to be on the next Accelerated Promotion Course.'

Chapter 9

Pollokshields, like many places, is a neighbourhood of contrasts. Established in 1849 on land bequeathed by the Stirling-Maxwell family, and feued in a large part by Edinburgh architect, David Rhind, vast sandstone mansions, home to many of Glasgow's great and the good, sit alongside elegant streets of spacious and stylish flats. Alexander 'Greek' Thomson designed villas and Harry Clifford's magnificent Pollokshields Burgh Hall, that stands on the eastern edge of Maxwell Park, leave their own mark on this charming Victorian suburb. There is, however, a darker side to the Shields and you don't have to venture far to find it. Decaying tenements and litter-strewn streets become increasing the norm as you venture north towards Albert Drive and Kenmure Street. The wealthy and the poor, the fortunate and the not so fortunate, separated at most by a few hundred metres. Sitting astride the two on Nithsdale Road is a small enclave of shops. An artisan baker, a florist, and several trendy coffee shops, sit next to a specialist grocer and a gift shop brimming with soft furnishings, scented candles and other frivolous stuff that nobody needs but everyone desires. And then two of life's essentials, a pharmacist and a butcher's shop.

Cranston's family butchers have been operating from the same premises on Nithsdale Road since 1885.

Started by the current owner's great grandfather, the Cranston family have been purveyors of high-quality meat to the denizens of Pollokshields for nearly 120 years. Magnus DeVilliers, and his wife Isobel, had been regular customers since they first moved to Glencairn Drive back in the early eighties.

It was approaching ten when Campbell found a parking space across the road from the butcher's shop. For this morning's enquiries he was accompanied by Natalie Mellish, Asif had a mid-morning appointment with the Divisional Commander, just a quick meeting to congratulate him on his successful application to the AP Course. So, for this morning at least, Campbell had a new neighbour.

The two officers waited patiently as the old lady at the counter fumbled in her purse looking for the elusive ten-pound note that she was sure was in there.

The rosy cheeked bespectacled man in the stripped apron and white coat behind the counter smiled knowingly, he had been here many times before.

'Don't worry about it, Mrs Lavery, you can pop it into me when you're next passing. You said you brought a different bag with you, perhaps the money is in a different purse in the other bag. I think that's happened before, hasn't it?'

Mrs Lavery smiled.

'I think you're probably right. I'd forget my head if it wasn't screwed on, this old age is no fun. But that's very kind of you Mr Cranston. So how much is it I owe you?'

Mr Cranston took a pencil from his coat pocket and wrote on a piece of paper. It's on the receipt I gave you, but I've written it out bigger here, it's a lot easier to see,

£3.80. But there's no hurry, just drop it in when you're passing.'

'I'll do that.' replied Mrs Lavery stuffing the quarter of mince and sausages into her bag.

'That's very kind of you, and I'll not forget, I'll come round with it later.' With that the old lady about-turned and bustled out the shop.

'Occupational hazard?' asked Campbell showing Mr Cranston his warrant card.

'Yeah, you could say that we get all sorts in here. I've got a lot of elderly customers. Very faithful customers, but some, like Mrs Lavery can be a bit forgetful, but it all works out in the end. She'll be back with her money before lunchtime I expect, you just need a little come and go in this business. Now Detective Inspector, Connell Cranston's the name, what can I do for you?'

Campbell removed the receipt from his folder and handed it to Mr Cranston.

'I'm making enquiries into an incident involving a Mr Magnus DeVilliers, he stays in Glencairn Drive and since he had a receipt from you in his house, I'm assuming he may be one of your customers.'

Mr Cranston looked over his glasses and gave the officers a knowing look.

'You don't work in the same shop for 42 years without getting to hear things officer. At least three customers this morning must have told me about the goings on at the DeVilliers house yesterday. Dreadful business, everyone is now assuming that the body that your boys recovered last week from Queen's Park and that's been all over the news is Mr DeVilliers.'

The merest of nods was all the confirmation Mr Cranston needed. He shook his head.

'Lovely man, always so polite. I knew his wife Isobel better; she was very regularly in here. It was only after her death that I got to know Magnus better. I believe she died of cancer. Must be well over a year ago now. It all seemed to happen very quickly, so very sad, as I said, just a lovely couple.'

Campbell nodded sympathetically.

'I'd like to ask you a few questions, if that's ok, it shouldn't take very long.'

'Sure, fire away, I'll help in any way I can.'

'The receipt you've got there is dated the 11ᵗʰ April, that was the day before we found Mr DeVilliers body. Do you remember him coming in? And how was he, was there anything different about his demeanour?'

Mr Cranston thought for a moment.

'No, nothing I can think of. It was all very normal. He bought his usual steak pie and some liver; I remember I asked him if he was golfing as weather-wise it was a reasonable day. I know he and his wife used to be keen golfers; I think they had a place in the Algarve that they regularly visited. Mr DeVilliers was a retired Consultant. Ear, Nose, and Throat, specialist, I think. He worked mainly from Ross Hall; you know, private work. Quite lucrative, must have been to live in Glencairn Drive and have a place in Portugal. And his father had been an admiral in the Royal Navy, he was also a decorated war hero, that was pretty well known around these parts. Boats and ships were another passion of Mr DeVilliers, he used to talk about it a lot.'

Natalie jotted down some notes in her folder.

Campbell continued. 'So, nothing unusual about his behaviour. He didn't seem worried or concerned?'

'Nope. He was the same as he always was. Bright, quite upbeat. There was nothing out of the ordinary.'

'One last question if I may. Did the DeVilliers have any family? They would be grown up now, but I wondered if there were any children.'

Mr Cranston pursed his lips.

'Not that I'm aware of. Neither he nor his wife ever mentioned children. But I can't be 100% sure. You should try at the bowling club, it's right across the road from his house, I don't know if he bowled, he may, of course, just have been a social member, he told me he liked to stroll across the road for a glass of wine and chat to friends. Subsidised bar, cheap drink, what's not to like even if you were wealthy like Mr DeVilliers.'

Cranston handed back the receipt which Campbell returned to his folder.

'Thanks for that I'm grateful to you, that's been most helpful. And mind and let us know if the old lady doesn't return with her money, that's just the sort of crime I reckon we could get a detection for, what do you reckon Natalie?'

For a moment the remark caught her off guard, she wasn't sure if her colleague was being serious.

'Ah, sure, yes, well I suppose technically it would be a fraud?'

Campbell shook his head and chuckled. 'Crikey, you've got a lot to learn, even Asif would have got that joke, and he's as slow as a stopped watch when it comes to getting jokes.'

Natalie blushed with embarrassment. Earlier that morning the DCI had told her that she'd managed, with the agreement of the Sub Divisional Officer, to get her seconded to the enquiry team for the duration of the investigation. This was not the best of starts, she desperately wanted to make a good impression, the last thing she needed on her first morning was to come across as some sort of airhead.'

Campbell sensed her discomfort.

'Look, I'm just joshing with you, and no need to panic, none of this will find its way back to the DCI.'

Natalie smiled weakly and decided to move the conversation on.

'Are we heading to the bowling club? There might be people there, friends perhaps, who could potentially give us useful information.'

'Yeah, we will be going there but all in good time. First, I want to finish checking the house, and particularly the study, there's still a considerable amount of paperwork to go through.'

Back at the property, Campbell got busy ploughing through the various piles of paperwork on Mr DeVilliers' desk. He'd asked Natalie to go and try and locate a set of car keys for the BMW X5 that was parked in the garage. To his knowledge nobody had come across the keys, so the vehicle had not been searched. Fifteen minutes passed then a voice shouted up the stairs.

'I've got them, I've found the keys, they were hanging on a hook behind a curtain in the utility room, strange place to leave them but close to the backdoor and handy for the garage I suppose.'

Campbell stuck his head out the door.

'Good stuff, well done. Now you crack on, I'll be down when I'm finished here. Just unlock the car and check the boot and the glove compartment. In fact, just have a right old root about. I'll be down in five.'

The garage was cavernous. The X5 is a big car but Natalie reckoned there was room for at least another two vehicles. She glanced round the inside of the brick-built building. It was typical of most garages, although it was three times the size of her own and considerably tidier. A lawnmower and various pieces of gardening equipment were neatly stacked against one wall. Tins of paint, oil cans, and car cleaning products filled the shelves next to the window. Standing against the other wall was a set of golf clubs, in a white and pink bag. The tag on the bag read Lady Member 2002, Whitecraigs Golf Club. Natalie didn't need the affirmation from the tag, she was a golfer herself, quite useful in her youth and student days. She didn't play as regularly now but she recognised the Wilson Ultra clubs immediately, she had a very similar set herself. These were ladies' clubs, and it was clear that they had belonged to Mrs DeVilliers. A wide wheeled golf trolley stood folded up next to the bag. In a box next to that was a black golf travel bag, the type you use when taking clubs abroad on a plane. Natalie examined the travel bag, attached to the handle were old flight labels. Faro/Glw and a bar code still clearly visible.

Natalie pressed the key fob to unlock the car. She opened the passenger door and checked the glove compartment. Other than the car's handbooks, a bag of wine gums and a locking wheel nut in a blue velvet bag there was little else to be seen. The same was true for the rest of the interior. Judging by the smell of polish it appeared that the vehicle had been recently valeted. The only thing on the back seat was a box of tissues.

Natalie opened the boot. Lying on the floor was a set of golf clubs in a large red bag. Next to the clubs was a pair of green wellingtons, a small shovel and some cleaning rags. And that was it. She lifted the bag in case she had missed it. Strange she thought. Closing the boot, she did another check of the garage, but it was nowhere to be seen.

The side door opened and in walked Campbell.

'Found anything of interest?'

Natalie tilted her head.

'Might have. There's nothing of particular interest inside the car that I can see, but something doesn't add up.'

'Oh, and what's that?'

'There's no trolley or travel bag. His wife's clubs are over there against the wall, as are her trolley and travel bag. But his appears to be missing. His clubs are in the boot but there's no sign of a trolley. It's a big heavy bag he's got. I play a bit of golf and I can tell you that you wouldn't be carrying a bag that size, certainly not a man DeVilliers age, you would have them on a trolley, yet it doesn't appear to be here. There's no travel carrier either. His wife's still got flight labels on hers, but again, there's no sign of his.'

Campbell rubbed his chin.

'Could he have left the trolley at his club?'

'It's possible but unlikely I'd say. But that can be easily checked. I think that most people would keep their clubs and trolley together, that's certainly what I've always done.'

Campbell nodded quietly; something was dawning on him.

'Show me the travel bag that's got the labels on it, will you.'

Natalie lifted the black bag out of the box.

Campbell examined the thick nylon bag.

'Hmm, you know something Natalie, I think you might have stumbled on something significant here.

I reckon we can answer the question as to how DeVilliers' body was removed from the attic. I think whoever killed him took his travel bag from in here and put the body in it, leaving the head behind of course. Then they've dragged the bag down two flights of stairs and out of the house, without, as far as we know, leaving a speck of blood anywhere.'

'And if the trolley's also missing it's quite possible that they put the bag on the trolley and just wheeled him away.' added Natalie.

'Now that would be a first, you don't ever see a murder like that on Miss Marple. But it's more than plausible. I know some of the team are checking the local CCTV footage, this will be just one more thing for them to look out for.'

Chapter 10

'Campbell, Natalie, grab a mug and join us. The coffee's just brewed, help yourself, but I think you're going to find this interesting. Go on Asif, tell them what you've just explained to me.'

Campbell poured himself a coffee and sat down while Natalie perched on the edge of a desk.

'It was Roisin that came up with it, so I'm really just the messenger. I can't take any credit for it. I had no idea that …'

Campbell took a large mouthful of coffee and put up his hand.

'Detective Butt, can I just stop you for a moment. If you're going on the next AP course, you're going to have to learn how to explain things plainly and succinctly. No waffle. So, here's an opportunity for you to do just that. What is it that you need to tell us?'

Asif took a deep breath and started again.

'Ok, let me try again. Last night, when I got home, Roisin asked me how my day had been. She always does that. I replied fine except for the number of frogs we encountered at the property and the strange letter and numbers that had been daubed in blood on the wall. I said it had freaked me out a little, and I'd had a mild panic attack.'

Campbell raised an eyebrow.

'I know, I know. The boss has already spoken to me about discussing police work at home, but honestly, I didn't tell her any names or addresses. Anway, she remarked that it sounded creepy, and it reminded her of the story of the plague of frogs from the book of Exodus in the bible. I had no idea what she was talking about, but as a good Catholic girl she knew all about it. Apparently, there were ten plagues, and the frogs were the second one. She told me what the first was, but I can't remember, but that doesn't matter. Anyway, she went and got her bible. She said that bible readings are often referenced by a letter, for the book it's taken from, and then two numbers. The chapter number and the verse it refers to.'

Campbell slapped his forehead hard. He was annoyed with himself, why hadn't he seen it. Hearing it now from Asif it was blindingly obvious, but with everything else that had been going on, he'd somehow managed to miss it.'

'Roisin's right, she's absolutely right. And as a boy brought up on Lewis in the Free Presbyterian Kirk, I should have recognised that. My old ministers will be spinning in their graves. 'D' 8, 5. It's a bible reference, but it's not from the book of Exodus.'

Asif nodded.

'No. We think it's a reference to Deuteronomy. Apparently, there are only two books in the bible starting with a 'D'. Deuteronomy and Daniel. Chapter 8 verse 5 of Daniel didn't make any sense but the reference to Deuteronomy does, I think.'

Asif opened his folder.

'Just to make sure I've got this right. Yes, here it is.

Take this lesson to heart: that the Lord your God was disciplining you as a father disciplines his son: and keep the commandments of the Lord your God.'
Deuteronomy Chapter 8 Verse 5.

'Well, it was some lesson right enough!' said Campbell sardonically.

Conway got up to pour himself another coffee.

'Terrific. So, we've got some religious nutter running around Pollokshields cutting folk's heads off like it's some bloody jihad.'

Mini looked perplexed.

'I think you're mixing your religions up Con, and as far as we know, it's just the one head that's been cut off.'

'Ah, but you see that's the problem with these religious nutjobs, they don't know where to stop, before you know it, we'll have a serial killer on our hands, mark my words.'

'How many cups of coffee have you had.' asked Campbell mischievously. 'Boss, you've not given him some of the Insomnia from the other day, 'cause whatever it is it seems to have tipped him over the edge.'

'Ok, that's enough everyone. Let's be serious can we. And thanks for that update, Asif. It's an example of another good piece of work by the team, well, not strictly by the team, but you know what I mean, it's close enough. Now, before we move on can I just clarify, for Con's benefit and everyone else's for that matter. As things stand, we've got no evidence to suggest that this isn't just an isolated murder. A very unusual one I'll grant you, but we've nothing to indicate that our killer might strike again.'

The others nodded in agreement. The DCI continued.

'Excellent. Now we've got agreement on that, I need you to step up Jan. You're gonna be a busy lady. I want all that written up and put onto the system. Not sure why our killer would be leaving references from the bible at the murder scene, but it's another line of enquiry that will require looking into. I'm going to get you an extra pair of hands, you're going to need some assistance, because this is going to take you a while. And Natalie, after this meeting, do me a favour and write that bible quote verbatim up on the whiteboard.'

'That's what I'm here for.' replied Jan logging onto her computer.

Natalie waved a dry marker pen in the air. 'On it, ma'am.'

'Ok, just one more thing. Can everyone ensure that their updates for this morning's actions are written up and left with Jan. No lunch till that's done. And then, this afternoon, door to door continues, and Campbell and Asif, you're making enquiries at the bowling club, unless you managed to get that done this morning. And apologies, I got sidetracked by that excellent bit of detective work by Asif's wife, was there anything else that I need to know about from this morning's enquiries?'

Campbell looked over at Natalie and smiled.

'Well boss as it happens there is, and that was largely down to Natalie's efforts, can I have five minutes to update you about a missing golf trolley and travel carrier?'

'You may indeed, but first I need another infusion of this rather mellow blend called Gevalia, which believe it or not, comes all the way from Sweden.'

*

A mixed pairs match was in full flow on the green to the left of the front gate when Campbell and Asif arrived at the bowling club. Sitting on a bench in a shelter next to the green watching proceedings were a pair of elderly gents, glasses in hand. Judging by the near empty bottle of wine that sat between them, they had been there for some time. Over on the other green two men wearing white pullovers and white caps were positioning scoreboards and rink markers at either end of the green. It appeared they were preparing for a serious match. The clubhouse, a one storied Arts & Crafts building with geometrically patterned black and white rendered walls had an impressive conical shaped roof immediately above the bay window of the lounge.

Asif opened the door just to the right of the front entrance that led to the lounge and bar. Two couples sat engrossed in a game of bridge at a table by the window which offered panoramic views of both greens. The bridge players seemed oblivious to the detectives' presence and to the goings on outside. Other than an old man who was sitting alone at a corner table nursing a half pint of Guinness and reading the Telegraph, nobody was in the place. Asif rang the bell at the bar. After a couple of minutes, a middle-aged man wearing a club sweater appeared behind the bar.

'Sorry about that, but I was round the back changing a keg of beer. Trying to get ahead of the game you see. First match of the season this afternoon and I won't get a chance to do it later when the bar gets busy. I'm the club steward here, David Beckett's the name, how can I help you?'

Asif showed Mr Beckett his warrant card and explained why they were there.

Beckett scrunched his nose up and gently shook his head.

'I was expecting that you would pay us a visit. It's all anyone's been talking about. Shocking news, and what a lovely man. A real old-school gentleman was Mr DeVilliers.'

Asif opened his folder and took his pen from his jacket pocket.

'Did you know him well?'

Beckett nodded. 'Yeah, I suppose I did. I've worked here eight years and he's been a member all that time. Funny thing is in those eight years I never once saw him play. He used to wonder across the road of an evening, usually about nine, stay for an hour or so, have a couple of glasses of wine, before heading home.'

Beckett chuckled pointing out the window.

'He didn't have much of a commute as he literally lived across the road, the house with the large beech tree.'

Campbell pulled up a stool and sat down.

'So, he was really just a social member?'

'Pretty much, although before his wife died, they both liked to come and play bridge. That was mainly on a Wednesday, we have a few that come in to play on a Wednesday. His wife was a nice lady, but I believe she was more into her golf, never saw her on the bowling green either.'

Asif scribbled down some notes.

'Did he come in much after his wife died, which I believe was about 15 months ago?'

Beckett thought for a moment.

'Perhaps not as regularly, but I did still see him, in fact I'm sure he was in a week or so ago playing bridge. That would have been the last time I saw him.'

'You're not the first person we've spoken to who's said what a gentleman he was, so in many ways he seems a most unlikely victim. Look, I'm going to come straight to the point, can you think of any reason why someone might want to kill him?'

'Woah, I wasn't expecting you to ask me that.' replied Beckett clearly taken aback by the directness of the question.

He thought for several moments.

'You know honestly, I couldn't give you a single reason why anybody wouldn't like Mr DeVilliers, let alone want do him any harm.'

Beckett rubbed his nose.

'The only thing that I'm aware of about him that was even remotely controversial was several years ago he got involved in a dispute with the Friends of Maxwell Park, Conservation Group. We called it 'Dabchick Gate' at the time, but really it was no more than a storm in a teacup, it was nothing serious and anyway, as I said, it was years ago.'

'Dabchick gate! What on earth was that about?' asked Campbell.

'The Dabchick, or Little Grebe as it's better known as is a bird, officer. Anyway, for many years Mr DeVilliers and a group of other enthusiasts, perhaps as many as a dozen of them, used to sail their model boats on the pond in Maxwell Park. They would be there every Saturday morning without fail, come rain or shine. I believe Mr DeVilliers was the group's co-ordinator, he was a real boat enthusiast, and extremely knowledgeable about them. His father had been a famous admiral in the Royal Navy, I think that's where he got his love of boats from.'

Asif looked confused.

'But what has any of that got to do with a bird. I think you called it a Dabchick.'

'I was about to explain that officer. One spring, it must have been about five years ago now, a pair of Dabchicks appeared at the pond. No one could recall ever seeing one before, well, not in Maxwell Park. The pair started to build a nest on the small island very near to where Mr DeVilliers and his friends launched their boats. And that's when Hilda Chisholm got herself involved. Chisholm was part of a small group of conservationists who took an interest in the park. They put up nest boxes, made bug hotels for insects, and planted wildflowers. You know the type of thing. Hilda Chisholm was the activist in the group. She was their leader. Years ago, she'd been at Greenham Common and was a vociferous and quite outspoken supporter of Greenpeace and CND. And if there were any type of local conservation campaign then you could guarantee that Hilda Chisholm would be at the head of it.'

Campbell scratched his chin.

'So, I take it that the arrival of the Dabchick put her and her group into conflict with Mr DeVilliers and the model boat enthusiasts? I presume she didn't want the boats disturbing the birds when they were nesting.'

Beckett smiled.

'You've got it in one detective. She was a bit of a firebrand, but she was able to get some important people to rally to her cause. The RSPB and the local council got involved. She even lobbied our MP, claiming the Dabchick was a protected species and that the model boaters were going to cause it to desert its nest. It was big news at the time, the local paper carried the story for weeks. Even the Evening Times ran a feature about it.'

Asif put down his folder.

'So, what was the upshot?'

Beckett smiled wryly.

'This I think takes us back to Mr DeVilliers being a gentleman. He really didn't want to cause a fuss and I know he didn't want to do the Dabchicks any harm, he told me that himself, so he decided to back down. That didn't go down well with everyone, some of the group wanted to ignore Chisolm and carry on sailing their boats. But Mr DeVilliers didn't see it that way, so the model boaters stopped coming on a Saturday. Most people, me included, assumed that they would resume after the breeding season had passed and the Dabchicks had raised their young. But they never did. I believe some of them might have moved to another pond, but I'm not sure of that. One thing's for certain though, they never sailed their boats in Maxwell Park again.'

Campbell took off and wiped his glasses.

'Hmm, interesting story. But there doesn't appear to be anything there that might raise concerns that somebody might want to do harm to Magnus DeVilliers.'

'What happened to Hilda Chisholm, is she still living around here? Because I think we should at least have a word with her.' asked Asif.

Beckett smiled again.

'Well, you can score her off your list of suspects. She was knocked down and killed by an MOD convoy a couple of years ago while on a CND demonstration at Faslane. How ironic is that?'

Campbell raised an eyebrow.

'And do you know the two other ironic things about Dabchick Gate.'

Campbell and Asif shook their heads.

'Nope, I think you're going to have to enlighten us.' added Campbell sarcastically.

'Well firstly, it turns out that the Dabchick was never a protected species, so there was no reason in law why Mr DeVilliers had to stop sailing his boats. And here's the kicker. That particular spring was the one and only time the Dabchicks ever nested in Maxwell Park. After they raised their young, they skedaddled, and they've never been seen again.'

Campbell stood up from his stool.

'Well, it's a rattling good tale, I'll grant you that. And it would make a half decent TV drama, but somehow, I don't think it's going to help us to find the killer of Mr DeVilliers, but never say never, stranger things have happened. But listen, we're grateful for your time, Mr Beckett, it's been a most interesting half hour.'

Chapter 11

For the first time in several weeks, it looked as though spring might finally have arrived. It was only just after 8am, but already it was several degrees warmer than it had been of late and the early morning sun and cloudless sky showed promise of a lovely day ahead.

Mrs Bartholomew had noticed the man standing outside the front door of the Royal Mail sorting office on Victoria Road when she passed on her way to Lidl's. She was an early morning shopper, and at least three times each week, she left her flat in Butterbiggins Road to pick up messages at her local supermarket. She must have passed the sorting office hundreds of times over the years, and it wasn't unusual to see a queue outside, it was a busy place. But it was unusual to see someone waiting at 8 in the morning, a full hour before the office opened. She needed to go to the sorting office herself, to pick up a parcel for her grandson's birthday, perhaps that's why she had noticed him. It had crossed her mind that he might be waiting for a lift, but as he was still standing in the exact same spot when she returned 45 minutes later, she decided that was perhaps unlikely.

It wasn't just the fact that he was queuing so early that had caught her attention, it was also the way the man was dressed. He looked like he was equipped for a polar expedition, it was quite out of place for such a mild spring morning. Quite small in stature, and perhaps in his early forties, he was sporting several days' growth. He was wearing a filthy padded blue jacket with straggly fake fur around its collar. The jacket was covered in dark greasy stains and was badly torn across the right shoulder. His trousers were made of thick serge and were far too long. The trouser hems were shredded where they had caught under his feet and dragged along the ground. His metal toecapped boots appeared enormous, certainly out of proportion to his height. His look was topped off by a black beanie hat pulled down tight over his ears.

Mrs Bartholomew had half thought about going home with her trolley of messages and returning later for her parcel. But as several other people had now joined the queue, including a friend who she saw most weeks at the Bingo, she decided to stay, and have a natter while she waited. Anyway, she wouldn't have to wait long, the office was due to open in five minutes, and it was just a joy to be outside on such a lovely morning and for the first time in months feel the warmth of the spring sunshine. She passed the time of day with her friend as she rummaged in her handbag for the card to reclaim her parcel.

The man at the head of the queue appeared agitated. He was constantly muttering to himself and shifting his weight from foot to foot. Something was clearly bothering him. From inside his jacket, he removed a small and rather nondescript brown cardboard box, about half the size of a shoebox, the side of the box appeared to be covered in small holes. The lady standing immediately behind him took a couple of steps back and turned her face away. The young man behind her was not so polite.

'Holy suffering fuck!' What the hell is that smell?'

Mrs Bartholomew and the other ladies in the queue fumbled through their bags looking for tissues as the rancid smell wafted slowly down the line.

Studiously avoiding eye contact the man muttered something inaudible and thrust the box back inside his jacket.

At that moment a man in a Royal Mail uniform opened the front door. Head down, the man with the box, brushed past him and entered the office. The others in the queue held back, no one, it appeared, was keen to share an enclosed space with the man and his malodorous box.

The Royal Mail man made a strange face as the first odours reached his nostrils.

'There's plenty room inside, if you'd like to come in.'

Nobody moved.

'The strange face now became more of a contortion. On second thoughts you're very wise, stay where you are.' he added.

The man removed a hankie from his pocket and wiped his eyes. He grimaced at the others in the queue.

'Pray for me, I'm gonna have to go in there and see what he wants.'

'Not sure a prayer is gonna cut it somehow, it's a bloody gasmask you'll need. Seriously, that's a damned health hazard.' said the young man in the queue.

It was difficult to make out what exactly was being said inside the office. But judging by the raised voices and expletives that filled the air, things were getting heated. A full-blown argument was raging inside. Mrs Bartholomew was transfixed, she hadn't had this much excitement in ages, this was like a scene from a movie.

Fully five minutes passed before the front door burst open and the man in the blue padded jacket stormed out. Head down and swearing.

'Fucking idiots, the lot of you. But you've not heard the last of this, I can fucking promise you that.'

And with that he was gone, crossing Victoria Road he disappeared along Coplaw Street.

The Royal Mail man appeared carrying a black bin liner bag tied with a bit of string. He was accompanied by another man wearing a suit. The badge on his breast pocket said manager.

'Sorry about that and for the delay. I'm afraid it's still rather unpleasant in there, but we've got the windows open, and I've sprayed a whole can of air freshener in the front office. Can I ask that you give it a couple more minutes before coming in, hopefully the worst of it will be away by then.'

The half dozen folk in the queue all nodded in unison. The manager turned to his colleague.

'Ok Davie, if you've sealed that properly, take it round the back and dump it in one of the black bins.'

'Roger that.' replied his colleague holding the bin liner at arm's length.

The manager smiled and made his way back inside.

'What the hell was that all about?' asked the young man in the queue when Davie reappeared from the back yard.

Mrs Bartholomew and the others strained to hear what was being said.

'Just some nutter coming in and shouting the odds. Claimed we should never have delivered the package and left a calling card as he was away for a few days. But he picked a fight with the wrong people, the box

111

hadn't been marked properly, we would never have left it if we'd known what was in it, but without the appropriate labelling there was no way that the postman could have known that it contained live insects.'

The young man made a face.

'Jeezo. I didn't know you were allowed to send live things via the mail!'

'You can send some types of insect. Universities and laboratories quite often do it. But there are strict regulations about the type of container that must be used, and it must be properly ventilated and clearly marked that the package contains live insects.'

The young man shook his head. 'Well, you learn something every day. I take it, judging by that stench, that they had all perished?'

Davie nodded.

'There was just a pile of mush at the bottom of the box when he opened it. He was trying to claim that he should never have been sent that box as he'd already received his order a week or so ago. We tried to explain to him that his complaint was with the company he ordered the damned things from and not us, but he wasn't having any of it. It was only when my manager threatened to call the cops that he backed off and stormed out the office.'

The young man puffed out his cheeks.

'Things you don't expect to have to deal with, eh. And I can tell you that's about the most horrendous smell I've ever encountered, and I say that as someone who's sampled the delights of the portaloos at 'T' in the Park, on more than one occasion.'

Davie laughed as he held the front door open.

'You and me both brother. Been there and got the T-shirt. But that box was on a whole different level, wasn't it?'

Davie leant into the office and sniffed the air.

'It's not completely away, there's still a lingering odour, but it's a hundred times better than it was. I think it's just about safe to come in. Now who's first?'

Chapter 12

The following morning it had just gone 7am but for once Conway wasn't the first in. Jan was already at her desk in the incident room updating actions from yesterday's door to door enquiries. She glanced up and held up her mug as Con came through the door.

'Kettle's just off the boil, and I'll take another cup of tea if you're making one.'

'No probs.' said Con placing a brown paper bag on the table. 'And I've brought croissants, freshly baked, they're still warm if you fancy one.'

'Tempting, but I'll just have the tea thanks. Too many calories in a croissant I'm afraid. When I'm stuck in front of this computer all day, I'm not burning anything off, so if I'm not careful the weight will creep on.'

Con took off his jacket. 'I don't think you've got much to worry about on that score, you look pretty trim to me. Anyway, not to worry, Asif will be in shortly and he's bound to take one, refuses nothing but blows that boy and there's nothing of him, he's built like a beanpole.'

'Ha. It looks like he must have heard you because here he comes now.'

Asif walked in carrying his folder and a large pile of mail.

'Perfect timing Detective Butt, your ears must have been burning, teas just made, and I've got fresh croissants from the Newlands bakery, I'll take it you'll have one.'

'You take it correctly Mr Niblett, I'll be delighted to relieve you of one.'

Con chortled as he passed Jan her tea. He'd liked Asif from the first time he'd met him. He had a ready sense of humour and while he could sometimes be naïve, he was hardworking and conscientious but still found time to have a laugh. Compared to some of the other detectives he was a breath of fresh air.

Asif took a bite of his croissant as he sorted through the mail.

'I wonder if this might be the report that the DCI was waiting for, she mentioned it to me last night. Forensics phoned her to say their report was ready and it would be with her today, looking at the envelope I reckon this might be it.'

'Could easy be.' said Con getting up and closing the door. Asif gave him a quizzical look and then started to chuckle.

'You getting a draught in those bones of yours old man? You're at a dangerous age, and what is it, six weeks till retiral, you can't be too careful.'

Conway looked a little sheepish. 'No, no. I just wanted a quick word while it's just the three of us.'

Jan swung round on her chair.

'Sounds interesting.'

'Look, I just wanted to run something past you both. I don't want to be a gossip, but I want your opinion on something, and it involves our new leader, DCI Cooper.'

'Ok, go on.' said Jan.

'I know it's really none of my business, but I was in Shawlands last night about 2130 hrs, my wife was visiting her friend in Minard Road, and I was picking her up. You see, I was parked just down from the junction at Kilmarnock Road, I looked up and who do I see coming out of DiMaggio's?'

Asif stated to laugh. 'I'm going to have a flying guess and say Mini Cooper.'

'Ok, smart aleck, I've already told you this is about her. But it was who she was with and what she was doing that I wanted to tell you about. She was with Natalie Mellish, they were both in civvies and...'

'Two work colleagues out for a bite to eat after work is hardly news Con.' said Jan turning back to her desk.

'No, that's true, but the full-frontal snog that followed might be don't you think?'

Jan swivelled back to face Con.

Con continued. 'I'm telling you this was no peck on the cheek, it was deep mouth stuff and they kept at it for ages. I had no idea that the boss or Natalie for that matter were that way inclined.'

Asif made a face. 'Does it really matter? They're both adults, they were off duty, and it is the 21st century, times have changed.'

Jan sighed wearily.

'You know in normal circumstances I wouldn't get too exercised about two consenting adults getting it on, that would be their business. But I suppose what makes this a little different is the circumstances. Department lead and junior officer, that in itself isn't very professional. The bosses would have a canary if they knew.'

Con helped himself to a croissant. 'That's kinda what I thought, and Mini did pull out all the stops to get

Natalie seconded to the department. I thought at the time that the speed it all happened at was strange. So, I guess we know the reason why she did it. My question then is, what do we do about it?'

Jan thought for a moment.

'Look Con, I'm not trying to wriggle out of any responsibilities, but Asif and I only have this second-hand from you. We only know what you've told us, so I suppose what I'm saying is it's your shout. But if you're asking me, I would say speak to Campbell in the first instance and get his opinion, but I think it's down to you how you want to play this.'

Asif blew out his cheeks.

'Blimey, tricky one, but I think what Jan's said is sensible, I would speak with Campbell, see what he has to say and take it from there.'

Con rubbed his face with his hands.

'Yeah, that sounds like good advice, but it'll have to wait a bit, that sounds like the boss and Campbell coming along the corridor now. So, not a word right, this is between us at the moment.'

For the next twenty minutes, Mini and Campbell were locked in earnest conversation in the Chief Inspector's office. Asif had been right; the envelope was from Forensics and now the DCI and her senior detective were poring over its findings. There were several things that were of interest. Firstly, the residue that Campbell had observed around the neckline of the corpse at the PM was confirmed as being lead, most likely the report said, transferred from the blade of a knife or similar sharp instrument. Tiny particles of lead residue had also been found during the examination of the head at Glencairn Drive.

Secondly, a thin smear of blood had been found on the edge of a skirting board by the stair carpet on the first-floor landing. It was the only blood found outside of the attic, but it had been confirmed as being blood from the murder victim.

And thirdly, and perhaps of most significance from Campbell's point of view, was the identification of a glue-like substance that was found at various locations on the staircase. A small section of a label, no more than a half a centimetre square, had also been recovered at the foot of the stairs in the hall. Examination of that had revealed that it was covered in the same type of glue that had been found on the carpet. It looked like his theory was correct. The body had been dragged down the stairs in some sort of bag, almost certainly the missing golf club carrier. The glue on the carpet was the same type used to attach flight labels.

But that wasn't the end of the good news. During yesterday's enquiries one of the team's detectives had finally got to speak to a park employee, who had just returned to work having been off for nearly a week with the flu. Mini handed Campbell a copy of the man's statement.

The man's name was Russell Evans, and what he had been able to tell them might prove to be highly significant. In his statement Evans told the detective how he'd encountered a man pulling a golf trolley at the entrance next to Langside Hall on the southwest edge of the park. It had been well after 8pm on the evening before Mr DeVilliers body was found. Evans was rushing to try and catch a bus, so he hadn't given it much thought at the time. And anyway, it wasn't that unusual to see someone with a golf trolley in the park.

Usually, they were heading up to the pitch and putt at the Victoria Infirmary end of the park to hit a few balls. People weren't supposed to bring their own clubs, but park employees tended to turn a blind eye and let them get on with it. They weren't really doing any harm. But what was unusual about this was the lateness of the hour, the light would have been gone in half an hour, so there was hardly time to play any golf. Then there was the way the man pulling the trolley was dressed. Evans remembered thinking he didn't look like a golfer. From what he could recall, he was wearing a woolly hat and a dark coloured heavy jacket. And the boots he had on were the type working men wore. He looked nothing like a golfer.

Mini rubbed her hands together and grinned at Campbell. For about the first time, she felt things were starting to turn in their favour. It might only be a couple of pieces of the jigsaw puzzle but nevertheless it was progress. Things were moving in a positive direction and that had to be a good thing.

Mini scribbled down a note and looked at her watch.

'Right, we'll have a meeting with the team at 0815 hrs. Bring them up to speed with the forensic report and this statement from Evans. And now we've got an accurate time and date we'll create an action to revisit the CCTV footage and see if we can't locate our man with the golf trolley. But before any of that that I think we've got time for a coffee and it's another good one today. This is a dark roast from Ethiopia, bit of an acquired taste I'll grant you, a little bitter, but I like it, a great cuppa to kick start your day with.'

Campbell looked unconvinced.

Mini handed him a mug.

'You look a tad unsure Detective Inspector, but in the same way that you shouldn't judge a book by its cover, you shouldn't form an opinion until you've tried it. Then if you don't like it fair enough, at least you will have given it a go.'

Campbell took a mouthful of coffee and swirled it around in his mouth. He looked surprised.

'Hmm, I quite like that. You're right, it is bitter, but not in an unpleasant way, packs a bit of a punch. No, I think it's pretty good.'

'Excellent, there's still hope then, you may not be a lost cause after all. Most people I've given it to haven't cared for it, so good for you. I think it shows you've got sophisticated taste buds.'

'That may be overstating things a little, but no I like it, it's one of the better ones you've brought in.'

Mini smiled, she sensed that her second in command might be warming to her. He certainly seemed less grumpy and argumentative which was a good thing, as she now needed him to do her a favour.

'And sorry I should have asked, how are your teeth?'

Campbell swallowed another mouthful of coffee.

'The pain's a good deal better thanks, I think the antibiotics are starting to have an effect. Two days ago, I wouldn't have been able to tolerate anything hot or cold. Still got a lot of treatment ahead, but the pain's nothing like as bad.'

Mini nodded sympathetically.

'Glad to hear it, toothache is one of the worst pains, it's that constant dull ache, wears you down, there's no doubt about it. Anyway, before you go there's something I wanted to run past you.'

'Shoot.' said Campbell drying his mug with some kitchen towel. 'What's on your mind?'

'This Monday coming is the initial meet and greet at the police college for all the new starts on the AP course, so it's important that Asif goes.'

'Don't have a problem with that, I'm sure we can hold the fort without him. How long will he be away?'

'From Monday lunchtime till Tuesday afternoon. There's a presentation from the course facilitator, a dinner at night where you meet and socialise with the other students on the course. But most importantly, you get to meet your mentor. That's usually someone at least a couple of ranks above you who themselves have been through the course. It's probably the most important part of the whole AP set up. If you can build a strong relationship with your mentor, then everything else just seems to fall into place.'

Campbell looked slightly confused.

'Not a problem. I'm delighted for the lad; I'll just be sorry when it's time for him to move on. But I'm not really sure why you needed to tell me this, if you're sanctioning it then he gets to go, simple as that.'

Mini twiddled her hair.

'Well, yes of course. But that's not why I'm telling you. You see I'm going to be away as well. It'll give me the chance to meet up with my own mentor, and network with some of my course members, whom I haven't seen in a while. I've cleared it with the Superintendent and assured him that the enquiry will stay on track with you overseeing it. It's not ideal and I wouldn't normally absent myself from a murder enquiry, but the stage we're at with no suspects in the frame yet, there was the opportunity for me to go and if you're happy to take

121

charge of things here then that's what I intend to do. If anything of any importance were to come up, we're just a phone call away and could be back down the road in an hour.'

Campbell smiled.

'Absolutely, and of course you should go. I know how these things work. Networking is a big part of the process, and I can understand you not wanting to miss out on that. I'm more than happy to cover things at this end, and as you say, if anything significant were to come up, you could be back down here in no time. So, it really isn't a problem.'

Chapter 13

For nearly 75 years, every newly appointed police officer in Scotland has undergone their initial training at the Scottish Police College at Tulliallan, an impressive 90-acre site of parkland and forest just north of where the Kincardine Bridge spans the river Forth. The castle at Tulliallan dates back 160 years. Built in the Gothic style with the assistance, it is said, of French prisoners of war, the castle was originally the home of Admiral Lord Keith, one-time senior officer in Nelson's fleet.

Nowadays no-one visiting the police college for the first time could fail to be impressed. As well as the castle, there are modern purpose-built classrooms and accommodation blocks, sports fields and a skid pan, where driving training courses are put through their paces. A modern swimming pool and sports complex sit to the side of the parade square, one acre of concrete where new recruits are drilled, inspected, and shouted at in roughly equal measure as they strive to acquire the skills necessary to be a constable in the Scottish Police Service.

For some, like Asif, their time at the police college can be a traumatic experience. 12 weeks of residential training, Monday through Friday, with just enough time if you were fortunate enough to live close enough to get home for the weekend, to touch base with your loved ones and get five shirts washed and ironed. Then for conscientious officers like Asif, there was the prospect of several hours study on Sunday revising the previous week's legislation ahead of the inevitable mock exam first thing on Monday morning. It was a stressful time. Prior to going to the college, an old sergeant had told, Asif, that Tulliallan was just a game, and that all you needed to thrive was to learn the rules of the game. Looking back, it didn't feel like much of a game. He hadn't understood what the sergeant meant, and as the sergeant hadn't bothered to explain what the rules were, he often felt lost, a little helpless, and completely out of his comfort zone.

At the college new recruits are constantly under pressure. You need to be up at seven to be washed, shaved and seated at breakfast for eight. Then for every minute of the day until the conclusion of your dinner at six, you are required to be somewhere. It's like being back at school. 50-minute periods with just five minutes between lessons to get to your next class are designed to put you under pressure. Those precious 5 minutes might include having to get from the swimming pool to the practical training area at the other end of the campus. And of course, you dare not run as that would incur the wrath of the ever-watchful instructors. It feels like everything you say or do is being monitored and assessed, others, it appears, are in control of your life. Then there is the discipline and petty rules, that are part and parcel of all uniformed organisations. If you're not used to it or expecting it, it can feel overwhelming and crushing.

There were always casualties along the way. Collateral damage as staff at the college called it. Policing isn't for everyone and dropping out of the course had crossed

Asif's mind on more than one occasion. The key to success at the college is learning how to prioritise your time effectively. As a wise man once said, you'll not be remembered for having the shiniest shoes on the course, but coming top in the examinations might just leave its mark. It's a balancing act, but in truth, it comes down to how you choose to prioritise the precious few hours that belong to yourself each evening. In that regard Asif had been fortunate, he had several advantages that others didn't. For a start he didn't need to spend any additional hours, as many others did, working on his fitness. He had arrived at the college as fit as a butcher's dog. It also helped that he found the academic demands of the course relatively straightforward. He was used to studying from his university days, learning volumes of legislation, both common and statute law, wasn't something he was accustomed to, but for the main part he found it interesting, and he was able to pass his exams with little difficulty.

It was the social demands of the job where he ran into difficulties. Unsurprisingly, Asif found himself in a very obvious minority. When he joined in the late 90's the job was still the preserve of white males. Significant progress had been made in the numbers of female officers joining the organisation, but progress in terms of ethnic minority officers was sloth-like in comparison. Out of an initial intake of 78, Asif was one of only two officers from an ethnic minority background. There was still much work to be done. The discrimination he experienced both from staff and students was never overt, but it was nevertheless still there, lingering like a bad smell. He never felt truly accepted. He was an outsider, standing on the sidelines looking in.

On top of that he found it difficult adjusting to the cultural norms of the college. He didn't drink, so the bonding sessions over a couple of beers with his fellow students in the Copper Lounge for the hour before lights out was never his scene. His biggest frustration by far, however, were the collective punishments meted out as part of the college's discipline regime. More than once, he found himself, along with the rest of his course, being paraded on the drill square at 7am in best uniform. The whole course then received a verbal tongue lashing from the Drill Sergeant for some minor misdemeanour that he'd had no part of. That, and the bollocking he received for leaving his shower gel in his shower, was in his book, beyond petty. Where else are you supposed to leave your shower gel bottle? It was infuriating and the ridiculousness and unfairness of it never left him.

Mini Cooper's experience of Tulliallan could not have been more different. She thrived in the environment from the day she arrived. After spending her teenage years at boarding school, this was water off a duck's back. It was just like being back at school. The petty rules and strict discipline didn't bother her, she understood the rules of the game. It helped, of course that she was sporty and bright. She excelled in all aspects of the course and to nobody's surprise was awarded the 'Baton of Honour,' as the outstanding student on her course. She even saw the fact that she was one of only 13 females out of a course of 68 as an advantage. It just allowed her to stand out and shine even more. Mini certainly left her mark at the college, she was identified as a high-flyer, destined to reach the upper echelons of the organisation. There wasn't much not to like from her perspective. Tulliallan had been the launch pad for her career aspirations, she had nothing but the fondest memories of the place.

Asif felt his heart rate quicken as Mini turned off the main road and started the long drag up the driveway towards the main castle building. This was the first time he had been back to the college since his pass out parade nearly eight years ago and coming through the entrance he felt the flutter of butterflies in his stomach.

Mini turned and smiled at him.

'Well Detective Constable Butt, how does it feel to be back?'

Asif puffed out his cheeks and exhaled loudly.

'Feels like a return to Colditz if I'm being honest.'

Mini scoffed theatrically.

'Colditz! You've got to be kidding me. This place is more like Hogwarts. And I mean that seriously, the Scottish Police College is a magical place, and I can assure you that your experience this time round will be a very different. I can guarantee you that.'

Asif looked sceptical.

'On the AP Course you'll be part of Senior Division, it's a completely different experience from probationer training and Junior Division. For a start, your classes will be in the castle, and you get to take your coffee in one of the grand lounges after dinner. Same in the evening if you're having a drink at the bar, you get to use any of the lounges. I've stayed in four-star hotels with poorer facilities and I'm not joking. You're going to love it. And do you know what the best bit is?'

Asif shook his head.

'As an AP student everyone will know who you are. You are one of the elite, chosen for your brains and leadership potential, I think I'm right in saying there are only going to be eight on this year's course. Eight officers from all the Forces in Scotland. If that doesn't make you feel special, then I don't know what will! There were only six on my course, when I was accepted. We're now down to five, one guy with a Law degree left to go into private practice, but the rest of us are all doing well. Two substantive Chief Inspectors and the other three are due to follow very shortly. So, you see it's a wonderful opportunity you're being given, one that most officers could only dream about, so don't fuck it up, you've got to grasp this opportunity with both hands. And I'm only going to give you one piece of advice. The AP Course is no place for faint hearts. You must stand tall and be prepared to fight your corner at all times with complete conviction and unwavering self-belief. That, above everything else, is the key to success, mark my words.'

Asif didn't reply.

If he had been unconvinced about accepting a place on the course before, he now had grave doubts about the wisdom of all of this. Mini's rallying call had done nothing to persuade him that this was a good idea. He had joined the police to make a difference to peoples' lives. To help make communities safer and better places. Sure, he wanted to get on. But not at any cost. And tramping over others in pursuit of the next rank held little appeal. But at the same time, he had never been a quitter, and he'd experienced his fair share of ups and downs since he'd been in the police. He would give the course his best shot, try his hardest as he always did and just be himself. It was all he knew, and anyway, it had got him this far so he couldn't be doing too much wrong, so that's how he intended to continue. He didn't really have a choice, there was no way on this earth that he could be like Mini Cooper, that's not how he was wired, and deep down he was very grateful for that.

After checking in at reception, Asif and Mini went their separate ways. They agreed to meet in the Kinnear Room at 1830 hrs, for the drinks reception ahead of dinner, but before that, Mini had a meeting with her own mentor, Chief Superintendent Nick Taylor, from Tayside Police while Asif had to attend the lecture theatre for the official welcome and opening presentations. That wasn't until 1630 hrs, so he had nearly an hour to find his accommodation and settle in.

As he walked through the connecting corridor from the castle to the new building where the classrooms and practical training areas are located, memories from his initial training course came flooding back. It was like being transported back in time.

His route took him past the vast dining room where all staff and students take their meals. Asif pushed open the heavy double doors and peered inside. All was quiet except for a couple of kitchen staff who were placing condiments and water glasses on the circular tables ahead of that evening's deluge of diners. He sniffed the air and his nostrils filled with a familiar aroma. Sausage casserole was on the menu. No doubt conjured up by the ever-resourceful chefs from the sausages left over from breakfast. Nothing was allowed to go to waste in the Tulliallan kitchen. It was said, and it was true, that more money was spent per meal feeding prisoners in Barlinnie than was spent feeding probationary officers at the Scottish Police College. Not that that mattered to Asif. He was just grateful for all the nourishment he could get as throughout his time at the college he was almost always as hungry as a bear. And little wonder, they worked you hard. After numerous classroom lectures, there would often be a course run to look forward to through the nearby forest to Rice Krispie Hill. Inevitably followed by endless shuttle runs up and down the steep sided muddy hill, aptly named, as it was there that many of the not so fit were known to deposit their breakfast. Then, at day's end you might find yourself on the parade square, freezing your bits off waiting patiently for the Drill Sergeant to inspect you in your best uniform. The list of deficiencies, and there would be many, in your uniform preparation would then very publicly be gone over in excruciating detail. It could be a humiliating experience.

Passing the assembly hall, Asif's route took him past the glass panelled corridor that ran along the side of the parade square. He paused for a moment to gaze upon the empty square. He was gripped by feelings of anxiety. Strange the effect that 5,000 square meters of cold concrete can have on you. To those ex-military personnel, who had seen service in the Guard regiments, the drill square was known as God's acre. To others, like Asif, who had no military background, it could be a place of nightmares.

His Drill Sergeant during his initial training was a man called McLaren. He had been a former Marine, highly muscled, tough as teak and with a temper to match, he appeared on the square resplendent in his red sash and tackety boots with toecaps so highly bulled you could see your face in them. The razor-sharp creases in his trousers and tunic defied explanation. How could anybody get such sharp creases using just an iron. McLaren never did reveal his secret, perhaps because he was too busy shouting abuse at Asif and the half dozen other students on his course who found drill particularly challenging. McLaren called them his Tick Tockers, as if they were some sort of family pet. Their discomfort seemed to provide him with endless hours of amusement, and he seemed to take sadistic pleasure ridiculing their genuine efforts to march. Tick Tocking is a peculiar phenomenon, it occurs when you swing your right arm in time with your right leg, or your left arm in time with your left leg. It looks utterly ridiculous and in truth is almost impossible to do. Nobody walking down the street swinging their arms has ever inadvertently tick tocked. It is such an unnatural movement and yet it happens repeatedly when officers are learning to march.

McLaren's attitude to female officers was equally appalling, some of the things he said to them would likely now get you arrested. He was a misogynist and a bully, but remarkably nobody seemed to bat an eyelid let alone complain. Incredibly, that had only been eight years ago. Asif shuddered at the memory and moved swiftly on.

His room on the first floor of the Tantallon building looked directly across to the swimming pool and sports complex. Unpacking his suit carrier and overnight bag, he smiled to himself as he watched a class of students, hair still wet from their life-saving class, scurrying towards the parade square en route to their next class. In one respect perhaps Mini's exhortation about the college had been right, and he'd seen a glimpse of it when he was checking in. The respect and friendly tone with which the staff greeted him was completely at odds to the way he had been spoken to when he first arrived as a probationary student. By way of justification, the college would argue that a strict discipline code and a slightly officious manner is necessary when dealing with new recruits to the organisation. The police service demands the highest standards of behaviour and personal integrity. Learning right from wrong, following orders, acknowledging and respecting authority, and upholding the law are pillars on which the reputation of the police college is built. It is non-negotiable and in truth these standards have hardly changed in nearly 75 years. It has served the organisation well, and as is so often the case in such circumstances, there is little appetite to change. If it ain't broken leave it alone is the mantra when it came to standards and college rules.

Just one example of these rules is the requirement for probationary officers to acknowledge everyone they encounter at the college. From your first day, it is drilled into you that every person you come across while moving about the college will be acknowledged with either a polite 'Sir', or 'Ma'am', according to their gender. Such greetings must be extended to all non-probationary officers, all members of staff and any visitors. It is done as a courtesy and as a mark of respect. There are no exemptions. It's a fine tradition that has long since disappeared from police colleges in other parts of the UK.

For an officer who is not a probationer it does have one significant downside. If you happen to be leaving the dining room when 150 probationary students are heading to the parade square for a drill lesson, you can find yourself returning the greeting 150 times. Perhaps that is one reason why you see people diving through the first available door, that being the only way of avoiding it. It might appear an antiquated custom, but for anyone who has been an officer in the Scottish Police Service it is one that everyone understands and respects.

Fortunately for Asif, the only students he encountered on his route to his accommodation was one class of 20 students who were leaving the officer safety training area. Even so, returning 20 acknowledgements still left him feeling like one of those nodding dogs that your grandparents used to have on the back shelf of their car.

After a quick shower and shave, Asif put on a fresh shirt with his favourite dark grey suit. He had decided to wear his green and white striped tie. They were the colours of Pakistan, his homeland, and also his football team. It was the very same tie he'd worn when he was appointed as an Acting Detective Constable. It was his lucky tie and it had served him well to this point, he just hoped that his luck would continue.

He still had nagging doubts as to whether he was doing the right thing, he'd only been away for less than a day, but he was already missing Roisin and Caelan. He thought about phoning, but decided that might only make things worse, he would save that call for later. Right now, he needed to banish any self-doubts and feelings that he didn't belong. He'd been given a place on the course by his own efforts, nobody else's, and in a matter of weeks it was likely that he was going to be made a sergeant. He just needed to believe in himself. If only he could bottle some of Mini Cooper's self-confidence he would be laughing. He looked in the mirror for a final time and straightened his tie. Right, he thought, this is it. Go out and make Roisin, Caelan, and your mother and father proud. Time to think of yourself for a change, this is a once-in-a-lifetime opportunity.

The words of introduction and welcome to the college were given by the College Commandant, a friendly and ruddy cheeked man who, prior to taking up his college appointment, had been the Chief Constable of Central Scotland Police. After the first few minutes of banal pleasantries and a potted history of the college, Asif's concentration started to drift, and he soon found himself studying the course programme. This included a short profile of all the students on his course. It was only a couple of paragraphs, but Asif had spent hours and a great many drafts agonising as he tried to find the right words to describe his career to date. He needn't have worried, reading the biographies of his fellow students it appeared that their careers were equally as bland as his own. The course comprised of eight officers, six male and two female. Interestingly, all but one were graduates. The exception being a male officer from Grampian who had spent 10 years in the army. There were four students from Strathclyde, Two from Lothian & Borders and one each from Tayside and Grampian. It hadn't taken long for the course 'Keener' to identify himself. Constable Mordaunt from Lothian Borders, 5 year's service and with a LLB from Edinburgh University, asked several long and very convoluted questions after each presentation. Judging by the course director's response to his seemingly endless need for clarification, it did not strike Asif as being the most sensible way to make a positive first impression. By contrast, Asif, and one of the female students seated in the row in front of him, hadn't said a word. He had understood what he was being told so he didn't see the need to say anything, although all the others asked at least one question.

By 1815 hrs the introductory presentations were done, and Asif found himself walking over to the drinks reception in the company of the female officer who had been sitting in front of him in the lecture theatre. She was short and slightly overweight. She wore a navy-blue trouser suit and a pair of black Doc Martin shoes. Her heavy dark rimmed spectacles and spiky gelled hair gave her a mildly nerdy look. She was not typical of the other female officers you encountered at the police college.

'Hi, I'm Suzi. Suzi Lessard, from Tayside Police.' she said thrusting out a hand in Asif's direction. Returning the compliment Asif introduced himself.

'If you don't mind me saying, your accent doesn't sound particularly Scottish and neither does your surname come to think of it, but I'm struggling to place where you might be from.'

Suzi laughed.

'And I suppose that Asif Butt is indigenous to Glasgow.'

Asif smiled.

'Good point. No, I was born in Lahore in Pakistan. My family moved to Glasgow when I was thirteen. But unlike you, I think I lost my accent, I speak pure weegie now, much to my parents' annoyance!'

'Accents are funny things don't you think. I left Canada when I was ten and have lived in Dundee ever since. I'm really half Scot and half French Canadian. My mother was born in Perth and met my father when she came over to Canada to study. My father was born and bred in Quebec, and as you might have gathered Lessard is a French name.'

'Hmm, interesting. I've never been to Canada, would certainly like to go one day, it's on my list, I hear it's a great country.'

Suzi started to chuckle.

'Well, I think we're even in that regard as I've never been to Pakistan, but hey, I hear it's a cool place, I'd like to visit someday.'

Asif wasn't sure if Suzi was being serious or just pulling his leg, deciphering other peoples' humour was not one of his strengths. Not that it really mattered, it had broken the ice and better still, he had made an acquaintance. He'd only known Suzi for five minutes, but in that short time she'd already made an impression. She was fun with a ready wit and from what Asif could tell, she ploughed her own furrow. In that regard, he thought, she was much like himself.

The Kinnear room was already busy by the time Asif and Suzi arrived. As well as the students on his own course, there were officers from previous years AP courses as well as a smattering of teaching staff. It was clear that most people seemed to know each other, and what with the grandeur of the setting, it had the feel of a rather exclusive club. In the far corner of the room standing with a glass of red wine in hand was DCI Cooper. She appeared to be deep in conversation with a tall dark-haired man who was stretched languorously across a chaise longue. Another female officer appeared to be part of the company, giggling as the man on the chez held court making exaggerated arm gestures.

Noticing Asif come into the room, Mini raised her glass and smiled. Asif turned to Suzi.

'If you're wondering who that is raising a glass and smiling at me well that's my boss, DCI Cooper.'

'Your boss.' said Suzi starting to chuckle, 'Well she better keep her wits about her, that streak of manhood stretched out on the settee is Chief Supt Nick Taylor. He's from my Force and I can tell you that his reputation as a womaniser is legendary, quite the lothario is Mr Taylor.'

Asif took an orange juice from the tray being carried by a waitress.

'Can I pass you a drink? There appears to be fizz, red or white wine or orange juice.'

'Just a juice for me please, don't do alcohol, it doesn't agree with me.'

Asif took another glass of juice from the tray and passed it to Suzi.

'Well, that's another thing we've got in common, I don't touch alcohol either, but that's more on religious grounds than any health reason.'

Suzi peered suspiciously at Asif over the top of her glasses.

'Another thing we have in common you said. Have I missed something? What is it you've discovered in the 15 minutes that we've known each other that we have in common?'

Asif flushed red with embarrassment. It was just a remark, a throwaway line, the sort of thing you might say when you're having an inconsequential chat with someone. Now he was being subjected to a forensic examination by someone he'd only just met. He wasn't sure how he should respond.

Sensing her colleague's discomfort, Suzi broke the silence.

'Look, if you meant that you and I might just be a little different from the other officers in this room, then you may have a point. I've always been a bit of an introvert, I don't do showy and I don't do needy, I just do me. So, I think it's best that we get that clear straight away. If you're gonna hang about with me, you ain't gonna be with the cool kids in the class, I just want you to know that.'

Asif beamed a great big smile. That was music to his ears. He didn't regard himself as being cool either. He could, like Suzi, be quite introverted. He liked his own space, and he had his own way of doing things, so on that basis he reckoned he and Suzi would get along just fine.

'Oh, and I don't think you need to worry too much about my boss being seduced by Casanova over there if you get my drift.'

Asif winked at Suzi.

'Hmm, interesting. So, she's a fellow worshipper then?' asked Suzi suddenly taking quite an interest.

Asif looked confused.

'Worshipper?'

Suzi smiled at Asif.

'Yeah, like me, she worships on the island of Lesbos?'

Asif scratched his head.

'Well, that's a new one on me. Never heard that before. Is it a Canadian expression?'

Suzi laughed but didn't confirm one way or another, so Asif continued.

'But if it means, and I think that's what you were inferring, that she prefers the company of ladies then yes, I'm pretty sure she does.'

'Well, that will certainly disappoint, 'I can't keep it in my trousers', Taylor. Not that knowing that would necessarily stop him. He simply can't help himself when he's around women. I know more than one colleague back at Force who was treated appallingly by him. And that's putting it mildly. But he's smart, I'll have to give him that, and of course he always thought he was fireproof. His father used to be an ACC in Tayside. Ended up as Deputy Chief Constable of Grampian. He only retired a couple of years ago, his claim to fame was he was the longest serving officer in Scotland at the time.'

'And was his father the same. I mean did he have a reputation as a womaniser?'

Suzi shook her head.

'Not that I'm aware of. He did have a reputation for being a complete arse though, he and several others in our Force could rightly claim that title. I don't know why I'm telling you all this, flies in the face of me claiming to be an introvert and not being showy. Yet here I am gossiping like some old fish wife. So please, not a word to anyone, least of all your boss. None of this conversation can get back to the Chief Superintendent or I'll be in big trouble, and do you know what the worst of it is?'

Asif shook his head.

'His room tonight is directly across the corridor from mine, so I don't think he'd have much trouble finding me.'

Asif started to laugh.

'No, no, your secret's safe with me. Right, it looks like we're heading through for dinner. Did you get a squint at the menu. Very impressive. Salmon or steak for the main course. None of that regurgitated sausage casserole that they were serving to the probationers earlier. Nothing but the best for those and such as those on the AP course.'

Asif stretched out his arm.

'Please, after you. Us Asian boys know how to treat a lady!'

*

Suzi was already sitting in the dining room when Asif walked in at 0745 hrs the next morning. He helped himself to a bowl of muesli and some toast and went and sat down next to her.

'Sorry I bailed on you so early last night, but after the dinner I just wanted to get back to my room and phone Roisin and then after that, I didn't think there was much point in heading back to just sit in the bar. Did you stay long afterwards?'

Suzi hit the back of her boiled egg with her spoon and shook her head.

'Left just after ten. The drink was starting to flow and as I found myself sitting at a table nursing an orange juice in the company of one Michael Mordaunt, I thought it was time to cut my losses and leave. God, that man is an insufferable bore. I made some excuse that I had a migraine coming on and left. Anyway, enough of that. Have you spoken to your boss this morning?'

Asif shook his head and looked at his watch. It had gone ten to eight and DCI Cooper was nowhere to be seen. She'd told him last night that she intended to have breakfast at 0730 hrs as she had arranged to meet with the officer, she was mentoring at 0830 hrs. By Asif's reckoning Mini was more than twenty minutes late, and although he hadn't known her long, he knew from personal experience that she was a stickler for good timekeeping. Yet there wasn't any sign of her.

'I don't think we could have missed her, how long have you been here?'

Suzi looked up.

'Ten minutes and she's definitely not been in.'

'Why are you asking, you look concerned?'

140

Suzi wiped her mouth with a napkin.

'I've hardly slept worrying about it, so much so that I was nearly phoning you at two in the morning.'

'Well, I wish you had, what the hell has happened?'

Suzi shook her head and sighed.

'I don't know for certain that anything has happened. But I was reading in my room as I couldn't sleep. It was quite late maybe 0045 hrs. Anyway, I heard voices in the corridor, a male and a female. I recognised Chief Supt Taylors voice straight away, it's very distinctive and he's loud. I could tell he was the worse for drink.'

Asif looked concerned.

'And do you think the female's voice was DCI Cooper?'

'I couldn't say, I've never heard her speak. The point is about an hour later I heard loud banging and a muffled scream coming from Chief Supt Taylor's room. Then it all went quiet.'

'Jeezo Suzi, I wish you had phoned me; this sounds serious. So, what happened after that?'

'Nothing for half an hour. I was lying awake worrying about what was going on. Then I heard the door opening. I jumped out of bed and opened my door; your boss DCI Cooper was standing in the corridor. She was dressed and carrying her shoes, but her hair was a mess, she looked quite dishevelled. She started to walk along the corridor. I say walk but she was quite unsteady, she'd clearly had a lot to drink.'

'And did you go out and speak to her?'

Suzi nodded.

'I asked if she was alright. She assured me she was. But she didn't look alright. She looked disorientated, she had a vacant, distant look about her, it's difficult to explain. She'd definitely been crying as she had mascara running down both her cheeks. But more concerning was the marks on the side of her neck. The light wasn't great but I'm telling you Asif, she had what looked like a significant bruise just to the side of her throat.'

'Bloody hell that doesn't sound good, and you're sure it was DCI Cooper?'

'100%.'

Asif was about to suggest that they should both head over to the DCI's room when he was aware of someone standing behind him. An arm leant over his shoulder putting a hand down on the table in front of him. It was DCI Cooper. The sleeve of her jacket rode up as she went to whisper in his ear. Both Suzi and Asif clocked the fingertip bruising that was wrapped around her wrist. Asif turned to face his boss. He wanted to see her neck. She had turned the collar of her blouse up under her jacket. It was a strange look and not one that Asif had seen his boss sport before. The edge of her crisp white blouse was covered in orangey brown make up. In fact, her whole face and neck were caked in the stuff. It was so thick it was impossible to make out any bruising on her neck.

'I need you back in your room and packed in ten minutes. Then meet me at the car. We're leaving. I've just taken a call from Campbell, they've found another body, a female this time, it looks like we're dealing with a serial killer!'

Chapter 14

It wasn't uncommon for officers on the early shift to find somewhere discreet where they could have themselves a cup of tea and a bite to eat. With a 0645 hrs muster ahead of the shift start at 0700 hrs, there weren't many who would have eaten anything prior to heading to their place of work. Who wants to eat breakfast at 0530 hrs?

For the most part, the first hour or so of the early shift is usually quiet, so you have time after the muster to head to your favourite doss and grab a bit of breakfast. It's a tradition that goes back decades. Today it is less common as far fewer officers walk the beat. In the old days most city officers patrolled their area on foot and if you were a cop who was worth their salt then you knew just about everyone on your beat and that included the owners of every shop, café, and pub. An experienced officer could always find somewhere to get out of the rain and have a cup of tea. Nowadays, with most officers patrolling in panda cars, it isn't quite as straightforward. Of course, most officers still know the places to go, but hiding a marked police vehicle, while you disappear for twenty minutes to have some scran isn't quite as easy as it once was.

It had just gone 0730 hours when Constable Chris McKenna parked his sherpa van around the back of the bus garage on Butterbiggins Road. His neighbour, Dave 'Slypig' Cunningham, was not in the prettiest of moods. He was mumping his gums because Chris had chosen the bus garage as this morning's breakfast venue. He wasn't complaining about the quality of the food, the sausage and bacon rolls the ladies served in the staff canteen were as good as any you could find on the southside. Slypig's issue with the bus garage was that you had to pay for your food. As a subsidised canteen it was cheap as chips and terrific value, but nevertheless having to dip into his own pocket still rankled. He preferred the dosses where you could eat for nothing. Being tighter than a duck's arse was just another thing to add to his list of unsavoury traits.

Chris started to laugh.

'Driver's prerogative, I'm afraid. Those are the rules. The driver gets to decide where breakfast will be had and today, I'm choosing the bus garage, 'cause you can hide the van round the back where the sergeant isnae gonna find us. And anyway, I think wee Sadie and her team do the best rolls. Tomorrow, if you decide you can be bothered to drive, you can get to choose. But as far as today is concerned, you're gonna have to suck it up.'

Slypig made a strange snorting noise indicating his displeasure.

Five minutes later the two officers found themselves a table by the window at the far end of the spacious canteen. Apart from half a dozen drivers who were all sat around one table near the servery watching breakfast TV nobody was in the place.

Slypig had just taken a bite of his second roll when his police radio burst into life.

'Govan control to Golf Mike 4.'

Through a furrowed brow Slypig glowered at his neighbour.

'Fuck's sake can a man no get a minute's peace to eat his breakfast anymore,' he spluttered with egg yolk running down both sides of his mouth. He grabbed several napkins from the container and wiped his mouth.

Smiling at his neighbour's predicament, Chris put down his mug of tea and pressed the receive button on his radio.

'Golf Mike 4 go ahead.'

'Golf Mike 4 your position please.'

Slypig's face was now flushed red with rage. The bloody control room were about to give them a call to attend. To make matters worse Chris appeared to be finding the situation amusing. Chris winked at his neighbour before replying to the control room with a little white lie.

'Golf Mike 4 we're approaching the junction of Victoria Road at Butterbiggins Road.'

'Roger that Mike 4. In that case can you attend at 7, Tankerland Road and see a Mrs Paton. Resides 1up at number 7. She's an elderly lady and appears quite confused. She's reporting an infestation of grasshoppers in the close. She says that some have now got into her flat. I know it's not really a police matter but given her age can you go and see her and find out what's going on?'

Slypig was now apoplectic with rage.

'It's not even a fecking police matter yet that idiot in the control room wants us to attend. Stuff like that gets right on my tits I tell you; it really does.'

Chris smirked and put on his hat.

'Roger that. 7, Tankerland Road, Mrs Paton, we should be there in ten minutes.'

Slypig held up his arms in despair.

'What about my bloody breakfast?'

'What about it!' replied Chris heading for the door. 'Look, you can either come with me now, or you can finish your grub and walk back to the office and explain to the sergeant why you're not at the call. That old lady could be your mother, she needs our assistance, is it not about time that you started thinking about the job and not about your belly. And I'll tell you another thing, if you're going to be working with me you better start taking some responsibility because your attitude is seriously starting to piss me off!'

Slypig continued his huff as they made their way to the call. He had wrapped the remains of his roll in a napkin, but that was now proving to be a serious mistake as he'd managed to drip most of the yolk all over his trousers.

Chris found a parking space on Newlands Road near to an old church building that had recently been turned into flats. Number 7 Tankerland Road was part of a small block of three storey red sandstone tenements typical of the type of flats that can be found all over Glasgow. Built from sandstone quarried in Locharbriggs near Dumfries, the spacious bay windowed flats with their high ceilings and 'wally' closes had been highly desirable properties since they were built more than a 100 years ago.

Chris locked the van and looked at his neighbour. Seeing the state of his trousers he started to chuckle.

'I wouldn't worry too much about a couple of egg stains, when was the last time you washed that uniform, I'm sorry but you look like a bag of spanners, a bit of egg isn't going to make any difference.'

'Well thanks for those supportive comments. Having had my breakfast aborted and now getting it thick from my so-called neighbour, this day just gets better and better.'

Chris ignored his colleague's sarcasm and strode up the hill towards number 7.

'Right, here we go number 7, Paton, Flat 1/1.'

Chris pressed the intercom which was immediately answered by Mrs Paton. She pressed the buzzer to let them into the close. They had only taken a few steps up the stairs when they were met by several flying insects.

'Yikes, look at the size of those bloody things.' exclaimed Chris. 'I don't know much about insects, but if that's a grasshopper it's a fecking huge one, look at the size of the thing!'

The winged insects were greenish brown in colour and nearly three inches long.

'Shit, they're everywhere.' cried Slypig as two more of the flying creatures landed on his uniform.'

Chris started to laugh.

'Perhaps they like egg, or any of the other food stains that you've got on that jumper of yours.'

Slypig flicked the insect off his shoulder in the direction of Chris.

'Flipping heck, I hate insects, especially big flying buggers, expect they bite or sting, probably do both.'

By now Chris had made his way up to the first-floor landing where Mrs Paton was waiting at her door. In her early 80's, she was small and wiry with a shock of white curly hair. She wore a blue checked housecoat over her tweed skirt and on her feet were a pair of purple velour slippers. It was apparent, after just a minute's conversation, that she was anything but confused. She explained how the insects had first appeared three days ago. At that time, she'd only noticed one near to the close door when she came back from the shops. Assuming it was a grasshopper, she hadn't thought much about it. Yesterday when she was going out, she encountered three more flying about the close. But today their numbers had multiplied to more than a dozen. They now seemed to be everywhere, including a couple that had found their way into her flat. She told Chris that she'd managed to corner one in the kitchen and dispatch it with a long-handled broom.

What was concerning her most was the fact that they appeared to be coming from her neighbour's flat immediately across the landing. Chris turned to look at the flat. Perfect timing, as another insect emerged from under the wooden storm doors. It immediately took off and flew up the stairs towards the second-floor landing.

Chris turned back to Mrs Paton.

'Have you had a chance to speak to your neighbour, what have they got to say about all of this?'

Mrs Paton shook her head.

'No, I haven't been able to speak to her. You see she's not in. Her name's Maureen Goodall but she's away on holiday and not due back for at least another week. She always seems to be away somewhere these days. I suppose that isn't so surprising given that she's now retired. This time it's a cruise in the Mediterranean. Don't get me wrong, she's a lovely neighbour and we hold spare keys for each other's flats. Maureen's always been very good to me, so I don't want to speak badly of her. I've lived in this flat for more than fifty years. Been here myself for the last twelve since my husband died, but it's a good close, always has been. We all keep it nice

148

and clean, but I can assure you we've never had an infestation of insects like this before.'

While Chris was speaking to Mrs Paton, Slypig began examining the storm doors across the landing. There appeared to be a slight gap between the two eight-foot-high wooden doors. He pushed the bottom of the doors with his foot. The left-hand door opened without difficulty. From what he could see there didn't appear to be any evidence of forced entry, nor did it appear that the door had been bolted or locked. He peered into the dimly lit space towards the glass panelled front door. Several envelopes and pieces of junk mail lay piled on a door mat. Slypig's eyes flicked upwards towards the front door. It also appeared to be lying ajar. He sniffed at the air suspiciously. He had thought he could smell something when he reached the first-floor landing. He may not be good at many things, but he had a sense of smell that would put a bloodhound to shame. Leaning in towards the door he sniffed again. Now he was sure of it. The smell of death is unmistakeable, it smells of rotting meat and has a musty slightly sweet undertone. It's very distinctive and once you've smelt it, you're never likely to forget it or mistake it for anything else.

Slypig turned round to speak to Chris as another flying insect fizzed past his head.

'Unless I'm very much mistaken, I reckon we've got ourselves a 'sudden puddin', and by the smell of it, one that's been lying quite some time.'

Attending the report of a sudden death is a common occurrence for uniformed patrol officers. It would be unusual to go a fortnight without being sent to one. Normally, they are quite straightforward. More often than not, an elderly person has died suddenly in their home. On most occasions they would be discovered very quickly, usually by a family member, or a friend or carer calling just to check they were Ok. Occasionally, if they lived alone, it could be several days before they were found. The police would always be called to such incidents and often there would be telltale signs that a dead person was inside. Unopened curtains, or more probably a pile of unopened mail with the front door locked from the inside, and at times that unmistakeable smell. If no-one held keys for the property, then the police would force entry. Even then most sudden deaths are not the traumatic experience that people imagine them to be. Invariably, the officers sent to deal with the incident will have no previous knowledge of the deceased. Consequently, there is little or no emotional attachment to the dead person. That, of course, can change according to circumstances. The death of a child, through cot death or a tragic accident is always a difficult incident to cope with, even for the most experienced officers.

Similarly, suicides or deaths that occurred through an act of violence can, for very obvious reasons, be challenging. But fortunately, such circumstances are rare. But no matter how the person died, the police have a job to do. There are strict procedures to follow. A supervisory officer must attend the locus and if there are any suspicious circumstances then the CID will attend. And in every case, be it straightforward or a sinister murder, a report must be sent to the Procurator Fiscal outlining the circumstances of the death. Dealing with death is part and parcel of being a police officer.

'Mrs Paton, can I ask you to go back into your flat please. I'll be back over to speak to you as soon as I can, but I'm going to have to go with my colleague just now and investigate what's been going on at your neighbour's flat. But before I go, can you confirm when you last saw Mrs Goodall, I think that's what you said her name was?'

'That's correct officer, her name's Maureen Goodall, but she's a Miss not a Mrs. She's a very attractive lady, I could never understand why she never married. I can't be 100% sure of when I last saw her, but it must have been about a week ago. It was the day before she left for her holiday. She told me she was away to get her hair done.'

The distance between Mrs Paton's front door and her neighbour's could not be more than 10 feet. While Chris had been speaking to Mrs Paton, he couldn't say he had been aware of it. But as he crossed the landing the sickly-sweet smell became increasingly intense. Slypig had called this one right. That was the smell of a dead body.

'Are you going first or am I?' asked Slypig slightly sheepishly.

'Senior man's prerogative I'd say, but I'll go first if you want me to, it's not a problem.'

Both officers knew why that question had been asked. Dealing with a sudden death was not the problem, the heart pounding moment is the few seconds that lead up to the discovery of the body. You just never know what you are going to find. It's a strange feeling, but one that all police officers have experienced.

'Right, no worries it's fine, I've got this.' said Slypig pushing open the front door.

Stepping into the hallway the officers were met by a wall of intense heat. Heat like you experience when you step off the plane for your summer holiday somewhere hot like Spain or Greece. It must have been at least 30 degrees. The smell inside the flat was also incredibly strong. It was not a pleasant combination. Slypig immediately reached for his hankie. He didn't do heat at the best of times. With his bulk he could work up a sweat in the middle of winter, let alone the spring or the summer. He simply detested hot weather. This, however, was on a whole different level. It was like stepping into a sauna. He dabbed at his face with the hankie.

'Bloody hell, Chris, It's like a sweat shop in here. Who the hell has their heating on that high? It must be nearly 90 degrees, and it's the middle of bloody April, it's not like it's cold outside.'

Chris hadn't heard his neighbour; he was crouched down looking at the carpet which appeared to be covered in some sort of vegetation. Wilted green leaves and stalks were scattered all over the floor. There were piles at the entrance to the lounge and yet more at the kitchen door. It appeared to be everywhere.

'This is fucking strange man; what the hell are all these leaves doing on the floor?'

Slypig shrugged and shook his head.

'This is starting to creep me out. I don't know what the hell's going on, but I tell you what, I think we should check each room together.' added Chris.

'Agreed. You'll not get an argument from me. And get your stick out, you just never know what we might find.'

Both officers removed their batons from their utility belts and unbuttoned the clip covering their CS spray.

'Right, let's start with the lounge.' said Chris tentatively opening the opaque glass panelled door.

There was nothing untoward about the room. It was just how you would expect a lounge in a nicely appointed and neatly kept flat to look like. There was certainly no body in it. The officers moved to the bedroom next door. It was much the same, although on the large double bed sat piles of neatly folded clothes and a sky-blue hard-shell suitcase that was lying open and empty. Chris slid onto his knees and checked under the bed. Apart from some sporting equipment, nothing. The same was true of the double wardrobe which contained an array of dresses, jackets and coats, all neatly hung on hangers and colour co-ordinated with light colours on the left and darker colours on the right.

The officers moved across the hallway to the kitchen-diner. It appeared that several of the flying insects had settled on the roller blind by the window. Still more were gathered round a large dish on the working surface by the cooker that appeared to be filled with balls of cotton wool. That apart, everything seemed normal. Slypig was about to suggest that that only left the bathroom to check when he glanced into the recessed area behind the kitchen door.

He gasped in horror hurtling backwards into Chris as he tried to distance himself from the horrific scene. The body of a middle-aged woman sat strapped to a kitchen chair. Her wrists and ankles bound by cable-ties and her head thrust backwards. A gaping angry wound of congealed blood ran round the base of her neck, it was clear that her throat had been cut.

The woman's mottled skin had formed a patchwork of squares like those found on a quilter's blanket.

Having sat for days next to a burning radiator she had turned the colour of charcoal. Her white round neck blouse now lurid pink and the blue cut-off jeans she was wearing were also saturated in blood. The wall next to the chair was speckled with blood trails, like those left by a bursting firework. Her only feature left untouched by the horror was her tumbling blonde hair, newly cut and curled.

The body was sitting behind a white topped metal legged table. It was smeared in blood with several unintelligible marks. What, however, was clearly visible and scrawled in large strokes was the capital letter 'D' and the numbers 8 and 5.

Momentarily stunned, Chris covered his mouth and nose with his sleeve, the stench was quite overpowering. Coughing and spluttering he stumbled across the floor and opened the window. He needed fresh air.

'Shit man that's just gruesome, I thought I was going to be sick. The smell and the heat are making me gag. I don't know what I was expecting to find but it wasn't this. It's horrendous, what a way for that poor woman to die.'

It had taken Slypig a few moments to regain his composure but now he was in 'action at the scene of a crime' mode. He needed to be switched on and thinking straight. He thrust his hands into his pockets to prevent himself touching anything unnecessarily, forensics would be going over the flat with a fine-tooth comb, so the preservation of evidence was now a top priority.

Dave Cunningham was the butt of many people's jokes. He knew that, and in a large part that was his own fault. Nobody was forcing him to eat and become the size he was. And, of course, being so overweight meant any physical task was an enormous challenge, so when he opted out it was often perceived that he was lazy. Truth be told it was a bit of a vicious circle. Until he could lose some weight, what he was able to do was quite limited. The lazy tag irritated him immensely, nobody enjoyed being made fun of, especially when it was done by your work colleagues. He might not have the greatest work ethic, but he wasn't stupid. He was a highly experienced officer, who knew the operational side of the job inside and out. When he did apply himself, he could do a decent job, there was no question about that.

'Chris, why don't you step outside and get some air, you'll feel better, and while you're at it give the control room an update and request the attendance of Inspector Brough and the CID.'

Chris put up his thumb. Covering his face with his hand he grabbed his radio and made for the front door. Slypig shouted after him.

'And tell them that the letter and numbers smeared in blood on the table are the same as those that were daubed on the wall in Glencairn Drive when they discovered DeVilliers' head. The M.O is exactly the same. I can remember the photographs that we were shown by DI Morrison at the briefing. The person who killed DeVilliers also murdered this lady, I can tell you that for nothing, and I'm not even in the CID.'

Within twenty minutes of the call being made Inspector Brough and DI Morrison were at the locus where they were met by Chris and Slypig.

'According to Mrs Paton, her neighbour across the landing, the lady's name is Maureen Goodall. She's a retired nurse apparently and she hadn't been seen for about a week. Mrs Paton thought she'd gone on holiday. There is an unpacked suitcase and piles of clothes in the bedroom which suggests she was about to pack to go somewhere. She's been strapped to a chair in the kitchen recess, blood everywhere, she's not a pretty sight.'

Campbell listened carefully to the update.

'Ok, guys thanks for that. Maureen Goodall, you said her name was. I take it she resides here alone?'

'She does according to Mrs Paton.'

'Fine. Right, I suppose I'd better go and take a look.'

Returning a few minutes later he went over to speak to Inspector Brough who had remained in the hallway.

'Bob, I don't think there's any requirement for you or any other uniformed officer to go in there, the poor woman's throat's been slit and she's the colour of coal. She's been dead for several days I'd say. Dave and Chris have already been through the flat, so we don't need to risk contaminating the crime scene any further before SOCO get here. But if you could get an officer to start a log and position them at the close door so nobody unauthorised gets in, I'd be obliged.'

'Sure, not a problem, I'll get that sorted. And what do you want me to do about the other residents in the close?'

'Get someone to contact each of them, get the details of everyone living there and ask them to remain in their flats until told otherwise by ourselves. I don't think you'll get any resistance but if you do then refer them to me.'

'Roger that.'

Campbell took off his Barbour jacket and wiped his brow with his shirt sleeve.

'Bloody hell guys it's absolutely roasting in here, I've been in colder Turkish Baths. Can we get the heating turned down without interfering with any evidence?'

Slypig grinned and pointed to the wall behind Campbell.

'The thermostat is on the wall next to the bedroom door boss. It's been turned up to 31 degrees and every radiator in the flat has been turned on full.'

Campbell walked over to the thermostat.

'Right. I can confirm that the temperature is set at 31 degrees. Dave, Chris, can one of you take a note of that in your notebook and include it when you submit your statement.'

Slypig removed his notebook from his pouch. 'Will do sir.'

'Right then, I'm turning the thermostat right down, nobody can work in that heat, and you can see the damage it's done to that poor woman, she's that colour because she's been left next to a red-hot radiator. Ok, so here's my next question, what's with all the old cabbage leaves on the floor? Is there a rabbit hutch or guinea pigs in here somewhere?'

Slypig and Chris looked at each other and shook their heads.

'Not that I'm aware of. I think it's connected to the grasshoppers; I think it's been left as food for them.' replied Slypig.

'What grasshoppers?' asked Campbell looking all around him.

A look of horror spread over Chris's face as he stared at the open window in the kitchen. The insects that had settled on the roller blind had all gone, and from where he was standing, he couldn't see any in the hall or bedroom either. His shoulders slumped as he realised what he'd done. The insects had escaped through the open kitchen window or through the open front door. While he couldn't shoulder all the blame for leaving the front door open, he could certainly be blamed for opening the kitchen window. It was an honest and simple mistake, but that one action now risked losing vital evidence. Evidence that might be crucial in proving who killed Maureen Goodall.

'Hands up boss I've fucked up. There were grasshoppers in here, well we think they were grasshoppers. Dozens of them. But what with the heat and the smell I opened the window to get some air in as I thought I was going to be sick. That was just plain dumb. Unless there's still a couple in the close, I think I've screwed this up good and proper. They've all flown away. I'm sorry, what can I say.'

Campbell gave a resigned shrug and shook his head. It was disappointing, but it was an honest mistake which Chris had immediately owned up to. He wasn't going to be giving any bollocking or lectures, that wasn't his style, and anyway, he'd made plenty of mistakes of his own in the past. That didn't mean Chris was off the hook. As soon as he'd received the information from the control room, Campbell had called DCI Cooper at the police college to apprise her of the circumstances. She was now on her way back from Tulliallan with Asif. God only knows what she'd have to say when she learned that one of her colleagues had literally let evidence fly out the window.

Noticing something sitting on the working surface Campbell moved back into the kitchen.

'What's with the dish full of cotton wool balls? And why are there two plastic containers turned upside down?'

Slypig looked at Chris and grinned. He may just be about to save his neighbour from the wrath of the DCI. While Chris had been in the close updating the control room, he had had the presence of mind to remove a couple of plastic containers from the drying board next to the sink and place them over the insects that were gathered round the cotton wool balls. While most had managed to fly away, at least two had been trapped under the containers.

'Don't lift the containers boss, I've got a couple of the grasshoppers trapped underneath them, so we've not lost all the evidence.'

The broadest of smiles spread over Chris's face.

'Oh, you little beauty, Dave. That's one I owe you. I'll buy your breakfast for the next week for doing that.'

Campbell patted Dave on the back.

'Good work Dave, that was smart thinking, and it might yet prove to be a vital bit of evidence. I'm certainly no expert, but I'm pretty sure we're going to find that these insects aren't grasshoppers.'

Slypig looked at him quizzically.

'You reckon? What makes you think that?'

'Are you familiar with the book of Exodus?'

Slypig and Chris shook their heads.

'I've heard of it. Is it not a book from the bible? But that's about all I know.' replied Chris.

Slypig scratched his head.

'If my memory serves me right, and I'm going right back to my Sunday School days, wasn't Exodus a book in the Old Testament, I'm pretty sure it was about

Moses leading the Israelites out of Egypt? It was something like that.'

Campbell smiled.

'Impressive Dave, so you're not just a pretty face. And yes, you're spot on. It was about Moses and the Israelites, but there was more to it than that. The book of Exodus also tells the story of the ten plagues of Egypt. And do you know what one of those plagues was?'

A knowing look spread over Slypig's face. Mrs McQueen's efforts in Sunday School when he was a kid had not been in vain, it was all starting to come back to him.

'Locusts!' he announced triumphantly. 'One of the ten plagues was locusts.'

Chapter 15

It hadn't taken long for word to get out. By just after 10am a small crowd of interested onlookers had gathered on the pavement across the road and, much to the displeasure of DCI Cooper who had arrived only minutes before them, the press had turned up. Like vultures circling a carcass on the African savanna, the press had an unerring ability to turn up when least wanted. Always on the lookout for breaking news or a scoop, they had a network of eyes and ears who would make a call, for a small gratuity of course, to their offices whenever something potentially newsworthy happened. Sometimes such calls were made by disaffected officers, perhaps someone who had been snubbed for a promotion, or had fallen out with the hierarchy. That wasn't the case today. More likely the call had been made by a passing taxi or bus driver, who had seen the police barrier tape and a uniformed officer standing outside the close. Whoever had made the call, the press hadn't been long in getting themselves organised. Two reporters, one from the Record and the other from the Evening Times had turned up along with a camera and crew from STV news.

The reporter from the Evening Times was an interesting character. He went by the name of Walter 'Scoop' McSorley and was a seasoned hack. For years he'd been a 'well kent' face around major crime scenes in Glasgow, and polis howffs, where he inhabited dark corners drinking and gossiping with his coterie of obliging detectives, whose tongues would loosen at the mere mention of a large dram. He was the journalistic equivalent of Joe Beltrami, Glasgow's famous criminal lawyer. But like many successful people, McSorley started to believe his own hype and got a little too greedy. He loved the notoriety of being Glasgow's premier crime journalist and grabbing exclusive stories from under the noses of other hacks. But in his thirst for the scoop, he overstepped the mark and betrayed one too many confidences. His police touts dried up and before long he found himself out of a job. That had been more than ten years ago. He'd moved down south, and for the last five years had been working for a provincial paper in Yorkshire. The chance to move back to Glasgow came with an offer from the Evening Times. He took it, and for the last six months had been slowly trying to rehabilitate himself and repair his damaged reputation.

As the officer in charge of the investigation, Mini knew that she would be required to give an interview to the press but there was no way that was going to happen until she was fully conversant with the facts. It was an unhelpful distraction on what had already been a difficult day. Trying to remain calm and professional she was now shut away in the lounge with Campbell, Asif, Inspector Brough and two members of the SOCO team.

Through enquiries with the other residents in the close, Inspector Brough had established that the last confirmed sighting of the deceased had been Mrs Paton's conversation about a week ago. Several residents were away at work when officers called, so they would need to be interviewed later, but for now it would appear that Maureen Goodall had been dead for approximately seven days.

Lucy, the senior member of the SOCO team, had explained that when the postmortem examination took place, the pathologist should be able to say, with relative accuracy, when Maureen Goodall had died. That could be calculated by assessing the level of decomposition and factoring in the temperature within the flat. Asif was scribbling endless notes as he knew his boss would want a thorough debrief of events when she got back to Aikenhead Road.

In a stroke of good fortune, it turned out that another of the SOCO team, a guy by the name of Hugh Sloan, had studied Zoology at university and through that had developed a particular interest in entomology. His expert knowledge was able to confirm that the insects caught in Slypig's containers were in fact desert locusts. Found in vast swarms in Africa, the Middle East and Asia, they are the insects associated with devastating huge areas of crops and vegetation. An adult locust could eat more than its own bodyweight in a day. In this country, most locusts are reared as a food source for other creatures, particularly lizards and some species of birds. The climate in Scotland is too cold for them to survive in the wild, hence they are kept indoors, in tanks heated to 30 degrees.

Campbell rubbed his chin.

'That's fascinating Hugh, and it would explain the piles of cabbage leaves and the thermostat being set at 31 degrees. But what about the dish full of cotton wool balls, I take it that's connected to the locusts too?'

Hugh smiled and nodded.

'I expect that had been left there as a water supply, the cotton wool balls would have been soaked in water, whoever left the locusts in the flat wanted them to survive.'

Campbell looked confused.

'But the dish and cotton wool were bone dry, hardly surprising given how hot the flat was. The water would have evaporated pretty quickly in that heat.'

Hugh nodded enthusiastically.

'The cotton wool balls are interesting, and, I think, a bit of a giveaway.'

'Oh, how so?' asked Mini who had been listening with interest.

'Whoever left the water really didn't need to. The locusts would have got sufficient moisture from eating the cabbage leaves, the water wasn't really necessary. An expert would have known that. The fact that they left the water suggests to me that they weren't aware of that. I don't think whoever brought them here was experienced in keeping locusts, that's just my opinion.'

'So, our killer isn't an expert on entomology then?' added Mini.

Hugh nodded. 'That's my theory.'

Campbell pursed his lips.

'Interesting, but I think that makes sense. I reckon its much more likely that our killer is some sort of religious nut or an expert on the bible, or someone who at least has a reasonable knowledge of it. If the letter and numbers written in blood at both murder scenes are, as we suspect, a reference from the bible, then I think it would be fair to surmise that both the frogs and the locusts are straight out of the Exodus playbook, they are two of the ten plagues mentioned in that book. And it's just my opinion but I think their presence are meant as some sort of allegory, they are intended to carry a hidden meaning.'

'A hidden meaning like what?' asked Asif.

'Like a plague on all your houses. Well at least the houses of both our victims. Both Magnus DeVilliers and Maureen Goodall have been deliberately targeted and sadistically murdered. Whoever did it would appear to have a deep-rooted hatred of both of them. Must have to inflict that level of violence. I've been a detective a long time and I've never been involved in a case quite like this.'

Mini held up her hands.

'Ok, can we call a halt to this discussion for the moment fascinating as it undoubtedly is. We'll revisit this when we've got time and everyone together. We've got lots to talk about. But first can we make sure that we've got everything covered here, I want to be bloody sure we don't miss anything. And after that I've got the press conference to think about.

Campbell, can you hang fire here with Asif, at least until SOCO and the photographer are finished, that will let me get back to the office. No doubt the Chief Super will be champing at the bit awaiting a full update, I wouldn't be surprised if the press haven't already been in contact with his office looking for a comment.'

'Not a problem. And while we are here, we'll try and see if we can find any evidence that would link Maureen Goodall to Magnus DeVilliers. Two murders with almost identical M.O's, there's got to be a connection. Chris told me that Goodall had been a nurse, so with

165

DeVilliers being a retired consultant that's an obvious place to start. We'll see what we can turn up.'

'Ok, fine, but don't hang about too long, we need to get things rolling back at the office. Lucy, before I disappear, can I have a word in private, I'm looking for some advice and potentially a favour, it's nothing to do with this enquiry.'

Asif raised an eyebrow; he wondered if what the DCI just said was connected to what happened yesterday at the police college. If it was, he wasn't being allowed the opportunity to find out as Campbell was ushering him, Inspector Brough and Hugh out of the room.

'Right, we'll leave you to it boss and we'll catch you back at the office in an hour or two.' said Campbell.

'Thanks. Appreciate that.' said Mini closing the lounge door.

Asif looked at Campbell and frowned.

'And what are you looking so pissed off about? asked Campbell. 'I thought you'd be delighted to get your teeth into a juicy murder enquiry like this, you were always banging on about getting the chance to be involved in a proper whodunnit, well now's your chance, so less of the petted lip, eh.'

'Look, I'm sorry, but it's got nothing to do with this enquiry, honestly, I'm delighted to be involved, but I need to talk to you and get your advice about something. Later perhaps after work, but it's important, it's about something that happened at the college, as I said, I need your advice about it.'

Campbell smiled. 'Sure, no problem, why don't we grab a bite to eat straight after work, nothing fancy, maybe a KFC and we can talk about it then.'

'Sounds good. Roisin is away to visit friends with Caelan today and will have eaten with them, so that would suit fine. Ok, back to business, where do you want to start with this?'

'Let's check the bedroom, it's about the only room that isn't crawling with SOCO. Let's see if we can find out where she was supposed to be going.'

The two detectives began by going through the piles of clothes that were neatly stacked on the bed. Several items were brand new as they still had their labels on them. An Alexandra Miro red swimsuit with gold lace trim had a Silks of Netherlee tag while several Ralph Lauren pastel-coloured tops were wrapped in a House of Fraser bag.

'The lady had expensive tastes, this stuff is all designer labels and most of it appears to be new. Must have been a lady of means although didn't you say she was a nurse.' mused Asif.

'Recently retired apparently. But you're right, this is expensive gear, beyond the purchasing power of most nurses I would think, but perhaps she had money from other sources. She might have inherited wealth, lots of people do.'

'I wish I could. Even with Roisin going back to work part time money's tight. Having a child to look after makes all the difference I can tell you.'

Asif was sure Campbell hadn't heard that last comment as he was now going through some documents that were sitting next to the suitcase.

'Hmm, this is interesting. Her passport is here and according to her date of birth she was sixty. That must be a very old photo, no way does she look sixty. I'd say early forties at most, here take a look.'

Asif nodded. 'She was a fine-looking lady, not that you could tell if you saw her now in the kitchen, hope some poor relative doesn't have to ID her for the PM.'

'They'll try to get a fingerprint ID first, you never know, she might have some indiscretion in her past, failing that they'll try for dental records. Anyway, enough of that. It isn't just the passport that's interesting, it's the other stuff, or should I say the lack of other stuff that might be significant.'

Once again Asif had lost his boss's thread. He always seemed to be at least one step behind Campbell when it came piecing bits of evidence together.

'You've lost me again, what might be significant?'

'Well, the fact that there's a passport, a travel insurance document and a wallet that has 200 Euros in it, but no itinerary, no tickets of any description, or nothing that says where she was going. That's just a bit weird don't you think?'

'It is strange, and 200 euros wouldn't get you very far these days, but perhaps she was taking a credit card, and the euros are just petty cash.' added Asif.

'Yeah, could be.' Campbell scratched his head. 'But I wonder if the lack of anything with an address on it suggests she was going to be travelling with someone else. Perhaps they have all the details of where they were going. Seems plausible don't you think? Most people go away on holiday with somebody. I wonder.'

'Wonder what?'

Campbell shook his head. 'Never mind, it'll keep for later. Right let's check the rest of the room, time marches on and Mini will be wanting us back ASAP, so we better crack on. You check under the bed; I'm going to check her bookcase, see what she's been reading.'

Asif got down on the floor and pulled several items from under the bed.

'It seems that she was right into her fitness. She's got a yoga mat and blocks under here and there are at least three tennis rackets and several tubes of balls, but other than that, nothing out of the usual.'

'Ok, that's all noted.' said Campbell removing a couple of books from the bookcase by the window. He leafed through both books, then turned to Asif.

'Am I right in saying that the fellow Beckett who we spoke to at the bowling club said that Magnus DeVilliers occasionally played bridge at the club?'

Asif Nodded. 'Affirmative, yeah, I can remember him saying that. Why you asking?'

'Just putting two and two together and probably making five, but Maureen Goodall has two books about bridge. Bridge for dummies and a beginner's guide to bridge. Don't know about you but I've always regarded bridge to be a bit posh, I never learned how to play, and I certainly don't know any cops that play, or retired nurses for that matter. But I'm wondering if that might be a connection, perhaps DeVilliers and Goodall knew each other through playing bridge. Both these murders are clearly linked, you don't need to be Poirot to work that out. But what is it that links Magnus DeVilliers to Maureen Goodall?'

Campbell held both books aloft. 'If it's not through their work it could be bridge, don't you think?'

Asif shrugged his shoulders.

'It's possible, it certainly can't be discounted.' He picked up a photo that was propped up on a dressing table.

'This looks like her in her tennis gear, she certainly looks the part, very athletic. We should show this to

Beckett at the bowling club, see if it rings any bells. She doesn't look like the type of lady you would forget easily.'

'Yeah, that's a good shout, but I still think that both of them having a medical background is a more likely connection, but you never know, they might know each other through bridge, it definitely needs exploring.'

Campbell put both books back on the shelves. Outside in the hall there was the sound of voices and equipment being moved. Moments later Lucy stuck her head around the door.

'That's us done for now, so if you want to arrange for the shell to remove the body then that's fine by us. I want some more photographs of the blood splatters on the wall immediately behind the chair in the kitchen, but that will best be done when the body has gone and we have better access. There's still work to be done in the other rooms but that can wait till tomorrow. We're done in the kitchen for now.'

'Sounds good to me Lucy. And while you're here, and given that we haven't found blood or any sign of a disturbance in any other room, I take it that the murder has occurred in the kitchen?'

Lucy made a face.

'As you know I can't be 100% sure, but it's the only explanation that makes any sense. Given that the pool of blood is restricted to the recessed area, it would appear that's where the poor woman was strapped into the chair and had her throat cut. Chilling, isn't it?'

Campbell and Asif nodded in unison. There wasn't much more to be said.

'Right, time for me to get back to the lab and get those samples analysed.' added Lucy looking all around her. 'And has anyone seen where I put my case, I better not forget that as it's got the DCI's bottle in it.'

Asif made a mental note of that comment. He looked at his watch.

'Any chance we can run past the Inglefied Dairy on the way back to the office and pick up a couple of rolls? I never got breakfast this morning as Mini wanted to get straight down the road after she took your call.'

Campbell patted his colleague on the back as they walked down the close stairs.

'Sure. I'm a bit Hank Marvin myself, and as our erstwhile old colleague Conway might say, an army doesn't march on an empty stomach, so that sounds like a decent plan to me. Right, where the hell did I put my car keys?'

Standing on the pavement outside the close, Campbell checked his trouser and jacket pockets. Then he rummaged through his folder. He screwed up his nose.

'Shit, I must have left them up in the flat. I think I put them down when I was looking at those bridge books. Do me a favour and get the Cop keeping the log to put in an entry that I had to return to the flat for my keys. Better do this by the book or there might be bother.'

'No probs, I'll speak to him, but hurry up, I'm famished.'

Chapter 16

By the time that Campbell and Asif got back to the office it had gone 1330 hours. Jan was at her desk busy updating the action log while Con and another DC were carrying computers and boxes of stationery into an adjacent empty office. Mini Cooper was nowhere to be seen. She had informed Con that on the instructions of the Divisional Commander, and in light of the second murder, the enquiry team was being expanded to include another 4 detectives and an additional Holmes operator. That explained why Con was busy setting up another office.

'Where's the DCI?' asked Campbell unpacking the bag of rolls on his desk. 'I'm having a brew, you want one?'

Jan passed Campbell her mug. 'Please.'

She glanced at her watch.

'The DCI's in a meeting with the Div Com. She's been away at least half an hour. Hope everything's alright.'

Campbell switched on the kettle. 'Why wouldn't it be?'

Jan shook her head.

'It's not like the Div Com to have lengthy meetings, it's just not his style. I've known the man a long time, I worked for him for nine months when he was a

Chief Inspector in Pitt Street, I don't expect he'll have changed much. He liked a light touch. He certainly didn't like to get too involved in any enquiry, he just wanted the bare bones, a basic overview of the salient facts. You see it's much easier to distance yourself from an enquiry if things go belly-up if you're not embroiled in the nitty gritty. It's the little details that will catch you out, so you don't want to get too hands on. I watched him do it countless times, he's an absolute master of the craft and of course he's not alone. There's a Divisional Commander in the East who apparently has made it all the way to be a Chief Superintendent without ever having to give evidence in a court of law. And the man wears it as a badge of honour. Quite incredible. If he's never been to court, it's likely he's never had to deal with an angry man. And yet here we are. Half the senior officers in the Force are the same, nothing more than pen pushers, and that's certainly the category our current leader falls into. An obsequious, pen pushing nonentity of a man. Concerned about nothing except his own career. And that's our so-called leader. So, yeah, the fact that the DCI's been locked away in his room for more than 30 minutes causes me some concern.'

Campbell scoffed as he took a large mouthful of roll.

'And I hear that the Div Com speaks very highly of you as well. Who knew you held the man in such low regard. But I must say I enjoyed that; it was quite a rant.'

Jan blushed as Campbell handed over her tea.

'Ok, I might have been a little over dramatic, but I really don't care for the man. There aren't too many, whether they are pen pushers or not, that I don't have any time for, but he's one of them. I wouldn't trust him as far as I could throw him, and that's not far I can tell you.'

Con, who had come back into the room carrying a box of paper for the photocopier, had heard most of what Jan had said.

'I know exactly what you mean. There's something of the night about the man, I never feel relaxed when I'm talking to him which isn't very often right enough as he spends most of his time locked away in that ivory tower of his. No idea what he spends his time doing. But hey, who's the mug, he's picking up a Chief Superintendent's salary while a mere CID clerk like me is scratching about trying to earn a crust.'

Jan and Campbell both laughed. Conway was one of those characters who could always make you smile. Just weeks away from retiral, he could be a cantankerous old bugger at times, especially when someone, usually a boss, had annoyed him. But most of the time he was tremendous fun with a ready wit and a seemingly inexhaustible store of amusing stories of his time in the job. His story about the escaped lion from the Oswald Street Zoo, told after a few drams at many a polis leaving doo, was the stuff of legend, even if it was an apocryphal tale.

With nearly 30 years service in the bag, he still had a commendable work ethic. At his desk at 0715 hours every morning to prepare for the morning meeting, he was invariably still in the office well after five, a full hour after he should have gone home. He was part of a dying breed, if there was work needing doing you stayed until it was done, that was just the way it was.

Campbell held up the bag of rolls.

'There's a couple of spare rolls going if anyone fancies one. Cheese and tomato or a ham and salad, take your pick.'

Jan's eyes lit up.

'You, sir, are a life saver. I'll take one if that's Ok, I was rushing to get the kids out for school this morning and didn't pick anything up for myself. Con, what about you? I'll only be having one of them.'

'Sure, whatever, but you choose, I'm easy with either. And thanks Campbell, that's generous of you.'

Campbell chuckled.

'Not a problem. Always happy to help an impoverished old CID clerk who's just trying to earn a crust.'

Conway got up and put on his jacket.

'Right, before I have my roll, I'm popping over to Asda to get some fags, anyone need anything when I'm over?'

The others shook their heads.

'Nope you crack on, it would appear that we're all good.' said Asif wiping mayonnaise from his chin.

The newspaper counter in Asda was surprisingly busy given that it was just after lunchtime on a Thursday. There were at least six people in the queue ahead of Con waiting to be served, most of whom appeared to be clutching the early edition of the Evening Times. Two elderly ladies immediately in front of him were deep in conversation.

'Well, that's all we effing need Senga, another 'Bible John' type maniac murdering people in the southside. I'll tell you Senga, that's me done with the Bingo till the polis catch the bastard. I'll not be oot after dark, apparently some religious nutter nearly cut aff the poor woman's heid. Look, it's on the frontpage of the times.'

Con glanced down at the pile of papers on the stand.

'Is this the return of Bible John?' City gripped by fear as second murder victim found with throat slit. Times

exclusive by Chief Crime Reporter Walter McSorley,
pages 2,3 and 4.

Conway swallowed hard. It wasn't just the macabre headline that sent a chill down his spine. More concerning than that was the realisation that someone directly involved in the murder enquiry had leaked the story to McSorley. But who the hell would be stupid enough to do that, the body of Maureen Goodall had only been discovered that morning, it was, quite literally still warm. Con was old enough to remember McSorley's first incarnation, and the stories he broke over his many years at the Record. He didn't know the man personally, but he was aware of former colleagues who had had their fingers badly burnt in their dealings with McSorley. A lesson for any would-be police officer. Never trust anybody who tries to curry favour by giving you free drink. There's always an angle, nobody befriends cops out of the goodness of their heart. As sure as night follows day, there's always going to be a quid pro quo.

Con picked up a copy of the paper and quickly turned to page 2. Two paragraphs in he confirmed what he had already suspected. There it was the anonymous quote.

'A senior detective involved in the enquiry said the murder had all the hallmarks of a religious fanatic. Drawing similarities to the infamous 'Bible John' case, which today, 35 years later, remains an unsolved mystery; the detective said two almost identical murders have now ...'

Con felt a sinking feeling in the pit of his stomach. A senior detective, surely not. The only senior detectives who had been at the scene were Campbell and the DCI. No way on this earth would it have been Campbell.

The DI was a wily old fox who had been around the block a few times. There wasn't a cat's chance in hell that he would have made an off the cuff remark like that to someone as notorious as Walter McSorley. So that only left the DCI. But that didn't make any sense either. He hadn't known Mini Cooper long, but it had been long enough to realise that she was smart. Extremely smart and hyper ambitious. She wouldn't dream of compromising her career with a stupid unguarded remark to a gnarly old hack. Nope, he was almost certain it wouldn't have been the DCI or Campbell. So, who did that leave? For a heart stopping moment Con didn't want to answer his own question. The only other detective that he knew had been at the locus was Asif. And for all his brains and likeability, it had to be said that Asif was notorious for thinking out loud and saying daft things. But there was another thing that might point the finger of suspicion in Asif's direction. It was a trick used by most journalists when they reported serious crime stories. Any officer of rank, no matter how junior, was invariably reported in the paper as 'A senior officer said.' It was good for a headline and added gravitas to the story, even though it was often a barefaced lie.

This had all the hallmarks of a PR disaster for the enquiry team. Judging by the way the paper was flying off the shelves the Evening Times must have thought all their Christmases had come early. The exact opposite would be true for the police. The story would quickly grow arms and legs and before long, every news organisation in the land, and beyond would be onto it. Con had seen it happen before, it would become an enormous distraction, and even though Media Services at Pitt Street would pitch in to help, the newshounds would be wanting interviews with the officer in charge of the enquiry, and at this precise moment that person was DCI Mini Cooper.

It was a classic example of shooting yourself in the foot and it would have been largely avoidable if only the loose-tongued detective had been able to keep their mouth shut. The press would still run their stories no doubt with lurid and salacious headlines, they were in the business of selling papers. The police couldn't stop a free press from writing what they liked. But they could have stopped it using non-attributable quotes. The press can't just write a police spokesman said if in fact nobody had said it. They must, as they say in the media, be able to stand a story up. If they can't then they shouldn't print it. By restricting who talks to the press the police can, to some extent, manage the message. It still isn't a perfect situation, but it is a whole lot better than what had happened this morning. This story had the potential to turn into one almighty headache. Of course, there were other potential consequences. If it did turn out that Asif was the source, then he could likely kiss goodbye to his hope of being made a sergeant anytime soon.

'Fuck me.' sighed Con as he scurried back over the road to the office with the paper. 'And to think I only came over to get a packet of fags, it's a funny old world right enough.'

By the time he got back up the stairs the only person in the office was Jan. She raised her hands and with a worried look pointed to the DCI's office next door.

Con held up the paper and pointed to the headline.

'I take it they already know about this then?'

Jan nodded and immediately winced as a slamming door was followed by a tirade of high-pitched expletives. Neither Jan nor Con needed to be told who was doing the swearing. The shrieking voice was unmistakably that of the DCI.

'I take it that was why she was in for so long with the Div Com, he had her in reading the riot act.'

Jan was about to reply when the next volley of swearing echoed down the corridor.

Con instinctively hunched his shoulders and ducked down as if he was trying to avoid some imaginary gunfire. He looked at Jan.

'Not good. I take it Campbell and Asif are in with her?'

'Yep, they were summoned just after you went to Asda.'

Con shook his head. 'God, I hope Asif's not gone blabbing his mouth to McSorley, you know what he's like, there's no harm in the boy, but he does say some stupid things sometimes.'

Jan nodded in agreement. 'Tell me about it. I've known Asif since the day he joined the job, and he's never changed. But I'll tell you something, neither he nor Campbell looked at all perturbed when she called them through, neither of them had the look of a guilty man.'

Con made a strange face. 'That's probably because Campbell didn't know anything about it and Asif, well he's just Asif isn't he. If he did do it, he probably hasn't appreciated that he's done anything wrong. Naïve I think is the word for it. Right, I'm having another coffee. I could really do with a fag, but I can't go for one while this is going on. The tension's unbearable.'

179

Jan handed Con her mug. 'Put an extra shot in it will you, I don't do nicotine but I'm certainly needing an infusion of caffeine. I just hope to God that Asif hasn't done anything silly.'

Five minutes had passed since the last bout of swearing and now all was eerily quiet, they hadn't heard another word from the DCI's office. Perhaps that was a good sign, but they were about to find out as just at that moment in walked Campbell with Asif following immediately behind.

Con and Jan stared at their colleagues searching for some clue from their facial expressions.

'Well?' asked Con holding up his hands.

'Well, what?' replied Campbell swinging his jacket over the back of his chair.

'Well, are you both still in a job?' asked Con with a degree of agitation in his voice.

Campbell started to chuckle.

'For the time being, at least until it's time for you to retire.'

Jan looked alarmed. 'Time being! That doesn't sound good at all.'

'Ok, ok, let's all calm down shall we. I'm just pulling your leg. Neither I, nor Asif, is in any bother. Though somebody, and that somebody is still to be identified, is deep in the brown stuff, but fortunately, it ain't either of us.'

Con and Jan let out a collective sigh. Campbell started to laugh; he was now starting to find the situation quite amusing.

'Just for once, Asif's notorious limpet like quality has proved to be something of a blessing. You see after he and Mini arrived at the murder locus, he never left my side. Seriously, for the whole time he was in the flat we were together. It was perfect. He could corroborate my movements as could Inspector Brough who I'd been with before Asif arrived, and I could do the same for him. And I can assure you that neither of us went anywhere near McSorley or any other journalist for that matter. We had too many other damned things to think about, most of which Asif has recorded in that notebook of his.'

Con grimaced. 'So, what was all the shouting and swearing about? Honestly, I expect the cops in the canteen could hear her, she was blowing a gasket.'

'She's been under a lot of pressure, and I think she just lost it for a bit.' added Campbell. 'She had obviously got it in the neck from Captain Courageous. I guess she wasn't expecting that, got blindsided and wasn't thinking straight.' Campbell glanced at the paper on Con's desk. 'I take it you've read the article. Typical exaggerated nonsense from McSorley, but that's his bread and butter, he's been writing that type of copy for over 30 years. That said, the fact remains, someone at the locus fed him those lines and the DCI has been given till the end of the day to find out who it was.'

Jan rolled her eyes and frowned.

'I can just imagine how old 'baw jaws' would have reacted. He'd have hated getting the call from Pitt Street so it would be just his style to take it out on the DCI. That's how it works in the police, when the brown stuff hits the fan it trickles downwards, there's always someone junior to pass the blame onto.'

Clearly unimpressed Con made a strange snorting noise.

'Well exactly. And it appears that the DCI tried the same tactic on Campbell and Asif. I thought she was better than that. It's always easy to have a go at someone junior in rank in this job. I should know, I've had my share of bollockings, and only some of them were justified. But you just have to stand there and take it, because if you don't, it only makes matters worse.'

Up until now, Asif had been strangely quiet, but now it was his turn to speak up.

'Look, I think you're being a bit harsh on the DCI, when Campbell explained that it couldn't have been us, she did calm down. She's clearly under stress, what with two unsolved high-profile murders on her hands and now this, she doesn't have her troubles to seek. In my opinion I just think she's had a rotten couple of days, simple as that.'

Con didn't look convinced. 'That's mighty benevolent of you, but I still say there wasn't any need for her to sound off at you like that. We all have stressful days doing this job, and she's a Chief Inspector, there's no excuse, not in my book.'

'So, if it wasn't either of you, are we any the wiser who it might have been?' asked Jan rinsing out her mug.

Campbell scratched his ear.

'It would appear that it wasn't Chris or Slypig either, they had been hauled in to see the DCI before us. Inspector Brough is in with her now. It's not going to be Robert, that isn't his style, but I reckon the suspicion is swinging towards whoever did the door to door in the close or was running the log. Robert will be able to give Mini their details.'

Con shook his head. 'Naw, I'm not buying that. McSorley said it was a senior detective. Those cops were all in uniform. McSorley wouldn't make a mistake like that, he's only just tholed his assize and been brought back into the fold, no way would he risk writing something completely spurious.'

Asif rocked back in his chair; a thought had suddenly come to him.

'Someone else was at that flat, she wasn't there for very long, but I know she was there. I saw her name in the log. She was delivering a folder with statement paper for Inspector Brough. Natalie Mellish was definitely at the flat this morning?'

Campbell, Jan and Con all looked at each in amazement.

'Wow, no shit Sherlock! Now if that does turns out to be the case that really would set the cat amongst the pigeons.' said Con unwrapping the cellophane from his fag packet.

Chapter 17

For a Thursday evening, the KFC on Pollokshaws road was surprisingly quiet. Asif found a table by the window overlooking the car park while Campbell waited at the counter to pick up their food. It had been an interesting day. The DCI had been locked away in her office all afternoon trying to establish who had blabbed to the press. By five o'clock it became clear as to who had been responsible as Jan had seen a tearful Natalie leaving the DCI's office. Understandably she was too upset to speak, she headed straight for her car to head home.

Campbell and Asif had held on at the incident room until the DCI made an appearance. They didn't want to just disappear. Campbell, particularly, understood the awkwardness of the situation, so they wanted to hang about to show their support for their new boss.

If it had been a traumatic experience for Natalie, it had been equally tough for the newly promoted Chief Inspector. Nobody liked to have to take sanctions against one of your own. Least of all when it was someone you were fond of and who was part of a small tight-knit team. But in the circumstances the DCI was left with very little choice. Natalie had to be removed from the team and returned to uniform duties. Mini knew that the Div Com would have insisted on it, and being truthful, in her heart of hearts she knew it was the

184

right course of action. It sent out a strong signal that team discipline was both necessary and important. Talking directly to the press without clearance from the boss was taboo, it simply couldn't be tolerated.

Constable Mellish had paid a heavy price for her indiscretion, but in her case, it wouldn't necessarily be a career stopper. She was still young both in age and in terms of her length of service and, most importantly, it was her first glaring mistake. She would recover from this setback, six months or a year back in uniform and she could realistically expect to be offered other opportunities. The important thing from today's events from her point of view was how she responded and learned from her mistake. So long as she didn't hide away in a prolonged sulk, she would be fine. She just had to pick herself back up and get on with things, there really wasn't any other way of dealing with what had happened.

'Right here we go. One boneless banquet and a diet Coke for you and a fillet box meal and hot wings for me. Great, I think that's us sorted, tuck in, you'll be ready for it, it's been a long day.'

Asif looked at his watch. It had just gone seven thirty. A lot had happened in the 12 hours that had passed since he'd left his room in Tulliallan to go for his breakfast that morning. If ever there was an example of how quickly things can change in the police, then today had been a good example of it.

'I'm gutted for Natalie though.' said Asif unpacking his box. 'She was hardly in the department and now she's been put back to uniform. Doesn't really seem fair, she wasn't deliberately trying to do any harm, she was just naïve and made a mistake. What do you think? Would you have dealt with the situation any differently?'

Campbell pushed a straw into the lid of his coke and thought for a moment.

'You know, I don't think I would have. I don't really think Mini had much of a choice. But I must give her credit, she acted swiftly, and if she is in a relationship with Natalie, she didn't let sentiment get in the way.'

Asif looked up. 'Perhaps that's why she acted so quickly. I mean to avoid the spotlight remaining on the issue for any length of time. That seems like a sensible decision if you ask me, draw the sting and then quickly move on. Strategically smart as you might say.'

Campbell's expression suggested he was impressed.

'Good grief, you'll only been away for a day, and I can already see the difference. You're starting to sound like a supervisory officer, mixing with those other bright sparks up at the college must be rubbing off on you. But you make an excellent point. If she is in a relationship with Natalie, then I'm pretty sure it would have been a major factor in her decision to act so quickly. It'll help keep the attention away from their relationship and in a strange way it will also help me.'

Asif grimaced and pursed his lips. Up until that last remark everything, for once, was making perfect sense. But now he was perplexed. What did Campbell mean?

'My newly discovered depths of perception seem to have left me as quickly as they arrived. You're going to have to explain, how is it going to benefit you?'

Campbell smiled knowingly.

'Think about it. If Natalie is no longer part of the team, then the fact that they're in a relationship becomes largely irrelevant. It might not be encouraged but having a relationship with someone else in the job, even someone working out of the same station is far from unique. The situation might have become a serious issue if they were part of the same small team. Up until today that was the case, but it isn't the case any longer. The fact that they've now been split up has saved me having to have a conversation with the Chief Inspector. There's now no need for me to tell her that we are aware that they've been seen out together. Now that they're working in different parts of the organisation, I don't feel I need to become involved.'

Asif scratched his head.

'But you would have if they had still been part of the same team?'

'Yep.' Said Campbell nodding.

'If you're close to somebody, and I mean close because you're in a relationship with them, not close because you just happen to work together, then your ear is always on the radio should they be sent to a call, you're always worrying, you want to be sure they are safe, not in any danger. It's like a parent looking out for their child, you just become much more invested, and that can be a distraction that prevents you doing your job professionally. Your judgement becomes too emotional which in turn leads to poor decision making. Rational and sensible are your watchwords, Asif. You don't want emotional baggage when you're a supervisor and trying to make good decisions. Does that make sense?'

Once again Asif was in awe of his mentor. None of that had occurred to him, and yet in a matter of weeks he could find himself promoted and having to make decisions about the interests and welfare of subordinate officers. One of yesterday's presentations at the college had been at pains to point out that by far the biggest transition in terms of responsibilities in the police was the move from constable to sergeant. As a cop, you are only ever responsible for yourself, or a probationary officer if you've been given the responsibility to be a Tutor Cop. You don't have to worry about anyone else. But when you become a sergeant, that situation changes immediately. From the get-go you will be required to assume responsibility for making decisions on behalf of your team. As a uniformed sergeant that could mean running a team of upwards of fifteen officers. Male and female, old lags, and starry-eyed probationers, fresh from Tulliallan. It's an awesome responsibility and one that Asif was yet to get his head around. It was a sobering thought; he knew he still had oodles to learn. He let out a heavy sigh.

'I'd never really thought about it in those terms before, but I can see your point. One of our presentations yesterday at the AP seminar was saying much the same thing. Being in a relationship and having that person working so close in a job like ours isn't ideal, yep, I totally get that. But while you might not have to have that chat with the Chief Inspector about Natalie, there's something else that I urgently need to get your advice on, and I think this time it might well require you to speak privately with the Chief Inspector.'

Campbell put down his chicken wing and wiped his mouth.

'Go on. I hadn't forgotten that you wanted to discuss something with me, and this sounds intriguing. So, crack on, I'm all ears.'

Chapter 18

If yesterday's media fiasco had been an unnecessary distraction, this morning's meeting had gone some way to getting the investigation back on track and focussing on what had now become a double murder enquiry. With laser-like precision, the DCI had given the team a detailed overview of what had been established so far. According to Mary the cleaner, Mini had been at her desk since 0530 hrs. She had covered two white boards with photographs, maps and action points. Her focus, which was written in large red pen on a separate flip chart was establishing the link between the murder victims. In the absence of any leads that would point to the identity of the killer, the focus, for now, had to be on establishing why Magnus DeVilliers and Maureen Goodall had been targeted in such a ruthless and callous manner. That, as she repeatedly stated, was the key to unlocking the mystery of the murders.

Campbell didn't disagree, but despite his vast experience, he was at a loss to explain what that link might be. He was sure that the most likely connection was through their work, but then again, the fact that they both appeared to play bridge might also be significant. As could the bible references and the presence at the loci of the frogs and locusts. It could, of course, be a combination of all those things. There was just too much information swirling about in his head, his brain was scrambled, it felt like he was wading through treacle so slow was the progress being made.

The focus of today's actions was to visit all the hairdressers in the local area. They knew, according to Mrs Paton's witness statement, that Maureen Goodall had had her hair done the day before she was due to go on holiday. As Mini had pointed out, hairdressers were famous for gossiping with their clients. She felt, as someone who enjoyed a juicy chat with her own hairdresser, that it was extremely likely that Maureen would have discussed her upcoming holiday with whoever was cutting her hair. Who wouldn't want to chat about your holiday? She'd be excited and looking forward to it. Campbell was no expert on ladies' hairdressers, nor on the conversations they had with clients, but the DCI's explanation seemed logical and to that end two of the newly appointed detectives were tasked with visiting all the local hairdressers.

Another two detectives had been given the task of trying to establish if the two murder victims had ever worked together. That was a more onerous and time-consuming task. It had already been established that for the last 11 years, Magnus DeVilliers had worked as an Ear, Nose and Throat Consultant at Ross Hall, a private hospital in the Crookston area of Glasgow. While according to neighbours, Maureen Goodall had spent her entire career working at the Victoria Infirmary for the NHS. No one had any knowledge of her working anywhere else, but that, of course, would need to be checked. It had all the prospects of being a time consuming and tedious task.

With Mini's agreement, Campbell and Asif were going to call at Whitecraigs Golf Club. They wanted to establish if Magnus DeVilliers golf trolley and travel carrier might be in his locker. They weren't hopeful, but as it remained a major line of enquiry it had to be bottomed out. Disappointingly, the trawl of all CCTV cameras located in the vicinity of Queen's Park and Pollokshields had not found any evidence that could corroborate the witness statement that they had from the park employee who stated he had seen a dark clothed figure pulling a golf trolley on the evening before DeVilliers' body was found. It was all very frustrating but in truth not that unusual. You had to get lucky with CCTV trawls, a camera pointing the wrong way and your opportunity was lost, it was a game of chance, and on this occasion the enquiry team appeared to have drawn a blank.

*

The club secretary was a tall man with a jowly face and a red bulbous nose. He was drinking tea in the lounge with a couple of members when the detectives arrived. Campbell introduced themselves and stated their business which the secretary acknowledged in a clipped RP Edinburgh accent. Each of his syllables stressed and signalled by a rise in pitch. His George Heriot's tie was another give away as was his disinclination to offer his visitors a cup of tea. He was clearly a man from the east.

'You'll need to wait while I go and get the master key. The locker room is down the corridor on the right, you can meet me there in a couple of minutes.'

Asif wasn't sure what to make of his last remark. It was clear by the way that the secretary had looked down his nose when addressing them that he was unimpressed by their presence. But Asif wondered if it were more than that.

Was his brown skin offensive? It wouldn't be the first time that Asif had encountered lazy slightly understated racism, that in Asif's experience was far from uncommon in men of a certain age and social status. He didn't bother mentioning it to Campbell as they made their way down the corridor to the rather well-appointed male locker room.

The secretary appeared brandishing a key. 'Magnus DeVilliers, locker number 117. It's the top locker just over here on the left. I'll open it and leave it with you if that's alright. I've things to be getting on with in the office. Just return the key when you're finished. My office is two doors down from the lounge.'

Strange, thought Asif as he watched the secretary disappear. Complete indifference, and not a word of sympathy about the loss of one of their members. He was still thinking about how strange the secretary's behaviour had been when Campbell pulled something from the top shelf of the locker. It was a large buff coloured envelope.

'As we suspected there's no trolley or travel carrier. And apart from this envelope the only thing in here is a fusty old pair of golf shoes and a set of waterproofs.'

Campbell opened the envelope and pulled out several pieces of paper. His face lit up as he examined each piece of paperwork in turn.

'Ah ha.' he said triumphantly handing Asif a stapled set of A4 paper. 'We may have just got lucky. This appears to be a travel itinerary and guess what, he wasn't travelling alone. Look at the name of the other passenger.'

Asif smiled. 'I'm guessing it's Maureen Goodall.'

'You've got it in one. And there are flight tickets in both their names, Glasgow to Naples. And look there's more. There's a smaller envelope in here with Euros in it.'

Asif looked up. 'How much?'

Campbell started counting the cash. 'One thousand euros in mixed notes.' He put the money back in the envelope. 'Well, it looks like Mr DeVilliers may have been a bit of a dark horse. Perhaps he wasn't quite the paragon of virtue that David Beckett and Connell Cranston suggested he was. And I wonder why he kept the travel information in his golf locker, why didn't he just keep it at home. It's not as if his wife was going to find out, she's been dead over a year.'

Asif shrugged his shoulders.

'Who knows. Perhaps he had a guilty conscience about going away with another woman so soon after the death of his wife. And keeping it here, well, out of sight out of mind, and all that. Anyway, it's not like you to moralise. At least we've made a definitive connection, the two victims clearly knew each other.'

'Yeah, clearly, but we're still none the wiser as to how they met or why anyone would want to murder them, we're still a long way off solving this mystery, but at least it's a start. Right, time to get back to the office and give Mini some good news for a change. And I haven't forgotten about our conversation last night, I just haven't had an opportunity to talk to her privately yet. But you were right about one thing, she is laying on the make up pretty thick, I hadn't noticed till you said, but you're spot on, she's caked in the stuff.'

Back in the incident room Jan was busy inputting statements onto the Holmes system while Con was checking intelligence logs at his desk. He looked up as Campbell and Asif walked in.

'If you're looking for the DCI then I'm afraid you've just missed her. She's put on her big girl pants and is away to Pitt Street to see the ACC Crime. She's been summoned and I think she's expecting a bit of spanking after yesterday's carry-on.'

Asif took off his jacket and sat down.

'You're joking, I mean about the pants?'

With a look of exasperation Con nodded his head.

'Of course, I'm joking. Well, I am about the pants, not about being summoned to Pitt Street. She made that joke herself, but you could tell she was concerned. It's easy to forget that she's only got 11 years service, that really isn't much. She's still a baby in management terms and she's got a lot on her plate. And that fecking imbecile along the corridor won't be any help. He's about as much fecking use as a handbrake on a canoe. According to Mary the cleaner, he leaves orange pips on the carpet behind his curtains and if she doesn't find them when she's cleaning his room, he goes off on one.'

Jan turned round from her desk and peered over her glasses.

'I know where I'd like to stick his orange pips, and it's somewhere where the sun don't shine.'

Campbell chucked.

'You really, really don't like that man, do you?'

Jan turned back to her computer. 'Nope. I really, really don't!'

Campbell tapped his fingers together; he'd had a thought.

'Right, I know everybody is busy, but while the boss is away and it's just the four of us, I want us to take the opportunity to take stock of where we are with this enquiry. I want Asif, Con and you Jan, next door with no distractions for the next hour or so. On the principle that four brains are better than one, and if any of you haven't read the Wisdom of Crowds by James Surowiecki then I recommend you do so. It's an excellent book, the best I've read in years and its premise is that on most occasions the collective wisdom of the crowd will outperform that of a single person. So, folks, with that principle in mind, and as my brain is absolutely mush right now trying to make sense of these murders, I think we should try and put Surowiecki's theory to the test. And no holds barred, no ideas a bad idea, everything goes no matter how off the wall it is. So, what do you say, who's in?'

Asif nodded. 'Sure, sounds good, let's do it.'

Jan got up from her desk. 'I'm in.'

Con rubbed his hand gleefully.

'No holds barred, eh. Now you're talking. We're taking it into the hurt room folks, where everything goes. It must be 10 years since I was last involved with one of these, but I think it's a cracking idea, let's do it.'

For the next hour and a half, the four colleagues discussed the circumstances surrounding the murders of Magnus DeVilliers and Maureen Goodall. Nothing was out of bounds. Ideas were tossed in then picked apart. The early part of the discussion was centred on motive. That had been Asif's suggestion, and it was a good one. He felt that too much emphasis up until now had been placed on trying to make a connection between the two victims. That remained an important line of enquiry, but there needed to be more focus on the motive. Why did someone want to murder DeVilliers and Goodall?

Jan offered up the not unreasonable suggestion that sex may have been a motive. Was the killer a spurned lover of Goodall, who had been dumped in favour of her new beau, Magnus DeVilliers? It was certainly possible, after all, they were going away on a cruise together. Inevitably it had been Asif who threw in the curve ball. Perhaps the relationship had been between the killer and DeVilliers, it was 2004 after all, same sex relationships were now ten a penny. The others thought that unlikely as DeVilliers had been married for many years. Ah, but without ever having family, added Asif, as if that made it more likely that DeVilliers may at least be bisexual. To and fro went the discussion and the time just flew by.

After more than an hour of earnest debate, some themes were starting to emerge. More focus on motive got the thumbs up from everyone. And everyone also agreed that this enquiry was suffering from a significant intelligence gap that needed to be addressed as a priority. To date next to nothing had come in via intelligence logs and that was seriously hampering the investigation. Intelligence is the lifeblood on which much of policing, and particularly detective work is built. Without it any investigation will start to struggle, that was certainly the case with this enquiry. Campbell wrote both suggestions on the flipchart as action points to be taken forward with the DCI.

Changing the subject completely, Con said he wanted to raise something that had been bothering him for a while. No one, it appeared to him, was paying sufficient attention to, as Con put it, the killer's egomaniacal tendencies. The chatter in the room immediately stopped. Everyone's attention suddenly turned towards

Con. This was something completely out of left field, everybody, it seemed, was intrigued to hear what he had to say.

Campbell scratched his head. 'Egomaniacal tendencies, well, that's a new one on me, but we're all ears Con, the floor's yours, please, take it away.'

For the next ten minutes Con made his case as to why he thought the killer was an egotistical attention-seeking maniac. He began by explaining the significance of the body in the boating pond. The killer, Con said, wanted that body to be found. That was obvious. If he hadn't he would have hidden the body, burnt it or perhaps buried it. No, he wanted that body found as soon as it got light. Also, he went on to explain, that the frog being found in a zipped pocket of De Villiers jacket was again a deliberate act by the murderer. They knew we would find that frog and start wondering why it was there. Con surmised that the killer would get some sort of perverse satisfaction, sexual or otherwise, knowing that the police wouldn't know its purpose or significance. The killer, he said, was deliberately taunting us.

Asif was transfixed. As far as he knew Con had never been a detective, he was a cop appointed to be the CID clerk. The clerk's function is primarily the day to day running of the office. Con was not a hands-on detective. But what this showed was you couldn't beat experience. Nearly 30 years of policing had clearly left its mark. Con maybe wasn't a real detective, but he'd worked with dozens of them over many years and sat in during endless briefings about murders and other serious crimes. It had obviously rubbed off. Listening to Con it was clear that he thought like a detective. This smart and original thinking which from Asif's point of view made perfect sense. He opened his folder and started to scribble down some notes.

Con continued his hypothesis. 'And the killers taunting behaviour can also be observed from the messages left at both locations. I'm still of the opinion that he's some sort of religious nut, must be if he's quoting bible passages'. He turned to the board where Natalie had written up the quote from Deuteronomy. He read it aloud.

'Take this lesson to heart: that the Lord your God was disciplining you as a father disciplines his son: and keep the commandments of the Lord your God.'

'This maniac thinks he is God, or at the very least he's doing God's bidding. And for what it's worth I'm pretty sure our murderer is a man. He thinks he's speaking directly to us through that bible quote. It says, 'Take this lesson to heart'. That's a threat, it's a warning shot across our bows. You've been punished because you needed to be punished. It's crazy but I think he thinks the murders were an act of compassion, like a father disciplines his son the quote says. This nutter believes the victims brought this on themselves and needed to be punished. The scary bit in all this is that I don't think he's necessarily finished. He could easily strike again'.

Campbell puffed out his cheeks. What Con had said had cut through. There was every possibility that this spree of killings could continue. As ever, time was of the essence, they needed to catch this killer, and catch him soon.

Campbell stood up and switched the kettle on.

'I'm grateful for that Con, I think you've profiled our killer fairly accurately. Of course, there are other examples that you didn't cite that I think also point to his mental state. The front door and storm doors at Goodall's flat in Tankerland Road had deliberately been left ajar. The killer could easily have closed them, yet he chose not to. It was as if he wanted that body to be found, you know, by a neighbour or perhaps the postman.'

Campbell tapped his forehead. A thought had just occurred to me.

'Asif, who was the cop running the log outside the close yesterday? I know you spoke to him.'

'It was Brian Stuart, why you asking?'

'Any idea if he's working today, I'd like to speak to him.'

Asif looked at his watch and nodded. 'I saw him earlier; I think he must be day shift. I could check the canteen; it's just coming to the end of piece time.'

'Yep, that would be useful thanks.'

'What's on your mind?' asked Jan as Asif scurried off down the corridor.

'I'm just thinking about what Con just said, about the killer being egotistical. It's just prompted a memory from one of my lectures at my last detective training course. We got an input from a psychologist, a strange looking fella with crazy fly away frizzy hair. He was talking about how murderers, will sometimes re-visit the scene of their crime, or hang about and watch as the police and forensics go about their business. Apparently, they like to relive the feeling they got when they committed the crime. It's a well-documented phenomenon, and it's happened before on enquiries I've been involved in, so I was just wondering if our killer, with an ego the size of a planet, may have made an unexpected appearance. Just a thought.'

Con removed his glasses.

'Not a bad shout. Well worth exploring. It's just a pity we don't have better CCTV coverage. There's next to nothing in Glencairn Drive and the same's true for Tankerland Road, so that ain't gonna help us much.'

Just then the door opened and in walked Asif and Constable Stuart. Campbell looked up and waved at them to come over.

'Brian, isn't it?'

Constable Stuart nodded.

'I don't think we've met but I'm DI Morrison. I just want a quick word with you about yesterday. I believe you were keeping the log at Tankerland Road.'

'That's correct sir, I did it all morning except for an hour when I was relieved for my piece break.'

'Good, that's what I thought. Can you cast your mind back and think about the crowd of onlookers who'd gathered across the street and were watching what was going on. I'm not so interested in the press, I know about them, I'm more interested in members of the public who might have been there.'

Brian screwed up his nose and thought for a moment.

'I'm particularly interested in anyone who may have been acting strangely and were most likely there on their own.'

Brian's eyes opened wide.

'There was a strange looking character who was there for quite some time. He appeared to be on his own, I certainly didn't see him talking to anyone else. He stood a little away from the rest of the crowd, with his back to the wall, just along from the chip shop.'

'You said he was a strange looking character, what made you say that?' asked Campbell.

'He was just a bit weird. Quite short, but I suppose it was more the way he was dressed that drew my attention. He had a beanie hat pulled down over his ears and he was wearing a dark heavy jacket. A heavy winter jacket, not the kind of jacket you would wear on a warm spring day like yesterday. Well, I wouldn't anyway. I think it was the way he was dressed that made me notice him because I didn't see him do anything.'

Asif noted down the description.

'Anything else you can tell us about his clothing, trousers, shoes?'

Constable Stuart rubbed his chin.

'I think he was wearing boots, but I'm not 100% sure, and dark coloured trousers I think, but again I wouldn't want to swear on it.'

'That's helpful.' said Campbell trying to sound encouraging.

'Can you try and picture his face, is there anything you can tell us about how he looked?'

Constable Stuart shut his eyes. 'White male, unshaven, a few days growth I'd say, and not wearing glasses. And I'm sure he had a canvas bag over his shoulder, it was dark, maybe grey coloured, you know the type of bag you see workmen carrying. And that's about it, I'm sorry but I think that's all I can tell you.'

Campbell smiled. 'That's been very useful. One last question if I may before you go, are you able to say how long he was there?'

Brian thought again. 'He must have been there about an hour and a half, maybe even a bit longer. He was there when I got back from my piece break and that was the back of eleven. And he disappeared just before I got relieved at one, so it was perhaps nearer two hours now I think about it.'

'Listen, that's been most useful. I'd like you to give me a statement if you don't mind and include what you just told us in it. If you could get it done either today or tomorrow that would be perfect and just leave it in the tray on Jan's desk over there, she'll see that it gets put onto the system. And thanks again for your help, that's filled in a couple of blanks for us.'

'No problem, just happy to help.' Constable Stuart opened the door to go out. 'Morning ma'am, I mean afternoon ma'am, oh, I'm sorry, excuse me, I'll just get out of your way.'

DCI Cooper stepped aside to let the flustered young constable past.

'What was all that about? You've not been interrogating young impressionable officers again Asif, have you?'

'What me ma'am, no, certainly not.'

Campbell and Con both started to laugh. Even though the subliminal messaging had again been lost on Asif, it was clear from the DCI's use of humour that things might not be quite as bad as they had feared.

'How did things go up the road ma'am?' asked Campbell.

A smile threatened to break out across her face as Mini removed her jacket.

'Much better than I thought it would, being honest. It still wasn't the most pleasant of experiences, but I'm still in a job and it turns out that the ACC doesn't care for our illustrious leader any more than you do Con. So, I think he's keeping some of his wrath for his meeting with the Divisional Commander tomorrow.'

Con and the others started to laugh. 'Nice one. Couldn't happen to a nicer bloke. Jan and I would pay good money to be a fly on the wall for that meeting. Time that man got a bit of a comeuppance, it's been a long time coming.'

Mini glanced at the headings written up on the whiteboard.

'Motive, Intelligence and Egotistical Maniac! What in God's name have you four been up to?'

'Best hour and a half I've spent in ages ma'am, a no holds barred, everything goes and no ideas a stupid idea kind of a meeting. If every day was as productive and fun as this then I'd be tempted to put off my retiral. But seriously, I think we've made a bit of progress. And constable Stuart who you bumped into when you arrived has given us some useful information.'

Mini searched her desk for her coffee mug.

'Excellent news. A good old fashioned 'Hurt Room.' I had a boss when I was a DS who swore by them, get everything out on the table, look at the pros and cons, identify the weaknesses and try and fix them, all before you take your ideas or recommendations to the boss. It requires complete honesty and trust, but in a small tight team it can work well and pay dividends. Yeah, that takes me back.'

'Well, perhaps we should do it again soon, I didn't realise I had a fellow devotee, but first, when you're ready I can brief you on the findings of this one.' said Campbell.

Mini handed Asif the cafetiere from her desk. 'Sounds good, just let me get an infusion of caffeine and I'll be right with you. Four heaped spoonfuls Asif, and I think we'll have the black insomnia, seems appropriate, it's in the jar with the red lid.'

Just then the phone on Jan's desk rang. It was Lucy from Forensics in Pitt Street.

'Yes, she's here, can you hold the line and I'll get her for you?

Ma'am, it's Lucy Harper from the Lab for you.'

Jan handed Mini the phone. Perched on the edge of Jan's desk Mini gestured to Con to get her a pen and notepad.

'Yes, yes, I can speak carry on. Ok, yes, I've got that, you're saying the sample you took from Maureen Goodall's neck contains lead residue that matches the lead found on DeVilliers body. So, there's every chance that the same weapon has been used to kill both victims and that that weapon has also likely been used at some point to cut lead. Excellent. Yeah, that is interesting Lucy. Very interesting.

Ok, yes, about that other matter, yes, fire away, I've got a pen and notepad.'

For a few seconds there was silence, then she wrote something on her pad. Asif approached the desk with his boss's mug of coffee. He couldn't help but see what she had written in bold capital letters.

CONFIRMED: KETAMINE & ROHYPNOL.

Chapter 19

Having dropped Campbell at his dentist in Shawlands for the next round of his treatment, Asif made his way to Glencairn Drive where he found a parking space just down from the bowling club. He had the photograph of Maureen Goodall with him which he wanted to show to David Beckett, the club's barman, to see if it rang any bells. It was a warm April morning and as he glanced across the road to Magnus DeVilliers' front garden, he noticed that the azalea and rhododendron bushes were now in full bloom. In fact, all the gardens that he could see as he looked up the drive were a riot of colour. Spring, it seemed, had finally arrived.

It was still early, and nobody was playing on either of the greens when Asif made his way up the path. He wondered if the place was closed as there didn't appear to be anybody about. The front door, however, was open so he made his way to the lounge where he found David Beckett on his hands and knees behind the bar trying to fix a leaky pipe. Beckett looked up clutching a spanner, he greeted Asif with a ready smile.

'Ah, detective, good morning. Just give me a minute and I'll be right with you. Help yourself to a coffee, there's a percolator on the end of the bar, it's freshly made.'

'I'll do that thanks. Can I get you one?'

'Sure. And just milk please. It's not real milk it's just those silly wee cartons I'm afraid, they're in a box next to the cups.'

Asif poured the coffee and went and sat down at a table by the window. Beckett joined him a couple of minutes later.

'Quiet today, where is everybody?'

Beckett started to chuckle. 'You're not familiar with the game of bowls then?'

'No, not really, I've never played.'

Beckett smiled. 'No, I thought not. Play won't start for another couple of hours, most of our members are retired and they don't like early starts. But more to the point a later start allows the groundsman to cut both greens and generally get things tidied up before play starts. It's not like golf or tennis for that matter. If you look out that back window you can see that they're already out playing at the tennis club, it's only a couple of hundred metres from here. Bottom of the drive and turn left. But Bowls is a much more leisurely game, a social game, and you don't need to end up all sweaty like you do playing tennis.'

Asif hadn't appreciated that the tennis club was so close by. It just hadn't been on his radar, but it was now. Maureen Goodall had been a tennis player, in fact the photo he was about to show Beckett was of her in her tennis gear. Asif scratched his ear and wondered. Perhaps it was the tennis club where DeVilliers and Maureen Goodall knew each other from. That would be his next port of call when he was finished here.

Asif took the photo from his folder and handed it to Beckett. He examined it closely and then shook his head.

'Terrible business. I heard all about it on the news last night. I must say I was impressed with your female Chief Inspector who did the interview. Crikey she looked young, but very professional. No stumbling over her words, and the appeal she made, it was as if she was speaking directly to the murderer, it sent a shiver down my spine I can tell you.'

Asif took a mouthful of coffee. 'That's good to know, I'll pass that on to my boss, DCI Cooper. She did the broadcast and will be pleased to hear that's how it came across, that was a deliberate tactic, to make the appeal as if she was speaking directly to the killer. Anyway, getting back to the photo. Have you ever seen that woman at the club?'

Beckett shook his head. 'No, I can't say I recognise her, I don't think she's ever been in here, well not while I've been working. And I don't think I would have forgotten her, she's a stunning looking woman, I hope that isn't inappropriate.'

Asif took the photo and returned it to his folder. 'No, you're ok. You're not the first and I'm sure you'll not be the last to make the same comment, she was an attractive lady, there's no doubt about that.'

Asif drained the last of his coffee and thanked Mr Beckett for his hospitality.

'So, bottom of the drive and turn left.'

'That's it. Titwood Tennis Club. Ask for Mary. Mary Sharp. She's kind of my equivalent down there, she should be able to help you, if anyone can it will be her.'

Mary Sharp was a bright and energetic lady with a beaming smile who seemed to do everything at breakneck speed. She reminded Asif of a P.E Teacher he'd had when he was at Hillhead. She moved almost as quickly as she talked, and Asif was in danger of lagging behind as she led him through the clubhouse to the all-weather courts behind.

'Yes, yes, she's definitely been here.' said Mary brandishing the photograph in the air. 'And on more than one occasion. But I can categorically tell you that she's not a member, nor has she ever been. She's played here as a visitor, somebody's guest, that or she's been here for a team match, you know as part of a team from another club playing our ladies' team. There's a league you know, very competitive one too, and this year there's a big push on to do well, maybe even win it.' Spraying words like a geyser and barely pausing for breath, Mary ploughed on.

'It's been over twenty years since we last won the league, and Jill and some of the other ladies are intent on changing that. That's four of them playing on the faraway court. You wait here officer, and I'll get Jill. If anyone knows the lady, it'll be Jill Smith. Nearly sixty now but what a player, 11 times ladies' champion at this club, you'll have seen her name up on the board as we came through the lounge. And it would have been more, but she's had surgery on both her knees in the last five years. Of course, she blames that on her badminton. That's her winter sport you see. Terrific badminton player as well. Now, as I said you stay here, and I'll get her for you.'

Asif slumped down onto a bench and took a deep breath. Good grief, what in God's name had that been all about? Asif was sharp and usually quick on the uptake. But Mary's verbal onslaught had lost him by her second sentence. She fired out words like bullets from a machine gun. They just kept coming.

Compared to Mary, Jill Smith appeared to be an oasis of calm. Fortunately, Mary had other things to do and had left Jill and Asif to their own devices. Jill quite understandably had been shocked when she'd heard the news of Maureen Goodall's murder. For her it had been a double blow, as she was also an acquaintance of Magnus DeVilliers who, while not a member of the tennis club, had many friends who were. She would occasionally see him in the lounge when he joined with friends to make up a four for bridge. She also knew him through Titwood Parish Church where they were both members.

With regards to Maureen Goodall, Jill explained that she had only been back in touch for about the last year. They'd known each other as youngsters and played tennis against each other as juniors at competitions and for their respective clubs. She explained that Maureen was a more than useful player and had been the ladies' champion at Newlands Tennis Club several times. Their paths had crossed last year when Maureen turned up with her Newlands teammates to play a team match. After a gap of nearly 40 years that reignited their friendship and since then they had played socially at each other's clubs on a couple of occasions. In fact, they were due to play again in a fortnight at Newlands after Maureen returned from her holiday.

It was clear from the way Jill spoke that there was fear as well as a deep sadness about what had happened. Jill, and many others from the local area were concerned that the killer might strike again. The endless gory headlines being spat out daily by Walter McSorley and other members of the media was doing nothing to dampen those fears. And as Jill had known both victims she was understandably concerned about her own safety.

Asif did his best to assure her that the likelihood of her becoming a target was remote. Miniscule even, but in his heart of hearts even he couldn't say for certain that the killer wouldn't strike again. Trying to remain sympathetic to her predicament, he was keen to find out if Jill knew how Magnus DeVilliers and Maureen Goodall knew each other. Jill had already told him that they had bumped into each other in the bar after Jill and Maureen had finished a game of tennis. That was sometime last summer. According to Jill, after they had got over the surprise of meeting each other, they chatted away like old friends. Jill had later asked how they knew each other, and Maureen had said that they had worked together for a time a number of years ago. Jill was adamant that she had no idea that they were planning to go on holiday together. During their last phone conversation, Maureen, had mentioned that she was going on a Mediterranean cruise, she had told Jill it was with a friend, but she most definitely didn't say she was going with Magnus DeVilliers. But why would she, it really wasn't anyone else's business.

It wasn't much but at least it was something to take back to Campbell and the DCI. Two of Asif's colleagues were already working on trying to establish if the victims had known each other through work. He'd feed the information he'd gleaned into the system and see where that took them.

*

After work that evening, Campbell and Mini found themselves a table by the window in the Granary pub in

210

Shawlands. Campbell had decided to strike while the iron was hot. After Asif had explained what Suzi Lessard had told him at the college, he knew he needed to speak to his boss as a matter of urgency. Given the sensitive subject matter, he felt that would best be done away from the office. In recent days their own relationship appeared much improved after what, it had to be said, had been a rocky start. It had been his suggestion to go for a glass of wine after work as something important had come up that he needed to speak to her about.

'Just a small one, thanks, I'm driving and it's an early start as usual tomorrow.'

'Fine, it's going to be the same for me. Red or White?'

'Red preferably, and just whatever, it's not like coffee, I'm not an expert on wine.'

Campbell returned with two glasses of Shiraz and a couple of bags of crisps which he opened and placed on the table.'

'Please, help yourself, I just needed something salty. Not good for my blood pressure according to my doc but I'm a sucker for salt and vinegar crisps.'

Mini smiled and helped herself to some crisps.

'You said that you wanted to speak to me urgently and I take it it's a private matter as we're sitting here in a pub and not the office.'

Campbell clasped his hands and leant forward across the table.

'Well, yes, it is a private matter and it's a sensitive issue. Also, it's not about me, it's about you boss, so I'm going to come straight to the point.'

Mini sat back in her chair and pointed a finger at her chest.

'Me! It's about me?' Her confused look suggested this had come as a complete surprise.

For the next five minutes Mini sat listening intently as Campbell explained what Asif had told him, not only about what was alleged to have happened at the college, but also that he knew what she had written down when Lucy Harper had phoned her with the lab results. Apparently oblivious to what she was doing, Mini fingered the bruise on the side of her neck as Campbell quietly and calmly explained how concerned he and Asif were for her well-being. By the time he had finished speaking Mini's fingers were heavily stained from the taupe coloured make up she had taken to wearing to cover her bruise.

Mini swallowed hard. For a moment the lump in her throat ensured that no words came. She felt suddenly exposed and vulnerable. Through mist filled eyes, tears rolled slowly down her cheeks. Campbell fumbled in his pocket for a tissue. Wiping her eyes and the makeup from her fingers she started to quietly sob. The last few days had been an emotional rollercoaster. With the murder enquiry taking a sinister and unexpected twist, and then the fallout from Natalie's indiscretion with the press, she had deliberately focussed all her energies on the investigation. As a professional officer that is what she had been trained to do. That, at least, had allowed her to shut out the trauma of what had happened at Tulliallan. But now, knowing that two of her closest colleagues knew the circumstances and wanted to help, all the pent-up emotions of the last 48 hours came tumbling out. The protective shell she used so effectively to repel threats and unwanted behaviour cracked open. Like a river bursting its banks, her defences could no longer hold. Tears flowed in waves as she sobbed uncontrollably.

Campbell shifted the position of his stool slightly, so his back was to the three punters who were drinking at the bar. He wanted to create a barrier, give his boss some privacy. Her pain was raw, and writ large on her face. She needed time and some space.

Campbell didn't know how long she had been crying, but when she stopped, he leant forward, and with the awkwardness that comes from being a middle-aged bachelor, put his hand on her arm.

'Boss, I know this is nobody's business but your own. But Asif wanted you to know, that he's more than happy to give a statement on your behalf, he can speak to seeing the bruises on your wrists. And the same goes for Suzi Lessard. She's offered to come through from Tayside and speak directly with you if that would be helpful. I think that's admirable on her part and shows how much she wants to help. But, as I said, it's your shout, only you can make that call.'

Mini dabbed her eyes and looked up.

'Thanks, that's most kind, I appreciate it. You're a good man Campbell, and that goes for Asif too, I'm lucky to have you on my team. I hadn't appreciated that Asif knew anything about any of this, but now thinking back I have a pretty hazy memory of speaking to someone in the corridor that night. And what you said makes sense, that someone must have been Suzi Lessard, although I didn't know that was her name, but I'm guessing it was the girl who sat next to Asif at the dinner, I'd seen them chatting in the bar beforehand, they seemed to be getting on well.'

'Yeah, that would appear to be the case from what Asif told me. He also said that Suzi personally knows other women who have been treated dreadfully by Taylor, well I think that's what he said his name was. He didn't know any specific details, but I'm suspecting that they may have been assaulted by him.'

Mini sighed wearily, it was as if all the stuffing had been knocked out of her.

'Yeah, Taylor's his name. Nic Taylor. He's just been made a Chief Superintendent in Tayside. And he's been my mentor on the AP course for the last couple of years. Huge ego and of course he thinks he's untouchable because his father was the DCC in Grampian, only retired a year or so ago, he couldn't be more establishment, he's very well connected.'

Campbell scoffed. 'Well, that shouldn't count for anything, I don't care if he's related to Pope John Paul himself, and it doesn't matter who his father is, that's irrelevant. And anyway, with Asif and Suzi you've got witnesses, good solid credible witnesses.'

Mini raised an eyebrow.

'This is the police we're talking about; they don't go after one of their own lightly. Not one as senior and well connected as Nic Taylor. But you're right, I know you're right. That scumbag put Rohypnol in my drink and raped me. He may think he's untouchable, but he's going to get one hell of a surprise!'

Chapter 20

As members of the enquiry team started to take their seats ahead of the morning meeting, there was a vibe and sense of optimism in the office that hadn't been felt since the enquiry started. The couple of hours they'd spent in the 'Hurt Room' the other day had helped consolidate people's thinking. Mini had acted swiftly and got Con to produce a new electronic briefing for use by all uniform shifts in the Division. Its focus was on intelligence, or rather the gap in intelligence that Campbell and others thought was holding the enquiry back. It seemed to have had an immediate impact. In the 24 hours since the new briefing went live, there had been five new intelligence reports related to the murder investigation. Two had initially seemed promising, as they included named individuals who officers had thought, from the profile they had been given, were worthy of investigation.

Unfortunately, they had proven to be a false dawn. The first individual named, a local man in his fifties who had left a career in teaching to train for the ministry, had recently been removed from the course for punching and threatening one of his theology lecturers. He had died three months ago, from complications arising from a peptic ulcer, brought on by years of alcohol abuse. He could not have been the killer.

The second possible suspect initially looked even more promising. He was a man in his early thirties, with a recent conviction for serious assault and connections to the southside. There was even a separate intelligence report, from some months earlier, stating he was a born again Christian and linking him to the activities of a far-right evangelical group who had established a church community in Springburn, on the north side of the city. Con's initial enthusiasm was quickly tempered when he discovered that the man was currently detained at her majesty's pleasure in Saughton Prison, in Edinburgh, and had been throughout the timeline of the murders. He wasn't the murderer either.

But it was an intelligence log that had been submitted by a uniformed cop, who had been working nightshift last night on the Cathcart beat that had caught Mini Cooper's attention. According to the report, the cop had seen two men, dressed in dark clothing carrying what appeared to be a large tubular bag into the common close at 24, Tulloch Street near to the junction with Holmlea Road. The cop stated that the men had taken the bag from the rear of a Blue Transit Van, Reg No T45 WMG. The van had McMenemy Roofing Services emblazoned in white writing on the side. The cop said that the bag appeared to be heavy, as the men had to put it down and take a rest before they were able to continue.

Mini gave a wry smile and passed a copy of the log to Campbell.

'Interesting don't you think? Two thirty in the morning and two men in dark clothing remove a heavy bag from the rear of a transit van and then struggle across the road with it to the common close. It could be innocent enough but it's not the kind of thing you see every day. Thoughts?'

Campbell re read the log and nodded.

'Certainly interesting. And I'll tell you one thing I know about the roofing business, they often use lead for flashing, especially if they're working around here where most of the roofs are made of slate.'

Mini stroked her chin. 'Hmm, I didn't know that. I know lead's a soft metal and can be easily cut, but I didn't know it was used so extensively in roofing. Now that is very interesting don't you think? Both our victims had traces of lead on them. We're going to have to get this one checked out, that is for sure.'

Mini took a large slurp of her coffee. 'After the briefing, I want you and Asif to do a recce at that close. See what you can find out. And without wanting to teach my granny to suck eggs, gonna check and see if the van's still there. Doubt it somehow, but we'll need to check it.'

Campbell picked up a fluorescent marker and pulled the top off with his teeth.

'Roger that.' said Campbell highlighting the Reg No with the green pen. 'And Con, do us a favour will you, and run a registered keeper check on this van? The number's highlighted on the log.'

An hour later Campbell and Asif found themselves parked up in Holmlea Road. Unusually for Asif, he was annoyed and having a moan at his DCI.

'If I'd known she wanted us to do some covert surveillance, I would have worn my jeans and bomber jacket. This car coat's all I've got to put over my suit, I'm going stick out like a sore thumb.'

Campbell started to chuckle. 'Look, I'm in exactly the same boat. Well maybe not quite. At least I've got the old Barbour. But don't be too hard on Mini, this was very spur of the moment, but it needs to be done. Anyway, folk will just think we're a couple of estate agents, that's what we look like.'

Campbell pursed his lips and nodded several times. 'And you know something, that's a stroke of genius on my part, we'll cut about carrying our folders and we'll look at the property. We'll pretend we're checking out the roof, windows, and the downpipes. And I'll guarantee you that's exactly what people will assume, they'll think we're a couple of estate agents, we won't even have to try and be discreet, nobody will give us a second thought.'

Asif didn't look convinced. Campbell continued.

'Trust me on this one will you. I'm ex Surveillance Unit, we did this sort of thing all the time, it'll work like a wee sweetie, believe me, it will.'

Asif raised his eyebrows and made a face. 'If you say so, but if we get burnt, you're on your own, I'm not copping the flak from Mini for this one if it all goes Pete Tong.'

Campbell got out the car and zipped up his jacket. 'Don't be such a wuss man. Sometimes, to get results in this job you've got to take a risk, not that this is much of a risk you understand. The trick to being a good detective is knowing when it's worth taking a risk and when it's not, you weigh up the pros and cons, and I've done that, this is hardly a risk at all.'

Campbell wasn't sure if Asif had heard any of his sage advice as he appeared to be peering through the front lounge window of a ground floor flat further down the street. Asif moved to the close door which had a Cathcart Housing Association For Sale sign on a wooden pole propped up against the wall beside it.

'I reckon that for sale sign is for this flat, looks like it's become detached from that lamppost. It's got to be the ground flat; it's unfurnished, it appears to be completely empty.'

Campbell looked bemused. 'You appear to be taking this estate agent lark a little too far. I said we only had to look like one, I didn't mean we had to start checking out all the property in the street!'

Asif had now positioned himself immediately in front of the flat's lounge window.

'Perfect. I reckon this would be perfect. Look, you can see the entrance to 24, Tulloch Street from here.' Asif then pointed to the next window. 'And that must be either the bedroom or bathroom window, and the view from there would be even better. This would be an ideal Ob's post, don't you think? It looks directly across to the close we're interested in.'

Campbell had to hand it to Asif, that was a sharp bit of work, and he was correct. The empty flat would make a perfect Observation Post. It was a tactic he'd used several times himself when he was part of the Surveillance Unit. It had proved particularly useful when trying to gather evidence that a flat was being used as a cannabis factory. It wasn't cannabis production that they were after this time, their investigation was potentially much more serious. They just needed to find the Housing Association's office holding the keys for the flat and sweet talk them into letting them borrow them for a short period so they could discreetly watch the goings on across the street.

Asif took out his mobile phone and googled Cathcart Housing Association. 'According to this their office is in Rhannan Road. That's perfect, it's just quarter of a mile from here. We can call in on our way back to the office and see if we can persuade them to give us a loan of the keys.'

Campbell rubbed his hands together. 'I don't think we'll have a problem there, in my experience housing associations or estate agents were usually very helpful when we made such requests, keen to keep on the right side of the polis I suppose. But before we do that, let's see if we can find the van and then check out the close at number 24.'

Asif wandered a little further down Holmlea Road, he turned and waved at his boss.

'Down here Campbell. The van, it's still here. Just down from the bus stop.'

Not wishing to draw attention to himself Campbell ambled down the road pretending to read something in his folder. 'Psst, Asif keep walking, we're supposed to be covert remember.'

Noticing that both rear windows of the transit van had been blacked out Asif kept walking till he came to the pedestrian crossing. He pushed the button as he waited for Campbell catch him up.

'I take it you saw that both rear windows had been blacked out?' remarked Campbell as he joined his colleague at the crossing.'

'Yeah, I noticed that. And what do you think those two spotlights on the roof at the front of the van are all about. Strange place for a couple of spotlights isn't it.'

Campbell looked back at the van as the red man changed to green.

'Hmm, good question, to be honest I haven't a scooby, but I'm not sure it's that important. Right let's get across before the lights change again. I want to get a look at that close. And remember, we're a pair of estate agents so make sure you appear to be checking out the building.'

There was nothing particularly remarkable about the close at number 24 Tulloch Street. All flats except one had names on the controlled entry box at the close door. The exception was flat 1/1 which had been left blank. Campbell pushed at the close door, no luck, it was locked. He pressed the service button which immediately buzzed allowing them entry to the close. Campbell looked at his watch, it had just gone twenty past nine.

'They must get a late postal delivery round here. If this was Aunt Chrissie's close the service button would have been off an hour ago, but as always, the sun shines on the righteous. And after you.' said Campbell holding the door open for his younger colleague.

24 Tulloch Street was an old fashioned 'wally' close, typical of many tenement buildings found all over Glasgow. Highly glazed green ceramic tiles ran to a terracotta border of smaller tiles about halfway up the close wall. Unlike many of the neighbouring closes it was very clean and tidy. On the wall, just above the tiles was a notice outlining the weekly cleaning schedule. Each flat appeared to have been allocated a particular week for cleaning the close and washing the stairs. There was a large tick, the initials ST and a date which suggested the close had been cleaned four days ago. The rear close door that led out to the bins and the communal green was lying open.

Noticing a small smear on the wall near to the stairs, Asif crouched down to take a closer look.

'Come and look at this. I'm not saying it's blood, but it could be don't you think? It's certainly the right colour to be blood. And if the close was cleaned four days ago that would suggest it's fresh, the rest of the walls look pretty clean.'

Campbell hunched down on his hunkers and stared at the smear. The mark was about three inches long and about a foot off the ground.

'It certainly looks like blood. It's definitely not paint, so I'm not sure what else it could be. Take a photo of it will you, so we can show Mini. I expect she'll want SOCO to come and swab it, it'll need to be checked out.'

Asif took out his phone and took several photos of the suspicious red smear. He was putting the phone back in his pocket when there was the sound of a door slamming shut from the floor above followed by footsteps coming down the stairs. Instinctively, Asif moved towards the rear door at the back of the close out of sight. Campbell opened his folder and leafed through some paper as if he was looking for something. As the person reached the bottom of the stairs Campbell looked up and smiled.

'You're not by any chance, Mr Khan, are you? I'm supposed to meet him here to do a flat survey.'

The man stopped and did a double take. Campbell's question seemed to have thrown him. The man was in his early thirties and sporting a couple of days growth. Wearing jeans tucked into a pair of brown Caterpillar boots and a dark blue sweatshirt, he had a brown beanie hat pulled down over his ears. He looked at Campbell suspiciously.

'Are you taking the piss? Do I look like a Mr Khan, wrong colour of skin don't you think?'

The man didn't wait for a response. He brushed past Campbell and headed out across the street in the direction of Holmlea Road. Campbell watched as he got into the blue van. Asif appeared from the shadows in time to see the van driving away.

'Ah, Captain Brave, glad you could join me. Where did you disappear to?'

Asif shook his head. He wasn't impressed by his mentor's sarcasm.

'I think it's probably just as well I did, or we might have blown our cover. And where did that Mr Khan idea spring from?'

Campbell pointed at the controlled entry and then tapped his finger against his temple.

'Smart thinking you see, I'd noticed when we came in that one of the names on the controlled entry was Khan. Here, look, flat 2/1. When I saw that the guy coming down the stairs was white, I reckoned he definitely wasn't Mr Khan. So that's why I used his name. It was just a cover; I was just trying to act normally and not arouse any suspicion. And I think I achieved that, he's gone on his way and thinks I'm an estate agent. The plan worked just as I said it would. Anyway, back to you fearty, where did you get to?'

Asif had heard enough, he didn't usually fall out with his boss, but on this occasion, he was nearly ready to explode. But if he were going to make his point the way he wanted, he needed to remain calm and in control.

'I think it's just as well I made myself scarce because I think I've identified a flaw in your cunning plan.'

Campbell looked at his colleague sceptically, he hadn't a clue what Asif was suggesting.

'Ok Einstein, fire away, I'm all ears.'

'Ok, fine, I will. The reason Mini asked us to come down here and recce the place was because of that intelligence log that came in yesterday, right?'

Campbell nodded. 'Correct.'

'And by implication she also thinks it could be connected to our murder investigation.'

'Correct again. Keep going you're on a roll!'

'So, it's possible that the guy we saw leaving in the van could theoretically by our killer.'

'It's possible.'

'And he could also be the same guy that Brian Stuart saw leaning against the wall when we were at Tankerland Road for the murder of Maureen Goodall.'

Campbell smirked. 'Also, correct, but can you get to your...' He stopped mid-sentence and his face fell. Suddenly he knew where Asif was going with this and the realisation of how stupid he'd been hit him like a ton of bricks. He looked at his feet slowly shaking his head.

'Fuck. Shit the bed that was stupid, what a fecking clown I am. You and I were both up and down that close a couple of times. You had to stand at the close door waiting for me while I went back to look for my car keys. I even got you to make sure Brian recorded it in the log. Bloody hell, I think I was even wearing this suit. If that guy is our man, he might have clocked both of us at the locus. And I don't mean this in a racist way, but you would have stuck out more as the only person there that wasn't white. God, how could I not have anticipated that. Apologies Asif, that's the dumbest thing I've done in a while. And you were smart keeping out of the way. God, if I've blown this operation Mini will have a hairy fit.'

Asif sighed and leant against the wall. 'Let's just hope it doesn't come to that. He only got a fleeting glance of you, no more than a few seconds and it was out of context, so he's probably not given it a second thought. And I wouldn't beat yourself up about it, everyone, even you, can make a mistake, you're only human.'

Asif could tell that Campbell was hurting. He prided himself on his strategic thinking, and so he should, he was damned good at it. He didn't live in the moment; he was always thinking five steps ahead. This, as far as Asif could recall, was the first time he'd seen him make such a stupid error.'

Campbell looked up and smiled weakly. 'Well, I'll say one thing for you, you've only been appointed to that AP course a week, but your decision making, and detective work are fair coming on, I'm going to have to up my game.'

'Aye, if you say so.' replied Asif trying to bring things back to an even keel. 'So, what's next?'

Campbell pointed towards the rear door. 'We'll take a squint at the back court, then I want to check the rest of the close. Then it's back to the office, via the housing association office to brief our leader. We've got lots to tell her.'

The two detectives made their way to the back court where they stood staring at the back of the building.

'Only two flats with the original wooden framed windows and that one there, flat1/1 is the flat with no name. And why do you think the glass has been covered with brown paper. Why would you do that.' asked Campbell.

Asif took a moment to look around him. 'I suppose it might be to stop anybody seeing into the flat. I know there's some trees at the back here, but they're not big, and those flats in the street behind look directly onto here.'

Asif didn't have to wait for Campbell to suggest it. He already had his phone out and was busy taking photographs of the back of the property.

Campbell scribbled some notes in his folder. 'That seems a plausible explanation to me, someone doesn't want people seeing in that flat. And another thing, all its windows are shut, most of the other flats have at least one window open.'

'Perhaps the brown paper is trying to keep the flats cool, this is south facing, must get plenty of sunshine on a warm day, it's pretty open here, not much shade.' added Asif.

'Yeah, could be. Right, anyway, it's given us plenty to ponder, but let's go back and check inside, I particularly want to have a butcher's at flat 1/1.'

The grey coloured storm doors of the first-floor flat were bolted shut. There was no nameplate on the doorframe and the paint on the wooden doors appeared old and flaky. On the bottom right-hand panel, the paint had peeled away altogether exposing the bare wood underneath. By contrast the two locks, spaced two feet apart, appeared new.

Asif carefully examined the locks. 'Both these locks are Ingersoll's and I can tell you that the top one is designed especially for storm doors, I remember them from my time as a crime prevention officer, we used to recommend them a lot for this type of property. Almost impregnable, but really expensive. Looks a bit out of keeping with the rest of the flat don't you think?'

'I'd say.' said Campbell who was now studying another red coloured smear on the wall to the left-hand side of the storm doors. 'Same colour as the one downstairs, but this one looks a little bigger, I'd say five inches and again if I was a betting man, I'd wager it's blood. Ok, I think we've seen enough, time for us to head back to the ranch, I've got a feeling in my water about this one young fella, we may have just struck gold.'

Chapter 21

Judging by her reaction, the young girl at the reception desk of the Cathcart Housing Association seemed to have quite a thing about the police. Giggling, she squirmed on her seat when Campbell showed her his warrant card. Bizarrely, she then told him that he looked a bit like Taggart, something he didn't regard as a compliment. Regardless of Campbell's indifference, she appeared thrilled at having two real detectives in her office. She slid out from her desk and went over to her manager's office and knocked on the door. Informed of the officers' presence, the manager, a short overweight man in his forties, came over to the reception desk and listened carefully as Campbell made his request.

As he had predicted, the manager was more than happy to lend them keys for the ground floor flat on Holmlea Road. The young receptionist was tasked with locating the keys. Curious, she asked why the police should need them. Campbell smiled benignly and stared at his phone. Not taking the hint she repeated her question. The blank expressions she received in response to her second request still didn't put her off, she was like a dog with a bone. Changing tactics, she fluttered her eye lashes and asked for a third time. In times past, Asif would have probably just told her. Now, with eight years' police service under his belt he was more savvy.

Poker faced he tapped the side of his nose and leant towards her.

'Covert operations.' he whispered. The girl looked a picture of confusion. Covert didn't appear to be a word in her lexicon. Asif chuckled as he watched her google 'Covert Operations' on her phone at her desk.

Armed with the keys, and an assurance from the manager that there was no pressure to return them as there were no viewings scheduled for the next week, they thanked him and headed for the door. Asif paused by the desk and winked at the receptionist. He tapped his nose again and whispered, 'Clandestine and surreptitious operations.'

'Now that's not nice.' said Campbell putting a hand on Asif's back and ushering him out the door.

Back in the office Mini was reading a progress report at her desk. Despite having Jill Smith's statement telling them that DeVilliers and Goodall knew each other from work the two detectives who had been tasked with following up that particular action had come up with precisely nothing. Despite checks at their respective hospitals, they could find no record of them ever having worked together. It was all rather frustrating.

There was better news from the door-to-door enquiries carried out in the streets in the vicinity of Magnus DeVilliers' home address. A witness had been traced who claimed he saw a man pulling a golf trolley on the footbridge that crossed the railway line from Darnley Street to Moray Place. The date and approximate time appeared to corroborate the statement given a week ago by the park employee. Unfortunately, the description of the man pulling the trolley was vague and not a great deal of use. But what it did do was suggest that Campbell's theory that DeVilliers body had been taken from the house by means of his golf trolley and travel bag was most likely correct. If you were intent on dumping a body in the boating pond in Queen's Park then the route over the footbridge into Moray Place was both logical and plausible. It was another small piece in this seemingly enormous puzzle.

There was a knock on the door, it was Jan, and she was carrying a pile of reports. Mini looked up, and gestured for her to come in.

'Ma'am, these are the most recent door-to-door reports that you asked to see.'

'Great, just leave them on the desk please, I'll get to them after I've finished reading this report.'

Jan smiled. 'And just for your information, that's Campbell and Asif back, I've just seen them drive into the rear yard. I know you'll be wanting a word with them, so before they appear can I give you a quick heads up?'

'Sure, fire away, what's on your mind?'

'I've just found out that it's Conway's birthday a week on Friday. I know he's retiring in a few weeks, but I thought it might be nice to do something to mark the occasion. I know he likes a curry; I wondered about a drink and then some food at Shimla Pinks, it's handy and I've heard the food is really good although I've never been. What do you think?'

'I think it's a great idea, let's do it. Nothing like a bit of team bonding over beer and a curry. Are you going to tell him or is it going to be a surprise?'

Jan laughed. 'No, I'll be telling him, he'll need to give his wife plenty notice because if she had other plans there would be hell to pay. I know who wears the trousers in that household and it isn't Con!'

Mini laughed. 'Fine, I'll leave it with you. And send Campbell and Asif in will you, I can see the pair of them lurking in the corridor.'

For the next half hour Mini and her two detectives sat discussing the findings of that morning's reconnoitre. All three were agreed that time was now of the essence, if the goings-on at Tulloch Street were in any way connected to their investigation, then they needed to act quickly. In an ideal world Mini would have liked time to get the blood smears swabbed and examined. She would have liked confirmation that it was human blood. That would still get done, but it would have to wait, the priority was to identify who had been using the van and what they'd been up to. The registered keeper check that Con had done yesterday hadn't really told them much. The van was registered to a roofing company based in Cambuslang; it gave no indication as to the identity of either of the two men who had been seen removing the large bag in the small hours of the morning.

Mini agreed that the observation point seemed perfect. It was her suggestion that two members of the Divisional Flexi Unit should undertake the surveillance. They worked in plainclothes; this type of work was bread and butter to them. As it was a pre-planned and a directed surveillance operation, a RIPSA[2] permission would be required that would need to be authorised by a Superintendent. Mini would organise the necessary paperwork for that while Campbell undertook to brief the Flexi officers who would be doing the surveillance.

---

[2] Regulation of Investigatory Powers (Scotland) Act, 2000

The last aspect to be discussed was the requirement for a search warrant. That would be straight forward enough to organise, and the initial plan was to execute the warrant as soon as the team received confirmation that someone had been seen entering the property. Asif quite shrewdly, had pointed out that given there were six flats in the block, there would be plenty of coming and going from other residents so they would have no way of telling who their target was. Mini, however, had thought of that. Her contingency was to suggest that they would only force entry to the target flat when they had confirmation of someone entering the close having come from the van.

Campbell leant back in his chair and put his hands behind his head. 'Not trying to rain on your parade Chief Inspector but there is a rather obvious flaw in that plan, I'm afraid.'

Mini lowered her eyebrows. 'Oh, how so?'

'Well, you might not be aware because you are new to this Division, but Holmlea Road and Tulloch Street are a nightmare for parking, always have been. There is absolutely no guarantee that the OB's point will have a line of sight on where the van parks, being truthful it could end up being parked several streets away, so I don't think that part of your plan will necessarily work.'

Mini sat back and thought for a moment. 'Fair point, and it's good to get these things identified and ironed out before we make any move. Yeah, thinking about it again, there are several imponderables about this operation, things that are not in our direct control. So that being the case I think it's best that we treat this operation as an evidence gathering exercise, certainly in the first instance, the guys in the OB's point will just run a log, recording all activity around the target flat. If anything of particular significance turns up, like men carrying a bag out of the van, then that will immediately be relayed back to us, and I'll make a decision accordingly. Can you make sure they're briefed to that effect.'

Campbell scribbled a note in his folder and nodded. Mini continued.

I'll be on call throughout the night, and you'll have your phones switched on at all times, we can be back at the office and ready to go within an hour of getting the call, should that prove necessary. We'll still have the RIPSA and warrant in place, so we'll be good to go if and when required.'

Campbell nodded in agreement. All of that was eminently sensible. In the space of just a couple of weeks he had seen a big change in his DCI's management style. Her abrasive and dictatorial style was much less evident, she was now in listening mode, and making good and well considered decisions based on what she was being told. They still couldn't catch a break in terms of the murder investigation, progress in that remained stubbornly slow, but the enquiry team she had put together had bonded well and were working long punishing hours in their efforts to bring the killer to justice.

'That sounds like a reasonable plan, to me ma'am, I don't think you can be too prescriptive with these things, not with the number of variables we're dealing with.' added Campbell.

'I'll go and organise the night vision binoculars and other equipment and then grab a word with the Flexi Sergeant to see who he's got on duty that could take this on. Asif, do us a favour and go and have a word with

Malcolm in productions, see if he can organise a couple of chairs, preferably something like those collapsing fabric chairs, you know the ones you take to a BBQ or to the beach, a couple of them would be ideal. There isn't a stick of furniture in that flat, so the troops are going to need something to sit on.'

Asif was gathering up his things and about to leave when Mini looked up. 'Just one more thing gents before you leave. I spoke to Suzi Lessard on the phone last night, we had a very interesting chat. And following on from that she's arranging to come through and see me next week, on her day off which is above and beyond and very kind of her. It's still to be confirmed but it'll likely be Wednesday. I would have gone up to see her, but with this enquiry ongoing that's a little difficult. Anyway, I thought I'd let you know, things are progressing on that front, and it's you guys I've got to thank for that.'

Chapter 22

In the front lounge of the ground floor flat at 325, Holmlea Road, Constables Stuart Kerr and Derek McKinnon were making themselves comfortable. As well as the two folding chairs that Asif had organised, they had brought a rucksack stuffed with provisions. Two flasks of tea, a packet of Jaffa Cakes, four Mars Bars and several bananas as well as a two-litre bottle of Irn Bru. It was set to be a long night and they didn't want to go hungry. In addition to their snacks, they had a pair of back-to-back radios so they could speak directly to their supervisor back at Aikenhead Road, a logbook, and a set of night vision binoculars. They also had a small digital radio, set to Heart FM. As experienced plainclothes officers, they knew how tedious a job like this could be, especially one that was going to run through the night. The radio would at least provide some relief from the inevitable boredom.

Constable Kerr, ten years older than his colleague and originally from Peterhead, poured out two mugs of tea. 'And just to cap it all, it's started to rain, look at it, it's absolutely pissing down. I don't think there's going to be much action tonight, not if the weather stays like this.'

He placed Derek's mug on the window ledge as his colleague scanned the flats in Tulloch Street with the night vision binoculars.

'Ah damn it. There might not be much action out on the streets, but the girl on the top floor at number 32 looked like she was primed and ready to go if you know what I mean, but now she's gone and closed the curtains, so that's that!'

Stuart opened the packet of Jaffa cakes and took a sip of his tea. 'I hadn't you marked down as such a perv to be honest, did you ken that one of the CCTV operators at Carnwadric got his jotters recently for doing exactly that. Apparently, he spent the second half of the nightshift looking for windows to peer through. He scanned the street with one of those fixed site cameras and zoomed in when he found something interesting. Those CCTV cameras are powerful, they can pick up the smallest detail. He usually targeted unsuspecting females who had forgotten to close their blinds. Of course, his victims were oblivious to what he was doing, he only got caught when one of his colleagues fired him in.'

Derek put down the binoculars and started to garble some excuse. He'd only meant it as a joke which he now regretted; he flushed red with embarrassment.

His older colleague shook his head. 'Look, dinna fash yersel, I ken you meant it as a joke, but it just shows you, eh. Things like that can get you in a heap of trouble. And that operator at Carnwadric got what he was due. Also, it turned out that he'd been accessing porn on the works computer, hours of the stuff. Sounds like a right dangerous individual, the job's well shot of him.'

'G43 calls G47.'

Stuart picked up his radio. 'G47 go ahead. G47 just to let you know that's myself and G39 checked all surrounding streets within a half mile radius of the target flat. There's no trace of the blue transit van. Repeat no trace of the van.'

'Roger that G43, that's all noted. I take it that's you boys now standing down.'

'Affirmative, heading home to watch the Rangers' game, got it recorded from earlier. Might manage a beer or two at the same time. Now you boys have a quiet one, you're at a dangerous age Stubo, can't get too excited, not at your stage of life.'

Derek laughed as he updated the log. 'I'll keep an eye on him Stevie, but I don't think we'll see much action at this end, not if this rain keeps up, it's like a monsoon out there now.'

For the next half hour, the two colleagues sat drinking tea and demolishing the packet of Jaffa Cakes as they put the world to rights about all that was wrong with the job. From crap bosses to drowning in needless paperwork, the two friends did what all cops do when they've got time on their hands, they moaned about the job.

Outside it was deadly quiet. Apart from a young couple dressed head to foot in waterproofs who were walking a bedraggled black spaniel, nobody had walked past the window. Even the road was eerily quiet, for a Thursday night there was very little traffic, there was next to nobody about.

Derek looked at his watched and sighed. It was only just after midnight; they had another eight hours of this to go.

'Ah ha.' said Stuart getting up from his chair to get a better look. 'Check out the old boy in the pork pie hat bouncing down the street, look at the state he's in, must have had a right skinful.'

The two cops watched as the old boy, who looked like he was in his mid-seventies, weaved his way down the road. He stopped at the bus shelter about fifty yards past the flat and stepped in out of the lashing rain.

'Don't you think he's a dead ringer for Popeye Doyle in that hat and coat? I think he looks just like him.' said Derek.

'Yeah, I can see where you're coming from, but he's a lot shorter. Gene Hackman must be well over six foot. That joker's lucky if he's 5'7". And look at the state of him he can hardly stand up.'

The old man's luck appeared to be in, he had only been in the shelter for about a minute when a number 6 bus pulled up at the stop. Straightening his hat, the old man staggered towards the bus waving his hand wildly at the driver suggesting he wanted to get on. His other hand was thrust deep into his coat pocket searching presumably for his bus pass.

His hand reappeared clutching a large rectangular shaped package wrapped in white paper which he immediately dropped as he stepped onto the bus. The bag split disgorging its the contents across the floor.

Derek burst out laughing. 'Oh God, you couldnae make it up, it's like a scene from 'Chewin' the Fat,' he's just gone and dropped his donner kebab and now he's slipped on it trying to pick it up.'

'What a fecking state he's in.' cried Stuart with tears of laughter rolling down his cheeks. 'God, he's now wiped it all over his shirt, salad and sauce everywhere.'

The man's white shirt now had a large red stain covering most of his chest. 'He could have been in the French Connection.' added Stuart, 'he looks like some dude's just shot him.'

Derek snorted. 'What is it with drunks, he's not giving that kebab up is he, look he's mopped up the rest of the meat off the floor and stuffed it back in his pocket. Ah shit, the bus driver's seen enough, he's not going to let him on.'

'Not surprised.' added Stuart. 'Steaming drunk and covered in bloody kebab sauce, I wouldn't be letting him in any vehicle of mine.'

The bus drove away leaving the old boy slumped on the ground with his back against the glass window of the shelter.

'Well, that was fun while it lasted, well for us, not so much for him. And what are we going to do now? We can't leave him lying there like that, he'll be soaking wet, he'll freeze to death. Should I go out and check he's alright?'

Stuart narrowed his eyes and stared at his colleague. 'Nope. First rule of covert operations, never give your position away. No, we'll radio it in and get the uniforms to come and hoover him up. A night in a warm cell and he'll be right as rain. He'll be charged with being D&I, but it won't go anywhere, the Fiscal will bin the case.'

Twenty minutes later the marked police vehicle had been and gone. The old boy appeared half asleep when the officers arrived. But with help from two burly cops, he was able to stand up and get into the rear of the van which he did without complaint. If he was able to provide the officers with his name and address, and if there was someone going to be at home, they may well decide to take him straight there. If he lived alone, it would be a night in the cells. They couldn't risk leaving someone as drunk as him alone, it would be too risky.

After the amusing incident with Popeye Doyle the rest of the night proved to be deadly dull. And each hour that passed seemed longer than the previous one. There were still two hours of the shift to go and with the last of the tea and the Jaffa cakes now gone Derek found himself desperately trying not to fall asleep. With a nine-month-old baby daughter at home he wasn't getting much sleep at the best of times, and yesterday, after he'd received the call from the Sergeant telling him he was required to work a nightshift, he'd tried to grab a couple of hours kip in the afternoon when the baby was napping. That hadn't been too successful, he'd been wide awake and ended up watching afternoon repeats of 'Only Fools and Horses.' He was paying for it now; he could hardly keep his eyes open. Fortunately, his neighbour was much more awake. Stuart Kerr was a nighthawk, he went to bed late and got up early, so rarely slept more than five hours. He put that down to his time living in Aberdeen prior to joining the police, when he'd worked at the Hacienda Nightclub, where he regularly didn't finish work till 4am. He just seemed to be able to get by with very little sleep.

'Look, just put your feet up and shut your eyes, I can see you're knackered. I've got this covered, it doesn't take two of us to watch nothing happening. Grab some kip while you can, I'll wake you if anything happens.'

That was music to Derek's ears, and a favour he now owed his colleague. Stuart had barely finished speaking when Derek drifted off into a deep sleep.

The rain that had been falling steadily throughout the night had now eased to a light drizzle. It was ten minutes to seven and in the early morning light of a late April morning the world appeared to be waking up. A group of early commuters were gathered at the bus stop across the road. The young among them had their headphones on listening to music or were absorbed staring at their mobile phones. A well-dressed young woman, in a camel-coloured coat and red ankle boots, appeared to be applying lipstick with the aid of a very small mirror. Two older men had their noses buried in the football pages of the Daily Record. It was a snapshot of a scene that could be repeated in every city in the land, day in and day out.

Stuart sighed deeply. Watching those unfortunate souls heading for another day of doing exactly what they had done the day before made him glad he was in the police. He may have spent the first couple of hours of this shift moaning about his lot, but tomorrow would be another day, filled with unpredictability and perhaps even excitement. It was the variety of work that being in the police afforded that appealed to Stuart, something that was probably true for most officers. No two days were quite the same. He may be bored sitting in an Observation Point watching nothing happening, but it was still better than being one of those commuters caught up in the rat race, he certainly didn't envy them.

He was in the process of peeling a banana when he noticed the blue van pull into Tulloch Street. He watched as it parked on the other side of the street, about 50 metres down from the target flat. Stuart reached for his notebook just to double check the registration number. T45 WMG. It was the same van. Stuart kicked the feet of his sleeping neighbour who woke with a start.

'We're on. That's the blue van just parked up. See it, outside the flat with the red curtains one up.'

Derek nodded reaching for the binoculars. 'I see it. And two guys have just got out and now they're taking something out the back.'

The two officers watched as two men, dressed head to foot in dark clothing and wearing beanie hats, removed a large black bag from the rear of the Transit van.

'That looks heavy, the two of them can barely lift it, whatever they've got in there must weigh a ton!'

Carrying the bag between them, the two men struggled across the road and up the street towards number 24.

'That's better, I've got a good view of them now. Two males, both white and of medium build, one slightly taller and I'd say both look in their mid-thirties, no older.'

The two men put down the bag as they reached the close door. The taller of the two fumbled in his pocket and produced a set of keys.

'Stuart, there's something leaking out the bag, take a look, you can see it on the steps, I'm pretty sure that's blood.' Derek handed his colleague the binoculars.

'Yeah, sure looks like it. Ah fuck, the other guy's got a hankie or a cloth and is trying to wipe it up. I'm not sure what the fuck is going on but it's time to radio in and get some back up down here sharpish.'

Chapter 23

By 8am the incident room was a hive of activity as members of the enquiry team took their seats ahead of the morning briefing. Because of the nature of the operation, Mini had requested the assistance of six Public Order trained officers. Tall and dressed all in black, their Kevlar stab proof vests and 14 eye Doc Martin boots gave them a quasi-military look. They stood at the back of the room with their arms folded across their chests accentuating their highly tuned biceps. As well as carrying all the normal kit of batons and CS spray, they would be wearing helmets and protective leg and arm guards. They would also be in possession of full-length heavy-duty shields. But most important of all, were the skills they would bring to the party. As highly trained Public Order Officers they were specialists in forcing entry to buildings should that prove to be necessary.

The officers at the observation point had reported seeing a light go on in the front room of the target flat shortly after the two men had entered the building. That was all the confirmation that Mini was looking for, they had their search warrant at the ready and for the last 45 minutes, Mini and Campbell had been going over the plan. There really wasn't a great deal to it. Uniformed officers would be positioned in the back court should anyone attempt to escape via a rear window.

Accompanied by the public order officers, Campbell and Asif would attend the front door in possession of the search warrant. If the occupants refused to open the door the Public Order Officers would take over and force entry by means of a Ramit. A large and very heavy metal cylinder with a handle on the top that is used to break down locked doors. Once entry was gained all occupants within the flat would be handcuffed and detained. Mini would be the officer in charge and command the operation from her position inside the Observation Post in Holmlea Road.

The team headed out in a convoy of marked and unmarked vehicles which were parked at the rendezvous point in Spean Street, just a block away from Tulloch Street. By 0830 hrs everyone was in position and ready to go.

'DI Morrison to Govan Control. Request talk through with DCI Cooper for the operation in Tulloch Street.'

'Govan Control, that's talk through now enabled, go ahead DI Morrison.'

'DI Morrison to Chief Inspector Cooper.'

'Go ahead Campbell.'

'Ma'am that's the Public Order Officers, Asif and myself now in the common close. Just for your information and the log, there are several of what looks like blood spots on the stairs leading to the first floor. The storm doors are closed over, but they're not bolted, and we can see lights on in the flat.'

'Ok, that's all noted Campbell. We'll proceed as planned. And remember any resistance or suggestion of weapons, withdraw immediately and let the Public Order cops do what they're trained to do.'

'Affirmative, understood. And stand by, we're about to knock the door.'

For several minutes nothing was heard. Then the radio sprung back into life.

'DI Morrison calls Chief Inspector Cooper.'

'Go ahead Campbell.'

'Chief Inspector, that's us gained entry to the flat. No forced entry required, and occupants were compliant. The flat has been thoroughly searched, two persons, both male now handcuffed and in custody. They're now being removed to a police vehicle as I speak.'

'Excellent. And what about the flat, what have you found?'

'It's a blood bath ma'am, an absolute blood bath.'

Mini's face drained of colour, she stood rock still, that was not what she was expecting to hear.

'What! You mean there are more bodies in there?'

'Yep, it's quite literally a blood bath. Fortunately, the bodies are sheep and not human. There are two freshly slaughtered ones in the bath and more hanging up on hooks in the kitchen. They've skinned them and the fleeces are piled up in the bedroom. I'm telling you, it's like an abattoir in here. The bold boys have been away sheep rustling during the night and then the dead sheep have been brought back to the flat and butchered in the kitchen. There are at least six carcases hanging up, it's quite a business they've got going by the looks of things.'

Mini blew out her cheeks and slumped back against the wall. Just for a moment she really did think they'd met their Armageddon.

*

245

An hour later the team re-convened back at the incident room. Mini made a large cafetiere of coffee. Black insomnia with two extra shots in it. They could joke about it now, but for a heart stopping moment Mini really did think they were about to discover their third or even fourth body. It was still early days, but from the information coming up from the custody suit, it didn't look likely that either of the two men who were now in custody were in anyway connected to the murders. A search of the van had revealed a map and two high powered rifles. The two lights on the roof of the van were spotlights used to illuminate their targets. A circled area on the map suggested the sheep may have come from a hill farm, three miles south of Eaglesham. It was likely that neither of the men held a firearms licence. That being the case they would be charged with firearm offences as well as the poaching.

Sheep rustling was not something that Campbell or Asif had any experience of. It wasn't the sort of crime you came across when you worked in a busy city Division. Inspector Brough had already indicated to the DCI that Sergeant Pearson and one of his cops would take over the case. Sergeant Pearson had worked in Girvan, South Ayrshire before he was promoted and had experience of reporting similar crimes. The offer was appreciated, there was no way that any of the detectives could get themselves involved in such a case, there was still a killer on the loose and two murder investigations to solve.

'Well, that's been an interesting start to the morning.' said Mini pouring out the coffee. 'Doesn't help the enquiry any, but we couldn't ignore it, it needed to be checked out.'

Campbell opened a packet of Hob Nobs and passed them round. 'Absolutely, a first-class intelligence led operation I'd say. And it's a cracking case for the uniforms. Something different, I always enjoyed reporting unusual cases when I was a young cop.'

'Same here.' said Asif munching on a biscuit. 'My particular favourite was the Civic Government Scotland Act, 1982. Lots of weird and wonderful offences in that. I used to love bamboozling the sergeant with some of the one's I came up with. Section 49, 'Keeping a Dangerous or Annoying Creature,' was one I used quite successfully a couple of times to charge people who'd let their dog attack another dog. The sergeant said that wasn't what the legislation was designed for, but the Fiscal disagreed, and I got a conviction. Yep, happy days, I used to love finding obscure statutes.'

'You do surprise me.' said Mini sarcastically. Asif looked puzzled. She was about to explain what she meant when there was a knock on the door. It was DC Thomson from the enquiry team. Mini gestured for him to come in.

'Come in Bob, coffee's not long made if you want one.'

Bob pulled up a chair and sat down. 'No, no I'm fine, just had one thanks.'

'Suit yourself, but you're missing out, this stuff's got a kick like a mule, two mugs and you won't sleep for a week. Anyway, sorry, I digress, what can I do for you?'

Bob produced a photocopied sheet from inside his folder. 'I think you may be interested in this ma'am.' He held up a photocopy of a bank statement. 'You know how our initial enquiries with Ross Hall and the Vicky failed to establish a link between DeVilliers and Goodall.'

The DCI nodded.

'Well, we decided to take a different approach and I think it's just paid dividends.'

Mini raised her eyebrows. 'Sounds intriguing, so what you got?'

'Fortunately, Maureen Goodall appears to have been a fastidious record keeper. She had box files in a cupboard with receipts and bills for just about everything. I was going through a file of her old bank statements and I have discovered a couple of things that I think you'll find interesting. Firstly, there's this.' Bob handed the DCI a sheet of paper.

'I've highlighted the relevant entry. Halfway down the page, it's nearly ten years ago, September 1994. You see I recognised the code. It's the same one that's all-over DeVilliers' bank statements. It's a pay code for Ross Hall hospital. It would appear that Maureen Goodall did work at Ross Hall, but only for a very limited time, in fact just five days. The 5th to 9th September. When I went back to the hospital, I got them to double check their records. They eventually found it in their accounts' records, she was paid for five days work, although it still wasn't showing in their employee schedules for those dates. They couldn't say why it didn't appear, but they did suggest it was likely to be human error, nothing sinister.'

'Hmm, good work Bob, that is most interesting. But do you know why she was working there and more particularly why for only five days?'

'From what the hospital was able to tell me she must have been working as agency staff. Apparently its quite common for staff in NHS hospitals to do a bit of moonlighting in the private sector in their spare time, or during their annual leave. Allows them to earn a bit of extra cash. And we know Maureen Goodall had expensive tastes, so that part at least makes a bit of sense. And that leads me onto the second thing, which is also, I think, quite intriguing. You see for about the next five years, give or take a month or so, Maureen Goodall was depositing £500 cash into her account every eight weeks, regular as clockwork. The day of the week she deposited it varies but every eight weeks in it goes and it was always for £500. On her bank statements it just shows as money in, there's nothing to indicate where it came from. Then after about five years it suddenly stops. There's no more deposits.'

Campbell put down his mug and chewed on the end of his pen. 'Hmm, so we can prove that she did work at Ross Hall albeit only for five days. That's helpful, it establishes a positive link with Magnus DeVilliers. It's also interesting to know that she was in receipt of additional money, that might partly explain how she was able to support her lavish lifestyle. It's just a pity we can't say where that money came from. I take it you checked DeVilliers' statements, I remember looking at them and not seeing anything particularly unusual.'

Bob nodded. 'I couldn't see anything suspicious; he did regularly withdraw cash though. A hundred here, a couple of hundred there, but he was a very wealthy man, there were certainly no regular withdrawals of £500 or more, so no, nothing unusual that I could see.'

Mini leant back in her chair. 'I appreciate your efforts Bob, and that's an excellent piece of work, it's filled in some blanks, but it still doesn't explain why someone might want to murder the pair of them.'

Bob gave a knowing look. 'That, I'm afraid, is a question I can't answer.'

He checked his watch. 'Is it alright if I leave it with you ma'am, we've got a couple of actions to follow up at nail bars on Clarkston Road. They were held over from yesterday, but the owners should both be in this morning.'

'Yeah, you crack on Bob and thanks again for this, it's another small piece of the puzzle on which we can hopefully build. It's only marginal gains at the moment, but a breakthrough might not be far away. We've got to stay positive.'

'Always.' said Asif helping himself to another coffee.

Mini's eyebrows narrowed. 'Careful tiger, remember what I told you, it's akin to rocket fuel that stuff.'

Campbell took out a hankie and cleaned his glasses.

'The key to this is finding the motive. I know that sounds obvious and we've discussed it before, but nearly two weeks in and we're really no closer to understanding why the killer wanted them dead.'

Asif took a large mouthful of coffee.

'Are we perhaps coming at this from the wrong angle. Perhaps we should list the things that we're pretty sure weren't a motive. Like theft or robbery. Our murderer appears not to have stolen anything from either victim and DeVilliers was wearing a Rolex Yacht Master worth thousands. Also, we can't find any evidence that suggests the two of them were in a relationship. Well not a physical one. And we now have dozens of statements from friends, neighbours and former work colleagues. Oh, I don't know, it was just a thought.'

Mini started to scribble some notes. 'No don't stop. This is a bit like the 'Hurt Room', no idea's a bad idea, just get it out there. So, not money. I think we're agreed on that. But I'm not so convinced that sex isn't involved, we know they were about to go on holiday together. But what else do people get murdered for?'

Campbell removed his glasses and leaned forward. 'Revenge, I would have thought. Most murder enquiries I've been involved with had revenge as the primary motive.'

Mini nodded as she wrote more notes. 'Revenge. Yeah, I like that. A consultant and a nurse. Why would someone wish to take revenge on them? I wonder what happened during the five days they worked together?'

Chapter 24

Wednesday 5th May

Zander Muir was up early, and it was just before seven when he parked his Range Rover Vogue next to the captain's space in the empty carpark. He had arrived at the course so early that he had to wait the best part of ten minutes for the first of the greenkeepers to arrive so he could get access to the shed where his electric golf cart was kept. He had a tie to play at eleven in the McPhail trophy, a competition he had made the final of before but had still never won, that was something he was keen to rectify. Getting to the course early to play a few holes followed by an hour or so on the practice ground to fine-tune his game was typical of him. He took his sport extremely seriously, he simply loved to win. His competitive nature had first showed itself when he was a very young boy running races at school sports day, and it was something that had remained a constant all through his life. Whether it was on the rugby field, cricket pitch or golf course, Zander Muir was in it to win it. There was no such thing as just a friendly game in his book. Nobody remembered who came second, coming second was for losers. Winning was what was important, and for most of his sporting and professional career he had been pretty successful at it.

At secondary school at Glasgow Academy he had been a dashing fullback, very much in the mould of JPR Williams, strong and powerful in the tackle and with an impressive turn of pace. He had been good enough to represent both Glasgow and then Scottish Schools in his final year, perhaps still his proudest sporting achievement. Golf was a game he turned to when he was much older. Now in the twilight of his professional career as a successful lawyer, he could afford to indulge his passion and had played all the championship courses in Scotland and some of the finest courses in other parts of the world. His membership of Greenbank had always been one of convenience. He would readily admit it was not even the best course in the neighbourhood. In his book, that distinction went to East Renfrewshire, a rolling moorland course a couple of miles south of Newton Means. But with a house in Whitecraigs, and a back garden that literally backed onto Greenbank, a membership there made perfect sense.

The use of a golf cart had become a necessity more than ten years ago. The legacy of an old rugby injury that had finally caught up with him. For a man now in his late sixties he was otherwise extremely fit, but the 'gammy knee,' a consequence of being on the receiving end of a fierce tackle while playing FP rugby for Glasgow Accies, had ruptured his cruciate ligament. Two failed operations meant his rugby career was over and the many hills and slopes of Greenbank meant walking and pulling a trolley were now a distant memory.

Colin Grimes, one of the assistant greenkeepers, knew exactly what Zander Muir was waiting for when he drove into the car park at just after 7am. He parked up next to the shed and unlocked the large green double doors. He looked at his watch.

'Morning Mr Muir, you're here early, even by your standards.'

Zander smiled as he removed his clubs from the rear of his vehicle.

'A tie to play at eleven. Graeme Forbes plays off six and is nearly twenty years younger than me, so I'll have my work cut out. He'll be giving me four shots, which I'll need to make the most of. I thought I'd get here early, get half a dozen holes under my belt, and then head to the practice ground. I take it the pins will be as they are, you're not changing them today, are you?'

Colin shook his head. 'No, the pins will be staying the same, but all the greens are getting cut this morning, so they will be running that bit faster. I'm cutting the practice putting green first so spend a bit of time on there. That'll give you a good feel for the speed of the greens.'

Zander pulled a golf glove from the side pocket of his bag and put it on.

'Don't worry about that. I'll have at least half an hour on the putting green later. Remember what they say, drive for show but putt for dough. It's the putting and your short game that wins you matches in this game. Forbes will be hitting it 50 yards past me off the tee, but he won't beat me on the greens, I'll make damned sure of that.'

Zander carefully manoeuvred his buggy out of the shed and loaded his golf bag onto the back.

'Will you be giving your opponent a lift on the cart? Plenty room for two on there.' asked Colin mischievously.

Zander lowered his eyes. 'Ah no. That won't be happening. He can walk and the further the better. I'm needing every advantage I can get. He'll be lucky if I even speak to him. And I'm only half joking. Golf is a serious business. Well, mine is anyway, and this is a match I've no intention of losing.'

'Well, I'll wish you luck.' said Colin filling the tank of one of the grass cutting machines with petrol. 'Oh, and I should have said. There's fresh sand in all the bunkers. Bob and I spent yesterday putting it in. So be aware of that if you're in any, they'll play like real bunkers should, they've been like concrete for months and we've had endless complaints about them, but there's little point refreshing the sand till late spring and the better weather arrives, but there's at least three inches of new sand in each, so they should be perfect.'

Zander put on his skip cap. 'Thanks, that's useful to know, I'm needing every bit of help I can get.'

By twenty past seven Zander had reached the third tee. A monster par five called Devil's Dyke. 572 yards long and all downhill. With your drive you had to be sure and keep away from the stone dyke that ran down the right-hand side of the fairway. Go over that and you were out of bounds. As the hole was stroke index 4 on the scorecard, Zander knew he would be receiving a stroke at that hole. He must make the most of it and aim well left. Then there was the burn to negotiate before you reached the green. With a stroke to the good Zander intended to play safe and land well short of the burn with his second shot. He would then hit his third with a pitching wedge onto the green and be there for net two. That would give him every chance of winning the hole. Good course management would be key to winning his match.

Just behind him on the second hole, Colin was making good progress cutting the greens. With only Zander out on the course he had already cut the practice putting green and the first and second holes. He intended to do the first six holes and then stop for his breakfast. After replacing the pin on the second green he made his way to the third tee at the top of the hill. Sitting astride his John Deere, he peered down the sweeping slope of the third hole towards the burn that ran across the fairway in the far distance. He squinted his eyes and did a double take. It was a few hundred yards away, but if his eyes weren't deceiving him, he could see Zander Muir's golf cart lying at an angle of 45 degrees and half in the burn. More alarmingly, he couldn't see any sign of Zander. Shit, he thought, if he's slipped and fallen into the burn he could easily drown. It wasn't particularly deep but after recent rain it was running fast.

Colin jumped down from the John Deere and raced down the hill towards the stricken cart. Overweight and out condition he was a spluttering red-faced mess by the time he reached the cart. He vomited on the spot. Slumped across the bench seat was the body of Zander Muir. His pale grey Lyle and Scott sweater saturated in blood had taken on the colour of the cherry blossom trees that spread over the rear fences of the gardens to the side of the third hole.

Colin could see Zander's spinal column through the gaping open wound. His throat had been sliced open. Shaking and disorientated he fell to his knees and emptied his stomach for a second time.

*

256

'Excuse me ma'am but can I ask what time's your appointment with Suzi is today? asked Asif as he handed over the updated action log. 'It's just that if I'm around the office when you're finished then I thought it might be nice to grab a coffee with her if she's got time before she has to head back. It would be good to see her again, we seemed to hit it off when we met last week and as you'll recall we had to rush off and get back here when they discovered Maureen Goodall's body. Suzi must have wondered what the hell was going on and I've not had a chance to speak to her since.'

DCI Cooper glanced up at the wall clock and smiled. 'She's supposed to be coming in early. In fact, anytime now. She came down last night and stayed over with an old university friend, so we made the appointment for first thing. I didn't want to take up too much of her time, not when she's come all this way and it's her day off. I'll give you a shout when we're done. I take it you're going to be in the office this morning?'

Asif nodded. 'For most of it I should think. I've got statements to finish off and a few phone calls to make regarding the action around places of worship. Campbell's convinced the murderer has some religious affiliation and has got me contacting every church or place of worship on the southside. I never thought there were so many, there are literally dozens of them. And see trying to get hold of a minister or pastor, or anyone for that matter connected to the church, well it ain't easy, let's put it that way. I've left endless messages but they're not the best at getting back to you.'

Mini chuckled. 'The joys of being a junior detective, Asif. I make sure that young foot soldiers like yourself get all the plum jobs, and as I've told you before, you've got to make the calls if you're going to get a result. It's all about perseverance.'

Asif looked at his boss doubtfully. That particular line of enquiry had so far produced the sum total of nothing. But he wasn't about to argue with his boss, it was on the log, so it had to get done. If he were shortly to become a Sergeant, it would most likely be in uniform and he'd be in charge of a shift. That was a daunting prospect, but at least it would spare him the tedium of following up actions that mostly led up blind alleys. That would be a part of detective work that he wouldn't miss. He headed back to the incident room in search of Campbell, who seemed to have disappeared. He hadn't seen him for the last half hour.

Ten minutes later the DCI was deep in concentration reading through a pile of witness statements when there was a polite knock at the door. It was Jan and she had somebody with her. 'Ma'am, I've got Suzi Lessard here to see you, she's got an appointment with you this morning. The kettle's not long off the boil, can I make you both a coffee?'

Mini got up from her desk and gestured for them to come in. She handed Jan a small jar of coffee that was sitting on the windowsill.'

'Is coffee good for you Suzi, or would you prefer tea?'

'Not so keen on tea so a coffee would be great thanks, and just black, no milk or sugar.'

'Ah, a woman after my own heart. I'm the same as you, don't care for tea. Too wishy-washy for my taste. And Jan, there's a tin of shortbread in the top cupboard in the kitchen if you don't mind bringing that as well.'

Jan smiled and headed off towards the kitchen.

'Please, come in and have a seat. And it's very good of you giving up your time to come and see me. And before I forget, don't let me let you leave without saying hi to Asif, he's keen to grab a word with you, if you don't have to rush off.'

Suzi smiled. 'Jan and I bumped into him in the corridor two minutes ago. He's a really nice guy, and not, I should imagine, your typical hardnosed Glasgow detective, that's probably why we hit it off, although we hardly got a chance to get to know each other last week before he had to rush away. So, I'll have time but I'm not sure he will. I've been following your murder enquiry when it's been on the news or in the papers. I saw your last media broadcast when you were appealing for witnesses to come forward. I thought you were really good, very professional.'

'Kind of you to say and yes, it's been a bit full on. Luckily, I've got a great team, but it's long punishing days. We're making progress but it's painfully slow and it's beginning to turn into a real whodunnit. Ah, Jan, many thanks can you just put the tray over there on the table.'

Over coffee, Mini and Suzi continued their conversation.

'You must be getting a bit tired of all the media attention though. My friend had the Evening Times in her flat, that guy McSorley who writes the crime features seems hellbent on making your enquiry the second incarnation of 'Bible John.' If he mentioned it once he must have mentioned it a dozen times, the man seems obsessed, it must be a huge distraction?'

Mini rolled her eyes and scoffed.

'Bane of my life that man, fortunately I've got Media Services assisting me, so they take a lot of the flak.

He must phone twice a day every day looking for updates. My partner rather naively fell foul of him, but she's getting over that now. I've no time for the man, all he's interested in is his next sensational headline, it's really quite tiresome. Anyway, that's not what you're here to talk about. And just for your information, Asif, and my DI both know about the incident at the college. They're both good guys and have been very supportive. Asif told me that you know people in your Force who have had similar experiences with Ch Supt Taylor. Before we talk about what happened last week at the college, I'd like to hear more about that if you don't mind. So, what can you tell me about Nick Taylor?'

*

Campbell had spent the last half hour with the Divisional Intelligence officer, checking out a number of names that had appeared on statements obtained during the last week's door-to-door enquiries. Once again there appeared to be nothing on the intelligence databases to link them in any way to the enquiry. It was hugely frustrating. No matter what they tried they couldn't seem to catch a break. Campbell had over twenty years' experience as a detective, but he'd never dealt with a case that had so little information about the possible identity of the killer. They had conducted hundreds of interviews, obtained significant forensic evidence and enormous quantities of seemingly relevant information, but none of it had pointed to who had murdered Magnus DeVilliers and Maureen Goodall.

Campbell was making his way back up to the incident room when he met a rather panicked looking Asif standing at the top of the stairs.

'Where the hell have you been? I've been looking for you for the last 10 minutes.'

'I was down with Simon in intel, why, what's happened?'

Asif blinked several times in quick succession.

'Looks very like we've got our third murder. Uniforms are up at Greenbank Golf Club right now. One of the greenkeepers found a body about 45 minutes ago. A male, late sixties, found with his throat slit in a golf cart. Got to be the work of our man, the M.O is almost identical to Maureen Goodall's murder.'

Without a flicker of emotion, Campbell took a moment to absorb the information.

'Does the DCI know?'

Asif nodded. 'Yeah, I told her. She's got Suzi Lessard in with her just know. She's asking for us to go to the locus and then provide an update. She'll come up as soon as she's clear.'

*

A uniformed officer was stopping cars as they entered the driveway that led from the main road to the golf club. Sensibly, the officer was advising the motorists to drive up to the car park and then do a U-turn and come straight back down. As it was now just after nine, several members were arriving at the course for their regular midweek game. Her system seemed to be working and it saved cars backing up on the busy Mearns Road as she explained that the course was temporarily closed because of an ongoing police incident.

'That young cop seems to have a proper grip of things, she's avoiding any build-up of traffic and it's a dangerous bend here. She's done well.' said Campbell as

261

he waited behind the car in front to gain entry to the car park. Asif wound down his window.

'For your information that officer is Natalie Mellish, and you're right, she's got it under control, she's doing a grand job. It's good to see her again, I still feel bad about what happened to her.'

Campbell stared through the windscreen. 'Gosh, so it is. I didn't recognise her in uniform. And I wouldn't beat yourself up about it if I was you. I'm afraid it's all just part of the learning curve as far as Natalie's concerned. She messed up and paid a heavy price for her indiscretion, but if she gets her head up, and it looks like she has, and just gets on with things, her time will come again, I'm sure of that.'

With the car in front safely turned around, Natalie smiled at her former colleagues and waved them through. They parked up and approached a uniformed sergeant who was standing at the entrance to the clubhouse. He explained that the greenkeeper who had discovered the body was currently upstairs with the club secretary and by all accounts was badly shaken by his experience. He was needing some time to regain his composure.

'Ok, we don't need to talk to him right now, we'll give him some space. But can you let the secretary know that we'll be wanting to speak to him and the greenkeeper after we've finished viewing the body. Have we been able to establish who he is yet?'

The uniform sergeant took his notebook from his pouch.

'Yep, and I've written it down. It's Zander somebody. Just give me a sec, the greenkeeper told the secretary the name. Ah, here it is. The deceased's name is Zander Muir.'

The significance of the name hit Campbell like a dump truck. He thumped his forehead in frustration several times. Muttering obscenities under his breath he turned to his younger colleague who was none the wiser as to what was going on.

Campbell shook his head. 'Zander Muir. Fecking hell, how stupid am I?'

'Not very.' replied Asif looking confused. 'And what are you on about, I'm not following?'

'Feck, feck, feck.' Campbell tapped at the side of his temples in frustration. 'Zander. It's an abbreviation for Alexander. Zander Muir. Alexander Muir!'

Asif's eyes lit up. He'd never come across the name Zander before, but he now understood the significance of what Campbell was telling him.

'Ah, yes, I see. Were we a little premature giving the secretary his list of names back?'

Campbell blew out his cheeks and sighed wearily. 'It appears so doesn't it. With my bloody toothache I wasn't on top form that day, but even still that's a stupid silly mistake on my part.'

Asif could see that his boss was deflated. He needed to say something positive.

'Well, we can't undo any of that, but at least it firms up the connection with Magnus DeVilliers and Zander Muir. Well, I think it does. I take it you're assuming that the AM on the scorecard we found in DeVilliers' pocket refers to Zander Muir.'

Campbell smiled. Six months ago, Asif would still be scratching his head trying to make that connection. But not now. Now he was putting two and two together and making four. He'd come a long way in a short time and

Campbell was going to miss his friend when he got his promotion.

'I'd say that's looking likely and someone wanted both of them dead. There's a lesson in there for us. Don't assume, and don't take shortcuts. It can be a pain in the arse sometimes, but if I'd gone through that list more methodically, then who knows, our third victim might still be alive.'

'No, don't say that this isn't down to you, so let's have no more talk of that. Sergeant, can you point us in the right direction, we need to go to see this body?'

Five minutes later the two detectives found themselves standing by the edge of the burn looking at the cart that was lying at an angle of 45 degrees. The body of Zander Muir was still lying slumped across the front seat of the vehicle. Asif walked round to the other side to get a better look.

'Seems he may have smacked his head off the windshield when he crashed, his forehead is all cut. And what's with all the sticky yellow tape, he's got a bit stuck to his cheek and there's another piece on his sleeve?'

Campbell leant into the cart to get a better look. 'Don't think he's hit his head, there's no blood or marks on the windshield. Those look like cuts made by a knife to me. Oh shit, yeah, that's what it is.'

Campbell turned his head to the side as he stared at the deceased's forehead. 'Yep, no doubt about it, from this angle you can see it's the letter 'D'. The numbers are more difficult to make out, but I'd say that looks like an eight and the other one certainly could be a five. That sadistic bastard's done it again. He's cut his throat and then left his calling card carved into the poor bugger's forehead.'

Asif shook his head despairingly. 'He couldn't have survived very long, not with a wound like that and the amount of blood he's lost. And the yellow tape, that's just weird don't you think? It looks like it's all covered in dead flies.'

Campbell nodded. 'That's exactly what it is. Pieces of flypaper covered in dead flies. It's another metaphor, just like the frogs and locusts were. One of the ten plagues in Exodus was a plague of flies. As Con pointed out last week, our killer is trying to play mind games with us.'

Asif sighed ruefully. 'God only knows what McSorley's going to write when he gets hold of this story.'

'We'll worry about that later. But for now, let's get a tent organised ASAP and get this locus protected. It's pretty open and there are already half a dozen rubberneckers over by the dyke wondering what's going on. And as sure as bears shit in the woods the press will be along shortly, so let's not give them any unnecessary photo opportunities.'

Asif took out his radio. 'I'll give the control room a shout and get that organised and I'll see if they have an ETA for the DCI.'

Campbell bent down to examine something that was lying in the footwell underneath the steering wheel. 'Hmm, interesting. Come and have a swatch at this, I think we're going to find that our man wasn't murdered here.'

Asif came back round to the other side of the cart.

'See that large rock? I reckon whoever killed Zander Muir placed that rock on the accelerator and sent this cart hurtling down that hill behind us. That would explain how the cart ended up being half in the burn.'

Asif stared at the large rock that was still lying over the cart's accelerator.

'Yeah, that would make sense. And it would also suggest that whoever killed him probably cut his throat up there, next to the tee. Look how close those trees are to the dyke at the top of the hill. They can't be more than a few yards from the tee box. Perfect cover. You could attack your victim and be back over that wall in no time.'

Chapter 25

DCI Cooper had arrived at the golf course shortly after 0930 hrs. She'd had to cut short her meeting with Suzi Lessard but that couldn't be helped. With a third murder now on her plate she had other more important things on her mind. Suzi wasn't put out in the slightest. As a fellow officer she understood the demands of policing only too well. Circumstances and priorities could change in an instant, it was the nature of the job, it came with the territory.

Mini hadn't stayed long at the locus. As usual Campbell and the team had things well under control. SOCO had arrived and were busy setting up their kit and the photographer who had arrived first had already taken general shots of the location, the cart, and the deceased. As predicted Walter McSorley and the rest of the media circus had turned up only minutes after Mini's arrival. It was uncanny how quickly they managed to find their way to a crime scene. Once again, the 'Jungle Drums' had done their work.

Several long-lensed cameras on tripods had been set up on rough ground by the side of the dyke. It was more than a hundred yards from there to the cart, but it was the closest the press could get to the crime scene. Much to the annoyance of the camera operators the white tent that had been erected was largely obscuring the cart and preventing any opportunity of a photograph of the deceased. McSorley had arrived wearing a black fedora hat and a blue checked sports jacket, with his pencil thin moustache he was a dead ringer for one of those on-course bookmakers you encounter if you ever go to the horse or dog racing. Much to the amusement of Asif, Mini was doing her level best to avoid eye contact with the hack, who was cutting an increasingly frustrated figure prowling up and down the side of the dyke waving his arms and gesticulating wildly trying to attract the DCI's attention. Mini was having none of it, she knew McSorley would write his own story anyway, she wasn't about to indulge him with any face-to-face interview. The removal of Natalie from the team for speaking inadvisably with McSorley after Maureen Goodall's murder still rankled, she wouldn't be doing any favours for him or his paper anytime soon.

Mini had left Campbell and Asif at the course. They were going to be interviewing the secretary and the greenkeeper who had discovered the body. She had arranged to meet them back at the incident room when they got clear. She also had an irate Divisional Commander to try and placate. With a third murder in little more than two weeks he was starting to feel the pressure and it was showing. And like many weak-minded senior officers he was keen to pass his responsibilities onto someone junior in rank. And in this case that person was DCI Cooper.

*

Con was busy preparing the duty rotas for the following week when Campbell and Asif arrived back at the office. Asif was munching on a roll that he'd picked up from a café on Clarkston Road. He couldn't remember when he'd last eaten a proper lunch or any proper meal for that matter. A murder enquiry was not proving conducive to eating regular meals or having a normal family life. He had hardly seen Caelan these last two weeks. He was away early in the morning and invariably not home till late. His son was often in bed fast asleep by the time he got home. Roisin had been very understanding; she didn't complain and understood the demands this enquiry in particular was putting on her husband. But the relentless hours were starting to take its toll on both of them. This was Asif's first experience of a protracted murder investigation and with the hours he was working and poor eating habits he could feel his energy levels dipping, he was more irritable, and his concentration wasn't what it should be. It was a strange existence and shone a light on the reasons why so many detectives ended up divorced. Birthdays, anniversaries and social occasions all played second fiddle to the demands of the job.

'Any idea where the DCI is Con?' asked Campbell.

Con looked up from his desk. 'Still in with the Div Com. I expect he's giving her a hard time. He was in here earlier in a foul mood picking fault with everything. He told me the office was a disgrace. Untidy, unprofessional, and unhygienic he said. There were half a dozen dirty mugs and I had just dropped a packet of Quavers all over the floor, so the place wasn't looking its best but come on, it was hardly a midden. The man's a buffoon, an enquiry team knocking its pan in trying to solve three murders and he's worried about some crumbs on a carpet. He didn't say so, but I expect the ACC had been on the phone and given him a verbal spanking. That's how it usually works isn't it? Then they go and find

269

someone junior in rank and vent their spleen at them. He's pathetic, he couldn't pour water out of a boot if the instructions were on the heel. Anyway, I bet you're glad you asked.'

Campbell smiled and patted Con on the shoulder. 'Aye, you won't miss nonsense like that when you retire. We must be the best organisation in the world for making the job harder for ourselves. And as for Captain Courageous up the corridor, he's about as much use as a chocolate teapot.'

Asif sniggered as he finished his roll. He always found the patter between Con and Campbell entertaining; they were the office equivalent of Statler and Waldorf from the Muppets. Curmudgeonly at times, but funny, nevertheless.

The door opened and in walked a smiling Mini.

'Well, I wasn't expecting to see you looking so chipper.' said Con switching on the kettle. 'I thought the Chief Superintendent was going to read the riot act with you.'

'He tried, but I was ready for him. And then almost immediately he started backtracking at a rate of knots, it really was quite amusing.'

'Wish I'd been there to see that.' added Asif.

'Just a little something I learned on the AP course. Get on the front foot early and don't back down, hold your nerve. I just told him as a newly promoted DCI this was my first experience of such a complex investigation, but I was more than willing to listen to his advice. I asked him if he'd like to brief the team as to the tactics, he thought we should be adopting to progress the investigation.'

Campbell snorted theatrically. 'And what did he say to that?'

'Absolutely diddly squat. He folded like a cheap suit. It was classic. He certainly wasn't expecting me to ask for his advice, I think it would be fair to say that he was a tad disconcerted.'

Con started to laugh. 'Nice one boss, I love it when pompous gits like him get their comeuppance, couldn't happen to a nicer man.'

Campbell rocked back on his chair. 'So, what was the outcome?'

'He muttered something about bringing in extra resources and having daily meetings with him to keep him abreast of our progress and that was it. He ushered me out the room after that, couldn't get rid of me quick enough. Anyway, enough about our illustrious leader, where are we with Zander Muir, what can you tell me about him?'

Campbell pulled a couple of pages of rough notes from his folder.

'A fair bit as it happens. The secretary was particularly helpful. Seems like our man Zander, and it is Zander, that's the name on the membership register and Zander Muir was the name on his locker. Anyway, it turns out he's a bit of an acquired taste if I can put it that way. Not universally liked by the other members. Apparently, he had a run in with an opponent some years ago who accused him of cheating in a competition. The allegation didn't go anywhere, but it's left a bad taste if you know what I mean. No smoke without fire. Same could be true of his domestic and professional life. According to the secretary he's been married and divorced twice and has had a string of short-term relationships, some with lady members of the club. As for his professional life, he's a lawyer, got a practice in Fenwick Road, Giffnock. Strange but I don't think I've ever come across him.'

Con and the others all shook their heads.

'A few years ago, he had a run in with the Law Society. Seems like he was investigated for misappropriation of clients' money. He wasn't struck off, but he did receive a formal warning. Well, he did according to the secretary and I've no reason to think he's lying. I thought Asif and I would head over to Muir's office, when we're clear here ma'am, see what we can dig up.'

Mini ran her hands through her hair deep in thought. 'Was the secretary able to make any connection between Muir and Magnus DeVilliers or Maureen Goodall for that matter?'

Campbell shook his head. 'No, not a thing. If Zander Muir is as we suspect the AM on the scorecard that DeVilliers had on him, it would suggest that DeVilliers was there as Muir's guest, and it was a one off. Nobody seems to know DeVilliers at the golf club and the same goes for Maureen Goodall.'

'Ok, fine. Yes, you and Asif head over to his office. I'm going to give Lucy at Forensics a call, I'd like an early heads up as to whether there was any lead residue found on Muir's throat, that's been a common denominator for the other two murders and it's something that I think we should focus more on. Anyway, we'll see.'

Just as Campbell and Asif were getting ready to leave Jan stuck her head around the door. 'Ma'am, quick word if I may. What do you want to do about the curry night on Friday. Given what's happened today I thought you might want to cancel. If that's the case, I thought I'd better give the restaurant a call.'

The others turned and looked at Mini. 'Nope. Just leave the booking as it is. We've all got to eat, and we can't work every hour of the day and more importantly, we're going because it's Con's birthday. We'll go easy on the beers as Saturday will be another working day, but I don't see any reason why we have to cancel.'

Con's face lit up. He'd negotiated a late pass from Mrs Niblett for that evening and was looking forward to it. 'Nice one boss, although I'm not sure that the Chief Superintendent would approve.'

Mini smirked. 'Well fortunately it's got fuck all to do with him!'

Campbell picked up his folder. 'I'm not going to be of much use on Friday I'm afraid. I've got court in the morning and the last of my dental appointments scheduled for four o'clock. Hopefully I'll be able to eat something, but if the anaesthetic hasn't worn off, I'll be dribbling curry sauce all down my shirt!'

Chapter 26

Zander Muir's office was above a Chinese takeaway in a row of shops not far from the railway station. To access the office, you had to navigate a steep and rather dimly lit flight of stairs. Muir & Reid, Solicitors & Notaries was etched on the glass panel of the door in large gold lettering. A bell rang as Campbell opened the heavy wooden door. A bespectacled lady in her early forties wearing a smart green trouser suit looked up from a desk on the far side of the room. She smiled, took off her glasses and switched off the radio on her desk. Campbell reached into his jacket pocket and removed his warrant card which he showed to the lady.

'DI Morrison and DC Butt, Aikenhead Road, CID.'

The woman looked at them knowingly. 'Can I help you? If you're looking for Mr Muir, I'm afraid he's not here. He's golfing today, he had a tie to play. He's at Greenbank Golf Club but I rather suspect you may already know that.'

That remark took Asif completely by surprise, how would she know that they were already aware that Zander Muir was at the golf course.

Campbell looked at her quizzically. The woman continued in a calm and controlled voice.

'Look, officers, it was on the lunchtime news, they've found the body of a middle-aged man on Greenbank Golf

Club and now the two of you have turned up here. I've tried his mobile phone several times, and he isn't answering. My dad was 35 years in the job and my brother is in the Fraud Squad in Edinburgh. I know the score. You've not just turned up here by coincidence. Am I right?'

For all Campbell's experience as a detective, he hadn't seen that coming, but now that she'd said it, he didn't see any point in trying to avoid telling the truth. It was the first time that anybody he had cold-called had presumed to know why he was there. It was a strange opening gambit; he didn't even know the woman's name. But he sensed an opportunity. With her straightforward, matter of fact approach, perhaps she would be a rich source of information. Time to put that to the test.

'Sorry I didn't catch your name.'

The woman grinned. 'Perhaps that's because I didn't tell you DI Morrison. I'm assuming you are DI Morrison. Butt's an Asian name, so your colleague will be DC Butt and you'll be DI Morrison. I'm Susan Blain, Mr Muir's secretary, PA, general dogsbody, you know the type of thing.'

Asif opened his folder and scribbled down the name. This was one impressive lady. Most civilians didn't talk like that, and they hardly ever remembered names first time, she was clearly sharp and on the ball.

Taking a leaf out of his DCI's playbook Campbell decided now was the time to get on the front foot.

'Fine, I like plain speaking. The body we've found is Zander Muir and he didn't die of a heart attack. If you don't mind me saying, you don't seem overly upset at that news.'

She shrugged her shoulders. 'I'm not a very emotional person Detective Inspector, so that's part of the reason, and I suppose being honest with you, it's not a total surprise, Mr Muir sailed close to the wind at times with the company he kept, if I can put it that way.'

'What do you mean by the company he kept; do you mean his clients?'

Susan Blain nodded. 'Let's just say some of them were acquainted with the inside of a prison cell.'

'I see. And do you know of any reason why any of them might want him dead?'

Susan shook her head. 'Nope, and I'm sorry I can't give you any specific information.'

She got up from her desk and went over to a filing cabinet and removed a large green coloured folder from the bottom drawer which she handed to Campbell.

'This is his list of clients so you might want to start there. Not sure if any of them wanted him dead but I suppose it's possible, I wouldn't like some of them anywhere near me or my family. As I said to you, I know some of them had spent time in jail. There's a lot more stuff on computer, but Mr Muir, like many older solicitors, still liked his paper records. It's a bit of unnecessary duplication as far as I'm concerned, belt and braces I suppose. I expect you're going to find a few names in there that are familiar to you.'

'Interesting.' said Campbell sitting down in a chair by the window. He started to sift through the paperwork that had been filed alphabetically. He snorted and gave a wry smile. Every page he turned seemed to reveal the name of a known criminal, drug dealer, or southside gangster. Every ne'er-do-well operating south of the Clyde appeared to feature in the folder.

Campbell blew out his cheeks. 'That's quite a collection of clients Mr Muir had accumulated. And you're right, I'm familiar with quite a few of the names in here. And yet, I've never encountered your boss at Aikenhead Road office or at court and believe me I'm there often enough.'

Susan bit her bottom lip. 'I think you'll find that's because Mr Muir specialised in Tax Law. We stopped doing criminal work after his partner, Donald Reid died more than ten years ago. Mr Muir decided there were more lucrative ways to earn a living, so he started to specialise in tax matters. His second marriage had broken up and with two divorces to pay for he needed money, and he needed it quickly. And then there was the bother with the Law Society!'

'Yeah, we're aware of that. Misappropriation of clients' funds, given a formal warning I believe. I take it that was to do with his need to get quick money?'

'Got it in one Inspector. After the Law Society enquiry, clients, or should I say normal clients, became a lot harder to get. It had been in all the papers, so everyone knew what he'd been up to. So, he was forced to diversify. And the names in that folder are the result. Those people pay well and don't ask too many questions. Business picked up and he started doing well again. In fact, so well he was able to move to a large house in Whitecraigs. I'm not complaining, he was good to me, paid me well, more than I could get anywhere else. But I kept our relationship strictly professional. He had an eye for the ladies, can I put it that way, and I've never known anyone as competitive as Zander Muir. He loved winning and he was a very successful sportsman in his younger days. If you go through to his office, you'll see what I mean, he's got photographs all over his walls.'

Campbell looked across to Asif who as usual was busy writing down copious notes.

'We'll do that if you don't mind but before I forget, you said he was twice divorced. Did he have any children? I'm just wondering who his next of kin would be.'

Susan looked at Campbell over the top of her glasses.

'No children from either marriage. And his next of kin would be his mother, Georgina. Formidable woman. Recently turned 90. Lives in a ground floor flat at 23, Queen's Drive. Beautiful view of the park from the lounge window according to Zander. Met her a couple of times, sharp as a tack and with a temper to match. Not someone you'd want to get on the wrong side of. Mr Muir's father has been dead for a long time, I know the family lost a lot of money through a business deal that went sour. They used to live in a huge house in Pollokshields, but after the business got into difficulties, his mother had to sell the house and move to the flat in Queen's Drive. She also found religion much later in life. Became a member of some obscure church in the area, much to the consternation of her son. He wasn't in the slightest bit religious and felt the church was taking over his mother's life and probably much of her money.'

Asif looked up from his notes.

'Can you be any more specific about the church, where it is or what's it called?'

Susan shook her head. 'Afraid not. I only know it was somewhere close to where she lived. She didn't drive so she used to walk there. I believe she organised the flowers for the church, I think that's what annoyed Zander. He thought his mother was funding all that from her own pocket.'

The wall next to the desk in Zander Muir's office was covered in photographs and other sporting mementos. On a set of shelves near the door sat two sparkling silver cups and a small shield. The cups shone as if they were new, someone was taking great care looking after them. The engraving on the shield read Glasgow Academicals, Young Player of the Year, 1958.

A set of three rugby photographs, all dated from 1955, and identically framed, hung immediately above his chair. Asif studied each of the photographs carefully. The first one was of The Glasgow Academy First XV, the middle one was of the Glasgow Schools' team, while the last one was of the Scottish Schools' side. Taken, it said, at Inverleith, Edinburgh, before a game against English Schools.

Asif went back and studied the names at the bottom of the first photograph, he had remembered something. Magnus DeVilliers had also gone to Glasgow Academy. His face lit up when he saw it. It was confirmation that Muir and DeVilliers must have known each other. A.C. Muir was standing third from the left in the back row while seated in the front row on the right-hand side of the captain was M.G.R. DeVilliers. The two men had played together in the same school team.

'Campbell come and have a look at this photo, Zander Muir and Magnus DeVillliers, knew each other as we suspected, they were at school together and played in the same rugby team.'

'Just give me a sec will you, I think I've found something that may be significant scribbled on the blotting paper on his desk. You've got a good memory; can you remember the dates that Bob Thomson said proved that DeVilliers and Goodall had worked at

Ross Hall at the same time. I'm sure he said it was nearly ten years ago.'

'I can't remember off the top of my head but just give me a moment I wrote it down somewhere.'

Asif turned back several pages of his notepad. 'Yep, here it is. Bob said it was between the 5th and 9th September 1994.'

Campbell tapped his fingers together. 'Excellent, then we might just be onto something. Take a look at this.'

Written on the blotting paper in black ink was the following.

Mildred Donaldson, 6th September 1994, Ross Hall.
Magnus DeVilliers 0141 423 3431

Asif looked at the message and then flipped back several more pages of his notepad.

'0141 423 3431 is definitely Magnus DeVilliers' telephone number, I've got a note of it here. And give me a moment I'm going to check that date.'

Asif took out his phone and googled the date. '6th September 1994 was a Tuesday. I wonder what went on at Ross Hall on that date that involved a Mildred Donaldson.'

Campbell was now busy leafing through the green folder. 'I was just wondering the same thing. Damn it, there's no Donaldson listed here, in fact there are no surnames beginning with D.'

Campbell stuck his head back round the door. 'Excuse me Susan but does the name Mildred Donaldson ring any bells with you. Client or perhaps an associate of Mr Muir?'

Susan gave a wry smile as she tapped on her computer. 'Ah, yes, Mildred Donaldson, the file with nothing in it, all I have is a name and a date.'

'The 6th September 1994 per chance.' asked Asif smugly.

Susan frowned. 'No. Miles out. The date I have is 11th March this year. Just five weeks ago. I remember it well. A strange guy appeared at the office late that day. I'm certain it was a Friday; you see I finish at three on a Friday as I have to take my son to his guitar lesson in Burnside. I was putting on my coat when the guy arrived, he said he wanted to see Mr Muir. He said it was urgent and about his mother, Mildred Donaldson. I was going to send him away because he didn't have an appointment, but Mr Muir came through and said he would see him. I only had time to create the file with the name and date before I had to leave. I thought I'd do that, so I didn't forget about it when I came back in after the weekend.'

'Ok, so what happened when you did come back in?'

'Well, nothing really. When I saw Mr Muir the following Monday and asked him about it, he said that it was now all sorted, and we weren't going to have any further involvement. Hence, it's just a file with a name and a date. A bit strange, but these things do happen.'

Asif was scribbling furiously trying to ensure he hadn't missed anything.

'And the guy who came in that day, what can you tell us about him?' asked Asif.

Susan eyes narrowed as she thought. 'Not much really. I must have only spoken to him for less than a minute. He seemed a bit odd though. Dressed in dark clothing, workman's clothing and he was wearing a beanie hat. Hadn't shaved either, he had several days growth. I hate that, makes men look dirty I think.'

Asif looked up from his notepad. 'Age, height, build? And did he give you a name?'

Susan shook her head. 'Sorry, but I don't think he gave his name. Might be Donaldson of course, he did say Mildred Donaldson was his mother. As for age I'd say late thirties maybe, and not that tall. Couldn't tell you his build, he was wearing a chunky jacket and I think boots, but that's about all I can remember.'

Campbell nodded his approval. 'I'd say that was pretty good for a meeting that only lasted a minute. You should see some of the descriptions people give us, and that's for people they've known half their lives. I just want to double check what happened on the Monday when you spoke to Mr Muir, that conversation could potentially be very important to our investigation.'

Susan shook her head again. 'No, I'm sorry, I don't think he elaborated, he didn't say anything else. He just told me the matter was sorted. I didn't give it any other thought.'

*

Back at the office Mini was going through the updated action log with Jan when the phone rang. The call was from Lucy Harper at the Forensic Laboratory at Police Headquarters, and she had some interesting information for the DCI. She informed Mini that unlike the first two murder victims, no trace of any lead residue had been found around the wound that had killed Zander Muir, although the cut itself was very similar. An incised straight cut with no ragged edges most likely done by an extremely sharp bladed instrument. The next thing she said was potentially the most significant piece of information. A small fragment of metal, almost certainly the tip of the weapon used to murder Zander Muir had been recovered from the inside of the victim's throat. It had most likely broken when it came into contact with bone. Zander Muir's throat had been cut all the way through to his spinal cord. The poor man was very nearly decapitated. The recovered piece of metal was only 2mm in size and it was still undergoing tests to distinguish what it was and what it was made of. She wouldn't normally do it, but Lucy wanted to give the Chief Inspector an early heads up, she knew how difficult an enquiry this was turning out to be.

On first examination, it appeared that the piece of metal had come from the tip of a craft knife rather than a scalpel. That could be ascertained from the shape of the tip which was rounded. The blades of medical scalpels tend to be curved and are made of surgical grade stainless steel. They have a much higher carbon content than craft knives and are more durable. The tip that had been found was currently being examined by a metallurgist, but the early suggestions were that a craft knife had been the murder weapon.

'Lucy, I'm most grateful to you. That's a couple of favours I now owe you. Obviously, I'd like an early sight of the report as soon as you get it. Will the metallurgy side of things take long?'

'I'm told not. According to Peter who's doing the testing he should have something for you by tomorrow. Fingers crossed.'

'That would be good if he could, I'm hoping the PM will be done tomorrow so that would tie things up nicely. And thanks again for getting things progressed so quickly, it really is a big help.'

'Not a problem just glad to be of assistance. Oh, and just before I go, how are things going with that other matter we discussed? I hope whoever spiked that sample is going to get their just deserts. Despicable that people do that sort of thing.'

'Bubbling away it would be fair to say. It's been difficult with everything else that's going on at the moment. But I'm just waiting to speak to an ex-colleague of mine who's now a solicitor in Edinburgh, I'll know more when I've spoken to him, but I'll keep you in the loop Lucy, don't you worry about that.'

Mini had only just finished her call with Lucy when the phone rang again, this time it was Campbell, who was phoning from the car park of Ross Hall hospital. After speaking to Susan Blain, he'd decided to strike while the iron was still hot, he carefully explained to the DCI what they'd discovered at Zander Muir's office. He very much wanted to check with the hospital's administration office and ascertain what had happened at the hospital on the 6th September 1994. All his instincts told him it was important, he was just giving his boss her place before he took things any further.

'Ok, that's fine. See what you can find out and then get back here ASAP. I've had Lucy Harper on the phone and there are things I need to update you and Asif on.'

'Roger that. I don't think this enquiry will take us particularly long, but since we're now here could you get a couple of the team to deliver the death message to Muir's Mother. Asif has updated the incident with all the relevant details. We'll pick it up again tomorrow. She's going to need to be properly interviewed, but for now, the priority is to let her know what has happened to her son.'

'Right, consider it done. Bob and Sally are somewhere in the office, I'll get them to do it. Ok, best of luck, I'll see you back here in a bit.'

Chapter 27

There were two women working in the hospital's administration office. The older of the two, an overweight woman in her fifties with stiff back-combed dyed blonde hair and a sour expression, spoke with a faux posh accent. It was a peculiar mix of Kelvinside and Kinning Park, with more a leaning towards Kinning Park, as she lapsed into the vernacular the more aggrieved, she became. It was almost as if someone had flicked a switch. Her rant had started as soon as Campbell had identified himself as a police officer. That was like a red rag to a bull. Her annoyance, it transpired, was on account of a fixed penalty ticket that she received last year for driving through a red traffic light in Shettleston, an offence, at least in her own mind, that she was clearly not guilty of. It obviously still irked her as, much to the amusement of her younger colleague, she went on and on about it. As miscarriages of justice go, it was on the lower end of the spectrum, but for some strange reason she didn't seem able to let the matter lie. Campbell wasn't sure what she thought he could do about it, but it had clearly jaundiced her view of the police and she didn't appear to be in any mood to co-operate. Fortunately, her workmate seemed a great deal more accommodating. And as old sour puss huffed and puffed at her desk, she busied herself trying to find the file that would tell them what had occurred on 6th September 1994.

The girl returned to her desk with a black box file. 'I think I might have found what you're looking for. This is all the paperwork for that particular week. Do you happen to know the patient or the Doctor's name?'

Campbell removed his glasses and smiled. 'I believe we know both. The patient's name was Mildred Donaldson and the Doctor, or Consultant I should say, was a Mr Magnus DeVilliers.'

The young receptionist searched through the file. 'Tuesday, 6th September you said. Ah, here it is. Mildred Donaldson. She had a Nissen Fundoplication operation to cure a severe acid reflux condition. She also had surgery to repair a hiatus hernia. And Mr DeVilliers was her surgeon.' The young woman's demeanour suddenly changed. Her brow furrowed and a worried look swept over her face. 'But from the notes here, it would appear that Mrs Donaldson died two days later. While she was still in the hospital.'

Campbell and Asif exchanged glances.

'What does it say she died of?' asked Asif.

The young woman looked up sheepishly. 'Myocardial Infarction.'

'Heart attack. She died of a heart attack.' added Asif.

'I'd like a photocopy of those notes please, everything you have in that file, that pertains to Mildred Donaldson's operation.'

The older woman looked up from her desk and snarled. 'You're gonna need a warrant if you want anything from this office, it's confidential.'

Asif sighed to himself. Another civvy who's watched too much crime drama on the T.V. and thinks they know everything there is to know about the law. The younger woman who was perched on the edge of her desk was clearly embarrassed and was now looking at her feet.

Campbell fixed the older woman with an icy stare. 'There are two ways we can deal with this. The easy way or the hard way. And may I point out at this juncture that if my colleague and I have to return to your office with a warrant, and that's the hard way, then it won't only be a couple of box files that will be getting removed to our office. You'll be coming too, as will your colleague. You are both potentially witnesses in a very serious police investigation. It matters not to me which way you want to play this, and being the reasonable guy that I am, I'm going to give you a couple of minutes to consider your response.'

The younger woman had heard enough. She took the paperwork out of the file and marched across to the photocopier.

'Senga don't you even think about it. I've got a date later with Russell which I ain't missing, were going for an Italian and then to see Troy at the Quay. So, let's give these officers the information they're looking for and be done with it. No ifs and no buts.'

Well, that's Senga told thought Asif as the older woman grabbed a packet of cigarettes from her desk and stormed out the office bristling with indignation.

The younger woman photocopied the file and handed it to Campbell. 'Sorry about that officer, she's a monumental pain in the ass. As well as being all fur coat and nae knickers as my grandma might say. Now is there anything else I can help you with, and I'm Sarah by the way. Sarah McCann?'

Campbell smiled. 'No. Your intervention was just perfect if I may say so. We will likely have to come back another day and get a statement from you, but that can wait. I'm grateful for your assistance.'

Asif took the copies from Campbell and put them in his folder. 'Hope you enjoy the film, it's just out, isn't it? I'm hoping to go see it myself when I get the chance.'

Sarah grinned. 'If it's a good film then that will be a bonus. But I'm only really going to see Brad Pitt, he's my secret crush, just love everything about him.'

Asif smiled. 'Best keep that to yourself, not sure Russell would be too impressed.'

Sarah giggled. 'Well, I'll not tell him if you don't.'

'Deal.' said Asif with a wink, 'Your secret's safe with me.'

Back at the car the two detectives started to read through the file. There were several pages of notes to digest. Campbell scratched his head.

'Mildred Donaldson was only 63 when she died. Not old by any means, but I suppose there are many people in their sixties who die of a heart attack. I wonder if she was a woman of means because here's the invoice on page two. £6,385 was the cost of the operation ten years ago, don't know if that's expensive or not. Account was paid in full and there's a signature at the bottom, quite faint but it looks like G. Donaldson. Could be her husband, or perhaps a son or a daughter? Who knows.'

Campbell removed a page and handed it to Asif. 'Now this is interesting, it's a copy of her death certificate and look who signed it to certify the death.'

Asif studied the piece of paper. 'I didn't think consultants would sign a death certificate. Thought that would be a job for a more junior doctor. And she was

Magnus DeVilliers' patient, he did her operation, is that even ethical?'

Campbell shrugged his shoulders. 'Perhaps things are done differently in the private sector. It's funny, but with all my years in the job this is the first time I've had an enquiry that's had any involvement with private medicine.'

Campbell continued reading. 'I was wondering if we might come across her name and here it is, bottom of page 3. This appears to be the names of the medical staff who assisted at the operation. Maureen Goodall and a woman called Lesley Craig were the nursing staff, and as well as DeVilliers, there was an anaesthetist called Kenneth Sheridan.'

Asif looked at his boss and raised an eyebrow. 'Two of those names are already dead. Does that mean that Sheridan, and what was the nurse's name, Craig, I think you said, are the next in line?'

'Bloody hell, don't say that, but tracing Craig and Sheridan's whereabouts is going to have to be a priority.'

'Definitely.' replied Asif who was now deep in thought. 'Look, what I'm about to say is slightly left field, but I want to run something past you. I've been thinking about it since we were in Zander Muir's office. It's to do with the lady's name, Mildred Donaldson.'

Campbell put down the papers and turned to his colleague.

'Ok, shoot. I'm all ears, what's on your mind?'

'I'm wondering if we might have made an error. Well not an error as such, more of an assumption that might not be accurate.'

'Ok, and why would that be?'

Asif took a deep breath. 'You know how we found Zander Muir's body with the letter 'D' carved into his forehead.'

Campbell nodded.

'Well, the letter 'D' was smeared in blood at the other two locations as well.'

'It was.'

'Ok, so here's the thing. We assumed that the 'D' was a bible reference, taken from the book of Deuteronomy, we've even got the bible verse written up on a board in the incident room. But couldn't the 'D' just as easily stand for Donaldson, left as a warning by someone taking revenge for her death. I don't know it's just a thought.'

Campbell looked sceptical. 'The woman died of a heart attack in hospital two days after an operation. That doesn't strike me as being particularly unusual. Or for that matter a good enough reason as to why someone would then go on and murder three people. We are going to need to find out more about the circumstances of that operation, no question about that, so tracing the two people who were present and who we assume are still alive will become the focus of this enquiry. The DCI will insist on it. Now I'm not dismissing what you're saying, but there are two things that suggest to me that the bible theory is correct. It was the numbers that we found at all the murder locations that pointed to the actual verse. Remember, Deuteronomy Chapter 8 verse 5. And I also think you're forgetting the significance of the frogs, locusts and flies that were found. I'm as certain as I can be that they are bible allegories. It's possible that both theories could be correct, but I'm as sure as I can be that this is the work of some religious nutter.'

Asif wasn't deflated by Campbell's response. The points he made were valid. Keeping an open mind to other possibilities was key to being a good detective. He'd learnt that watching how Campbell operated. He was finding it difficult to explain, and it could of course be nothing more than coincidence, but he had a nagging feeling that the 'D' and the name Donaldson were inextricably linked.

Campbell opened the driver's door. 'Right, before we head back to the office, let's see if Sarah McCann is still around and see what she can tell us regarding the whereabouts of Lesley Craig and Kenneth Sheridan.'

Chapter 28

Outside the front entrance of Aikenhead Road Police Office a sizeable crowd had started to gather. The crowd comprised mainly of schoolchildren, making their way home from Holyrood Secondary that was only a quarter of a mile down the road. They had been joined by a couple of elderly ladies pulling matching tartan shopping trolleys heading home from the Asda supermarket on the other side of the road. A middle-aged couple walking a beige coloured cockapoo dog had stopped to see what was going on as had a young couple with a toddler in a pushchair who, much to the amusement of the schoolchildren, was throwing a tantrum about not being allowed to have a second packet of Mini Cheddars.

In the middle of the throng stood Walter McSorley, wearing his blue sports jacket and trademark fedora hat. He was accompanied by a photographer who was busy taking shots of McSorley speaking to various members of the crowd. DCI Cooper and Jan, drawn by the noise outside, looked down on the scene from a first-floor window.

'This is all because I refused the chancer a face-to-face interview. He's pissed off after what happened at the golf course. He arrived at the office with his photographer in tow, looking to get a word with me.

He must think I button up the back. There's no way on this earth I'm going to give McSorley an exclusive interview, not after the nonsense he's been writing for the last couple of weeks. This is his way of trying to get back at me. Whip up the crowd and then get a hysterical quote from someone that suits their narrative, so they can splash it on the front page of the Times tonight. The man's a snake, and he's got no scruples, Jan. He'll write what he wants to write, that's what he always does.'

'Sometimes I'm glad I'm just a cop, you don't have to worry about people like McSorley. He's not interested in speaking to the likes of me, which is perhaps just as well. I don't know how you've got the patience to have to deal with folk like him. It must be so distracting when you're just trying to …'

Jan broke off mid-sentence, she had just noticed who was striding across the road at the zebra crossing. It was Conway, on his way back to the office with some milk and a box of teabags.

'Boss, Con's on his way back and he's now making a beeline towards, ah, too late. He now appears to be having an altercation with McSorley.'

'Yeah, I see him. Open the window will you, let's see if we can hear what he's saying. Oh God, he's now jabbing his finger into McSorley's chest. This is in danger of kicking off.'

Jan opened the window, but it was impossible to hear what was being said. 'The crowd of schoolkids had surrounded Con and McSorley and were jeering and egging the pair of them on. It was like two schoolboys squaring up for a fight behind the bike shed, this had the potential to get ugly very quickly.

'Jan, phone the uniform bar and tell them to get a couple of cops out there sharpish. Con looks about ready to punch him!'

As she was speaking the front doors of the office swung open and into the fray stepped Asif and Campbell.

Mini turned to Jan who was now speaking on the phone to someone. 'Shit, tell them to hurry up, Asif and Campbell are now out there, and someone's just knocked the photographer's camera out of his hand.'

Mini watched speechless as Campbell reached out an arm and grabbed Con's jacket by the collar. With one mighty heave he pulled him backwards away from McSorley and with the assistance of Asif pushed him through the double doors and into the sanctuary of the office. Within seconds, a uniformed sergeant and two constables appeared on the pavement. Whatever warning was given it had the desired effect, the crowd scattered in all directions leaving only the photographer and McSorley arguing their case with the sergeant, who didn't seem in the slightest bit interested in what they had to say. Two minutes later it was all over, with their pleadings falling on deaf ears, the journalists sloped off, retreating to their vehicle parked in the Asda carpark. It remained to be seen what headline would appear in the late edition of that evening's paper.

Mini was sitting at her desk when a rather red-faced Conway came into the incident room accompanied by Asif and Campbell. Con slumped down at a desk.

'Boss, I'm spitting feathers, and I'm no kidding.' Con held up this forefinger and thumb. 'He was that fecking close to getting the jail. I told him he was obstructing the footway and if he didn't move, he'd be getting charged. He called me a baldy bastard under his breath, and no bugger's gonna call me that and get away with it. I'm telling you he was that close to getting the jail.'

Mini leant forward on her desk. The others looked at her as she contemplated her response.

'Well Con, let me tell you what I saw. I saw an experienced officer with only weeks to go before his retirement let his emotions get the better of him. You've got many fine qualities, you're shrewd and intelligent, but the truth be told, you can also be an irascible old rascal with a fiery temper. And five minutes ago, you let that temper get the better of you. I'm not disputing that McSorley's an arse, I think we'd all agree that's a given, but you let yourself down there. If it hadn't been for Campbell's and Asif's quick thinking, you could have found yourself on the wrong side of the charge bar. I've seen it happen before as I'm sure you have. But the red mist never helps. I want you to just take a moment and reflect on that.'

The red face of anger was immediately replaced by the red face of embarrassment. Con hadn't realised that the DCI had witnessed what had gone on. But she was right. He'd reacted far too quickly, and things could easily have spiralled out of control. It was a character fault that had plagued him throughout his police career. And it was without question a major reason why he had never been promoted. Suddenly he felt quite ashamed, he'd let himself down in front of his colleagues and friends and now he didn't know what to say. Not for the first time, it was Campbell who found the appropriate response.

'Look Con, we've all been there. There by the grace of God and all that. And show me the man who hasn't made a mistake and I'll show you a liar. But a lesson learned eh, and thankfully no harm done. Even though McSorley's a complete dick, he ain't stupid. He won't pursue this; he'll not make a complaint. He knows it's not in his interest, so that'll be the end of the matter, ok.'

Con nodded quietly and shook his head. 'Thanks Campbell, and you too, Asif. But I just want you all to know if it had come down to a fight, I'm confident I could have taken him.'

Mini smiled. 'That, I'm sure we'd all agree, would not be in doubt.'

With the fracas with McSorley now over Con decided to make himself scarce in the CID general office getting on with the plethora of other admin jobs that were not related to the murder enquiry but had been piling up and now needed attention. Jan also sought to excuse herself. She had a mountain of statements to put onto the Holmes system, a tedious job but an important one. She got up and handed Campbell a handwritten note.

'Fiscal's Office were on the phone looking for you earlier. They want you to attend a Fiscal's precognition at the Sheriff court tomorrow at 1030 hrs. I've written the Crime Reference number down for you. It's that drugs case from November last year, the one where the accused spiked that young cop with a needle.'

Campbell took the piece of paper. 'Thanks Jan. Well, that's tomorrow morning taken care of, I'll need to dig out the case and statements, but I'll be glad to see this one go to jail. Utter scumbag. He knew he was banged to rights when he spiked that cop, but he did it anyway, he's getting everything he deserves that one.'

Mini smiled at Jan as she got up to leave. 'Much obliged once again for all your efforts, Jan. I know you're wearing three hats at the moment, but we appreciate all your help, it makes a big difference, everyone's lives are just that little bit easier.'

When Jan had gone Mini asked Campbell and Asif to wait behind. She wanted a full update about what they had discovered at Zander Muir's office, and during their visit to Ross Hall. There was a lot to catch up on. She grabbed a dry marker pen and started to write names and headings on a whiteboard as Campbell took her through the events of that morning. Writ large on the board were the names Lesley Craig and Kenneth Sheridan. She agreed with Campbell, they had to become the major focus of the enquiry. They needed to be traced and spoken to, and that needed to be done urgently. To that end she tasked two of her other detectives to get on the phones and establish their whereabouts. Finding them might prove to be the key to unlocking the mystery of who killed Magnus DeVilliers, Maureen Goodall, and Zander Muir.

Asif had been listening carefully to what Campbell and the DCI had been saying. As usual he was noting everything down in his folder. He was an assiduous note taker, and it was not only Campbell who had cause to be thankful for his diligence. Everyone in the department looking for a date, a name or a particular address, knew to check in with Asif. He had a formidable memory, but if that failed for any reason, he could normally be relied upon to produce the answer from somewhere in his notepad. He was turning into a highly skilled and knowledgeable detective. He had come a long way in the nine months since he'd been made substantive. He looked up from his notes.

'Ma'am, do you have any word on how the troops got on delivering the death message to Zander Muir's mother? I'm hoping to go and interview her tomorrow, perhaps when you're with the Fiscal, Campbell. I was just wondering if she might not be fit enough to do that, the news of her son's death and the circumstances must have come as a shock.'

Mini looked up from her desk. 'Interesting you should ask that. I spoke to Bob and Sally an hour or so ago. They said she was remarkably calm, stoic even. There were certainly no tears. According to Bob she was upset, but in that matter of fact, controlled way that elderly people often are. Personally, I think it's because they lived through the war, you don't get to be that age without experiencing some form of tragedy or heartache in your life. Older folk just seem a bit more resilient when it comes to dealing with death. But still, to be quite so calm when your own son has died, is a little strange, but there you have it. Oh, and one more thing. Apparently, she lives with a companion, a lady in her sixties, who does the cooking and general housekeeping. Cheaper than going into full time care I suppose, but you might want to try and speak to her as well when you're there.'

'I'll make a point of it, she might be able to shed more light on Zander Muir's lifestyle, which according to his secretary was, shall we say, colourful, at least it was when it came to the ladies. Twice married and a string of girlfriends since his last divorce, apparently, but there's absolutely nothing to link any of them to his death. Everything we know would suggest that Mildred Donaldson's death is at the centre of this, it's the only thing we've got that links the three deaths in any way. Nothing else makes any sense.' added Asif.

Mini got up from her desk. 'And the motive? What would the motive be?'

Asif shrugged his shoulders. 'Revenge I suppose.'

'Revenge for what? The woman died of a heart attack.'

Asif raised an eyebrow. 'Allegedly!'

Mini shook her head. 'It's still all too tenuous, we've got nothing concrete. We need to find some hard evidence to make those connections otherwise I'm afraid it's all just supposition.'

While Mini and Asif were still deep in conversation, Campbell went over to the whiteboard and picked up a marker pen. He started writing a list.

1. Water to blood
2. Frogs (1)
3. Lice
4. Flies (3)
5. Livestock pestilence
6. Boils
7. Hail
8. Locusts (2)
9. Darkness
10. Killing of firstborn Child

Mini and Asif watched on in interest. 'Those are the ten plagues that you've listed, aren't they?' asked Mini. Campbell nodded.

'And is that the order they appear in the bible?'

Campbell nodded again.

'So, what's the significance of the numbers in the brackets?'

Campbell put down the marker pen. 'They are the three that we think are connected to our investigation, in the order they occurred.'

'Interesting.' said Asif copying down the list. 'But our three don't follow the biblical order, they're just three from that list of ten.'

'Exactly.' replied Campbell.

Mini twiddled her thumbs. 'I'm not sure I'm following what you're trying to tell us.'

Campbell sat back down. 'I'm not sure I'm trying to tell you anything specific, it's just a bit of blue-sky thinking. But here's the thing. Given that our murderer has struck three times already, we can't discount the possibility that they'll strike again. So, I want you to take a close look at that list, pay particular interest to the seven that our killer hasn't involved themselves with yet.'

'Ok, I'm doing that.' replied Mini.

'So, of the remaining seven plagues, I'm pretty sure tuning water into blood is beyond even the capabilities of our killer. And likewise, I think it's unlikely that they could cause pestilence in livestock, or an outbreak of boils. And I don't think they could affect the weather to cause hailstorms or perpetual darkness for that matter.'

Mini started nervously biting the end of her thumb nail as she looked at the board. She wasn't stupid, she could now see where Campbell was going with this.'

'That being the case, that only leaves lice and the killing of …'

Mini put up her hand to stop Campbell in mid flow.

'Ok, enough. Don't even go there, that's too horrendous to even contemplate, surely whoever is the killer, wouldn't be that evil, would they?'

Chapter 29

Asif had decided that he would walk to Queen's Drive. He'd declined a lift from Campbell who was on his way to his precognition at the Sheriff Court. Anyway, it was only a 15-minute walk from the office, and it was a glorious warm sunny day. For about the first time that year Asif could feel the warmth of the spring sunshine on his back. It reminded him of early March in Lahore when he was a boy. There, the dense fogs that settled over the city during January and February gave way to warm sunny days and the start of spring. Today's weather felt just like that. The air light with just a hint of breeze, the southside was coming out of its winter hibernation.

As he entered Queen's Park by the gate near to the Battlefield monument his route took him through an avenue of rhododendron bushes, their bell-shaped flowers a riot of red, pink and purple. The bluebird sky meant that the coats of winter could finally be cast off and T-shirts and shorts became the order of the day. Everywhere you looked people were peeling off clothes exposing their fair Scottish skin to the first rays of a blazing sun. This was 'Taps Aff' weather. Turning north, Asif headed up the hill towards the flagpole, the oak and chestnut trees that hugged the fence by the allotments were alive with small birds. Bluetits, chiffchaffs, and a passing flock of long tailed tits flitted from branch to branch hoovering up juicy caterpillars and aphids from high up in the verdant canopy. The birds had hungry young mouths to feed, and like the young mums nursing their infant children on a blanket next to the children's swings, they were busy nurturing new life.

By the time Asif reached Queen's Drive it was approaching half past ten. The steps leading up to number 23, like many of the flats in the attractive terrace, was festooned with terracotta pots brimmed full of colourful begonias and geraniums. Each set of steps seemed more colourful and extravagant than the last, it was as if the green-fingered residents of Queen's Drive were in competition with each other, this part of the city was very much in bloom.

Mrs Muir's flat was on the ground floor, which was something of a misnomer as all the flats in the terrace had basement properties. This meant that the bay window of the ground floor flats sat eight feet above the height of the pavement. That was ideal, for as well as affording privacy, it meant you enjoyed unrestricted views over the busy road to the park beyond.

The front door was opened by a small dark-haired lady wearing a housecoat and carrying a yellow duster. Asif produced his warrant card and introduced himself. The lady's name was Alison Holgate and, as she explained, she was Mrs Muir's live-in housekeeper. She invited Asif to come in. Expensive patterned rugs sat on highly polished wooden floors and on the walls hung ornate mirrors and paintings, mainly done in oils, of land and seascapes. An imposing grandfather clock, made of walnut, stood in the corner of the hall which struck the half hour as Mrs Holgate ushered Asif into the front room. He sat down on an elaborately upholstered gold coloured chair looking towards the bay window. Immediately to his right and standing in front of an impressively large wooden fire surround was an embroidered fire guard. It depicted a large tree, with various colourful animals and birds sitting on its branches. Lions, elephants, and monkeys, there was even a pair of mice, alarmingly out of proportion as they appeared to be nearly as big as the other animals. A peacock with its iridescent tail feathers spread wide, perched on the top branch of the tree. Blemish free, it was a magnificent example of intricate cross stitching. Asif leant forward to read the inscription at the bottom of the tree.

In the beginning God created the heavens and the earth: Genesis Chapter 1

'Isn't it just perfect.' said Mrs Holgate noticing Asif's interest in the work. 'It's probably Mrs Muir's favourite thing in this flat. And if you look around, I'm sure you'll agree she's got some lovely things. I have to hand it to her, she does have exquisite taste, but the cross-stitched fireguard holds a special place in her heart. It was given to her as a gift, by a lady she met not long after she moved here. Mildred Donaldson was one of her dearest friends, but she sadly passed away about ten years ago, so Mrs Muir likes to have it in pride of place in the front room, as a reminder of Mildred.'

He'd only been in the flat a matter of minutes, but this meeting had the potential to be extremely fruitful. Without even having to ask he had already established a firm link between Mrs Muir and Mildred Donaldson.

'Is Mrs Muir about? I think my colleagues who spoke to her yesterday said someone would be calling this morning.'

Mrs Holgate looked a little embarrassed. 'Yes, they did, but I'm afraid Mrs Muir has gone out. She had a longstanding engagement to meet two friends in town for coffee then lunch. She went away in a taxi about 15 minutes ago, and she won't be back until late afternoon. I'm sorry if this has wasted your time.'

Asif took out his folder and scribbled down some notes. 'No, that's ok, I can catch her another time. I just thought that she would be in, given the circumstances, and it being so close to the death of her son.'

'Yes, you might have thought. What a terrible business, I saw it on the news last night. I watched it in my room so as not to upset Mrs Muir. But going out this morning is in many ways so typical of her. She's a strong-willed lady, always has been, and she wouldn't want to let her friends down. What's done is done, she told me at breakfast, and she can't change that. She'll mourn in her own way. She was down at the church yesterday for several hours, praying for his soul, she told me. It's the Church of the Temple Mount on Maybank Street, I believe it's quite evangelical, fire and brimstone and all that. Her friend Mildred, the lady who embroidered the fireguard, also went there.'

Mrs Holgate sighed and shook her head. 'It's perhaps not the way you or I would mourn the loss of a loved one officer, but it's her way, and who am I to say she's wrong, she's grieving in her own way. Gosh, how rude of me, I haven't even offered you a cup of tea, or would you prefer coffee?'

Over a cup of tea, served in delicate bone china cups, and a slice of lemon drizzle cake, Alison Holgate explained how she had become Mrs Muir's companion and housekeeper. When she was first married, Alison had lived in a tenement flat in Leslie Street, Pollokshields. At that time the Muir family lived in a five bedroomed mansion in Sherbrooke Avenue less than a mile from her flat. Replying to an advert in the local paper, Alison had initially started working for Mrs Muir as a cleaner, but that role quickly developed into other responsibilities. Although Mrs Muir didn't drive, she did have access to several cars belonging to the family, so it wasn't long before Alison started chauffeuring Mrs Muir to various appointments and social events. This arrangement continued for many years until the Muir's family firm, a drapery business making curtains and soft furnishings, ran into cash flow difficulties and had to be sold. Shortly afterwards Mr Muir's health deteriorated, he developed cancer, and he passed away leaving Mrs Muir and her son Zander with a property they could no longer afford to maintain.

After the sale of the Sherbrooke Avenue house, Mrs Muir moved to the flat in Queen's Drive. That was 12 years ago, and Alison continued to clean the flat a couple of times a week. Three years ago, her own circumstances radically changed. Her husband died suddenly of a heart attack and, being a man who had always been partial to a drink and a bet, he left Alison with next to nothing. She was almost bereft and survived on a meagre widow's pension and the money she earned from cleaning Mrs Muir's and a couple of other flats. It had been Zander Muir's suggestion, that she move into the spare room at Queen's Drive and become Mrs Muir's companion.

Three years younger than Zander, Alison had known him for nearly 40 years. They hadn't always seen eye to eye and their relationship had its ups and downs, but on this occasion his suggestion seemed to make perfect sense. He had someone reliable and trustworthy to look after his aging mother and better still, Alison had always been someone his mother got on well with. Being honest, the move to Queen's Drive also suited Alison. She had a roof over her head and a regular salary, it was more than enough money to allow her to enjoy a comfortable lifestyle as she headed towards her pensionable years. Their relationship though was purely professional. Mrs Muir spent a lot of her time at the church in Maybank Street, just a short walk from the flat. For many years she had organised the church flowers, a role she had taken over from Mildred Donaldson after she died. Church was not something Alison got involved with. She wasn't religious so she never went. In fact, other than her Tuesday night Bingo she hardly went out at all socially. She was happy in her own company watching the Soaps.

Mrs Muir's affiliation to the church was something of a wedge issue with her son, an avowed atheist. She had never gone to church when he was growing up, it was only something that she had taken up when she had moved to Queen's Drive. And it had been her friendship with Mildred Donaldson that had led to that. Most days, Mrs Muir had been in the habit of taking an early afternoon walk in the park. She very often stopped at the same bench for a rest and to watch the men sailing their yachts on the boating pond. It was there she used to meet Mildred Donaldson. Within weeks they became firm friends, and at Mildred's invitation Mrs Muir started to attend church on a Sunday with her. To begin with, she only went about once a month, but as time passed, she found herself attending more frequently and before long she was going every Sunday. Encouraged by the pastor she also started attending mid-week bible study and prayer meetings. Her son wasn't overly concerned about his mother's church attendance, that was up to her, but he resented how much of her income she was giving to the church. As well as giving a substantial offering each month, he was convinced that she was funding the weekly flower arrangements that she assiduously arranged to brighten up the church, out of her own pocket. He knew for a fact that she had commissioned several replacement-stained glass windows over the years and in this, the 50th anniversary of the founding of the church, she was paying for a series of stained-glass panels that would be displayed in the vestibule. Mrs Muir refused to tell her son how much she was giving to the church, but Zander knew it was running into thousands of pounds.

'Would you like more tea, officer? There's plenty left in the pot.'

Dabbing the crumbs from his mouth with a napkin, Asif politely declined.

'I'm interested to find out more about Mildred Donaldson and her relationship with Mrs Muir. I know you told me that Mildred died some time ago, I was just wondering if you knew what happened?'

Alison thought for a moment. 'I know she died in hospital, after an operation I believe. But that's about all I know, Mrs Muir didn't talk much about it.'

'I'm presuming she must have lived close by if she went to the same church, and what about her family do you know anything about that?'

Alison screwed up her nose. 'Again, not really. I think she may have had a son but I'm not 100% sure, I could be getting mixed up with some other of Mrs Muir's friends. For a lady who has just turned ninety, she had a remarkably large circle of friends. As for where she lived, I really couldn't say, she died a long time ago.'

Asif thanked Mrs Holgate for her help and hospitality. He had learned some useful information, but he really needed to speak with Mrs Muir in person. She would surely be able to tell him much more about Mildred Donaldson and the circumstances surrounding her death.

'Do you think you could let Mrs Muir know that I'll try and call again tomorrow. Is there a particular time that would suit best?'

Mrs Holgate checked the diary on the telephone table in the hall.

'She doesn't appear to have any appointments that I can see, so she should be around. Late morning, 11 to 1130 might be best. Mrs Muir takes a while to get organised in the mornings. Oh, and don't come in the early afternoon, if its dry, that's when she likes to walk in the park.'

*

Back at Aikenhead Road, Mini Cooper was in her own office with the door firmly shut. She was deep in conversation on the telephone and had been for the last five minutes. She was speaking to George Maxwell, a friend and former colleague from Edinburgh, who she knew from their time on the AP Course together. George, who had studied Law at university prior to joining the police, had decided to leave the job and pursue a legal career. That had been a risk, as a sergeant on the AP Scheme he was giving up a lot, but as it happened, it turned out to be a shrewd move. Five years down the line he was now a successful criminal lawyer with an up-and-coming law firm who had developed a reputation for tenacity and ingenuity. They were shaking off the old image of staid and stuffy lawyers. They were forging a new path and had achieved some stellar results that had the legal fraternity's full attention.

'Again, sorry for the delay in getting back to you, Mini. Like you, things have been a bit hectic recently, but the trial ended yesterday, another not guilty verdict so that was pleasing. But I've now had a chance to read your e mail properly. What an absolute charmer Ch Supt Taylor seems. And for charmer read scumbag, he sounds a bad one right enough. But before I tell you what I want to tell you, let me say how impressed I've been with your media broadcasts. A triple murder enquiry and having to deal with this on the side, you've been terrific and, may I say, utterly professional. And that's not just me saying that as your friend, our senior partner mentioned it last week. He had no idea that I knew you, but I can tell you, praise from him is praise indeed. So, you must be doing something right.'

'That's kind of you George and I'm lucky I've got a great team, they're very capable and supportive, but it will count for nothing if I don't get a result, you know how these things work. It's largely irrelevant that it's my first murder enquiry, if I don't get a detection, it's possibly going to be my last. They'll move me into some admin role at Headquarters and I'll become the forgotten woman, and as you know, it would do nothing for my promotion prospects. God, that's depressing, so let's not go there. You said you'd read my e mail, and apologies for it being so long, but I wanted to cover everything, so you were conversant with all the facts. I'm interested in your thoughts.'

'Right let's get to it shall we, and I want you to understand I'm now speaking as a lawyer and not your friend. We can't let sentiment get in the way of this, it's too important.'

'Understood.'

'Ok, firstly, it's unlikely that you're going to be able to use the fact that he spiked your drink with Rohypnol at any trial. Any lawyer, and they won't even have to be a good lawyer, will drive a horse and cart through that evidence. I'm afraid, Mini, that as it stands it's inadmissible, nobody can corroborate that your urine sample was a consequence of what happened in that room. I'm just playing Devil's Advocate now, but that sample could have been taken anywhere and the drug put into it at any time. You can see where I'm going with this, that's what any defence lawyer worth their salt is going to argue. It would undermine your entire case if we were to try and lead that as evidence in court, it just isn't going to fly, and as an experienced officer I'm pretty sure you are already aware of that.'

'Yeah, I thought as much. Having the sample checked was more for my own benefit, I needed to know for sure what that bastard had done to me. But I understand what you're saying. On a more positive note, I'm assuming you're happy with Suzi Lessard's testimony, she can speak to my demeanour and the bruising on my neck when I came out of Taylor's room.'

'Absolutely no problem with that. Her evidence is going to be key and she's one brave lady. Taylor's from her own force and will have his own coterie of supporters, she's not going to have an easy time of it.

311

But she's clearly made of strong stuff, the Police Service needs more people like Suzi Lessard in it. Which leads me nicely on to perhaps the most important question of all. You mention in your e mail that there are several other women from his home force who have been victims of sexual assaults, and that Suzi was undertaking to speak to them to see if they would be prepared to testify against Taylor, do you have any update on that?'

'I'm due to speak to Suzi early next week, she messaged me a couple of days ago to say she's spoken with three of the women. Two have said they are prepared to give statements about what happened to them while the other one, a very young PC is still considering it. Suzi has one more woman to speak to, an older civilian who works in the Force's media office. She's been on annual leave but is now back at work, so as I said, I'm hoping by early next week to have a much better idea of where we stand. I take it you're thinking of using the Moorov Doctrine if we take this all the way?'

'You've got it in one. Moorov is ideal for this type of case. A series of offences connected closely in time, character and circumstance where the evidence of one witness in a series of two or more separate offences is capable of providing corroboration for the evidence of a witness in the other cases. It's perfect Mini, you couldn't wish for a better set of circumstances to go after someone using the Moorov Doctrine. And I'm now going to contradict what I said earlier. If it transpires that Taylor is alleged to have drugged any of his other victims, then the spiked sample could come back into play, but only if he's tried the same tactic on one or more of the other women. That's the beauty of using Moorov as the basis of our case.'

'Excellent, that's what I thought. I've never actually been involved with a case that has used the doctrine before, but I've read all the case law regarding its use, it's an absolute lifeline in terms of prosecuting sexual offences cases which are notoriously difficult to prove.'

'Ok, let's not get carried away, there's still a long way to go before we get Taylor in a court of law. And I need to say to you that if you're going ahead with this then it needs to be done properly. You need to lodge a formal complaint and then let an enquiry team be appointed and give them space to do their job. Once the complaint is raised you can't be involved. You are the complainer and a principal witness, everything must be done strictly by the book, we don't want to give the man any wriggle room whatsoever, I can't stress that enough.'

Chapter 30

Friday 7th May

The morning meeting that had been scheduled to start at 8am was now more than two hours late. Mini had conducted the latest of her media briefings from the conference room at Aikenhead Road first thing that morning. Unusually, for this morning's briefing, she had been accompanied by the ACC Crime. Perhaps that was an indication of the seriousness of the case. Even for a Force the size of Strathclyde, a triple murder investigation was something of a rarity. That, and Walter McSorley's relentlessly linking it with the Bible John Murders of thirty years ago, meant it was now attracting media attention from all over the world. Once again Mini Cooper had been on top of her game, answering a plethora of questions from the BBC, STV and Sky News. Most of the national print media had representatives present and again she took time to answer each of their questions in turn. Unruffled and assured, it had been a masterclass in how to manage the media. Jan who had been watching at the back door had to step out for a moment to suppress a laugh as she watched Mini quite deliberately ignoring McSorley's frantic efforts to catch her eye. Jumping up and down like a demented jack in the box only made matters worse, there wasn't a snowball's chance in hell that he was going to get to ask a question.

The Evening Times might lay claim to being the only evening paper printed in Glasgow, but that cut no ice, McSorley came way down the pecking order when it came to who got to ask questions at a media briefing of international interest. McSorley was incandescent with rage as, not for the first time, he found himself being very publicly ignored. It might have been unprofessional and unnecessarily petty on the part of the DCI, but who cared, this was payback time. Slighting McSorley gave Mini a warm glow, it was a small victory even though most others in the room were oblivious to it.

At the conclusion of the media briefing, it was straight back down to business. Mini grabbed the daily briefing note that as usual Con had prepared for her and left on her desk. It gave a brief outline of everything else that was going on in the Division that was not directly related to the murder enquiry. She needed to keep herself apprised of all matters that were relevant to the CID, so she digested the two-page document as she headed along the corridor to the incident room. Bob Thomson was already sitting at a desk when she got there, and he had some interesting news for her. From his enquiries, it appeared that Lesley Craig, the nurse who along with Maureen Goodall, had assisted at Mildred Donaldson's operation, had passed away more than six years ago. From what he could glean there appeared to be nothing suspicious about her death. She had retired from nursing and had been living in West Kilbride, but a little more than two years after leaving Ross Hall she had developed ovarian cancer. She died less than a year after her diagnosis. That line of enquiry had come to a shuddering halt.

Bob also had some news on Kenneth Sheridan, the anaesthetist who had assisted Magnus DeVilliers during Mrs Donaldson's operation. Bob had spent hours on the telephone trying to track Sheridan down. That had been no easy task, but his perseverance had paid off, although he still hadn't managed to speak to Sheridan in person. That responsibility now lay in the hands of Interpol, but at least he knew where he was. It transpired that Sheridan had emigrated to Australia in 1995, a year after Mildred's operation. Initially, he had been working as an anaesthetist in a hospital in Perth, Western Australia. That had been until a year ago when he had left the medical profession to pursue an altogether different vocation. From what Bob had been able to establish, Kenneth Sheridan was now in training to become a Benedictine Monk and was living as part of a monastic community in New Norcia, a small town 130 km north of Perth.

Bob's doggedness had paid off, he had established the whereabouts of Kenneth Sheridan, but now Mini was in a quandary, and she really needed the assistance of Campbell, her most capable detective.

That wasn't a reflection on Bob, he was a tenacious and hardworking officer, the problem was he also had mild dyslexia. That affected his ability to write coherent reports, being brutally honest it was fair to say his written work left a little to be desired. If Interpol were going to interview Sheridan, she really needed Campbell's skills to accurately outline the circumstances of their enquiry and to provide very specific details on what they wanted their Australian colleagues to speak to Sheridan about. That, unfortunately, would have to wait as Campbell had already left to attend court. It was the third time in the last ten days that he'd been cited for court. That was an occupational hazard for a busy detective. The more suspects you arrested and reported, the more likely you were to be cited for court. With an ongoing enquiry of this complexity, it was something they could all have done without; regrettably, there was nothing anyone could do about it. Campbell had tried to get himself on standby, which would have meant he could have remained at the office, but as the Fiscal was confident that the trial would go ahead that day, he wanted Campbell at the court, primed and ready to give his evidence.

It was twenty past eleven by the time the morning meeting finally finished, there had been a lot to get through. As well as updating the team about the status of Kenneth Sheridan and Lesley Craig, Mini had hoped to provide an update on the findings of Zander Muir's postmortem that was taking place that morning. But by the time she had finished going over the rest of that morning's business the detectives who had gone to observe the PM had still not arrived back.

Asif looked nervously at his watch. He really needed to get going, Mrs Holgate had told him that the best time to catch Mrs Muir would be late morning, just before lunchtime. Early in the morning didn't suit as she liked a lie in and when she did get up it took a while to get her breakfast and get organised. She was also in the habit of going for a walk in the park or popping down to the church in the early afternoon so late morning or later in the afternoon were the best times to catch her. He was putting on his jacket and gathering up his paperwork to leave when Mini asked him to go through to her office, she needed him to do her a favour.

While Campbell was away at court, she wanted him to prepare the timeline of events that surrounded the death of Mildred Donaldson. It was urgent. Getting Interpol to interview Kenneth Sheridan was now her number one priority so this needed to be done quickly. She explained that with his unsurpassed reputation for remembering dates and times, coupled with his assiduous and accurate note taking, he could be of great assistance to Campbell in outlining the timeline of events. When Campbell got back from court, she was going to ask him to prepare their interview strategy outlining the questions they wanted their Australian colleagues to ask Sheridan.

With a rising sense of frustration, Asif tried to explain that he had still to interview Mrs Muir, and in the absence of knowing what she might be able to tell them about Mildred Donaldson, any timeline he could compile would potentially be missing a vital piece of the story. But it was too late. Jan had stuck her head round the door to say that the Chief Superintendent wanted to speak to the DCI right away.

Asif sighed as he watched his boss disappear down the corridor. He really wanted to speak to Mrs Muir before he undertook this piece of work, but circumstances had conspired against him, he just had to suck it up and get on with it. He lifted the phone and called Mrs Holgate; it would now be late afternoon before he would get a chance to get down to Queen's Drive.

Asif had just put pen to paper when his mobile phone rang. It was a call from his wife, Roisin. She rarely contacted him when he was at his work but as it was such a glorious day, she thought she would take Caelan to the park later, to play on the swings, and she wondered if he might be able to join them. At breakfast she'd remembered that he'd said that some of the enquiry team were going for a drink in the Bungo on Nithsdale Road before they went to Shimla Pinks for their curry. If he was going to be in the area, she hoped he might be able to join them, at the playpark next to Balvicar Street, even if it was just for a short time. It had been ages since Asif had been able to take Caelan to the park and he was missing his dad. Asif's heart ached as he listened to Roisin. He missed his son dreadfully; it had been far too long since they'd been able to do anything as a family. The murder enquiry was having a detrimental impact on all their lives. So right there and then he agreed that they would meet. It might only be for half an hour or so, but it would just be the tonic that they were all needing.

It had taken him the best part of two hours to prepare the timeline. He'd never been involved with anything that was going to be used by an overseas Force before, so it was important that it was done properly. He would have done that anyway; his professionalism would have seen to that, and he sure as hell wouldn't dream of giving Campbell or DCI Cooper any work that wasn't done to the highest standards. Reputations are hard-won but they can be very easily and quickly undone. He'd seen it happen to others, so he wasn't going to let his standards slip now. That meant every time, day, and date had to be checked and double checked. It was a slow and methodical process. Less than three pages wasn't much to show for his efforts, writing the actual paper had been straightforward enough, most of the time had been taken up going through his notes checking salient facts. But it was done now and as Mini was nowhere to be seen he photocopied it and left the original on her desk. He now had an hour to kill before he had to call on Mrs Muir, so he accompanied Jan over to Asda to buy a bottle of malt and a card from the money she'd collected for Con's birthday.

*

Asif loosened his tie and slung his jacket over his shoulder as he made his way up the steep incline of Prospecthill Road en route to Queen's Drive. For the second day running the temperature was in the mid-seventies and by the time he reached the junction with Cathcart Road he was sweating profusely. Large damp patches appeared under both armpits; his choice of a pale blue shirt now seemed a poor one on such a sweltering afternoon. Rivulets of sweat streamed down between his shoulder blades, collecting in the small of his back saturating the back of his shirt, it was most unpleasant.

It was two minutes to three when he arrived at his destination. Trying to make himself presentable he mopped his brow and neck with a handkerchief. He put on his jacket and rang the bell. The door was answered by Mrs Holgate. The look on her face told him all he needed to know; Mrs Muir had gone AWOL again.

'I'm really sorry officer but I'm afraid you've just missed her. I did tell her you were coming around three, but she said you could come down to the church if you wanted to speak to her. There's a wedding in the church tomorrow apparently and she wanted to get ahead with the flower arrangements. I feel bad that you've wasted your time once again.'

Asif smiled and shook his head.

'There's no need to apologise it's not your fault. And it isn't the first time it's happened I can assure you. It comes with the territory. But no harm done. I'll just pop down to the church and try and catch her there, I think you told me it was in Maybank Street, is that correct?'

Mrs Holgate smiled. 'Nothing wrong with your memory officer, yes the Church of the Temple Mount, it's on the corner of Maybank Street and Albert Avenue, it's only a five-minute walk from here.'

The Temple Mount Church was a rather plain looking single storey building. The dark green front doors were showing their age and in need of a lick of paint while the outer walls were covered in a dull rather non-descript brown harling. The roof appeared to be made of corrugated sheeting and the guttering, which hung down on the left-hand side of the building was missing a couple of brackets. Other than a weather-beaten maroon notice board that was partially hidden by an overgrown laburnum tree, there was nothing to distinguish that the building was a church. Asif peered at the faded board.

Sunday Worship 1030 am, Bible Study Tuesdays 7.30 pm, Prayer Meeting, Thursdays 10 am. Pastor: A.C. Rudd MSc,BD.

Pushing open the unlocked front door, Asif stepped into a small glass-panelled vestibule. The inside of the church could not have been more different than the drab exterior. The magnolia-coloured walls appeared to have been freshly painted as had the ceiling from which hung eight ornate gold lightshades. On each side of the building were three oblong shaped stained-glass windows, in the afternoon sunshine, streams of light poured through the south facing windows causing pools of colours to form irregular shapes on the opposite wall.

Running down the centre of the sanctuary was a royal blue carpet. On either side of the carpet sat eight rows of beechwood chairs with upholstered seat cushions that matched the colour of the carpet. At the front of the sanctuary two steps led up to the chancel on which stood a plain and rather solid looking oak lectern. An enormous leather-bound bible lay open on the lectern, two silk ribbons, one blue and one green, indicated the place of the last reading. Dominating the centre of the chancel was a large communion table, which also appeared to be made of oak. Immediately behind the table stood a high-backed wooden chair with intricate religious symbols carved into the arm supports and splat. Asif could make out the shape of a fish and a lamb and what he thought looked like a dove. Behind the chair was the pièce de résistance, a large arched shaped stained glass window depicting Christ on the cross with his mother Mary, Mary Magdalene, and Mary of Clopas weeping at his feet.

Asif was a devout Muslim, but he was married to a Roman Catholic and together they had visited several grand Christian churches. Few he'd been in could match the beauty and majesty of the window in this unprepossessing building. He stood for a moment soaking in the magnificence of the spectacular window. Distracted by its splendour, he hadn't noticed the old woman coming in through a side door carrying an armful of freshly cut flowers. The old lady, tall and remarkably erect for a woman her age, wore a smart dark green tweed jacket and skirt. Her brushed back hair, the colour of freshly fallen snow, sat stiffly around her face. She smiled at Asif as she started to stick the stems into a green oasis that was sitting on top of a black metal stand.

'I think I know who you are. Mrs Holgate said it had been an Asian officer who had called yesterday. Are you from around here? Because nowadays we have lots of Asian's living in this neighbourhood.'

The old lady's directness caught Asif slightly off guard, but he sensed that she wasn't trying to be rude, it was an honest question from a lady who, over the decades, must have seen innumerable changes in the city of her birth.'

'Crossmyloof, about a mile away Mrs Muir. I take it you are Mrs Muir?'

'You are correct, Georgina Muir's my name, and you are?'

'Detective Constable Butt, Aikenhead Road CID, ma'am. And first of all, can I offer my condolences about the loss of your son, his death must have come as quite a shock.'

Mrs Muir turned to face Asif. She spoke very deliberately and with no apparent emotion.

'It's never easy losing a close loved one officer, least of all when it's your own child, it's not how things are supposed to happen, the natural order has been disrupted, there will be a reason for it, but that's something only God knows, mere mortals like you and me, are just left to wonder. I'll have to wait until I pass into God's glory, he has dominion over all our lives. Only then will I understand why my son died.'

Zander Muir had suffered an untimely and violent death, Asif knew that Mrs Muir was aware of the circumstances surrounding her son's murder, but as

Mrs Muir appeared to be very much in control of her faculties and going about her business in much the same way she always did, he thought it appropriate to ask the very obvious question, did she know of anyone that might want her son dead?

Mrs Muir sat down on a chair at the front of the church. She thought for a moment then shook her head.

'Honestly officer, I've no idea. I can't give you any specific names, but I know that Alexander sailed close to the wind at times, through his work he dealt with some dubious characters, do you know about his problem with the Law Society?'

Asif nodded.

'Well after that he couldn't be too fussy where his clients came from, he knew I didn't approve so he didn't talk about it much, although it seemed to pay him very well, he moved house and went on expensive holidays with his numerous girlfriends. That was another thing I didn't approve of, twice divorced and he changed girlfriends more often than most folk change their socks. It really was most unedifying. Are you familiar with the expression 'If you fly with the crows then you get shot with the crows.'

'Yes, I've heard that expression many times.'

'Well, that's what I think happened to my son, he got in with the wrong crowd, a really bad crowd and got mixed up in something he shouldn't have, and now he's dead. What a waste, he was still relatively young and had his retirement years to look forward to. Now all that's gone and as I said to you earlier, only our gracious God knows the reasons why.'

Asif came over and sat down next to Mrs Muir, he felt sure she was telling the truth, she didn't have any idea who had murdered her son. But now Asif wanted to pursue another line of enquiry.

'Can I talk to you for a moment about Mildred Donaldson? I'm aware that she died in hospital several years ago, but Mrs Holgate told me you had been good friends, and she was the reason that you got involved with this church.'

The mention of Mildred's name brought a smile to Mrs Muir's face. 'She was just the loveliest person. Kind and gentle and oh so talented. Embroidery, flower arranging, she even did pottery at one time I believe. I met her in the park over by the boating pond the first summer I moved here, we used to watch the men sailing their boats. She was much younger than me, but we became firm friends, and you're right officer, it was Mildred who invited me to come to this church. I only knew her for about 18 months before she died. She used to do the flower arranging like I do now. Her death was so unexpected; she went in for a routine operation on her throat and died two days later of a heart attack. Nobody could quite believe it.'

'That was most unfortunate, I think she was only 63 when she died, so not old.'

'That's correct officer, 63, and she really was very fit. Of course, it hit her son Gabriel hardest of all. He was in his early thirties when his mother died, he was extremely close to his mother. Mildred's husband had died when Gabriel was just a young child, so their bond was strong, I know she worried about him a lot. He was always a bit of a loner, a bit sullen and quite introverted, he didn't say a great deal. He still comes to church, but it's not every week, although he still regularly attends Pastor Rudd's bible study group. Pastor Rudd says that

Gabriel's bible knowledge is better than his own, that's something handed down from his mother, she had an encyclopaedic knowledge of the bible. I could have introduced you to Gabriel, he was here earlier but he seems to have disappeared again, the same thing happened the other day when I was here, I'd literally just arrived when he disappeared without saying a word. Come to think of it he's been acting strangely for several weeks. As I said he's a bit of a peculiar character, quite deep. I've always tried to help him when I can, mainly out of respect for his dear mother. That's mainly been through financial support but not always. I gave him Alexander's contact details a couple of months ago. He came into church one Sunday in a right old tizz about something, he said he needed urgent legal advice regarding a family matter. So, I gave him my son's number. Not that I got any thanks for it, and he's been surly and evasive ever since. Anyway, I digress. I expect he'll be back sometime this afternoon; all his stuff is still on the table at the back of the church.

Asif opened his folder and scribbled some notes.

'What do you mean all his stuff, what is it he does?'

Mrs Muir pointed to the stained glass windows. 'He designs and makes stained glass windows. Some of the windows in this church are his including the large one at the back of the chancel. Beautiful, isn't it? Especially on a day like this with the sunlight streaming through it. It's a shame because most of his work used to be making windows for churches, he travelled all over the country doing it. But with dwindling congregations and when money's tight, there isn't the same demand anymore. I've tried to help where I can, I commissioned the window nearest the door, the one depicting Jesus with some of his disciples, and I've also commissioned him to do a series of ten small panels for our church's 50th anniversary which will hang in the vestibule. He doesn't know I'm paying for it; he thinks the money's coming from the church, which in a way I suppose it is, but I'm underwriting the cost of it. But I don't like to advertise these things, I'm going to dedicate the panels to the memory of Mildred.'

Asif got up and walked over to a trestle table that was standing against the back wall of the sanctuary. A series of small panels, each about 6 inches by 8, were soldered together to form one continuous tableau. Laid out on the table were various small hand tools and other pieces of equipment. A soldering iron, glass cutter, and various knives and scalpels. On the floor underneath the table was a coil of rolled up lead and a grey canvas bag.

Asif studied the various glass panels. The first depicted some red liquid being poured from a terracotta vessel, the next was a collection of frogs of various sizes and colours, the third panel was of a group of people who seemed to be scratching their heads.

'It's excellent, isn't it?' exclaimed said Mrs Muir who had joined Asif at the table. 'So intricate and delicate. The panels represent the ten plagues of Egypt. Before Moses led the Israelites out of slavery and crossed the Red Sea. It's from the book of Exodus. It was Gabriel's suggestion. He said we didn't have anything in the church from the Old Testament, everything we have is from the New, and mostly depicts the life of Jesus. Pastor Rudd thought it would be a most interesting project so that's how it came about. He still has four of the panels to do so it's very much a work in progress.'

Asif stood and stared at the glass panels. He glanced down at the coil of lead under the table. His eyes scanned across the knives and scalpels that lay in size order on the table. Then he saw it, it was the confirmation he was looking for, now he was absolutely certain. The large craft knife with a rounded blade was missing its tip. It hit him like a thunderbolt, he was staring at the weapon that had murdered Zander Muir. He swallowed hard as he tried to remain calm.

'Mrs Muir, do you happen to know where Gabriel lives? I really need to speak to him quite urgently.'

'I'm sorry but I'm afraid I don't and there's no one else here at the moment that we could ask. I know he lives locally. Mildred used to stay in Niddrie Road and she was always popping round to Gabriel's to take him some soup or a hot meal. As I said to you, she worried about him. He must live nearby, that's about all I can tell you.'

Mrs Muir thought for a moment.

'You know come to think of it, I've seen him in the park before, eating his sandwiches at lunchtime, or having a flask of coffee in the afternoon, it's possible he could be there having a break, it's literally only two minutes away.'

Asif looked at his watch. It was just after half past three. He had nearly half an hour before he was due to meet Roisin. Mrs Muir's suggestion that Gabriel might have headed to the park wasn't a bad one. He would check it out, but first he needed to know what Gabriel Donaldson looked like as he didn't have the faintest idea.

'Can you tell me what Gabriel looks like and if you can remember what he was wearing when you saw him earlier that would be very useful?'

Mrs Muir considered the question. 'He's not very tall, maybe 5' 6", medium build I'd say and a right scruffy individual. He's always unshaven, which I disapprove of, makes a man look untidy, and he will insist on wearing that silly woollen hat, even when he's in church. I think that's very disrespectful, but Pastor Rudd doesn't seem to mind. He says ladies wear hats in church so we shouldn't judge Gabriel if he choses to wear one.'

Asif jotted down his description. 'That's very useful Mrs Muir, but is there anything you can tell me about what he had on today?'

Mrs Muir made a strange snorting noise. 'He had on that awful T-shirt again, it's black and the front has a demonic looking angel on it, in fiery red and orange. Apparently, it's supposed to represent Abaddon, the angel of the abyss from the book of Revelation. It's the last book of the New Testament. We were studying it recently in our bible study group, but I stopped going, I really don't care for the apocalyptic nature of it, the four horsemen, and the beast with seven heads and ten horns. No thank you. I'm much more attracted to the Gospels and the Acts of the Apostles.'

Asif looked up. 'But I take it Gabriel liked it, is that why he wears the T-shirt?'

Mrs Muir sighed. 'He loved it. He kept pestering Pastor Rudd with more and more questions, quite dark questions, I found it a bit unsettling, that's why I stopped going. And ever since that bible study he's worn that infernal T-shirt, never seems to have it off, that can't be hygienic, can it? I know his mother would have disapproved.'

Chapter 31

Mini Cooper had not been expecting to hear from Suzi Lessard until early next week so her phone call on Friday afternoon came somewhat out of the blue. But what she had to tell Mini couldn't wait, it was urgent, and it was not good news.

The young Tayside officer, a woman by the name of Elspeth Baird, who had been thinking over whether she could give a statement and testify against Chief Superintendent Taylor had got back to Suzi to say that she wasn't, under any circumstances, going to get involved in any complaint against Taylor. That, in itself, was disappointing, but there was worse to come. It transpired that Baird worked in the same department as a female AP Inspector who, just happened to have been the other officer drinking with Mini and Taylor in the bar at Tulliallan ahead of the AP dinner more than a week ago. Having initially gone to seek her advice, what the Inspector told Baird left her completely floored and dispelled any notion that she could go out on a limb and contemplate pursuing a complaint against such a senior and powerful officer.

Over the phone Suzi Lessard explained what Elspeth Baird had said to her. Baird alleged that the Inspector had told her that after the dinner was over, she, and DCI Elaine Cooper, had accepted Chief Superintendent

Taylor's invitation to go back to his room for more drinks. According to the Inspector, over the next couple of hours the three of them consumed the best part of a litre bottle of vodka. That was on top of copious amounts of wine and port that had been drunk at the dinner. As a result, all three were much the worse for drink. But it was what Baird told Suzi next that was the bombshell. The Inspector alleged that along with DCI Cooper she had indulged in consensual sex with the Chief Superintendent in his room. She also insisted that she had been in the room the entire time that DCI Cooper had been there, and in fact, hadn't left the room until sometime after DCI Cooper. Nothing that the Inspector said suggested that any drink had been spiked by Taylor, it was never mentioned.

This new information of what was alleged to have happened on that fateful night had just turned the unfortunate episode on its head. This was a complete disaster. Any possibility that Taylor could be charged with rape, or any other offences for that matter, had almost certainly disappeared. Taylor had an eyewitness, a middle ranking officer, who was prepared to testify that the sexual activity that took place in that room was consensual. No court in the land would convict on that evidence, in fact the case wouldn't even get to court, the Fiscal and Crown Office just wouldn't entertain it.

Apoplectic with rage and with a face the colour of puce, Mini Cooper smashed her fist off her desk.

'Fucking hell, Suzi. Taylor's nobbled that Inspector, he must have, there's no other explanation for it. The lying bitch. I don't even think she was there, but of course I can't be certain because that bastard spiked my fucking drink! Shit, I can't believe this is happening, this is a nightmare, I want to be sick.'

'Ma'am, I'm so sorry, but I knew you'd want to know as soon as possible. Of course, and just for your information, I haven't approached or spoken to the Inspector as I didn't want to compromise any potential enquiry. But for what it's worth, her name is Clair Moodie, I don't know her personally, but I've got it on good account that she'd shag any boss if she thought it would help her career prospects, she's got history. I'm gutted to be the one bringing you this news, I know it's not what you wanted to hear.'

The silence that followed spoke volumes. Mini was stunned and fighting to control her anger. She took several slow and very deliberate deep breaths. Eventually she felt able to respond.

'First of all, Suzi, I want to thank you for all that you've done. You didn't need to get involved in any of this, but you still did it and that speaks volumes about your integrity, and I want you to know that I appreciate everything you've done for me. I just hope none of this is going to make your life more difficult, you know as well as I do how people close ranks to protect their own, so you be careful. It's an aspect of this job that I absolutely loathe, it's supposed to be 2004, but it might as well still be the dark ages as far as policing is concerned. And do you know what makes it even more hurtful and harder to deal with? It was one of our own, it was another female officer who sold me out. It's despicable, but I don't know why I'm surprised, in a male dominated job women acquiesce to their demands all the time. Just to be accepted and to get on, it's always been that way. You know, sometimes I don't know why I joined this bloody organisation.'

Their conversation had lasted less than five minutes but in that short space of time Mini's world had turned upside down. Putting down the phone she got up and put on her jacket. She was looking for her handbag under her desk when Jan stuck her head around the door.

'I'm making coffee for Con and myself would you like one? And for your information Campbell's just off the phone, he's clear from court but he says he's now heading for his dental appointment and will see us later. No idea where Asif has got to, so it looks like it's just you, me and Con. Can I make you a mug?'

Mini shook her head as she headed for the door. 'Not for me Jan, I'm needing to get out of this bloody office, get some air and clear my head, I've got some serious thinking to do. And anyway, it's alcohol rather than Coffee I'm needing right now. I'll see you in the pub at 1700 hrs as arranged and if you're there first, mine's a large Malbec.'

*

Queen's Park was teeming with folk when Asif entered the park through the gate on Balvicar Street. That was hardly a surprise as the temperature was nudging 75 degrees and there wasn't a hint of breeze. Everywhere you looked people were sunbathing or sitting on the grass enjoying picnics in the unseasonably warm weather. The swing park, alive with the shrieks of toddlers and young children was a hive of activity. Asif scanned the seats to the side of the swings and the queue of people waiting patiently for ice cream at a van parked near to the park gates. There was no sign of anybody fitting Gabriel Donaldson's description.

Following the line of the footpath Asif picked his way past innumerable dog walkers and kids on scooters as he headed towards the boating pond. Once again there was no trace of his target. He sat down on the only vacant seat next to an overweight teenager wearing headphones who was busy stuffing himself with Doritos from an enormous bag while slurping a lurid blue slush puppy drink through a straw. Asif doubted if the teenager had been anywhere near a shower in days as the smell of B.O was quite overpowering, you didn't need to be a detective to know why the seat next to him had been left vacant. Asif was about to move on when his eyes fixed on something unusual on the far side of the pond. He'd noticed a figure in a black T-shirt standing with his back to him holding a plastic bag. But it was what he was wearing on his head that made him stand out. He was wearing a black woollen beanie hat. On such a hot day, nobody else was wearing that type of headwear, the look was incongruous, he stuck out like a sore thumb. Asif watched as the man, slightly built and of below average height, turned round so he was now facing him. He was too far away to make out the figure on the front of his T-shirt, but it was definitely brightly coloured. That and the man's general dishevelled appearance could only mean one thing. He was certain he was looking at Gabriel Donaldson, the man he believed had killed Magnus DeVilliers, Maureen Goodall, and Zander Muir. His mouth felt suddenly dry, this was like a scene from a T.V drama, in his eight years in the job he'd never encountered anything remotely like it. His heart beat hard against his chest. Trying to remain calm he reached into his jacket pocket and removed his police radio, the next few minutes might just prove to be the most important of his police career, now like never before he needed to be thinking clearly, he needed back up and he needed it quickly.

Asif stared in disbelief at the blank screen on his radio. Shit, his battery was dead. In his haste to get to Queen's Drive after completing his note for the DCI, he had forgotten to put in a fresh battery. That was a schoolboy error, now he had no means of speaking directly to his control room. Reaching into his trouser pocket he pulled out his mobile phone, mercifully that was nearly fully charged, all was not yet lost. But his suspect was now on the move, he didn't have time to phone, he couldn't afford to let Donaldson out of his sight, he needed to see where he was going.

Asif retraced his steps back to the seats next to the swing park. He had assumed that Donaldson would be heading back to the church. He had assumed wrong. Coming out of the park gates Donaldson went left, in the other direction from the church and headed towards Pollokshaws Road. He glanced back as he reached the main road, and for a couple of seconds was looking directly at Asif. Frozen to the spot Asif felt his heart rate surge, what if he'd been recognised? It felt like an eternity, before Donaldson turned back and continued walking without quickening his step.

Asif exhaled deeply; he hadn't been recognised, his was just another face in the crowd. He felt slightly nauseous, if he'd blown his cover, he could have jeopardised the whole investigation, it didn't bear thinking about.

Using other pedestrians as cover he began to follow his target from a safe distance. It appeared that Donaldson was heading in the direction of Shawlands. They'd only gone a few hundred metres when Donaldson suddenly angled across the pavement to the edge of the kerb waiting to cross the road. Asif took cover behind a large Chestnut tree. Taking his chance between a bus and a van, Donaldson ran across the road and up the path of the tenement at number 85 Pollokshaws Road. A blond sandstone tenement almost directly opposite the boating pond.

From his vantage point behind the tree, Asif stared at the entrance to the close. Number 85, surely that had to be a coincidence. But was it? Asif's brain was now in overdrive. Con had been adamant that the killer was playing mind games with them. Perhaps Con was right? Why had Donaldson gone in the close at number 85, the very number that had been written in blood at each murder location? Had that been some sort of subliminal message, the more he thought about it the more possible it seemed. And as he'd pointed out to Campbell at Ross Hall, Donaldson begins with the letter 'D', was that just a coincidence as well? He didn't think so as he sprinted across the road narrowly avoiding an oncoming black taxicab.

Chapter 8 and verse 5 of Deuteronomy might prove to be nothing more than a convenient red herring, a clever ruse designed to confuse and throw the police off the scent. Whatever the motivation, at this precise moment it didn't matter. What was imperative was establishing the whereabouts of Gabriel Donaldson. Asif desperately needed to know which flat he'd gone into.

His eyes ran up and down the list of names on the control panel. But that didn't tell him anything, rainwater had penetrated the box causing most of the names to become completely illegible. There no trace of the name Donaldson. He stood back onto the pavement and gazed up at the bay windows of the three-storey building. All but one of the flats had been double-glazed, the one that hadn't, one up left, had decrepit rotting wooden frames, in fact the pane on the left side of the three windows that made up the bay, had a piece of cardboard covering a large crack. But it was what was sitting behind the centre pane that suggested it might be Donaldson's flat. Sitting on some form of stand was a large model ship. Gunmetal grey, it looked like some sort of gunboat of the type often featured in films about the Second World War. The letter D, number 85, and now a model boat almost identical to the one he had seen in Magnus DeVilliers study. Asif was certain he was looking at Donaldson's flat.

The controlled entry system didn't appear to be working so Asif pushed the door open and entered the close. Hugging the side wall, he crept his way up the stairs to the first-floor landing where he found both storm doors lying open. An official looking white envelope together with several flyers for fast-food shops lay on a coir door mat in front of a glass-panelled front door. He stared inside. The hallway looked Spartan. Against the far wall an old gateleg table stood on bare floorboards and other than a rack of empty coat hooks the hall appeared devoid of furniture. He picked up the envelope and studied the address. Gabriel Donaldson, Flat 3, 85 Pollokshaws Road. Asif never saw the man come up behind him, that was the moment when his lights went out.

*

Mini had phoned Natalie and asked her to meet her at the boating pond. She had made a decision but now she

337

needed her girlfriend's approval. She'd been thinking of doing it for a few days but somehow today's events had forced her hand. It felt appropriate to do it now. She needed a hug and after her distressing call with Suzi Lessard she needed to feel loved. She wanted Natalie to join her at the Bungo for drinks with the team. With Natalie's agreement, she was going to make their relationship public. No more having to be discreet, arranging clandestine date nights, she was done with that. Natalie had moved into her flat last week, they had nothing to hide, now was the right time to tell their colleagues that they were an item.

Mini found a seat on a bench on the side of the pond nearest to Pollokshaws Road. It was Natalie's weekend off, so she'd gone shopping in town, but she'd texted to say that she was now on the train to Queen's Park, she'd be at the park in less than ten minutes. Mini's heart skipped a beat, there was something affirming about announcing their relationship, a weight had been lifted off her shoulders, for the first time in quite a while she felt happy. More than fifteen minutes had passed before a waving Natalie came into view. They embraced warmly.

'Sorry I'm a bit late but I bumped into Roisin, Asif's wife near to the swing park. She had Caelan their toddler with her. I recognised Roisin straight away, I'd met her at a couple of shift night outs when she was going out with Asif, she's a beautiful looking girl, very striking.'

Mini raised her eyebrows.

'Stop it. You know I don't mean it like that, but she is very pretty, and Caelan is just the most gorgeous wee boy. Big brown eyes and a great mop of dark curly hair. Anyway, they were supposed to be meeting Asif at the swings at four, just for half an hour before he hooked up with you and the others at the Bungo, but he's failed to trap. She's tried phoning several times but he's not answering, it rings and then goes on to his voicemail.'

Mini looked at her watch. It had gone twenty-five past four. It wasn't like Asif to be late, and in her experience, he always answered his phone promptly.

'I know he was going to Queen's Drive to speak to Zander Muir's mother, but that was at three. He should be clear of that by now, and anyway that doesn't explain him not answering his phone, that is most unlike him.'

*

When Asif came to, he was strapped to a chair with cable ties pulled tight around his wrists and ankles. Several layers of gaffer tape covered his mouth forcing him to breathe though his nose, a process made more difficult by the early onset of his summer hay fever. His head hot and throbbing felt like it had been hit by a sledgehammer. Rivulets of blood trickled slowly from the wound on the back of his head down the collar of his shirt and between his shoulder blades. His instinct to squirm trying to loosen the ties had no effect. Each tiny movement caused the plastic bands to bite deeper into his flesh, blood started to ooze from the weals on his wrists. Asif knew he was in deep, deep trouble.

His seat had been placed in the middle of what Asif assumed was the lounge. It was difficult to tell as the walls were stripped back to ancient plaster and there was no carpet on the floor. A dust covered light bulb hung from a brown twisted flex above his head. Standing six feet away immediately in front of the bay window was a white Formica table on which stood the

339

grey coloured gunboat. Made of metal, the starboard side of the three-foot-long boat looked across to the boating pond on the other side of the road. From his chair he could see families enjoying the late afternoon sunshine, he was supposed to be there with his wife and young son, he felt tears welling in his eyes. He was fighting hard just to stay in control.

His police radio and mobile phone had been taken from his jacket and placed on the Formica table. Asif's eyes darted nervously from side to side, there was no sight or sound of his assailant. Looking over his left shoulder he could see a folded-up golf trolley and black canvas bag propped against the wall near to the door, next to a threadbare brown sofa. Pinned to the wall over to his right was what looked like a handwritten letter, and a series of newspaper cuttings, most, but not all, had been taken from the Evening Times, each one a more lurid headline than the last. There was even a double centre spread with a profile of McSorley, the Glasgow hack on the trail of a triple killer, screamed the headline. His smug face stared back at Asif; it was a face you wouldn't get sick of punching. D, 8 5 was Scrawled in red paint above the cuttings, everywhere he looked was confirmation that Donaldson was the killer. Helpless and alone he started to contemplate his own fate, he hated himself for doing it, he knew he needed to stay strong, but he was human and right now he was shit scared.

He turned back to face the window as he heard footsteps approaching. He sat rock still staring straight ahead as Donaldson walked to the table and picked up Asif's phone. He studied the screen saver and smiled as he crouched down in front of Asif only inches from his face. It was the second time that day a man with poor personal hygiene had offended the detective. His breath stank, a peculiar odour of rotten eggs and raw onion. Asif gagged and turned his face away just as his phone started to ring. Donaldson looked at the screen and pointed to the phone.

'It's Roisin, I take it she's your wife, or perhaps she's your girlfriend, is that the girl who's on your screen saver with the wee boy?'

Asif didn't respond, he stared right through Donaldson.

His show of defiance was not well received. Donaldson reached into his pocket and pulled out a red handled craft knife. He pushed the blade against Asif's throat.

'Don't play fucking games with me detective, I asked you if she was your wife?'

Asif made the merest of nods. The phone rang again, Donaldson moved to the window and looked across to the park. Something had caught his attention. Three women and a child in a pushchair were gathered around a seat by the pond. Gesturing and animated, the woman with the distinctive silver pixie cut hair had her phone pressed to her ear. She was looking directly at the block of flats opposite. Donaldson turned back and approached Asif.

'She's got a very distinctive look your wife, a pretty lady.' Donaldson pressed the craft knife hard against Asif's neck. 'And tell me this detective, is the child your first born?'

Without thinking Asif nodded again. Donaldson's eyes widened with delight.

'Excellent news, then I think It's time for Abaddon to pay another visit.'

Asif felt suddenly sick. God, what had he done? A momentary lapse and Donaldson had the affirmation he was looking for. He was going to enact the tenth plague and the intended victim was going to be his son. Shaking uncontrollably anguished tears streamed down his cheeks; this was a nightmare being played out in real time. He hadn't heard what Donaldson said to him as he left the room, his mind was lost elsewhere, but he was aware of the front door closing. Fuck! He'd never felt so helpless and alone. To make matters even worse, Roisin and Caelan were no longer with Mini and Natalie, they had moved further up the path. He could see his wife, crouched down by the pushchair, helping Caelan throw bread to the ducks.

Desperate, he knew he had to do something to alert them of the danger, but what could he do? He was strapped to a chair, immobile and mute, how could he possibly warn them?

*

Standing at Shawlands Cross, Campbell rubbed his numb jaw gingerly. He doubted he'd be able to eat a curry without spilling most of it down his shirt, but at least his final visit to the dentist was done. Hopefully, he wouldn't need to go back for at least a year, he'd had quite enough of dentists these last few weeks. He took out his phone and called Asif, he thought it was five, but he couldn't remember what time they were supposed to be meeting at the Bungo. The phone rang and then went to voicemail. Strange, he thought, not like Asif not to answer. He tried Jan's number, she answered almost immediately.

'Hi Campbell, yes meeting at five, I'm with Con we're just approaching the Battlefield monument, we should be at the pub in 10 to 15 minutes. Nope,

I haven't spoken to Asif, he's been away most of the afternoon, expect he'll see us at the pub. Same goes for the DCI, she left some time ago, said she needed to clear her head, she seemed annoyed and distracted, somethings up just not sure what, again we might find out later. I take it you're heading to the Bungo now?'

'Yep, I'm at Shawlands Cross, I'll head into the park, might meet you on the way down. Mouth's still a bit numb, but I'm looking forward to a beer or two, it's been a while.'

Asif could see Donaldson, with his distinctive black beanie, heading towards the park gates at Balvicar Street. Surely that maniac wouldn't attack Roisin or his son in the middle of a park in broad daylight. More likely he'd follow them home and attack them there, it was almost too horrible to contemplate, racked with fear he planted his feet to the floor and rocked backwards and forwards in his chair. He started to move forwards in tiny increments. Slowly, inexorably, he inched closer to the table. He had to try and do something, anything that might draw his colleagues' attention. Nearly two minutes passed, he'd only moved a couple of feet towards the table. For his plan to work he needed to get closer. Close enough so that when he threw himself off balance, he would crash into the table knocking the metal boat off its cradle and into the fragile looking single glazed window. The model boat looked like it might be heavy, he hoped to God that it was, he needed it to smash the bay window. Across the road on the path by the pond, Mini and Natalie were still deep in conversation. He could see their faces happy and smiling, unaware of his unfolding trauma. They were so tantalisingly close, they couldn't be more than 75 yards away, it was now or never, he needed to get their attention and pray that their police instincts would then take over. It was his only hope. He had no other options; he was going all in, and the stakes couldn't be higher.

By the time that Asif had got himself close enough to the table to execute his plan, Donaldson was striding purposefully up the path towards the pond. Mercifully, Roisin and Caelan had finished feeding the ducks and had moved away. He could no longer see where they were. He shut his eyes and said a prayer, he prayed to Allah that he would see his wife and child again.

Pressing down hard with the balls of his feet he manipulated the chair so that he was almost side on with the table. It was now or never. Building momentum by rocking on the legs from side to side he launched himself at the table. Catching the edge with the full force of his left shoulder he upended the table. Asif crashed unceremoniously to the floor smacking his head off the solid wooden floor. The sound of smashing glass took away from his pain, he lay dazed and helpless on the floor, like a fish out of water, there was nothing more he could do.

'Holy shit, what in the hell was that?' Momentarily disorientated, Mini scanned the flats opposite looking for the source of the noise as large shards shattered into tiny fragments on the concrete path below the window.'

Natalie was quicker getting her bearings, she pointed to the first floor flat across the road.

'It's the centre window of the flat one up, look directly across the road, Number 85, you see it? The one with the model boat stuck on the window ledge, looks like the whole window's come away.'

344

Mini stared up at the broken window. 'What in God's name would have caused that?' It wasn't making any sense. She gazed up at the bow of the boat perched precariously on the window ledge, then she fixed her sights on the number at the entrance to the close. Mini Cooper hadn't been made a Chief Inspector with only 11 year's service for nothing. She was sharp and renowned for her agile brain; she made connections quicker than almost anybody and right now something important was dawning on her. A moment's more thought, the fog of the last three weeks was lifting, the puzzle was starting to make sense. A model boat and the number 85, both these figured in her enquiry. Also, more than a minute had now passed since the window was smashed, yet no one had come out of the close, neither had anyone appeared at the window. Her instincts told her that was important, in some strange way all these things were connected to her investigation. Someone had deliberately smashed that window; she just didn't know why.

'Right Natalie, follow me, we're going to check this out, I've got a feeling about this. Hold my bag, will you? I'm going over the railings.'

Using the stanchion to pull herself up, Mini scaled the metal fence and was now standing on the pavement.

'Here, pass me the bags and put your foot between the spikes and be careful, I can't afford to lose you!'

Dressed in her jeans and Converse, the six-foot railings presented little difficulty for someone as athletic as Natalie, she negotiated the fence effortlessly and seconds later the two friends were sprinting across the road towards the close at number 85. There was still no sign of anyone as they made their way to the first floor.

345

Both storm doors were lying open, Mini pressed her hands against the glass of the inner door, shielding her eyes from the sunlight that filled the flat, she peered in. There was nothing particularly untoward about the property except that it appeared to be unfurnished. It looked like it might be about to be redecorated ahead of new tenants moving in, one thing was certain, there was no sign of any movement within. Out of the corner of her eye she noticed a crumpled white envelope lying face up to the side of the doormat. She bent down and picked it up, someone had stood on it, a footprint of a shoe was clearly visible. Her eyes opened wide as she read the name and address. With a sinking feeling she turned to her colleague.

'Shit, this letter is addressed to a Gabriel Donaldson, Asif had left the office to visit a lady in Queen's drive, he was making enquiries about a Mildred Donaldson. He failed to turn up to meet his wife and child and he's not answering his phone. And now we're standing outside a flat occupied by someone called Gabriel Donaldson. Something's not right Natalie, I just know it, I think Asif's in here and I think he's in trouble.'

The look of bewilderment on Natalie's face said it all, she held up her hands.

'I don't have my police radio, I'm off duty, I've just got my phone. You?'

'Same. But there's no time, we need to get into the flat. I don't think anyone else is in there, they would have come out by now or appeared at the window. But they haven't. Give the bell a ring and when they don't answer we're going through that door.'

Natalie rang the bell several times but as Mini suspected there was no reply. Natalie looked aghast at her girlfriend.

'You're not planning to kick in the glass panel, are you? You'll slice your leg to threads if you put your foot through that glass. Happened to a boy on my shift, nearly severed an artery, he could have killed himself, he was off work for weeks.'

Natalie picked up a wooden broom that along with a plastic bucket had been stashed behind one of the storm doors.

'You could use the end of the handle; it might do the job.'

Mini wasn't convinced. She looked around her. On either side of the front door of the flat opposite were two decorative ceramic pots containing red geraniums. Mini picked one up.

'This is a better bet I think, got a bit of weight to it, now stand back just in case any glass comes flying our way.'

The plate glass panel was no match for the ceramic pot. Hurling the pot at the door, it shattered the panel just below the level of the Yale lock. The large pot spun across the hall spilling its compost and most of the plants over the floor. Pulling the cuff of her jacket down over her wrist Mini carefully reached in and unlocked the door.

She turned and winked at her colleague. 'Might be an idea to keep hold of that broom, eh, just in case.'

Natalie had her serious face on. 'No worries on that score, I wasn't intending to sweep up the mess, any person coming at us is getting sconed right over the head with this, I've got your back.'

As they entered the hall, they could hear sounds coming from a room over to their left. Several dull thuds, one after the other. Natalie tightened her grip on the broom handle, somebody was in the front room. Holding their breath, they peered round the frame of the door. Lying on the floor, still attached to the chair was their stricken colleague.

'Fuck me, there's nothing wrong with your powers of deduction, you were right, it is Asif, what the hell has been going on?'

In a flash Mini was across the room and kneeling on the floor and at the side of her detective. She found the edge of the gaffer tape covering his mouth.

'Brace yourself my friend, this is likely to hurt.' With one swift pull, Mini tore away the tape.

Asif's face contorted with pain, bits of skin and countless hairs attached themselves to the inside of the sticky tape, his bottom lip ripped raw started oozing blood.

Grabbing an arm each, his colleagues lifted him and the chair back onto its feet.

'Oh, I'm really sorry Asif, that looks painful. Natalie, see if you can find a knife or some scissors to cut these cable ties.'

The pain was the least of his worries. Licking the blood from his lips he blurted out.

'He's in the park, he's over there right now, he told me he's going after Roisin and Caelan, you've got to stop him. He's the killer, his name's Gabriel Donaldson and he's trying to murder my wife and son.'

The seriousness of the situation had just ratcheted up, Mini felt a surge of nervous energy, but she needed to remain calm, lives might depend on it.

'Ok, Asif, we hear you and we're going to stop him.' Mini took out her phone. 'I'm phoning Campbell right now, keep speaking to me Asif, I need an accurate description of Donaldson, tell me what he was wearing, what does that scumbag look like?'

Asif spat some blood onto the floor. 5'6", medium build, several days growth, he's wearing a black beanie hat and a black T-shirt, it's got a picture of an angel on the front in bright red and orange.'

*

'Just give me a minute Roisin, I'd better take this, It's the DCI. Yes boss, what can I do for you?'

Calmly, Mini relayed the information and description that Asif had given her. 'Black beanie and black T-shirt, brightly coloured on the front with a picture of an angel. The man's name is Gabriel Donaldson, he's our killer and according to Asif he's armed with some type of knife. He headed into the park just minutes ago, he's going after Roisin and Caelan, they're his next victims.'

Campbell turned away from Roisin and breathed deeply as he processed what Mini was telling him. For a moment he was speechless. In more than 25 years in the job, he'd never received a message of quite that magnitude. He kept talking to Mini as he scanned the dozens of faces that were coming and going all around him.

'You said you were with Asif, well tell him his wife and son are with me and are safe, I bumped into them coming into the park, they were heading home. I'm next to the mansion house, I'll keep them with me, just assure him they're both safe and well.'

Mini turned to Asif and smiled. 'Roisin and Caelan are with Campbell, they're safe Asif, it's going to be alright.'

Asif didn't hear what Mini said next, the relief hit him like a tidal wave, shaking uncontrollably, be broke down in floods of tears.'

'Boss, you still there, is anyone with you?'

'I'm here.' Replied Mini. 'I'm with Natalie and Asif, I'm going to keep this line open, I'm putting you on speaker phone.'

'Good, well in that case get one of them to phone Jan, I spoke to her five minutes ago, she's with Con and they were just approaching the park, they must be nearby, let's get three pairs of eyes looking for this psycho.'

'I'm on it.' said Natalie scrolling her contact list.

Gabriel Donaldson stopped abruptly at the fork in the footpath near to the mansion house. On the right-hand path, next to the five-a-side pitches, he could see the lady with the distinctive silver hair and his target, sitting in a pushchair drinking from a plastic cup. The woman appeared to be with a slightly overweight man with brown curly hair who was wearing a lightweight blue suit. He had his jacket slung over his shoulder and was speaking to someone on his mobile phone. Donaldson stood rock still staring down the path. The man in the blue suit looked familiar, he had seen his face before. Then it dawned on him, he remembered where he'd seen him. He was a police officer; he'd seen him standing outside Maureen Goodall's flat in Tankerland Road a couple of weeks ago. From their body language it was clear to Donaldson that the woman and the officer knew each other. Her shoulders were shaking, and now her head was pressed into the cop's shoulder, she appeared to be crying. He cursed his luck; his plan would need to be aborted.

Campbell pulled a packet of tissues from his pocket and passed one to Roisin. He handed her his phone as she dabbed her eyes.

'Asif's on the line, I think he would like a word with you.' As she spoke to her husband Campbell crouched down to talk to the child who was still busy drinking from his cup. He had next to no experience of small children, so his interaction was stilted and a little awkward.

'And when your mummy's finished talking, I expect your daddy will want a word with you as well.'

Caelan didn't seem to notice Campbell's awkwardness, he simply smiled and chuckled, blissfully unaware of the danger he'd been in.

Campbell winced as he stood up, thirty seconds in such an unnatural position had been more than enough for his ageing hips. Tentatively, he stretched, straightening his back and legs. Looking straight ahead his detective's eyes locked onto a face in the crowd. The man in the black beanie hat and brightly coloured T-shirt, was no more than a hundred yards away. Campbell knew exactly who he was looking at.

Over on the other path Jan and Con were now approaching the mansion house. They had been apprised of the circumstances by Natalie, they were on edge as they eyeballed every passerby. They were hunting the crowds for their prey.

Con reached out an arm and wrapped it around Jan's shoulders.

'Just play along will you, I want us to act like we're a couple, it's an old trick but it works like a charm every time, nobody suspects. I used it loads of times when I was in plainers. So, let's see if we can't flush the wee bastard out, where the fuck are you hiding Gabriel?'

Donaldson wasn't hanging about to see if Campbell had recognised him, he was on the move again, he needed to make himself scarce, he turned tail and hurried up the other path. That proved to be a fatal error of judgement.

He never saw Conway's boot coming. The kick, delivered at lightning speed, caught him right between the legs, poleaxed, he went down like a tree being felled, writhing and groaning on the ground in agony. Conway Niblett may have been in his fifties, but there was still life in the old dog. Donaldson's torment was not yet at an end. In a flash, Con had rolled him onto his front. Wedging his knee between Donaldson's shoulder blades, he grabbed both arms by the wrists and pressed down hard on the back of his hands. Donaldson squealed like a stuck pig; Gooseneck holds are designed to inflict pain. A group of teenage boys on bikes and a couple of dog walkers stopped to gawp at the spectacle.

'Police!- stay back, don't move, stay where you are. This man is under arrest!' Shouted Jan holding her warrant card aloft. The crowd of onlookers moved back on her command. With her free hand she carefully dialled 999. Calmly and very deliberately she explained who she was and where they were, they required back up and they needed it quickly. Requesting the assistance of her colleagues had never felt quite so good. Marked police vehicles were responding from all over the southside, help would be with them in a matter of minutes.

Her second phone call was to the DCI. She was in the middle of relaying the good news to Mini when she saw Campbell striding towards her up the path. He broke into a jog, grinning from ear to ear. 'Brilliant guys, fecking brilliant, top work. I knew you'd got him; I was just the other side of the house, I could hear you shouting, what a bloody result.'

In the distance they could hear the wail of police sirens approaching. Con looked up and grinned at Campbell.

'Thank fuck you're here, if I have to stay in this position much longer, I don't think I'll be able to get up. I can't feel my right knee, it's gone all numb.'

'I know the feeling.' chuckled Campbell rubbing his swollen jaw.

Minutes later Donaldson was handcuffed by uniformed officers and bundled unceremoniously into the back of a Sherpa van.

Con hauled himself to his feet and slumped onto a park bench. Sweating and out of breath he'd had quite enough excitement for one day.

'Take your time old timer, Mini and Asif are on their way over, they'll be here in a couple of minutes. They'll want to hear all about your heroics, you're going to be dining out on this one for years my friend, and I have to say, as swansongs go, it's going to be hard to beat.'

Con sighed and shook his head, 'Aye, I suppose, but fuck's sake, what a pisser!'

Bemused, Jan and Campbell looked at each other and shrugged.

'What do you mean, fuck's sake?'

Con looked up and shook his head again.

'Just as I said, fuck's sake. I was really, really looking forward to that curry. Oh, and one more thing, who the fuck is Abaddon?'

Chapter 32

The following Monday morning, Campbell, Jan, and Con found themselves alone in the incident room. The weekend had been a whirlwind of activity. Donaldson had been charged with the murders of Magnus DeVilliers, Maureen Goodall, and Zander Muir and was due to appear at Glasgow Sheriff Court later that morning. There would be additional charges to follow, the assault and abduction of Asif for one, but they could wait. Donaldson would be remanded in custody after his appearance in court, there would be plenty of time to dot the I's and cross the T's.

It was, however, not all good news. According to the doctor who had examined Donaldson after he was brought into custody, it was doubtful if he would ever stand trial for the murders. The doctor suggested to Campbell that Donaldson appeared to be suffering from a severe mental disorder, most likely paranoid schizophrenia. He was delusional and hallucinating repeating stories about Jezebel, scorpion-tailed locusts and the apocalypse, he even referred to himself as the angel of death. He was clearly very disturbed. In all probability he would be found unfit to stand trial on the grounds of insanity, it was likely he would end up being incarcerated in the State Psychiatric Hospital in Carstairs.

On a more positive note, DCI Cooper and the ACC Crime were due to do a major media broadcast at just after nine. The story had been leading the local and National news over much of the weekend, but this morning's briefing was the big one. Judging by the number of media and outside broadcast vehicles that were parked up in the Asda car park, every news channel and newspaper from this country and beyond seemed to have sent representatives. There was even a delegation from NHK World, the Japanese news channel. Their cameraman had threatened to get the whole event cancelled as he'd sneaked into the toilets for a fly fag which set off the fire alarm requiring the building to be evacuated. Fortunately, the incident had happened early enough to allow the Fire Brigade to give the all-clear and allow people back in the building. The numbers attending the briefing were now so large the venue had to be changed to the sports hall on the ground floor. Perhaps as payback for their earlier misdemeanour, NHK news found themselves positioned at the very back of the hall.

Jan fetched three mugs and poured the coffee. 'Have you spoken to Asif this morning? I was just wondering how he was doing? That must have been pretty traumatic for him, bad enough being tied to a chair with a knife at your throat, but then thinking that psychopath was going to attack your wife and child, it doesn't bear thinking about.'

Campbell took a large mouthful of coffee. 'I spoke to him earlier, he said he's doing fine and would be in later. I told him not to hurry back but he insisted, said he wanted to get on with his statement, while things were still fresh in his memory, you know what he's like, never been afraid of hard work and always gives 100%, I don't think the boy will ever change.'

Con nodded reaching into the bag of doughnuts that Jan had brought in that morning.

'Gonna miss him when he gets promoted, but the boy deserves it, he'll be a cracking sergeant.'

'We're going to miss you and Asif being honest.' added Jan. 'The place won't be quite the same without the pair of you.'

Con blushed, he was very fond of Jan and touched by the sentiment.

'Anyway, changing the subject and while it's just the three of us, can you explain again how you worked out Donaldson was the murderer. I know Mini started to explain it yesterday, but I was up to my neck in Holmes actions and missed half of what she said.'

'And just as importantly, what was his motivation, why did he go on a killing rampage?' asked Con taking a bite of his doughnut.

Campbell put down his mug and took off his glasses. 'Well as the old song says, I should start at the very beginning. And this bit of the story comes from what Donaldson told me when I interviewed him yesterday.

And it starts when he was a small boy, aged about seven or eight. It appears that Donaldson's grandfather was in the habit of taking him to sail his model boat on the boating ponds in Queen's Park and Maxwell Park. Queen's Park because it was just over the road from where they lived and Maxwell Park because that's where Magnus DeVilliers sailed his boats. You see Donaldson's grandfather had been an Able Seaman during WW2 on HMS enterprise, that was the ship captained by Guy DeVilliers, Magnus's father. That is how Donaldson was first introduced to Magnus DeVilliers. You see Gabriel's grandfather held the DeVilliers family in very high regard. And although DeVilliers was much older, Magnus and Gabriel shared a common interest in model boats, a passion which would continue for more than twenty years, till Donaldson was in his thirties.

So, that establishes how they came to know each other. Then, about 10 years ago, Donaldson's mother, Mildred, became unwell with a chronic throat condition. Donaldson was aware that DeVilliers worked as an ENT consultant, so he approached him to ask his advice about his mother's condition. That conversation led to DeVilliers suggesting that Mildred's condition could be cured by an operation, so he took her on as a private patient. They agreed a fee, lower I believe than the going rate should have been, and used a combination of her savings and Gabriel's own money to pay for the operation.'

'Makes sense.' said Con brushing crumbs off his lap. 'So, what happened after that?'

'Ah, this is the bit where it gets really interesting. We found a letter pinned to the wall in Donaldson's flat, that's when the pieces of the puzzle started to come together.'

'You mean the letter you found that had been written by Kenneth Sheridan the anaesthetist guy who worked at Ross Hall with DeVilliers.'

Campbell smiled. 'The very one. It seems he wrote to Gabriel Donaldson a few months ago, it would appear with a view to clearing his own conscience about what had really happened during Gabriel's mother's operation. He said he needed the truth to come it, he wanted to get things off his chest, he could no longer live with the lie. Sheridan told Donaldson that he'd left medicine eighteen months ago, apparently, because he'd found religion. He sold his house and all his possessions and gave the lot to local charities. He's currently in training to be a Benedictine Monk.'

'Good grief, that is some career change.' remarked Jan. 'But why did he write to Donaldson, what was it that he needed to get off his chest?'

Campbell pursed his lips. 'There would appear to have been a major cock-up at the time of the operation. The staple gun DeVilliers was using to seal the incisions made during the surgery to Mildred's throat apparently failed. It seized and was stuck in the open position. They couldn't fix the problem and as they didn't have a spare gun, panic set in.'

'What do you mean panic set in?' asked Jan.

'In his letter Sheridan says they knew they were in a race against time, they needed to source a replacement staple gun urgently. The nearest one available was at the Southern General. Maureen Goodall was despatched in a taxi to go and pick it up. But all that took time, by the time Maureen got back to Ross Hall, Mildred Donaldson had been under anaesthetic for too long. It played haywire with her system, and according to Sheridan it was ultimately what caused her death.'

Con looked quizzical. 'I thought she died of a heart attack?'

'Yeah, so did I. And that is going to need further investigation. I can't say if they doctored the death report. But what we now know is that Mildred was under anaesthesia for much longer than anticipated because of the botched operation and that was ultimately why she died. It's a medical malpractice case.'

Con scratched his head. 'Ok. While that is all very interesting, it doesn't in anyway explain why Donaldson murdered three people. Or am I missing something?'

Campbell poured himself another coffee. 'It does start to explain it, I think. You see Donaldson long suspected that something had gone wrong with his mother's operation. We found copies of several letters he wrote to the hospital authorities years ago. But those letters went nowhere. It appears that the hospital authorities closed ranks to protect one of their own and Donaldson got fobbed off. Well, that part is my theory, I can't prove that yet, but I don't think I'm too far wide of the mark. Then three months ago, completely out of the blue, Donaldson receives Sheridan's letter, his confessional, explaining from his point of view what had really gone on during Mildred Donaldson's operation.'

Jan helped herself to a doughnut.

'So why did Maureen Goodall become complicit, I know you said she went in a taxi to pick up the replacement equipment. But that could have been entirely innocent on her part, she was just doing what she was asked, she thought she was helping out.'

Campbell made a face. 'Not so innocent if you believe what Sheridan says in his letter. You see Magnus DeVilliers had embarked on an affair with Maureen Goodall. A bit of a whirlwind apparently. According to Sheridan, DeVilliers was smitten from the first day he met her, and they struck up a relationship almost immediately. It turns out he wasn't quite the paragon of virtue we thought him to be.

Now this next bit is again just my opinion, but I reckon Goodall didn't know anything about any cover up, that didn't occur till much later on, well after her fling with DeVilliers had finished. But one thing we know for certain is that Maureen Goodall had lavish tastes. We also know for the five years following the operation she was depositing £500 cash into her account every two months. And remember, DeVilliers was a wealthy man, who regularly withdrew substantial sums from his own account. I'm convinced that for those five years he gave that money to Goodall, he used it to buy her silence. And as far as I can ascertain, Donaldson knew nothing about Maureen Goodall's role in all of this until her name appeared in Sheridan's letter.'

Jan shook her head. 'Wow. But what about Muir, how did he get himself embroiled in this, what connected him to DeVilliers and Goodall?

'A good question. And a most unfortunate piece of bad luck on his part. Muir doesn't get a mention in Sheridan's letter, he had nothing to do with the operation so I'm pretty sure Sheridan doesn't even know who he is. I'm also convinced that Muir had no connection with Maureen Goodall. No, Muir's involvement is solely with DeVilliers, and his misfortune was twofold. Firstly, he and Magnus DeVilliers knew each other from school. They were at Glasgow Academy together, they played in the same school rugby team and then again for the FP's when they left school. Then, in another twist of fate, a second weird coincidence occurred. It transpires that Zander Muir's mother and Mildred Donaldson were good friends. They went to the same church in Strathbungo, the one Gabriel Donaldson also attended.'

Con looked confused. 'That still doesn't explain why Donaldson would want to murder Zander Muir.'

'No, you're right. But I think I can answer that question. You see on receipt of Sheridan's letter Donaldson wanted to get some legal advice from a lawyer; he had received the affirmation he needed that his mother's operation had, as he'd always suspected, been botched. He became obsessed with pursuing a medical malpractice suit against DeVilliers and the hospital. And there's one final bizarre twist. It just so happens that Muir's mother had commissioned Donaldson to make several stained-glass windows that are now installed in the church. That's what Donaldson does you see, he makes stained glass windows, and apparently, he's very skilled at it.'

Con nodded knowingly. 'So that's where the traces of lead and the broken tip to the craft knife come in, they were tools of his trade.'

'Exactly. Then, during one of their conversations at the church Donaldson told Mrs Muir that he was looking for a lawyer. He said he needed to get advice about a family matter. He didn't disclose anything further and Mrs Muir, just wanting to help, suggested he should contact her son as he was a lawyer and might be able to assist him. So that's what he did. Donaldson went to see Zander Muir in person completely unaware that the person he wanted to take to court was a personal friend of Muir's. I think you can see where I'm going with this.'

Jan shook her head. 'So, he ended up getting fobbed off for a second time. This time by Zander Muir?'

'That's pretty much it. And that's the point I think when the red mist descended. His mental health had always been fragile, but getting the brush-off from Zander Muir was the straw that broke the camel's back. Donaldson had had a gut-full, he couldn't take anymore, he wanted revenge for what had happened to his mother, and well, you both know the rest. You don't need any more gory details.'

361

Jan blew out her cheeks. 'God, I'm exhausted just listening to that. But it's a tremendous result, and a great bit of detective work by you, Asif and the rest of the team. And not forgetting you Con; you delivered the coup de grâce. I bet Donaldson will be sore for weeks.'

Campbell smiled. 'And I think we should all acknowledge the part played by Mini, she was the one that worked out that Asif was in that flat. If she hadn't God only knows what might have happened. That was an impressive bit of deduction. She's proved herself to be one smart operator. I hold my hands up, three weeks ago, I wouldn't have given her a hope of bringing this investigation to a satisfactory conclusion. If you remember, we didn't exactly hit it off at the start. Just shows you what I know. That lady will go far, mark my words, and right now she's in her element, there's nobody better at giving media briefings.'

Campbell looked at his watch.

'Con, switch the monitor on will you? She'll be on in ten minutes; I want to see if she ignores McSorley again.'

Jan started to giggle. 'That would be excellent if she did, and it would serve him right, he's done nothing but fuel fear in this city, I can't stomach the man.'

Con was about to add his tuppence worth when the door opened. It was the Chief Superintendent; he was clutching a form and had his serious face on.

'Detective Inspector Morrison.'

'Sir.'

'I need you and Chief Inspector Cooper in my office immediately the press conference is over.'

He brandished the form in the air. 'Today of all days, I certainly wasn't expecting this, she handed me this resignation form just before she headed into the briefing. I need the pair of you in my office as soon as she gets clear of that meeting, is that understood.'

'Yes sir.' replied Campbell standing up.

Campbell, Jan and Con looked at each other in disbelief. That news had come right out of left field. None of them had seen that coming. Jan shook her head.

'I said to you on Friday that something wasn't right, she left the office in such a hurry. She said she wanted to get some air. And then with everything else that was going on I completely forgot about it. Shit, this isn't good.'

The news had certainly put a damper on what was supposed to be a day of celebration. They had just locked up a triple murderer, the case was watertight, thanks in a large part to the efforts of the DCI. Pacing up and down the bottom corridor, waiting for the briefing to finish, Campbell had time to think. He suspected he knew the reason behind the resignation. Sexual offences are notoriously difficult to navigate, invariably there are only two people present when the crime is committed. In the absence of any forensic evidence, it is difficult to secure a conviction. It is your voice against theirs. Who to believe? Then there is the mental torment experienced by those victims brave enough to pursue a complaint. When your assailant just happens to be a senior officer from your own organisation you can begin to understand how difficult a situation that is to manage.

It had gone twenty past ten when the doors of the sports hall were finally flung open. The briefing had lasted an hour and twenty minutes. Campbell hadn't seen any of it; he had spent the last hour wondering what on earth he was going to say to his boss. Some words of sympathy and understanding. He would certainly express deep regret that she was leaving. For a moment he had considered trying to persuade her to change her mind, but on reflection he decided that it really wasn't really his place to do so.

As the last of the media delegation drifted away, Mini appeared at the door. She looked tired and no wonder. Campbell stared at her face. It wasn't a smile as such, but neither was it a frown. Her look left him feeling slightly discombobulated, he wasn't sure what was going on?

'How did it go? Hope McSorley didn't hit you with a low bowler?'

'He didn't get the chance, I just ignored him, again!'

Campbell smiled. 'Nice one. Look, I know you must have other things to do boss, but the Chief Superintendent wants to see us both in his office right away.'

Mini scrunched up her nose and nodded gently.

'I assume it's to do with the resignation?'

'Yep, I'm afraid it is.'

Mini sighed deeply.

'I thought as much, I just feel it's such a terrible waste, what a talent to lose, Asif would have made a terrific Sergeant.'

Milton Keynes UK
Ingram Content Group UK Ltd.
UKHW032148260924
448786UK00004B/235